To: Dea

HAPPY CH

From: Joyce xxx

Connie Anderson, one of nine children, was born and bred in Malta. Her father, a carpenter, and her mother, a teacher, met during World War II when they were both working as Air Raid Wardens.

In the late sixties Connie met and married a British soldier. She gave up her teaching career when his job took them all over the world. While stationed in Germany they had two children.

When the family settled in Devon, they began to foster numerous children over a twelve-year period. They adopted two boys.

It was only when they stopped fostering that Connie finally found the time and energy to write the novel that was on hold for so long.

Connie has written stories and poetry from a very early age. Her earliest memory is when, at six years old, she was told off for writing a story instead of listening to her teacher!

THE MALTESE HOUSE WITH THE BRIGHT YELLOW DOOR

CONNIE ANDERSON

The Maltese House With The Bright Yellow Door

Vanguard Press

VANGUARD PAPERBACK

A CIP catalogue record for this title is available from the British Library

ISBN 1 84386 222 0

Vanguard Press is an imprint of
Pegasus Elliot MacKenzie Publishers Ltd.
www.pegasuspublishers.com

First Published in 2005

Vanguard Press
Sheraton House Castle Park
Cambridge England

Printed & Bound in Great Britain

Dedication

To my family: Trevor, Wendy, John, Jake and Zak.
Thank you for listening to me going on about it!

Last but not least to Mum and Dad from whom I got my writing bug.

Acknowledgments

My thanks go to Trevor – among other things for his help with p.c. hiccups, Wendy for her valuable input, John for his great idea for the cover and Marion for producing it. Thanks also to Joyce for reading it in batches and waiting eagerly for more! Marlene and Ray – thanks for helping with research and Katy for proof reading it.

CHAPTER 1

"Amy, it's your auntie!" called Jane urgently to her busy colleague. The youngest and newest member of staff was patiently sorting some files at the other side of the modern office.

"Quick," Jane called out again, covering the mouthpiece, "she sounds very upset."

There was no need to ask which one of her several aunties was on the phone, because Amy had always been especially close to her Auntie Meg and Uncle Jim who lived nearby.

The kind-hearted couple had no children of their own but their favourite niece had helped to fill that painful void. They were over the moon when they were asked to be godparents to little Amy. Both took the responsibility seriously and enjoyed their role. The devoted couple doted on their pretty goddaughter and saw her as often as possible.

As Amy got older, she started staying the odd night at their house. This became a bit of a treat for her, as it was a welcome break away from her boisterous brothers and sisters. It was lovely being spoilt a little into the bargain too! Amy loved all four of them dearly, but her siblings demanded too much attention and they kept their harassed mum constantly occupied.

When her dad wasn't on night shift, he was just as tied up with the children. So, Amy tended to curl up alone with a book or try to watch her favourite soaps. It was hard to follow anything, with all the chaos around her.

Meg and Jim's house, on the other hand, was a haven away from her brothers and sisters, who were often in competition with each other to see who had the loudest voice.

Being the eldest sometimes proved hard for sensitive Amy, especially since she had been an only child for eight years. Then her mum had four children in close succession and from an early age, the shy, conscientious girl had helped her mum to look after the others. But about six months or so earlier, things suddenly improved. Amy landed her first job and started gaining some independence. She was soon meeting people her own age and began going out more.

Her first day at Anderson's Estate Agents was quite a milestone for the whole family. It was a grey and wet Monday morning but that didn't dampen the family's excitement. It was Amy's eighteenth birthday! It was also the day when she started her new job and when the youngest in the family had started school!

Amy's mother soon began to look forward to regaining some independence and her eldest daughter relished her own new-found freedom.

One wonderful morning, Paul walked into the bright busy office and headed straight towards Amy's desk. Unusually chatty and confident, Amy surprised herself by responding so easily to his charm, agreeing to go out with him that same evening. Her first date with the cute client was the first of many and as usual on a Friday, they were going to the gym after work.

However, Paul couldn't make it so Amy went straight home to eat chocolate in front of the TV.

"I don't need you to help me love," her mother answered gratefully, when out of habit Amy asked if she wanted her to do anything.

"No love, you go to the pictures with Debbie. Go on, phone her back. She said to call her if you weren't doing anything and I promised her you would, as soon as you came in."

"Well, I had planned on going to the gym after work with Paul but he can't come now," she reasoned. "So I thought I'd stay in, but if you're sure…"

"Of course I'm sure. I keep telling you. Now, with the kids at school I can do all that needs doing during the day. There's no one under my feet so I tend to get finished in no time at all."

"I guess you're right. I noticed that when you tidy up now, it does stay tidy… at least until they come back from school. You'll be saying you're bored soon."

"Oh well, as it happens I might be looking for a little job soon. We'll see," she added with a smile. "At the moment I'm just enjoying being a lady of leisure!"

Amy had never minded helping at home, and now it was great to see her mother looking more relaxed and at the same time livelier than she'd seen her for ages.

Occasionally, she still helped with babysitting. She didn't mind that at all because Paul often came along too. If she didn't look after them occasionally, her parents would never go out as it was rather difficult to find someone to mind four energetic children.

Amy put the pile of papers down quickly and for a moment, she just stood there looking a little confused. She couldn't understand why her aunt was ringing at this time. She never called her during office hours. Jane had to urge her once more to pick the phone up and, frowning with concern, Amy finally did.

The other girls watched her changing expressions as she stood there with the receiver to her ear, then they eventually went back to what they were doing.

It was unusually quiet that morning at the Mutley branch of Anderson's Estate Agents. The modern office was one of the thriving businesses in the area. It was always busy with prospective buyers constantly trailing in and out. Plymouth University, which was nearby, provided many students, who were always looking for accommodation so there was never a dull moment in the bright, airy office.

"Are you still up for shopping at lunchtime?" Debbie wanted to know. She swung her chair round to face Jane. Her boss was using the quiet spell to file her nails.

"Of course. I want to get some new shoes. What are you after Debbie?"

"Nothing particularly, but I'm sure I'll find something. I love being so close to town but it's not good for my bank balance!!"

The three girls were a good team. Jane was the efficient but friendly office manager. Then there was Debbie, and Amy, who had only been there about six months.

Suddenly, the two girls heard Amy's raised voice.

"No, oh no!"

They both looked up in alarm as they detected the cry of dismay in their colleague's voice. Amy had turned pale and looked dazed as she clutched the phone. She was shaking as she listened to the voice at the other end of the line.

"Are you at the hospital now? ...Oh. Ok. No. Don't worry. I'll come at once... No, you stay there. I will...yes of course I will .... I'm sure Jane won't mind. Bye auntie, see you soon. Yes, I'll be careful." Amy stood still for a moment, then she looked at her boss.

"It's Uncle Jim. He's been taken to hospital. It seems that he's had a bad fall at work - slipped off a ladder. He's got a nasty head injury. Auntie needs me. Sorry, Jane, I have to go."

Amy replaced the receiver and was still talking and rambling on breathlessly as she rummaged in her handbag for her car keys. Jane reassured her that she must do whatever needed doing. Still murmuring her apologies, Amy put her coat on and quickly ran out of the office towards her car. As usual, her red Mini, her pride and joy, was parked conveniently in front of the tall building.

She was at her aunt's house in less than fifteen minutes. The worried girl sat at the edge of the big, comfortable armchair and sipped a soothing cup of strong tea as she listened to what her dear auntie had to say. Very calmly, Meg put down her cup and told Amy the whole story. She didn't do much without a cup of tea somewhere close by and this time was no exception. She told her niece how her darling Jim had slipped off a ladder and had injured his head. He was still unconscious, but when he came to briefly, he'd called out her name.

"As soon as we've finished this cuppa, love, we should go back to Freedom Fields Hospital," she said to her niece. "I didn't want to leave him but I had to come and get some clothes and some other bits and pieces."

Amy gulped the tea down as quickly as she could. She would have willingly left it and dashed straight to her beloved uncle's bedside. However, she knew better than to leave half a cup of her aunt's cure for all evil!

The fairly short drive to the hospital seemed endless to both women. Neither of them felt like talking, but Amy was trying to think of something to say to break the screaming silence.

"See auntie, my office is very close. Isn't it? I'll be popping in to visit Uncle Jim as often as possible. I could even do that in my lunch break," she volunteered.

"That would be good. I'll visit every day too. I want to be near him…"

"Here we are." Amy stopped at the entrance to let her aunt out quickly. "You go ahead while I find a parking space. It looks rather crowded," she went on, looking quickly around, "so it might take me a while. Go on. You told me where he is. I'll come straight up."

Soon the two worried women stood next to Jim, one on either side of the bed. Amy held back the tears as she looked at the sleeping man. She could hardly bear to look at his bandaged head.

"He's going to be all right isn't he auntie?" Amy asked

nervously. "Why won't he wake up?"

"I don't know love, but they've been doing some tests and I expect they'll let us know soon enough," said Meg, not much above a whisper. "Apparently, the longer he sleeps the better it is, because he's resting and not fretting. You know what he's like…he hates being ill." Suddenly, she remembered what she'd been advised earlier.

"Sorry Jim. I forgot that the doctor told me to talk to you. Go on Amy, you talk to him too."

"I don't know what to say," whispered her niece.

"Talk about anything. Same as you always do. You don't normally have a problem talking, love. I know… tell him about your new boyfriend. He doesn't know about him yet does he?" she said encouragingly to her niece.

"Amy hasn't mentioned Paul to you yet, has she Jim? Our Amy has found herself a gorgeous beau!" she teased.

"Oh, Auntie Meg, nobody says beau nowadays!"

"Well, it made you smile, love. When your uncle wakes up, he certainly won't want to see you looking sad," Meg added, trying hard to be positive.

"Sorry Jim. I keep forgetting to talk to you," she addressed her husband.

"Actually," she said, grabbing hold of his hand and giving it a good squeeze, "I'll try to make the most of it until you decide to talk back! It's not very often that I get your undivided attention. You're not the best listener in the world, are you dear? Now then, I think that you should be telling this young lady here that you'll soon be up and about and getting under my feet as you usually do. " Meg's voice started to break, in spite of her determination to stay calm for Amy's sake.

"I hope so. I really do hope so." Amy picked up where her aunt had left off.

"Auntie's right. I haven't told you about my new boyfriend yet, have I? Well, his name is Paul and he's a teacher. He teaches at the Comp, near the park."

"How… where did you two meet Amy?" asked her aunt.

"I met him when he came to the office. You see, he wanted to buy a flat in town. I was the one who helped him find one in the Barbican. He ended up buying it too. It's fantastic. Just five minutes walk from the Hoe."

Meg was looking at her dear niece and thinking how pretty she looked when she smiled. At that moment. Amy looked rather radiant as she talked about Paul.

"I was going to tell you soon, honestly," she continued quite easily now. " I just wanted to be sure first, 'cause last time, not long after I told you both that I was going out with someone, we split up."

"Yes, well, that chap wasn't as nice as we 'd thought," her aunt remembered. "He was a good looker, I grant you that, but he obviously knew it and he loved himself more than he loved you Amy. I'm right Jim, ain't I?" she said, trying to include Jim in the conversation. Meg then turned once more to her niece, and taking her hand, she apologised.

" Sorry, maybe I shouldn't have said that, Amy… but I'll keep an eye on this one. I don't want you to get hurt again, love."

"Keep an eye on Paul? How? Will you be following him around?" Amy was looking amused as she turned to carry on talking to the patient.

"Anyway. Uncle Jim, auntie has met him…sort of." Amy waited for her aunt to explain to her uncle.

"That's when she saw us together, quite recently."

"Yes, it was only a couple of days ago. When I went to town. I bumped into them literally!" laughed Meg. "I didn't say anything to you, Jim, because this young lady here, well, she wanted to tell you herself."

"Tell him how you met Paul," Amy nudged her aunt impatiently.

"Yes, I will love. Well Jim, I was on my way out of the main post office in town you know… the day before yesterday. I was walking away from the counter, but I wasn't looking where I was going and the next thing I knew, I bumped into the owner of a pair of big beautiful blue eyes."

"It was so funny," said a very amused Amy. "You should've seen her, Uncle Jim. Auntie didn't look very ladylike, and neither did I! We both ended up on the floor," Amy said with laughter bubbling in her voice. "Paul and I had gone in for some stamps. He suddenly stopped mid track to see where I had got to, because I'd stopped to look at some cards. Auntie wasn't looking where she was going and bumped straight into him. Then I bumped into both of them! So we both fell hysterically in a heap on the floor." Meg was laughing and wiping her tears as she recalled the comical scene.

"I suspect that the slippery floor didn't help much! It was raining and people were going in and out all the time."

"I'm sure you're right," Amy had to agree with her aunt. "I remember trying to stop myself falling, but the floor was too slippery, she said as she turned to her aunt again.

"Well, it's lucky that neither of us was hurt."

"I was more embarrassed than hurt," admitted Meg, "especially as I gripped his leg as I fell!"

Meg noticed that since they had started talking about Amy's new boyfriend her niece seemed a little less tense and not so worried. In fact, at that moment, Amy looked animated and a big smile lit up her face. Her aunt looked indulgently at her and she found herself hoping that this chap who could put such a radiant look on her niece's face, was really a nice bloke.

"Uncle Jim will like him, won't he auntie?" She turned towards the unconscious man and held his hand saying, "Do you know Paul likes your kind of music, strictly classical, nothing modern! You'll be able to impress him with your record collection." Meg also noticed that her niece was now much more relaxed when talking to her uncle.

" Oh, I just remembered something Paul told me yesterday…" It seemed that once she had started talking to Jim, there was no stopping the girl! Now, that was the Amy they both knew and loved. A chatterbox!

"…his dad was in the Army for a long time and they lived in Aldershot for a while. You two lived in Aldershot at one time, didn't you?" Amy asked. She wasn't finding it at all difficult now, to keep talking to her uncle.

"Yes," her aunt replied. "We lived there, but it was only for a short while before uncle left or rather before he was medically discharged from the Army. You certainly didn't like pen pushing did you Jim?"

"Paul said that they also lived in Malta for a couple of years. It seems that his dad was stationed there. I know you spent some time there too, uncle. I've never understood why you never want to talk about your time on the island. I've often wondered why."

"You're absolutely right. He never wants to talk about Malta. You didn't like it there, did you Jim? Well, I don't think you did anyway." She had given up asking her husband why Malta was taboo.

The two women stayed a little bit longer, each of them delaying leaving Jim behind. At one point Meg's eyes welled up. Seeing that her auntie was now feeling emotional, Amy became the strong one.

"Come on auntie, you look exhausted. We'll go now, Uncle Jim. I'll drive auntie home and I'll make sure she goes to bed early tonight. We'll see you again tomorrow." Bending over, she gave the unconscious man a kiss before she turned and started walking slowly out of the ward, leaving her auntie to say goodnight to her husband privately.

When they were on their way home, Amy asked her auntie if she wanted her to stop the night with her.

"No thank you love. I'm ok. Just exhausted," Meg was quick to reassure her niece. "I would like it if you stopped for a cuppa when you drop me home though. Then, after a few little jobs which won't take long, I'll have an early night because it's been a very long day."

"Do you know what, Auntie Meg? When we were talking about Uncle Jim's time in Malta, I thought that he was going to open his eyes. I wasn't sure, but it looked like it to me."

"Why didn't you say something, love? I would have..." her voice trailed away.

"Well, I wasn't sure. I'm still not sure if I imagined it or not. You were looking upset and I thought...."

"That's ok dear. I suppose that it's just as well really that you didn't raise my hopes. I used to get angry with Jim, you know, because if someone mentioned that blessed island, he always changed the subject. He even changed channels every time there was a travel programme about Malta. I asked why he did that more than once. I gave up in the end because he never gave me a straight answer."

"I wonder why. It's not like uncle to be cagey. He just comes out with things, doesn't he? Oh well, it couldn't have been a happy tour of duty there, could it?"

"It's supposed to be a gem of an island, though."

"Yes, Paul lived there for a while, and he's been there on holiday too. He loves it."

"Whereas Jim...well, it's always been obvious that Jim even hates the mere mention of Malta. I used to get upset and angry, but now I think it's simply because it brings back memories of the horrific accident which led to his losing a leg. What do you think?

I'm sure he loved the island. Everybody seems to love it there, so..."

"You must be right. Yes. That must be the reason... It must upset him when he is reminded... Poor Uncle Jim. Now he's hurt again. I just wonder how long he'll be unconscious..."

"No one can tell love. The doctor told me that all we can do is to keep talking to him, and that we must stay calm and casual around him. Apparently, he progresses while he sleeps. We just have to keep positive now. That's all we can do."

For Amy, the days that followed rolled into one another in the same pattern, work, home and visiting her uncle as often as possible. It was lucky that her office was just a short walk from the hospital.

Sometimes, she met her aunt at Freedom Fields, but at other times, Amy was alone while Meg was at home having a rest. That way, when it was possible, Jim had one of them with him all day. It was encouraging to see that he was looking much better and relaxed in his sleep. Occasionally, the women thought he was about to regain consciousness, but they were disappointed every time. It was so worrying to see him there, unaware of the surrounding hustle and bustle.

One wet Monday, about two weeks after the accident, Amy was on her way to the hospital. She had the day off work and being aware that her aunt needed some time at home, Amy volunteered to stay at the hospital all day if needs be.

"Thank you dear, you are so kind. It will probably be very late before I get to the hospital," she warned her niece, but Amy reassured her godmother that she didn't mind stopping with Jim a bit longer than usual. Very gratefully, Meg promised to take over from her niece as soon as she could.

Amy didn't mind helping out at all. She knew that her aunt was really very behind with all her chores. She had neglected her house because she had been spending every minute she could with her husband. Poor Auntie Meg, Amy thought, she was so house proud too! That particular day, Meg promised Amy that there would be a nice supper waiting if she went back home with her. Then, she added that maybe Amy would stay the night, if she had made no plans for that evening.

Amy thought that her aunt was feeling lonely and also very worried about her husband because she obviously needed company that evening. She was supposed to meet Paul later on, but she knew that her aunt wouldn't ask her to visit unless she really needed her to, so she decided to make her excuses to Paul.

As she made her way up in the lift, down corridors and towards the ward where her uncle was, Amy felt the usual sadness and frustration that she always felt when she visited him.

Every time she walked into the ward, she always found herself trying to look happy and to feel positive, otherwise she wouldn't be able to talk to him.

On this memorable day, when Amy entered the big ward, she had a big surprise. Jim was sitting up, propped up against snow-white pillows! He was being helped to drink by a very pretty nurse.

"Uncle Jim! Uncle Jim!" shouted Amy as she sprinted across the length of the room and nearly fell down on top of the patient. The other patients who were awake and all the visitors, looked at Amy in amusement and smiled indulgently.

"You're awake! Oh Uncle Jim, when did you? I had no idea..."

"Steady on lass, steady on."

"When did you wake up? I was here till late last night. So was Auntie Meg, but you were still..." Her voice trailed away as she hugged her uncle close.

"It was this morning, just in time for breakfast" said the nurse, before she went off on her duties. Before she turned away, she warned Amy not to tire her uncle too much.

"Auntie must know and yet she never told me...that's strange. I spoke to her on the phone. She said she's coming tonight. She never mentioned the good news!"

"That's my doing, lass. I didn't want her to tell you, even though she was dying to. I thought it would be a great surprise for you to see me back in the land of the living."

"Oh yes, definitely a great, wonderful, surprise. It's simply fantastic to see you awake. I just can't believe it. I really can't!"

"Well, I'm glad you didn't know...it was worth it, just to see that look of surprise on your face. Hey, be careful young lady. Don't smother me to death. I've only just come to! Now sit down Amy please. I need to talk to you."

"What's wrong Uncle? You look all serious, all of a sudden...What's up?"

"Shush now dear, be patient...please. I want you to listen very carefully because I need your help. Try not to interrupt me, love...

this could take a while."

"That's all right, I'll stay as long as you want me to. I can stay all day."

"Oh, that's marvellous. Meg'll be a while today because she has shopping to do as well, ready for when I go home."

"When, uncle?" Amy looked quite excited.

"I don't know yet love, but pretty soon I think. Anyway, young lady, I need to talk to you, quite seriously."

"Oh, what's the matter?"

"It's a long story, but I need to tell someone, someone I can trust. You're the only person I can tell. I trust you not to talk about it to anyone though ok?"

"What about Auntie Meg? Does she want you to tell me?"

"Your aunt doesn't know anything about this…about what I'm about to tell you. I must have your promise never to tell her."

"Ok uncle, don't look so worried. I promise. Whatever you say."

"Thank you. Please, love, just listen to me now. Please, let me get it off my chest. It's been worrying me for so many years, a lifetime, to be honest. I've always managed to keep it buried away. Then suddenly, this morning, when I woke up, it just hit me that I was alive and…I started thinking."

"I don't understand, but… this is so odd. I mean, it's strange that you've kept a secret from Auntie Meg. I've always thought you two are so honest with each other."

"We are honest. I hope that when you hear it all, you'll realise that it wasn't a question of being dishonest. At the beginning, it was just too painful for me. It was much too painful to talk about because I was feeling hurt and rejected by… Well, I'll tell you."

"By whom, who…?" interrupted Amy.

"I'll tell you in a minute. Like I said, I was feeling rejected and at the same time betrayed. It was just too much to cope with at the time and so I buried it all inside. I never spoke of it to anyone, until now."

"Was it that difficult to confide in someone…even in Auntie Meg?"

"Yes, it was. Then, as time went on, I was afraid to tell her."

"Why?"

"It was only because it would have been painful for Meg if I told her. I honestly thought that by keeping this secret from her, I was sparing her feelings."

"You're talking in riddles. Why now? Why me? I think I should phone her. She should be here…"

"Please, Amy, just listen. Your aunt would be hurt, very hurt and upset if she knew what I'm about to tell you. That's the last thing I want."

"Don't tell me then, please. I'd rather you didn't."

"Oh no, don't worry, it's nothing horrible. I haven't committed a crime or anything ghastly like that!"

"I'm glad, …not that I was thinking that for a moment! But what on earth is it then? What's this big secret that you can't even tell Auntie Meg? I just cannot…"

" Please Amy, just listen. Hear me out and then make your mind up. Is that fair enough?"

Amy nodded reluctantly and gave his hand a squeeze. Jim leant back against the pillows and had a few sips from a glass of water.

Just then, the nurse came back for the cups and glasses and with a stern look at Amy, she reminded her that her uncle was recovering from quite a nasty head injury and that she mustn't tire him.

Jim quickly reassured her that his niece would do nothing of the sort. He waited for the nurse to go, and then, when her squeaky footsteps faded away, he turned to Amy.

"You'll soon understand why I kept it a secret from your Aunt," he began. Amy was pleased to see a slow smile begin to spread gradually across his pale face at last.

"Well, it's great to see that cheeky grin of yours again. What's cheered you up?"

"Memories love, memories…"

"Must be good ones to make you smile like that!" Amy thought out aloud.

"Well, some certainly are…It all started in the sixties, the late sixties…those were days of love, laughter, great music, and a beautiful little island in the Mediterranean…"

CHAPTER 2

"I was only twenty years old when I found out that my Regiment had been posted to Malta for two years. Can you imagine me at twenty, Amy? Still wet behind the ears, but I was a new fully-fledged soldier on my first, my very first, posting abroad.

My family and friends kept telling me how lucky I was to be going to Malta, and my dad teased me endlessly. He kept saying that he wished that he was the one going to that little island in the Mediterranean for a couple of years.

I went home on leave before we flew out there and dad went on and on about Malta. I caught him winking at mum when he told me that there were lots of lovely and sultry, dark-eyed girls on the little island. He also told me that everybody spoke English. I wasn't quite sure what to believe!"

"Why, you're lucky. That island, well, it's a little England," he said. "Yes, it sure is, but without the rain. Oh, and guess what? They even have the same money as us!" He patted me on the back and, "you'll love it," he said for the umpteenth time."

"How did your dad know so much about that island then?" wondered Amy.

"He'd been there with his unit when he was in the Army himself, before I was born."

"Oh, I didn't know that, but anyway, carry on with your story…"

" Well, obviously, after all that, I looked forward to seeing it all for myself. I just wondered if all that I'd been told was true, or if it was all highly exaggerated, just to make me feel good. It worked anyway, because instead of feeling sad or anxious at going on my first posting abroad, I began to feel very excited and I even began counting the days to my flight to that little island in the Mediterranean.

As soon as we all got off the plane at Luqa Airport, the hot sunny atmosphere hit us. I remember feeling pleasantly wrapped up in warmth. Everything looked bright and golden. I know it sounds corny, but it actually seemed as if the early sun was coating everything around with a warm and wonderful yellow haze.

It was such a welcome atmosphere after the drizzling rain we'd cheerfully left behind in grey England. You'd have loved it, Amy. I know how you love the heat.

Anyway, we were soon on our way from the airport to the barracks, which were to be our homes for the next couple of years. The short trip was bumpy but very interesting. We all looked eagerly out of the windows. We were all surprised to see that all the houses seemed different. They were all painted in bright colours and looked so pretty."

"You remember what the houses looked like? Still… I suppose if they were unusual…"

"Yes, in fact it all looked very different to Blighty, but it took me a while to work out why."

"Why, what was so strange then?"

"Not really strange, but it suddenly dawned on me and the rest of us that there was hardly any green grass to be seen anywhere! It was all dried and brown. It obviously hadn't rained for a while. Mind you, there were masses of beautiful pink and white flowers on blooming Acacia trees. Rows of them lined the dusty wide streets. I'll never forget that first impression with colourful blossoms creating a bright, beautiful break from the surrounding brown grass verges. Of course that shouldn't have been a surprise 'cause this was early July. It probably hadn't rained for a couple of months."

"It sounds lovely and you obviously thought it was because you're sounding quite poetic. That's so odd when I think that until now you wouldn't even mention Malta! Ok, ok, don't look so exasperated. Go on with your story."

"I just want to get on with it in case your auntie turns up early. Where was I?"

"You were raving about the beautiful trees lining the streets," Amy reminded him because she still had the images in her mind's eye.

"Oh yes. We were on our way to the camp. Before we got to our barracks, the bus went past the beach which (I learnt later) was called St George's Bay. How more English a name can you get eh, Amy? I remember thinking, it's named after the Patron Saint of England, no less! The rattling bus trundled along past the crowded beach. I can see that sandy beach now - choking with all the sun worshippers and swimming bodies in the blue sea. Everywhere you looked there seemed to be rows of smiling faces and everyone looked so happy and relaxed. Finally, we were on our way up the hill to St Patrick's Barracks.

It looked like it was going to be a lovely Summer especially when I remembered being told that it wouldn't rain until September or even October…bliss, can you imagine that? Mind you, I did feel a little bit homesick in the early days, but I soon settled in and started enjoying myself. Before long, I'd got used to the perfect climate, and the warmth of the Maltese people."

"Was it all as you expected? Surely some things were disappointing?"

"Everything I'd been told about Malta and the Maltese turned out to be true, and in fact things turned out even better than my expectations."

"Really? Lucky you, but surely it was too hot?"

"It was all right if you took it slowly. Very soon, all of us squaddies seemed to have adjusted to the hot days and to the laid-back and relaxed way of living on the island.

Our camp, which was on top of a steep hill, was about twenty minutes walking distance from St George's Bay, the very same bay we'd passed on the bus from the airport. At the bottom of the hill, set among a row of houses and a couple of small shops, was a popular bar where we all used to drink after our daily swim.

The long hot days of that first Summer in Malta did wonders to help us enjoy settling in, slowly but surely."

"It must have been hard working in that heat," Amy (practical as always) wondered out loud.

"We only worked half days -it was always an early start at half past six in the morning. At that time, it was comfortably cool. Unless I had a guard duty, my working day ended at about half past twelve. After that it was just too hot to work. Well, it was in the Summer months anyway.

After lunch, a non-stop trail of soldiers walked regularly down from the barracks to the beach at the bottom of the hill. It was one of our favourite haunts because it was so handy. There was also another attraction, the Lido, a big café cum water sports centre. The beach was so popular with the soldiers because there were always lots and lots of lovely suntanned girls. We got to know them pretty quickly, as you can imagine.

"It seems that it was a hard life for you poor British soldiers away from home…Aaaah," said Amy sarcastically.

"It was good and it was getting better all the time. It was there, on that beach, that I met Gina and believe it or not, I knew straight away that she was special. She was sprawled out on a towel reading, and like all the other sun worshipping girls, she was obviously topping up her tan. There was something about her and, anyway, she had these amazing legs that went up to her armpits! "

"Really, I can't imagine you...you never mentioned her before!"

"What do you mean you can't imagine me...? I was young too once you know!"

"Oh ok. I was only teasing. Go on with your story Uncle Jim," urged his niece. "I'm getting curious now."

"I was walking along the sandy beach, on my way to the rocky side of the bay. You had to walk past all the people who were sprawled out on the sand to get there. Anyway, just when I was near her - I remember the embarrassment so clearly - I tripped up! Can you believe it? I felt a right prat! I nearly fell flat on my face."

"Poor you...how awful. Then what?"

"I blamed my new flip-flops of course. God, I managed to spread sand all over her book and towel. It still makes me cringe just thinking about it, even after all these years! I can just see her now. She stood up quickly and looked up at me. It seemed that she was just about to give me a piece of her mind, but then... I know, I know it's an old cliché, but our eyes met and she just stared at me for a few seconds. She didn't say a word...nothing! I was extremely embarrassed by my clumsiness and, to be honest, I felt awkward under her discerning scrutiny. So I mumbled an apology and carried on walking.

When I reached the rocky side of the beach I joined other new visitors dotted here and there in the afternoon sun. It was so easy to pick the newcomers to the island. Compared to the bronzed local boys, we all looked pasty. Since the working day finished at lunchtime, it was every serviceman's aim to achieve the quickest, best, bronzed look too, and to get it as soon as possible. It really felt as if we were on holiday, at least for half of the day!"

"How wonderful! You could spend every afternoon on that beach then. Huh, and all those girls there...hard life eh?" teased Amy.

"Practically as soon as their feet hit the island most of the soldiers were chatting up the local girls. It was so easy because there was no language barrier, but not me, oh no, not yours truly.. I was too shy really."

"I can't imagine you as some shy young thing Uncle Jim," laughed Amy.

"Oh well, I was." Jim closed his eyes and lay back on the crisp white pillows. Amy was concerned and tried to make him rest and have a little nap, but he just shook his head. When he opened his eyes again a few seconds later, he looked all alert and eager to go on. Determined to let Jim rest for a while, Amy used the toilet as an excuse to give him a well-earned break from his visit down memory lane. She could tell that it was extremely important to her uncle and so she had to humour him and let him get whatever it was that troubled him so, off his chest. What could it be? Who was this Gina? He'd never mentioned her before. Why all this reminiscing now?

"I remember it all like it was yesterday," he continued. "The very next day I went down to the beach again. I looked around to see if she was there. You know, the girl I'd covered in sand… It was difficult to pick someone out on such a crowded beach. Families with children and various friends and relations sat under brightly coloured beach umbrellas. Youngsters were busy building sandcastles. Ice cream vendors were parked on the roadside, which ran along the beach. Boys as brown as berries walked around the sun worshippers calling out to sell their packets of roasted peanuts and roasted broad beans.

I was so disappointed when I didn't see her amongst all the other girls who were sprawled on their large beach towels. I carried on walking till I reached the rocky side and after a vigorous swim in the sparkling blue sea, I started to work on my tan. In spite of a fair amount of sun cream, I'd managed to get burnt on my shoulders and arms. That day I learnt a very important lesson. Cover up, take it very slowly, especially in the middle of the day or end up looking like a beetroot."

"Oh you should have known better since you're so fair!"

"You should have seen my mate, Ginger. He really did look like a beetroot, instead of the usual carrot top. Anyway, I digress.

After spending a few hours near the sea, it seemed rather a long walk up to the barracks, but we (young lads that we were) were seduced by the music blaring out of a jukebox and the thought of ice-cold beers. The music was coming from a very popular bar by the looks of it. Tables and chairs with their big bright umbrellas gave some very welcome shade outside the bar. It was nestled in the corner. There were shops on one side, all displaying local products. We used to stop at that bar every day for an ice-cold beer. I remember the local beer, it was called, simply, Hop leaf.. Yes, I remember that first visit to The George Cross bar very clearly. I stood up and went to the jukebox to play my favourite song of the moment."

"Pop song? You?" Amy was surprised.

"Yes, don't look so surprised. It was Eleanor Rigby. I loved the Beatles, still do don't I? I know your Auntie Meg has all their hits, but they were originally mine! Whenever I hear that song now, it takes me back to the sixties, to Malta, and to the George Cross bar!"

"And to.... Gina?"

"No, I don't let myself.... anyway, as I looked up after feeding the jukebox...there she was, the girl...my girl!! I suddenly felt like an awkward schoolboy once again. I could feel myself blushing to the roots of my hair."

"Oh, it's you again!" Gina smiled. Then, with a cheeky grin, she asked me if I'd covered any other poor girls with wet sand. The conversation that followed was very stilted, on my side anyway, because I felt so very self-conscious compared to this vivacious girl. Somehow her teasing smile seemed to turn me into a tongue-tied idiot.

I kicked myself all the way back to St Patrick's Barracks. Why on earth hadn't I arranged to meet her again? Why hadn't I ask her out? I kept asking myself these questions. I could tell that she was interested. No, don't laugh Amy. Honestly, it was her smiling green eyes that said it all. Yet, for some stupid reason, I just felt awkward. Mind you, after that first visit, the bar soon became a regular welcome stop. After a few hours at the bay, I often stopped there to get a cold drink, but to be honest, it was mainly to catch a glimpse of her.

Most of us squaddies spent a lot of time propped up at the bar. Mind you love, it was a noisy joint, as we used to say, because the jukebox was never idle. Sometimes Gina was there, busy helping out but there was hardly ever an opportunity to have a few words. More often than not, you could hardly hear yourself think in that place. Like I said earlier, out in front of the bar there were a few tables and chairs that were topped with bright, gaudy, sun umbrellas. But these were taken very quickly. The place was always chock-a-block. Cold drinks, especially Hop leaf and Cocapina (a pineapple soft drink) were a must after a long session swimming, water-skiing or just sunbathing, or even all three!

"It does sound like you were hating it…not!" laughed his niece.

"Yeah, right…I'll tell you what was funny, shall I?"

"What?" Amy asked curiously.

"Well, we were all having such a good time in Malta, and making the most of it. Yet, all the time, one of our favourite songs went, wait for it... "We've Got Get To Out of This Place!" Everyone played it, and we made ourselves hoarse trying to outshine each other. I loved that song. I think it was by The Animals."

"I've actually heard it but I didn't know it was that old!"

"Anyway, the truth is we'd have happily stayed in Malta for much longer than the two-year stint!

Most days, we were still singing as we trailed up the hill to our camp. I remember my best mate Ginger pointing out that the darn hill seemed so much steeper after a swimming session."

"Ah, I suppose you were all tired after swimming and sunbathing, poor things," Amy said sarcastically.

"Yes, of course we were. It's hard work swimming and getting nice and bronzed into the bargain. Anyway, I'd better carry on otherwise I'll never finish my tale."

"Oh, all right, go on…," said Amy smiling widely now.

"Well, my dear. Eventually, Lady Luck smiled on me. It was a beautiful Sunday morning and Ginger and me were walking down to the beach. It was much earlier than usual and so we were hoping that it would be less crowded at that time. It wasn't too hot yet either. No, it was just perfect. Suddenly we heard someone calling my name… and, turning round, I couldn't believe my eyes. The gorgeous Gina was running to catch up with us."

"She knew your name then?" Amy said, smiling broadly.

"I actually wondered how she knew, it and showed my surprise, but do you know something? She never admitted how she found out. She was a great tease."

"Yes I'm gathering that. She sounds quite a feisty girl."

"You could say that. Anyway we waited until she caught up with us."

"Phew, I shouldn't run in this heat. I'm puffed out," she

managed to say as she wiped her brow with the towel she was carrying.

"Are you going swimming?" I realised straight away how stupid a question it was considering that she was wearing a bikini top and a pair of shorts…and she was carrying a colourful beach towel.

"Yes, I helped in the bar for a while but they're not busy now. I love it at this time of the morning, before it gets too hot," “she told us. Gina told us that the beach wouldn't be too crowded yet, which was exactly what we'd hoped for."

"Fingers crossed I'm right," she added, "but, the earlier I go, the less crowded it is usually."

Us lads had found out that the beach was always more crowded on Sundays, but as Gina said, it was early yet, so it was the quietest we'd seen it.

"You don't like it on the sand do you?" she asked, looking very sweetly at me, when we reached the sandy bay. She had the knack of looking through her dark eyelashes, and though it might sound corny to you, that used to - well it used to make me go weak at the knees!

Amy shook her head and smiled. "This doesn't sound like my Uncle Jim!

"Oh well, I've come a long way since then," he laughed. "When I finally found my tongue, I explained that it was less messy to sunbathe on the rocks. There were some flat sections to sprawl out on, on the rocky side. As soon as I got out of the water I'd go on to the rocks and dry off nicely without sand going everywhere.

Gina agreed with me, but she couldn't resist a sarcastic comment. It was something like," "Of course. On the rocks. There's no chance of anyone walking past you and covering you and your book with sand is there?" Her teasing dig made me blush again. Oh, how I used to blush in those days!

We were now at the spot where Gina always sprawled out. Me and my mate just stood there watching her drape the big colourful towel on the sand. Then she took her flowered shorts off and sat down on her towel. She looked lovely in her green bikini."

"I bet you two were staring, probably embarrassing the girl."

"No, not at all. She was so confident and laid-back...but then...Ginger made a gesture, which suggested that I stayed there with her. My mate left me there and he carried on walking to the

Lido for a spot of water skiing."

"Well, that was thoughtful of him wasn't it?"

"At that moment I could've kicked him, but soon enough, I was so glad that he did push me into it. For a change, I actually found myself talking quite effortlessly to Gina. Thinking about it now, it was amazing. In spite of being on a beach with people around, music blaring from transistor radios and the added calls of the ice cream vendors shouting to attract customers, I could only see this gorgeous girl in a green bikini…the colour complimenting her eyes perfectly. I was, in fact both of us were, totally oblivious to the entire hubbub around us.

"Do you actually live close by?" I asked her the question that I'd been dying to ask for a while. I said that I'd often seen her in the bar, helping out.

Then she explained that her brothers shared the upstairs flat above the bar. It wasn't huge but adequate for them and handy for work. Gina and her parents lived just next door. She went on to explain that a door under the stairs linked the two houses.

I was also ever so curious about a lovely old lady who sometimes served drinks. She was so quick and had a joke with every body. She seemed to love to chat to all the men and it looked like she knew everyone!

I found out that it was their Nanna, grandmother. Anna, the Nanna, lived a couple of doors down from the house with the bright yellow door. She and Nannu, the grandfather, originally owned the bar. She had always helped since she and granddad got married. They had worked together until the children came along. Her parents had done the same so it had been in the family for quite a long time."

"Well, Uncle Jim, with a bit of luck it's still in the family," Amy hoped.

"Anyway, the sprightly old lady was a widow, and she spent a lot of time in Gina's house. It seemed to work out well. If she got bored, she just walked through to the bar and helped out. She loved mothering all of us young servicemen away from home. Sometimes, she would sit and chat - if she wasn't clearing tables that is. Everyone loved Anna. We all called her "Nanna."

"She sounds lovely."

"She was that…she must be ninety odd now. Honestly Amy, she was such a great character. Yes, she definitely was that! "

"Hang on a minute Uncle Jim. Here you are. Drink this water 'cause you sound a bit croaky."

"Now, where was I?"

"You were talking about the grandmother."

"Where was I before that? Oh yes, I was saying how somehow I had managed to loosen my tongue that day. Gina and I talked and talked. I don't think we actually went in the water that day! Without much effort I found myself talking about my family back in Lincolnshire.

Gina wanted to know all about my brothers and sisters who, she said, must have been missing me. I told her that as I was the eldest, they looked up to me and they had all said how grown up I looked in my army uniform. I found myself relating little incidents that made home seem so far away. I remember feeling a little self-conscious too, but that didn't stop me taking my wallet out and showing her a snapshot of my dog. I felt a little bit sad when I talked about Rustler who was getting very old. I bet you didn't know about the dog I had?" Amy shook her head.

"No, I had no idea," she admitted.

"Anyway, Gina listened attentively. I knew about all her immediate family, and she'd told me that she had simply hundreds of cousins, uncles and aunts. Her two brothers were very protective of her and always watched out for their sister. Gina admitted that her parents were rather old fashioned.

"They hardly believe that I'm grown up even at twenty-two-years of age!" she often said. "Oh, did I mention that she worked in a bank?"

"I then asked Gina where she and her friends went of an evening, and she laughed out loud at that but then she did tell me that they usually went to Sliema or Valetta but that was a little far.

"Far?" I laughed. It wasn't far at all!

"Well, it's a bit of a drag on the buses," she said. Apparently it was ok if one of them had a car because then she wouldn't be late and so she didn't get into trouble with her dad."

"Trouble?"

"Yes, Amy, would you believe that she'd get a telling off if she got home after nine?

Honestly, it's true. She really had to be home by nine at the latest. I was really amused by this! Without thinking, I told her that if that was the case, then we just had to go out really early. Her lovely green eyes opened wide, her face lit up and, smiling up at me, she said that she wasn't aware that we were going out!

Afterwards, thinking about it, I couldn't believe that I'd actually plucked up the courage to ask her out.

To be honest with you, I'm not even sure if I did! I came to the conclusion that I must have been thinking out loud! However it had come about, I'd managed it and Gina seemed really and genuinely pleased to arrange a date."

CHAPTER 3

"You'd better pick me up from the house when we do go out. My parents will want to meet you properly. Yes, they do," she added when she noticed that I was shaking my head vigorously.

"I've met them haven't I?" I asked.

"I know you've met briefly in the bar, but taking their daughter out is another matter. They don't mind me mixing and talking to you lot in the bar."

"Why is that then?"

"I think it's because there's always someone around to keep an eagle eye on me there. To be perfectly honest they don't really like me going out with foreign boys."

"What's wrong with us?"

"Nothing Jim. It doesn't mean that there's anything wrong with you. It's just that they keep hoping I'll meet a good Maltese lad. A Catholic."

"So, I come to pick you up, and then what? Will I get the third degree?"

"It's not really like that at all. Well, not much," she was grinning at my frowning expression.

"My parents meet all my friends, boys and girls."

"All these get vetted, do they?"

"Jim, be serious. They just like to know who my friends are. If they think there's a boy I really like, in fact anyone that I'm remotely interested in, they tend to analyse him. Somehow, and I can't explain how, if they don't take to him I find myself totally convinced that he isn't the right one! "

"Crikey, how many did they reject?"

"I know that it sounds like there's been hundreds of boys, but in fact there were only two of them. I soon realised that they weren't as nice as I thought. I have to admit that thanks to mum and dad, I stopped myself from making a terrible mistake...Neither of them was the right one for me."

"You mean they weren't right for your parents! "

“Well, no, but I do love them dearly, and I respect their opinions because they only want the best for me. I admit that they're old fashioned in some ways."

"Mmmm...."

"You have to understand, I'm the only girl on my father's side. In fact, I'm the only girl for four generations. I suppose that's why they're, a little bit too protective of me"

"Well, from where I'm standing they seem very over protective, not just a bit. Goodness me! The girls back in England, girls younger than you, well, they stay out much later than that! Do you really have to be home by nine?"

"Well, this is Malta and all the girls go home around the same time as me. We're used to it. Like you said," Gina continued with a smile, "more than likely, we go out much earlier than the British girls do. It's probably because we only work half days ...at least in summer anyway."

"That's true I suppose. Girls back home go out around eight o'clock...when it's almost time for you to return."

"It's what we're used to. Anyway," she continued with a cheeky and somewhat provocative smile, "when are you taking me out then? Tonight?"

"Oh, hmm. Yes, yes, tonight is fine," I stuttered, not believing that this was really happening. Oh why was I blushing again?

"You don't have to take me out you know"...she quickly retorted when she saw how shy I was. I had needed a bit of prodding.

Later on, when we'd been out a few times, Gina mentioned that fact to me and often teased me about it.

"Oh, no, it's great. Tonight will be great. Sorry, it's just.... anyway," I quickly recovered, "I'll call for you at seven tonight."

"You know where I live. Next door to the bar. The house with the bright yellow door. Just come and say hi to my parents."

"Oh dear, I hope it won't be an ordeal - meeting your mum and dad properly, I mean. Of course, I've met in the bar. But everyone's done that. Whenever I saw them, they were helping your brothers out."

"Yes, they do sometimes but they try not to step on my brothers' toes too much. They give a hand and then they disappear through to the house."

"Well, I'll be there at seven sharp and, after my inspection, we can go and see the new ‘Carry on’ film that's showing at Sliema. It's supposed to be very funny...'Carry On Screaming'

"What's this inspection business? I like it! Well, let's hope you'll pass with flying colours eh?" I must've looked worried because Gina went on to reassure me that her mum and dad were really very nice and friendly. She tried very hard to convince me that there was absolutely no need to be at all nervous about meeting them.

"Oh, and Nanna might be there. She's there most evenings," Gina added.

"Oh no, not another officer to inspect me! "

Gina giggled as she explained that Nanna's opinions mattered a great deal, "especially where my mother is concerned. She's her mum. Nanna's still grieving for Nannu and she comes round for company. So it's not unusual for her to be at our house. Meeting you might give her something new to think about," Gina said with a big smile lighting up her face.

"Oh dear, that sounds worrying." I was gradually getting more nervous by the second. “Can't you meet me away from your house?"

"Well of course I can, but I would really prefer it if you call for me this first time." I realised then that Gina had already decided that this wasn't going to be a one-off! She just went on reassuring me.

"You see, that will save me getting the twenty questions later on, or even before I meet you. Besides, I really want you to meet them properly. Please don't worry. You'll like them, honestly."

"What twenty questions?"

"Oh, stuff like, what's he like, is he polite? Good looking? etc. etc. Oh and the big one, I don't suppose he's a Catholic? Then, the second big one, he's not married is he?"

"Oh all right then, so be it. Make sure you're ready please because I really don't know how long I'll be able to survive the scrutiny. I'll definitely get it all wrong, whatever I say."

"It's not like that at all, silly Billy. Look, I'm going now. I promised mum I'd do some chores in the house and I haven't done anything yet. See you tonight Jim."

"Bye Gina."

"See you…don't look so worried. They'll love you, you'll see," and off she went leaving me counting the hours until that evening.

Amy was mesmerised by the unfolding tale and she was surprised to see how animated her uncle looked. Usually, if anyone mentioned Malta, he changed the subject very quickly, or he just clammed up!

She asked him if he wanted to have a little rest but his reply was that he'd had a long, two-week rest, in fact.

However, Amy was pleased to see the dinner trolleys arriving.

"Oh, nice, it's lunch time. Here they come. I'll go down to the canteen and get myself something to eat too. You have your lunch and try to rest for a little while," she said quickly before he had time to argue. "I'll come back in about an hour. Don't look like that Uncle Jim," she laughed at his expression. "I must grab some lunch too and the canteen will be very crowded at this time. Then I have to make a couple of phone calls, one to mum 'cos I'm having supper with auntie and stopping the night so I must let her know."

"Oh, ok love. You get away. I'll tell you the rest later."

He had to be unselfish, the poor girl must be starving but he still felt he wouldn't rest until he'd told the whole truth to his niece.

When Amy walked back to her uncle's bed later, he was sitting up reading. He did look so much better and as soon as he saw her approaching he folded the paper and put it on his bedside table.

"Where was I?" he asked her when they were settled again. "See, I've lost my thread now."

"You were nervous about meeting the family," she laughed. Jim's face changed as he recalled that special day. He remembered it very well indeed.

"The evening couldn't come fast enough for me and yet I was dreading it, well aware that though I was only on my first date with Gina, first I had to pass an inspection by her possessive parents and her doting grandmother, and possibly her big burly brothers.

I knocked gingerly at the bright yellow door. The highly polished brass knocker in the shape of a serpent made a resounding noise.

"Hello, come in, come in," said the little old lady who opened the door wide for me to enter.

"You must be Jim. I've seen you in the bar. You're one of the quiet ones aren't you? Come on, in you come through to the kitchen," she talked fast and furiously.

"It's nice and cool in there," she said as she held on to my arm and led me through a long hallway into a huge bright and cool room. My eyes took a while to get accustomed to the darker indoors after walking for a while in the still bright, sunny outdoors. I looked round the big room which served as a dining room and kitchen. A long table surrounded by chairs was on the first half of the room and plants provided a dash of greenery here and there. Through the open door at the other end I could see orange trees in full bloom. Next to the back door I remember seeing a small shelf in front of a picture of Our Lady. There was always a red candle burning and some fresh flowers on that shelf."

"Sit down Jim, go on, "said Gina, as she introduced me to her parents. "You've met my Nanna. Nanna, this is Jim," she said unnecessarily.

"I did gather that Gina," said the old lady with a big grin. "I'm very pleased to see that this young man is not one of the rowdy ones," she said and succeeded in making me blush.

Gina smiled either at my embarrassment or because she saw her grandmother patting my hand familiarly. I found myself sitting with Gina on one side and grandmother on the other and I remember the music that was playing in the background. It was so appropriate and I thought it was a good omen."

"What was it then Uncle Jim?"

"It was a song from 'My Fair Lady' and it went on about "walking down on the street where you live." It was coming. from a Rediffusion set- that's what the radio was called - which sat in the far corner of the dining area.

Later, I found out that every household had a set. The Rediffusion, as the locals called it, was never turned off except at night-time and sometimes during siesta. Anyway, Gina's parents sat opposite me and soon we were all relaxed and drinking the famous "Hop leaf."

"Were you really relaxed or still very nervous?...It must have been daunting with all their eyes on you! "

"Not half! I must say though that afterwards, it felt like the time I had spent there on that first visit was almost a blur! After a little while, I relaxed and joined in the laughter and teasing that was going on. I actually found myself enjoying the attention and the easy flow of the conversation. In spite of the butterflies in my stomach, I'd managed to answer all the questions very easily, especially grandmother's direct ones. Later, I had to admit to myself that I'd found it all rather amusing and very quaint."

"You're certainly a hit with my Nanna, and mum and dad liked you too," Gina said generously as we walked to the bus stop.

"Did I not go on? I never stopped did I? At least I think I went on and on, when they actually gave me the chance to open my mouth!" I asked Gina when we left the house. "Thank goodness that I didn't have to deal with your brothers too!"

"Well, they were supposed to be there but obviously it must have been very busy in the bar. They were going to come through one at a time to interrogate you," teased Gina.

"Thank goodness for small mercies. Still, I've met them quite a few times now so it wouldn't have been too bad, I hope."

We didn't have long to wait for the green bus, that was to take us to Sliema.

After that first visit to Gina's home, I found that I quite enjoyed going to the now familiar yellow door. After a quick knock, I used to let myself into the lovely warm atmosphere and to an even warmer welcome that awaited me, every time I went to call for my girlfriend.

We were a happy couple, quite content to spend quite a few hours at Gina's house enjoying her parents' company. Granny was often there too and I was mesmerised by the treasury of stories and tales she was able to relate. More often than not it was some tale or other of bravery and courage during the war. One evening, with great pride in her voice, Anna related how the little island of Malta was awarded the George Cross for its great bravery during the Second World War. This explained the name of the bar to me. I also found out that if you write to an address in Malta you put GC at the end...The whole island was rewarded with the George Cross you see… Nanna kept me and Gina enthralled for hours and sometimes we were quite happy to stay with her until it was time for me to return to my barracks.

All too soon the long hot days of summer got shorter and shorter and September arrived with a big storm, which apparently always marked the start of autumn."

"Oh, I would have hated that!" exclaimed Amy with a shudder. Her uncle knew that she was still very scared of storms.

"Well this one was a beauty! I was walking down to Gina's house when the heavens opened and it started raining, then it started hailing. You should have seen them, hailstones the size of hazelnuts! They actually hurt my head and face and I ran down that hill as fast as I could with thunder and lightening all around me. Me and Gina didn't need much persuasion that night to stay in and watch 'The Prisoner' on television. It was my favourite programme and one Gina didn't like, but it was so cosy and warm in that big kitchen and so wet and cold outdoors that we gave up the idea of going to Sliema to see a film which we'd both wanted to see.

Later, when the wild storm finally abated and it was all quite calm again, we were soon strolling on the sea front.

It was strange walking down the deserted beach. It seemed very big without the usual crowds of families, friends and tourists. There were a few soldiers about though, all stationed at St Andrews and St Patrick's barracks. They had stopped at the George Cross bar for a beer and a play on the jukebox until the storm abated and now they were all running to the bus stop to catch the green buses to Valletta or Sliema. I'll always remember all the lovely coloured buses, which made it so easy to get the right one. Each city or village had a different colour bus service which was so useful especially in the early days of our stay in Malta.

Many a friendship started on the buses with the men sliding open all the windows and the girls with their long dark hair trying to close them, concerned about messing their hair up. It was so hot that a little occasional breeze was very welcome.

As the season changed - summer turned into autumn, our friendship changed too. Without either of us realising what was happening we were falling head over heels in love! It hit me suddenly when I found myself deciding to propose to her."

"You were that serious about her?"

"Yes, but I didn't know it myself at the time. Things came to a head when I was away on leave.

I'd gone back to England to spend my holiday with my family and friends back in Lincolnshire. One night, a rather drizzly cold night, we were all sat around the fire. Dad asked me if I'd got to know any Maltese girls. That was the opening I needed and soon I was talking ten to the dozen about my budding friendship with Gina. I caught my parents looking at one another and smiling, but they straightened their faces quickly when they saw me look up! I think they were glad to see me happy as I talked about this girl whom I was missing so much more than I thought I would.

"I think, in fact I know, that she is the one for me," I blurted out without even thinking.

"What do you think mum, dad? I want to marry her!"

"Well son, to be honest, I'd prefer an English girl for a daughter-in-law…simply because I could get to know her well before you…" said my mum being her usual frank self.

"As far as I'm concerned," butted in my dad, "if she's as great as you say, and you love her, it's all right by me… us… isn't it dear?" he asked looking at my mum.

"Of course son, if she makes you happy and you feel that she's the one for you then we're happy for you too," she said giving me one of her special big hugs.

I returned to Malta with my parents' blessing. I could hardly wait to see Gina again, because whilst I was away I realised just how much I'd missed her. My mind was made up. I was determined to propose to Gina as soon as I'd had a word with her father. Yes, I really felt that I couldn't live without her."

"You actually proposed to her?" asked Amy, her eyes wide open and a surprised look made her face look quite comical. "So you were actually engaged to this girl …this Gina! "

"No, no, Amy, don't rush me love. I'll tell you in a minute. .Oh, see what you've done now! You've just brought me back to the present with a jolt. Where was I? Oh yes, back to Malta…back to the sixties.

As it happened, as soon as I got back to my barracks I found out that we were going on exercise to Benghazi. We'd be away for two weeks training. I was feeling rather upset because it was all hands on deck after that and I was caught up in all the preparations and planning for the exercise with the rest of them. As the days were so busy I didn't see much of Gina before we left, but I was determined to ask her father's permission to marry his daughter before I went away. I only managed to fit in a couple of very short visits to see her and I had no opportunity to do what I wanted to do more than anything in the world. Her dad was on night shifts whenever I was at the house with the bright yellow door."

"Why did you want to ask him anyway? Gina was old enough wasn't she?" Amy looked highly amused.

"Don't laugh, Amy. You might think it odd, but things were different then. It was the done thing. Anyway I'd planned to speak to him the night before we sailed. Then, I'd ask Gina to marry me. I was sure she'd say yes and I'd go away knowing that we were engaged to be married. I had it all planned.

When I returned, I would then take Gina to choose the ring and we'd have an engagement party.

I just wanted to put a ring on her finger with no fuss. However, I knew that wasn't the way that Gina's family wanted it to be for her. They wouldn't be content without a good, rowdy and happy party for their only daughter. So I wanted to please them all.

Unfortunately, I didn't get the chance to talk to her dad, because the time of departure was brought forward and all my plans went up in smoke."

"Oh, how sad, and frustrating I should think."

"Very. I was really annoyed especially as I only managed a half-hour visit with her before I left. It took some will power not to ask her to marry me there and then but I had to do it properly. I didn't want to rush it. I couldn't risk upsetting her dad, because he was of the old school. In an effort to cheer myself up, I reassured myself that two weeks would fly by fast.

Gina and I went for a quick walk and all too soon it was time for me to return to camp. After a long, lingering kiss, I left her at the bright yellow door and promised to see her as soon as I returned. I can see her now with tears in her eyes. She went up on the front veranda and waved until she couldn't see me any more. That scene has been etched in my mind ever since then…Gina standing there, waving to me, and we were trying not to show each other how upset we were. We really tried!

Very early the following morning, we all boarded the troop ship with all the military equipment, rations, and vehicles. Soon, we were sailing out into the blue Mediterranean Sea. It was calm and shimmering under the rays of the early morning sun. Malta was getting smaller and smaller and me and my mates went down below decks to relax for the trip."

"Why, what's funny Uncle Jim? I'd have thought you were sad really, leaving your sweetheart behind." Amy asked seeing me smile.

"Of course I was sad, but something had made me smile just then. I suddenly remembered that I was one of the lucky ones who didn't suffer from seasickness. Not only did I keep my breakfast down, but I also had seconds because there were so many who couldn't even smell the eggs and bacon without turning green."

Amy could see that her uncle was getting tired and she didn't want him to tire himself out too much.

"Look Uncle Jim, let me go and get myself a cup of tea from the canteen. I'm rather parched," she said hoping he would take the opportunity to have a little snooze, at least for ten minutes or so. Jim nodded and letting go of her hand, gave in.

"Oh sorry lass, of course, of course, go on, I'll have a little shut eye till you return." With a relieved smile lightening up her face, Amy made her way slowly to the lift and to the ground floor where the canteen was buzzing with visitors and patients. She took her time to queue up and then sat down and slowly sipped the scalding hot tea. She wanted Jim to have a good break because she was aware that at times, he had been very emotional.

When Amy finally went back up to the ward, there he was sitting up. He was busy chatting to one of the friendly nurses who loved his teasing and sense of fun.

"You old rascal you. I turn my back and you start chatting up the nurses! " Amy laughed.

"Less of the old, young lady. I am only forty four. A mere youngster!"

"Of course you are uncle, and I'm a babe…a super model," retorted Amy as she smiled at the nurse who was turning back down the ward with the drug trolley.

"Well, you look rested now uncle."

"Yes, I must admit I needed a kip. Now where was I, love? Oh yes, of course, I was talking about my Maltese girlfriend. Oh, she was so lovely…but…."

"What happened to her?" asked Amy.

"I'm coming to that. Please pass me that glass of water. I'm so thirsty." Amy watched her uncle very closely. He took a few big gulps and then, leaning back against the snow-white pillows, he closed his eyes for a few moments. There was a sudden change in his face. He looked drawn and anguished, but he was still determined to go on so he took up where he had left off.

"You asked what happened to her. Why did I never mention her before? Is that what you meant?"

"Yes, it is, but please, I don't want you to get upset…." Amy was starting to get really concerned. He looked so sad and weary. His shoulders suddenly drooped and he looked very vulnerable.

"No love, it's all right. I'll tell you…

Well, you see, Amy, something terrible happened then.

Something awful enough to change the course of my whole life. Until then, I was thinking that everything was wonderful. I had a job that I really enjoyed, and I was in love with a gorgeous girl. I was positive that when I returned from the two weeks away she was going to agree to be my wife."

"Are you really sure you want to talk about it Uncle Jim?" said Amy. She pulled her chair closer so that she could hold both his cold hands. She saw the change in her uncle's face and as he spoke she just kept hold of his hands and listened attentively.

CHAPTER 4

Jim just wanted to get it over and done with and in a voice full of emotion, he carried on...

"You see, Amy, we had been away a week and of course I was counting the days until I would see Gina again. Everything was going smoothly and we were all so tired that we could have slept standing up. Then, halfway through our second week in Benghazi, on a routine live fire exercise, this..." said Jim, as he tapped his right leg, "well, this is the result of what happened that horrible night."

Jim looked pained as he related how he was accidentally shot in the leg, so very severely. It was so horrific that he was flown straight back to England to a Military Hospital in London.

"We were on a night exercise when a stray round bounced off an unseen boulder. In that split second my army career was signed off.

Unfortunately, they couldn't save my leg and because of some complication or other I had to spend a long time there. I was traumatised both physically and mentally. Believe me love, it was utter hell."

"Oh Uncle Jim," interrupted Amy close to tears herself, "don't go there. It's better if...."

"No love, I'm ok.... It's just..." and trying to control himself, Jim took a deep breath.

"I'd always wanted to join the Army. For as long as I could remember from a very young age, I always played at soldiers. Then suddenly, so early in my army career, I was forced to say goodbye to all that. It felt like the end of the world for me."

Amy knew about his horrific accident because she had been told about it when, as a young girl, she'd asked about his leg.

"I remember you always making jokes about your leg but you never seemed to be upset about it. Mind you, you've never said much about the events surrounding the terrible nightmare. I can't even begin to understand the trauma you must have gone through."

"Anyway, to get back to ...where was I? I was out of it for a long time apparently, drifting in and out of consciousness. My parents, brothers and sister were of course very worried and for a while it was touch and go. That's what I was told anyway. The only thing that kept me going was your Auntie Meg's encouragement, her constant coaxing, and yes, even bullying. She was special and stood out among all the others. If it were at all possible, she made sure that she was always there when I opened my eyes. Yes, Meg was my salvation…without a doubt."

"I know that Auntie Meg was a nurse. Both of you told me how you met and fell in love but, what about…what was her name again? Sorry I forgot…. It's unusual."

"Gina…I'll tell you in a minute. About your auntie first. Yes, your Auntie Meg was in the Queen Alexandra's. They're military nurses. She even helped when I was going through my rehabilitation. She was an angel, always there for me. Meg was great, even helping me to come to terms with my grief. Yes indeed. She was an anchor... I held on to her until I could stand up on my own two feet, literally; the old one and the newer model."

"I'm glad to see that you've got your sense of humour back. You must be well again, but what about Gina? I can't understand how you were virtually engaged to a girl whom you said you loved so much but then…. you married Auntie Meg!"

"You'll see in a moment," and, seeing a change in mood, Amy took her uncle's hand in hers again. She slowly and gently prised it open because she noticed it had turned into a fist and his knuckles were white. She could see quite clearly that he was still affected by whatever had gone on. As Jim slowly relaxed and lay back against the pillows, he picked up where he had left off.

"You see, after my operation I was unconscious for a long time. I kept everyone worried about me for a long time, or so I was told.

One morning, roughly about three months after my operation, I was sitting up reading the newspaper. I remember feeling good and thinking that I had finally emerged out of the black tunnel of depression where I'd been for weeks. I remember how, at long last, I was thinking positively. I also remember trying to convince myself that I could overcome my disability.

Then, Meg walked up to my bed. As usual, she had a huge smile lighting up her face and she handed me an envelope. She always looked happy when she brought our mail and we all loved that. Bless her, she thought I'd be pleased to get a letter from abroad.

"Here you are Jim," she said. "I'm sure you're quite capable of reading your own mail now heh? This one has some pretty Maltese stamps."

Until a few days before, Meg or the other QA on duty used to read my letters to me, so now it was a great relief and somewhat of an achievement to be able to read my mail myself. It was just as well! I would have hated anyone else, even my special nurse... especially my special nurse, reading that letter out to me!

I was prudently left alone to read it. It was a long time since I'd seen her handwriting, but I recognised it at once. I'd been waiting ages for this. She'd finally written to me. I must admit that for a couple of minutes I hugged the letter close to my chest. I didn't want to rip it open at once. I was just savouring the joy I felt to get a letter from my sweetheart at long last. However, I was in a fool's paradise until I opened that letter. I finally opened it, slowly and carefully. I didn't want to tear the envelope. I wanted to keep it all."

A pained look crossed Jim's face and Amy could see that he had obviously received bad news in that letter.

"Do you really want to carry on Uncle Jim?" the gentle girl asked softly. "It's obviously upsetting for you. Why not leave it for a while eh...maybe until you feel better?"

"No lass, no. Having this accident now and waking up properly today made me determined to tell somebody and I could only think of you. At the moment you're the only one I can tell, so I really must carry on."

"As long as you don't feel tired. Just stop before you get me into trouble with the nurses, ok? You were saying... The letter... it obviously didn't contain good news."

"Of course you're right,-it certainly didn't. I had often wondered why I hadn't had any mail from Gina, but being so ill and asleep most of the time, it didn't seem very odd. I'd even been dreaming that maybe she was planning a surprise visit to England. I used to imagine waking up and seeing her there at my bedside one day! What a fool I was, a young fool! I remember the sorry look the nurses had on their faces whenever I asked yet again if there was any mail for me. They made excuses and always brought me letters from my family with great big smiles on their faces. I appreciated those letters, my parents and brother wrote when they couldn't come to visit. However, I was waiting for a letter from Gina. I knew that she would have been told about my accident and why I wasn't back in Malta. Oh, I felt so depressed! I often found myself thinking that I hadn't had a long time on that gem of an island. It was hell for me, not being able to go back, and worse still, it was so puzzling having no word at all from the girl I had intended to marry. I just couldn't understand why even my mate Ginger hadn't written. It hurt, Amy, it hurt a lot! However, no letter came until the one I mentioned earlier."

"Well, Uncle Jim, since you insist on telling me all this, please tell me what was in the letter too. Try not to get too upset, but you might as well tell me what had made you so …hurt."

"It was a very cold letter. It was just like a note really, giving you some information. There was no feeling at all in those few lines."

"Cold? Had she dumped you?"

"My girlfriend and my best friend...huh…typical material for a song or a story, isn't it? Well, it seemed that my friend had gone round to see Gina and tell her all about my accident. Now that was nice of him of course, no disputing the fact. He felt sorry for her and told her that I wouldn't be joining the regiment back in Malta and how my army career was now no more. Understandably she was upset and it seemed that Ginger was there with his big shoulders for my girl to cry on."

Jim stopped and lay back for a few moments. It was just as well he did, because just then the nurse on duty came along with the drugs trolley. She told Jim that she hoped he wasn't tiring himself too much.

As soon as she was out of sight Jim told Amy what the rest of the letter said.

"It was the most awful experience for me, so terribly painful, especially after losing my leg." Amy held her uncle's hand as he told her the rest in a voice so full of sadness that she could hardly recognise it.

"The letter said that Gina had found out that she was pregnant and she'd wanted to tell me before I left for Benghazi."

"Why did she leave it until the last minute?"

"She'd had it confirmed on the day before the exercise but she'd decided to wait till after the two weeks, for the same reason that had stopped me proposing to her that very night! Do you remember me saying that I felt wretched when I found out that I could only spend half an hour with her? So, we both had something important to tell each other but...anyway love, it was all done and dusted. In that letter, Gina let me know that she had married Ginger a few days before she wrote it...apparently their friendship had turned to love. She did admit mind, that the marriage had avoided the scandal of an illegitimate child. Remember, we're talking about a very strict, religious family. I can't really describe how I felt."

"What did you do then?"

" I tore the letter up into tiny pieces."

"Did you ever hear from her again?"

"No, never. I never heard from either of them again."

"Why didn't she write to you before? I can't understand that! You said Ginger didn't write either."

"No, nobody wrote. I really don't know why she didn't write to me earlier. I did think at one time that it was because she couldn't face being with a cripple. I don't know.... that has got to be the reason. I thought of asking one of the nurses, maybe Meg or even my brother to write to her for me, but I was too proud. Too proud! Foolish young idiot! Then of course, when I did get a letter it was too late. Obviously I didn't want to spoil their little family or I would have gone to Malta and acknowledged my child. I just didn't want to cause trouble so I locked everything up in a corner of my heart."

"Poor you, and then because of this accident at work, you started thinking back..."

"Exactly. I had honestly thought I was alright about everything, and never talked about my time in Malta."

"Yes, I noticed that. Funny, I was only saying the same to Auntie Meg last night! "

Amy got up from her chair and gave her uncle a big hug. She looked at his pale face and felt quite emotional when she saw him close his eyes and lay back exhausted.

"I just needed to close my eyes for a few moments dear. It's not like me to show emotion...stiff upper lip and all that. To be honest, it's been a painful journey back down memory lane. I've rekindled the pain of rejection and betrayal, which had for so long been buried deep down inside of me. Thanks love. No Amy, don't shake your head, you're helping me by listening patiently to me."

"I'm glad but you are looking a little tired."

"Do I? To be honest Amy, the pain has begun to subside a little now. I'm feeling better and calmer because I'm actually talking to someone, finally, about my love child. Honestly Amy, for the first time I've finally admitted that many years ago I fathered a child. It's a huge relief now that I can talk to someone about it all. Maybe one day I'll feel peaceful again."

Amy opened and shut her mouth, not knowing really what to say without upsetting her uncle more than she had to. Well, fancy, her dear beloved uncle had a past that no one would have guessed! Oh dear, how would Auntie Meg react if she knew?

"Uncle Jim," she finally attempted to sort out her jumbled thoughts, "Auntie Meg wouldn't have been angry if you'd told her at the start, would she? I mean, it was all before you met her anyway."

"Well Amy, like I said earlier, as soon as I read that letter I tore it into shreds. I didn't stop to think then and I've never allowed myself to think about it ever since. Then, much later, after we'd been married for a while we decided to start a family. It was devastating to find out that it wasn't to be. That was the only time I actually thought of my son or daughter in Malta. I really toyed with the idea of telling Meg but I dismissed that very quickly. I feared that if I told her about my child, it would have been like rubbing salt into a wound. At that time she was really heartbroken to find out that she would never have a child.

Then, after we became your godparents, we started looking after you; babysitting when your parents went out. We used to take you to the park on Sunday afternoon. Then, when your mum had your brothers and sisters so close together, we started having you to stay over for the odd night. Your mum had her hands full with four kids close together in ages, so in a way we helped her a little. That's how you became like a daughter to us; the daughter we never had."

"Well, you might have one in Malta...but yes, I can now understand why you didn't want to tell Auntie Meg. I'm just surprised that you never said anything to her, confided in her, when she was nursing you. She seemed to have got close to you very quickly. I 'm amazed that she didn't realise that something had upset you."

"Oh, she did that all right! She guessed it was something in that letter especially when she saw the tiny bits I had reduced it to. However, I just couldn't talk about it. Not even to her."

"You must have missed her whenever she wasn't on duty."

"Well, luckily, Meg was a local girl and when she wasn't working at the hospital, she used to visit me as often as she could.

My family was too far away to travel back and forth very often. Yes, Meg and I saw each other almost every day. She somehow filled the void that was so brutally left in my heart by Gina."

"Oh I just wonder how you managed to keep in touch though. You said you'd been discharged from the Army so how did you two..."

"I know what you're thinking. Without either of us realising, what had started as a purely professional relationship between nurse and patient, somehow, slowly and surely, turned into a more meaningful one. I was in hospital for about four months and then I was sent to a Rehabilitation Unit to learn how to walk again and to start getting used to living with my disability. I was totally confused and so upset. I suddenly realised that Meg had become my right arm. It was indeed odd. I needed a right leg and found myself a right arm instead! "

Amy laughed with her uncle, feeling so relieved that he had found his sense of humour again.

"So what did you do then?"

"Well, there was only one thing to do. I asked her to marry me so that she could come with me and be there to help me and encourage me...Bully me more like...to start a new life. We had known each other for four months and had spent hours together every day talking, laughing, even crying together. When I was so near to desperation, it was your Auntie Meg who brought me back to sanity."

"Did she say yes...I mean, I know she must have done eventually, but at that time, did she decide at once? I mean, did she say yes straight away?"

"She said it was a shock, a surprise...but she wasn't against the idea. I just gave her till the next day to give me an answer. It sounds selfish I know, but I said that I didn't want to go without her. I didn't want to either."

"Then what? You got married?"

"Yes, it took about another month for the banns to be read, and for all the arrangements that followed. Our families pulled together and they came up trumps with the wedding and a lovely reception. The Army gave us a married quarter very close to the Rehabilitation Unit I was being transferred to. That was a great help. We were very lucky to be able to get a quick transfer for Meg too. Mind you, it was a bit sad for the poor girl, because she left all her friends behind, friends and workmates, but it couldn't be helped."

“I see, but you said you didn't stay in the Army after your accident. How come you were given a house?"

"Well, once I was able to get up and about again - getting used to my disability - I was offered a desk job. Of course, it was far cry from my old job in the infantry. However, Meg encouraged me to accept it and to start afresh. She was working and making new friends and I needed to do something and feel useful again. That's when we were given a house. Until then Meg had been living in the barracks."

"Did you never, in all these years, think of going to Malta again, on holiday? I've heard Auntie saying that her friends always go there on holiday. She often said that she wondered why you didn't want to go back. You must have said you'd been there, obviously."

"Of course she knows that I was stationed there. She also knows how my accident happened but I've never said much about it, as you know. If anyone ever mentioned Malta, I'd always try to change the subject."

"Now you mention it, yes you did, didn't you? You always said you'd prefer to go somewhere you hadn’t been before. Then, the funny thing is you always go to Spain."

"How would you like to go to Malta , Amy?"

CHAPTER 5

"Me?" Amy exclaimed, surprised and taken aback by the unexpected question.

"I'd love to! Why? Paul went to Malta last year."

"Paul who?"

"My boyfriend! I told you about him...Anyway, he's actually talked of us going there for a holiday one day."

"Has he really?"

"Yes. He had such a marvellous time when he went last year. I didn't know him then you see but I take his word for it." Suddenly, Amy felt very excited. She was thinking that her uncle wanted her to go on holiday with him and her Auntie Meg.

"So you've decided to talk about Malta from now on? That's fantastic and go there on holiday? You said you didn't want.... well," she carried on chattering excitedly, "it's great! I'm so glad you've changed your mind! Do you remember me telling you that Paul's dad was in the Army too? It was years before you, mind, but the family has fond memories of the island because their daughter, Paul's sister, was born there. I guess that's why they go there regularly." Amy just rambled on and on excitedly. She failed to notice how miserable her uncle was looking.

He was patiently waiting for his niece to stop for breath, yet hating having to deflate her excitement. He butted in quickly before she got carried away any further.

"Yes, I'm sure you're right, but..."

"Paul really loves it too. Especially, as he says, it's a very historical place. "Steeped in history," were his words. Did I mention that he teaches History?"

Her uncle nodded his head, afraid to digress any longer away from what he had in mind. As nervous as he was, he had to ask her to do him a great favour.

"Listen my dear, I'm sorry to disappoint you. There is no way that I'm going to Malta."

"Oh, why not?" and her face dropped.

"I thought you just said...."

"No Amy, I didn't explain properly. You'll understand soon.

I'm going to ask you to do something for me. It's a very big favour. I know I'm going to load you with a huge responsibility, and I'd be forever indebted to you."

"What is it…what can I possibly do?" Amy was looking quite puzzled and Jim noticed so he quickly carried on.

"It would be brilliant if you helped me. I feel that I've no choice because there's no one I can trust as much as I trust you."

"What are you saying then? You want me to go and…you want me to…?"

"Wait Amy, please. You don't have to decide to do anything straight away of course. I can wait. I will understand if you don't want to do it, but please hear me out first."

" But what…? What is it that you want me to do Uncle Jim?"

"Well it suddenly hit me that I could have died, you know, after that nasty fall at work I mean. When I woke up I took stock of my life and I found myself thinking of Malta, of Gina and of course, of my love child. Now I really feel that I must know if I have a son or a daughter in that little island. I must find out! I've thought of nothing else since I reached that decision."

"You want me to…to find out for you? Me? Why me?"

"I'd love to go myself, but I can't. You must realise that. However, darling Amy, you can! You said yourself you wanted to go. Your boyfriend told you how lovely it is there."

"Yes, that's true, but…."

"Don't dismiss the idea straightaway please love… Listen, if you went to Malta on holiday, I'm sure that while you're there you'll be able to find out for me... It's only a small island so it won't be very hard to find out. Please think about it. Don't make your mind up yet." Jim knew that he was begging and he could see how confused Amy was looking. He also knew that he was piling a huge responsibility on the young girl's shoulders.

"What I just can't understand," she finally wondered out loud, is how on earth did you manage to blot your son or daughter completely out of your mind for all these years? Didn't you think Auntie would understand? It was all before you met her anyway."

"I told you already why not, love. At that time she was just my nurse. She brought the letter to me and went away, but when she returned, she picked up all those tiny pieces that were left of it. She obviously saw how much it had upset me, so never asked me what was in it. All she ever said was, did I want to talk about whatever had made me feel so awful. I didn't want to talk about it, I buried it all. Now I do wish that I had opened up to her. You have to remember that I was so ill. That letter didn't help me at all. In fact it set me back quite a bit. Then, as time went by, it became almost a dream, a nightmare I should say. Of course, it became harder to broach the subject with the passing days, months, years."

"What a pity that you didn't confide in her before you two became so fond of each other. You did go and get emotionally involved with your nurse!"

"Anyway, we've been through all that. I must ask you again dear, will you go to the island and try and find out for me please?

I had almost forgotten something. I have a silver cross and chain, which Gina gave me on my birthday. The cross has her initials and mine engraved on the back. It's been hidden away all these years but now I'd love my son or daughter to have it. If you ever find him or her, I would love you to pass it on."

"I just think that it'll be so hard for me to keep all this from Auntie. Of course, I'd like to help, but how do I get to find out? I don't know my way around Malta. Even if I did find the place that you mentioned. What was it called…?"

"Sliema, but…"

"I can't just turn up …How will I…? What will I say? Unless Paul…"

"Slow down Amy. Just a minute, lass. Wait. Wait! It's not as difficult as you might be thinking. First of all, I was going to suggest that you go alone preferably, since you're the only person who knows about my secret. However, since your young man has been to Malta before, maybe he'd go with you. That would be perfect! Anyway, he'd be mad to refuse to go on holiday with a beautiful blonde girl like you. Wouldn't he just? You might suggest going there on holiday. Tell me dear, can we trust him to keep my secret?"

"Oh I'm sure we can, Uncle Jim. I do need to think about it though, and well, if I do decide to go it will be in about four weeks time, for Easter, because I've already booked my leave at work. I think it's better if I sleep on it and let you know tomorrow. I'll have spoken to Paul by then. Of course, it has to suit him too. I promise I won't mention why I would like to go to Malta, not yet, ok? I think it's best not to, not just yet."

"Thank you my dear. I feel so much better already. It's such a great relief that after all these years I've brought the subject up and spoken to someone about it. It had to be you my dear. There's no one else I could tell."

"Did you never even mention this to your parents or your brothers or sister? Weren't they curious when you started going out with Auntie Meg? You did say that you 'd told them about Gina and that you'd been intending to marry her!"

"Oh no, I never explained why that never happened. I never spoke about Gina again to any member of my family. Remember that I was very ill and they came to see me as often as they could. However, it was a fair distance from my home town to the hospital in London and they couldn't make it very often. Besides, it was rather a lot of money on the train with the six of them.

One day, weeks after I received the letter, and when I was just beginning to get over the relapse it caused me, my brother Mike and your dad, very cagily talked about it. He asked me if Gina had been told of my accident. I made it very clear to him and to the rest of my family that I didn't want to talk about her, ever. Thankfully they all respected my wishes."

"I see. I just wondered why it had to be me. It seemed strange that you never confided in anyone."

"Hopefully, when… if we find out everything, I might be able to tell Meg. For the time being, however, I don't think I should. There are my parents to consider too. Gran and Granddad have no idea that they have a grandchild in Malta - a grown up one too!"

"I think you're right there. I'll come and see you tomorrow and give you my answer. I'm stopping with Auntie tonight so I'll phone Paul later."

"You don't have to rush love. I mean, I've waited all these years. A few more days won't hurt."

"I know. Mind you, if he comes round tonight I'll try to bring the subject of holidays up and then ask him how a holiday abroad with me appeals to him. Then, I'll say that Malta sounds good. Don't worry, I won't mention the real reason."

Amy noticed that her Uncle was looking quite emotional and she gave his hand a gentle, reassuring squeeze. He also looked much calmer, she thought.

Suddenly, she remembered that her aunt had said that she would be late.

The young girl left her uncle's bedside to go to the phone box.

Going down the four floors, she found the telephone boxes near the main entrance to the hospital. Amy wanted to know if Meg was on her way or still at home because she needed some time to think and clear her head before she had to face her.

Meg knew her niece so well and she always seemed to be able to tell if Amy was worried about anything, however trivial it was. Oh well, she just had to try her hardest not to let on that she had such a lot to think about.

Auntie Meg was on her way, so Amy walked slowly back to the lift and on to the floor where her uncle was. She deliberately took her time. As she approached the ward she hoped that Jim was asleep because he had looked really exhausted. All that reminiscing and opening up of old wounds had taken their toll on him.

She was relieved to find him fast asleep and when she went closer, Amy was pleasantly surprised. She noticed how utterly relaxed and peaceful he looked then. It was a far cry from how he had been looking up until now. Going down memory lane had exhausted him. However, Amy was feeling happy because, although she now felt weighed down with such a big decision to make, her dear uncle had unburdened himself!

When Meg arrived she had a quick word with her niece and decided not to disturb her sleeping husband. She just put some fruit on the bedside table and dropped a gentle a kiss on his brow. Then, she asked the nurse who was on duty to make sure that when Jim woke up she was to tell him that his wife had been.

"Be sure to tell him that I'll be here again in the morning," she said as she lingered. She seemed to be finding it hard to tear herself away, but she must have finally thought that it was best to let him rest. As Meg walked away from her husband's bedside, she kept looking back over her shoulder in case he woke up. The two women then made their way back home in Amy's car, since Meg had got a bus to the hospital.

On the way home, Meg asked Amy lots of questions. She wanted to know if Jim had seemed better when he was awake.

"Did he talk a lot?" she wanted to know. She was hungry for any bit of information about her beloved Jim's welfare. I have missed him today but I needed time to catch up."

"Did you manage to catch up with the housework then?"

"Oh yes, finally! But I've been wondering all day how he has been. Did he talk much?"

Amy hedged about without telling any lies, saying that yes he did talk a lot, especially about his Army days. She went on to say that he'd told her how they'd met and got married. She felt that that topic was at least half, if not more, of what they had discussed, so that made it a safe subject to talk about.

"Really? I wonder why!" Meg was obviously surprised. "I mean, Jim doesn't often, if ever, talk about his days in the Army. At least not about the time before his horrible accident."

"Well he did say that he loved being in Malta."

"My goodness, he actually said that? I thought he hated it, because, as you know, he never talks about it!"

"He said how he and his mates settled quickly on the island and made friends." Amy was picking her words carefully. "Then he told me all about the freak accident.... when he..."

"Goodness, you are highly honoured! I only know because I nursed him. As you know that's when we met. He's never spoken of that terrible accident since!.. Oh I lie, he did sometimes talk to you about it when you were young and curious."

"Yes, but that was just to keep me from pestering him about his leg."

"You said that Jim talked about the Army?"

"Yes, not much really, but it was what he always wanted to do he said."

"Well, I think you know that once he was back home and working in an office he wasn't very happy, don't you?"

"Yes, uncle did say that he couldn't stand it for very long. In fact, he told me that he stuck it for a year simply because he really wanted to try and belong. Sadly, it made him unhappy wearing the uniform but not being able to be an active soldier."

"Yes, that was it exactly."

"You were still in the QA's though weren't you Auntie Meg?"

"Oh yes. I actually stayed another six years and left when I would have had to go to Germany."

"Oh I never knew that. Didn't you fancy going abroad then?"

"I did want to go but I didn't want to leave Jim. Besides, we had decided to start a family. Unfortunately that wasn't to be. Anyway I would've loved a son or a daughter; a daughter like you. Still, you've been like a daughter to us, not just a goddaughter. You know that."

"Yes, auntie of course I do." Amy turned and hugged her aunt as they were walking up the path to Meg and Jim's house.

As soon as she could, Amy was on the phone talking to her boyfriend. She needed to start the ball rolling even though she hadn't given herself time to make a decision about whether to go to Malta or not.

"Hi, it's me. Sorry, I only got back just a few minutes ago…No, no problem. Good news in fact. Uncle Jim is back to his old self. I've been there until now. No, I'm at Auntie's house. Yes, come round if you can. I'd like to... No, Auntie won't mind. Hang on Paul, I'll tell you the address."

"Are you sure everything is alright? You do sound rather…preoccupied," she heard Paul ask. It surprised her to think that he could actually tell that she was indeed worried about something. It was obvious that she'd have to try extremely hard to act as normal as possible, otherwise her aunt would certainly be asking questions as well.

"Auntie Meg, Paul's coming round in a few minutes. You don't mind do you?"

"No, of course not dear. I was wondering when I was going to meet this young man. Well, meet him when I'm not on the floor at his feet that is! You know that your friends are always welcome here. Especially such good looking men!"

Amy made a little effort to greet Paul by running a brush through her hair. She was just putting some lipstick on when the doorbell rang.

"Go on, Amy. Don't let him stand out there in the rain," urged Meg as she unnecessarily pushed her eager niece forward towards the hallway. Meg herself disappeared into the bright kitchen. As usual, whenever she needed to be busy, she put the kettle on and started setting a tea tray. This time, the best china was taken out because Meg felt that this occasion called for a lovely cuppa in her best china cups. When she returned to the lounge and joined the young couple they were sitting there holding hands and seemed oblivious to all around them.

"Oh, there you are auntie. Meet my boyfriend. Paul, this is my Auntie Meg."

"We met," he laughed. "You're a lot taller than I remember," he said and had both women giggling at his joke. Soon, the three were talking about Jim's great improvement and the relief the women felt now after the last few bleak days.

"You all need a holiday now," said Paul.

"When Jim is up and about again you must have a little break. You've all been through a lot!" he said thoughtfully.

"To be honest with you, it'll be just grand to have him home again. I very much doubt if he'll want to leave here for quite a while. It'll be just brilliant for us to be together again in this house. However, as for this young lady," Meg put her arm round her beloved niece, "well, she's really been a tower of strength and she deserves a break."

Amy was just staring open mouthed as she realised that here was the opening she needed. Paul had given her the opportunity to broach the Malta adventure, as she had called it in her mind. She forced herself to take a deep breath so as to talk slowly and rationally or she would quite easily give the game away.

"Well, I booked my leave last week and I was thinking, maybe this year I'll go abroad for Easter," she started to say tentatively.

"That's great Amy," said her Aunt." You should. That's a brilliant idea! Where are you thinking of going? Spain?"

" No, not Spain. I was thinking of maybe going to Malta. I've heard so much about it…you said you loved it there Paul."

"Oh yes, I really did. Mainly because we lived there when I was young and also because it's so historical. You know what I'm like about my pet subject."

"Yes, I do." Turning to her Aunt, Amy reminded her that Paul taught History at the local comprehensive school.

"Would you like to go Paul? You've raved so much about it." There, she'd said it!

"I feel I know it already."

"That's a brilliant idea," exclaimed Paul looking surprised. "As you said, Easter's coming up in a few weeks time and of course school will be shut. Have you booked your leave then? It would be great if we could go. I'd love to show you the island."

The conversation got rather animated especially since Amy knew that she had booked her time off for around Easter too!

"That's an absolutely perfect coincidence," said her aunt and Amy didn't want to disillusion her and tell her that the only reason she had booked those dates was because she knew that Paul would be on school holidays. For the first two out of the three weeks she had booked, she was going to be on leave at the same time as Paul.

Amy suddenly felt lucky. It was almost like a wave of relief descending on her just like a warm, comforting cloak. She hugged that feeling as she realised that there was no holding back now. It seemed that she had no need to sleep on it. The decision had been taken out of her hands without any effort. Amy was going to Malta!! She couldn't wait to tell her uncle and to see his relief as she let him know that she was ready to embark on the Maltese adventure.

CHAPTER 6

Next day seemed to drag on and on for Amy. She was feeling tired to start with because she had been too excited to sleep. That, and the fact that it had been very quiet with only a handful of potential buyers going in and out, made it feel like a very long day.

She'd been on tenterhooks since she'd decided to go to Malta, and when she finally got home after work, she made some excuse about having to go out straightaway.

There was certainly no hanging about for her that evening! She didn't get chatting to her mum and dad as she usually did. Nor did she play with her little sister who tried to get her to look at her new puzzle. Amy just couldn't wait to go and talk to her uncle and to put him out of his misery. She would have visited him at lunchtime but she knew that her auntie would probably have still been there.

Fingers crossed that he would be on his own, Amy hurried as much as she possibly could and she was soon walking towards the ward. She stopped, peered around the big door to see if Meg was there, then seeing that Jim was alone, she almost shouted in relief. Feeling really pleased, she hurried across the polished floor towards her uncle. It was marvellous to see him out of bed, sitting on a chair and reading a newspaper. It made his niece smile indulgently to see him looking like his old self, with his glasses propped up on the end of his nose.

"Hi uncle, you look so well!" she complimented him , giving him a big hug at the same time.

"Do I? I expect it must be all these pretty nurses coming to talk to me and bringing me cups of tea," he retorted quickly. "Mind you, they're nothing compared to my gorgeous niece," he added quickly.

"You old rascal. I bet you flirt all the time," Amy said knowing what her uncle was like. He loved his wife but he liked a pretty face and he did have the gift of the gab.

"You'll soon feel as good as you look - after I talk to you! I hope so anyway," she hinted with a big grin splitting her face in two. "No. I know for a fact you will," she promised smiling tantalisingly at him.

"Oh Amy! You've decided?" he almost shouted. Jim took his

reading glasses off, put the newspaper down and grabbed Amy's arm.

"You're going? You really are going to Malta? Oh my dear...." He was speaking very fast and his niece saw that his eyes had welled up. She tried as quickly as she could to reassure him that yes, she was going. Yes, she would look for his son or daughter, and yes, she would do her best to find this half cousin of hers on the island of Malta.

"Guess what Uncle Jim? Wait for it. It gets better. Paul is thrilled to come with me. It's lucky that we've both got the same holiday time available. There you are, see, it seems like a good omen to me! What do you think eh?"

"It's absolutely marvellous love. I'll pay your fare of course. No, no, don't argue, it's the least I can do. I can't believe it's going to happen. You, my dear, have made me a very happy man, and hopefully soon enough I'll be a very happy dad, to whoever...."

Amy could see how emotional her uncle was at her news and to avoid bursting into tears herself, she tried to be a little practical, which wasn't hard for her.

"Now you have to remember that I don't know much about Malta except that it's a very small island and what you told me..."

"Don't worry love. I'll tell you what, next time you come to see me, remember to bring a map. Your young man might have one."

"Yes, I'm sure he has. We need one to work out where Gina used to live and where the bar was."

"Of course, she and Ginger might have moved away after they got married. I doubt if they set up home with her parents, but then, who knows? I can't think straight. I'm too excited!"

"I think you should calm down Uncle Jim or the nurse will tell me to go if she sees you looking so flushed," Amy said with a giggle.

The two kept talking, planning and debating a few of the issues that came up as they both tried to pretend that each was cool, calm and collected about it all.

Amy kept looking at her uncle, mesmerised by the change in him. He somehow looked younger and much more alert since he found out that his niece was going to help find his love child. She had given her dear uncle that boost and it did feel good!

Finally, when it was time for Amy to leave, she left a very happy man behind.

As it turned out, Amy didn't have to take any maps to the hospital after all, because the very next day her auntie phoned her at lunchtime to say that she had some good news. Uncle Jim was going home in the morning. Wasn't that the best news ever? Of course Amy was overjoyed. Her beloved uncle was well and truly better. However, now she had the added concern of having to be extra careful and not letting her uncle's secret out before they had time to find some answers to any of his questions. At least when he was in hospital, Amy could go before or after her aunt's visiting times.

Even then, at times it had been rather dodgy. When she was discussing Jim's secret she used to be forever looking over her shoulder to see if Meg was coming into the ward. Now, it was bound to be even harder to talk about it, with Auntie Meg hovering about. Knowing her so well, Amy was sure that Meg would be fussing over Jim!

She hoped that she'd find a few moments alone with him now that he would have his wife like a mother hen around him all the time.

Lady luck was with them before too long. He'd been home just a couple of days when Amy turned up to see how he was and hoping for a chance to get the plan sorted.

"Oh this is a lovely surprise!" both Meg and Jim beamed at her. "We weren't expecting you today. Come on, sit yourself down. I was just going to make us a cup of tea."

"That makes a change!" laughed Amy. Then, turning to her aunt, she noticed that Meg was looking particularly chic in a navy blue suit and a pretty pink blouse just peeping from underneath her tailored jacket.

"You look nice aunt…going out?" asked her niece as she took in the smart suit her aunt had on.

"Yes dear, I am. I'm going to talk at the WI meeting this evening."

"What now?"

"Well, yes…in about an hour. We meet monthly in the village hall."

"Do you want me to drive you there then, since I'm here?"

"No thank you dear. It's only in the next street, and I call for my neighbour anyway. We always go together."

"Meg is the celebrity tonight Amy," teased her husband. "Doesn't she look the bees knees?"

"She does indeed," smiled his niece. "What do you mean, celebrity?"

"Oh, never mind your uncle. It's only that they wanted me to talk of my days in the QAs. I couldn't decide whether I wanted to or not, but this rascal here coerced me into saying yes. I'm feeling quite nervous now, but I have made notes. It's a good job I kept my old diaries really, because they helped enormously! Reading them brought it all back."

"Oh, Auntie Meg! That's great. I'm sure you'll get everyone interested. You've told me a few tales which had me in stitches and in tears! I expect that you'll be showing them your slides too."

"Well, Meg, you can go with a clear conscience now that I have this young lady to baby-sit me," laughed Jim. "Amy, it's a lovely coincidence, your turning up unexpectedly. Your aunt was actually going to ask you to come over and keep me company but I thought it wasn't fair to do that. You might have been going out with your Paul."

"You should've asked me. Paul has got parents' evening tonight at the school and he said he'd phone me when he's finished. I'll ask him to meet me here if it's ok with you."

"Of course, of course. You don't need to ask. We've always told you to treat this house as your second home haven't we?"

"Oh yes you have, I know but...."

"No buts, you phone him. Go on, do it now so that he can come straight here when he's finished with all the mums and dads."

It turned out to be an unexpectedly good opportunity. Just what Jim and Amy had been waiting for. They needed the time without Meg there so that they could plan the ways and means of trying to find Jim's unknown son or daughter.

When Paul arrived, they told him the real reason for choosing Malta to go on holiday. Between the two of them, they explained as much as they could about Jim and his unknown offspring. Jim then told Paul that since he was familiar with the island, he was ideal to help Amy in her search.

As they talked, Amy, being Amy, (always methodical), made notes in the notebook that she was never without. With the map of the little island spread out on the table, it soon became very clear to the girl that it wouldn't be as difficult a task as she had originally feared.

She'd been thinking that it would be hard to find out where Sliema was in relation to Valletta. She knew about the capital city because Paul had told her all about it and about its historical buildings…his pet subject. Now she could see that Sliema was fairly close. She could also see then that nowhere seemed very far on that tiny island! For most of the evening, the three were deep in conversation and plans.

Then the couple gave Jim the dates for their holiday. They told him they'd only be spending two weeks in Malta because Paul would have to return to school then.

"I actually have three weeks booked but I'll try and go to Somerset for a few days after, "Amy explained. Jim knew she liked visiting her grandparents whenever she could. She was really a lovely, caring girl!

"I'll book the flight and accommodation tomorrow morning," Paul said. "I'll have time at morning break. I just thought, Jim. Wouldn't it be absolutely wonderful if I managed to book one of the holiday apartments at what used to be St Andrew's Barracks?"

"Why, have the barracks gone?" a surprised Jim said. "I was stationed at St Patrick's, further up the hill from St Andrew's."

"Yes some of the buildings have been turned into holiday flats. Now you've said that, I'm a little confused…anyway one of those barracks is now holiday apartments. They're lovely. I've seen some adverts about them somewhere."

"I wonder if my old block is also converted into flats then. I suppose it makes sense. Of course, after the British Forces left Malta, there must have been many empty buildings about the island. Buildings previously used as barracks for the troops. You two must take some photos for me please, because I haven't got any at all."

"Yes of course Jim," Paul reassured him.

"Do you remember if it was a long walk from your barracks to the beach Jim? I seem to remember it was a very steep hill. Mind you, I was only six then, I think!"

"You remember it well Paul. It's steep and after a couple of bottles of the local beer at the George Cross bar, it always seemed longer and steeper!" It's quite a walk from there to the beach, but it'll still be spring when you two are there, so you won't be walking down, and back up to go swimming."

"Do you know, I think I know where the bar you mentioned is. There are about three of them fairly close to each other. I seem to remember the one you're talking about."

"Really? Are you sure? You said you were quite young when you lived there."

“Well, the name rings a bell anyway."

"There must be quite a few bars and pubs with that name Paul," Jim said knowing how proud the Maltese were that their island was awarded the George Cross Medal.

"Yes I'm sure you're right. However, remember that we lived in married quarters up at the top of the hill past the bay. I have a faint recollection of mum and dad and me stopping quite often at a bar that always seemed to be very busy. I can clearly remember sitting under the shade of big colourful umbrellas while mum fed my baby sister. Dad always got me a fizzy drink that tasted of pineapples."

It was obvious that Paul was all for a holiday in Malta. He had hardly stopped to catch his breath, his girlfriend was thinking very amusedly.

"That's great Paul," Jim was relieved. It did appear that Paul would make the task easier for his niece. "At least you'll be familiar with the area. If you know where St George's Bay is, then it's much less hassle for Amy, and you of course."

"Paul went there last year too, didn't you love?" Amy remembered.

"Yes, I was there on holiday just over a year ago. I stayed at a hotel that was only about twenty minutes walk from that bay. Mind you, I never went swimming there because the pool in the hotel was fantastic."

"If you do manage to book one of the holiday flats you saw advertised, you'll be close to the bar and of course close to the house with the bright yellow door." It was obvious that Jim was still mentally planning about the search for his offspring.

"It would be simply ideal Paul," said Amy, agreeing wholeheartedly with her uncle. "You're certainly going to be a great help and you're making things sound easier and better."

"I must admit that I'm feeling more nervous by the minute, but excitedly so," Jim replied.

"Me too!" Amy exclaimed.

"Initially I thought we'd stay at St Julian's because all the night clubs are there," Paul was still thinking about accommodation. "However," he seemed in a bit of a dilemma, " I think that since we need to be close to the George Cross bar, I'd better try to book one of the apartments I mentioned earlier. There shouldn't be a problem at this time of the year, since it's still spring. I wouldn't bet on our chances if it were in the middle of summer."

"Well, it would be fantastic if you two managed to get a booking there. I'll know then that you'll be going past the bar regularly. You have to, to get to and from the flats you mentioned. It's one long road starting at the bottom of a hill with the bar nestled in the corner. Ah, I can see it now!"

"I hope we manage to, Jim," Paul said smiling at the excited older man. "Then, knowing that it's close by, we'll be able to take our time and gradually, hopefully, get to speak to some member of the family. What I mean is, we have to take things slowly."

"That's if the family is still there - we're assuming that they are." Amy looked worried. "If it's the same family, whichever branch of it, we'll definitely meet some hostility. They're sure to get angry at some strangers turning up and asking questions."

"I do hope the family still lives there. The house is next door to the bar. Like I told this lass here, the door was a very bright yellow then." Jim was staying positive, mainly because knowing how small the island was, there was no doubt in his mind that they'd find Gina, and then his love child....or at least learn his or her whereabouts.

"Did the family own the bar then?"

"Oh yes. The George Cross bar has been in the family, or had been then, rather, for years. I remember someone, I think the grandmother, telling me that. Anyway, as you pointed out Paul, you can't rush things."

"I totally agree with you Jim," Paul said. "We have to tread carefully and first find out, of course, if the bar is still in the family. Then, we need to know whether Gina and that...that so-called friend live in Malta or not. He might have settled there you know; left the Army for all we know. On the other hand, they might be living here in the UK."

"I never thought of that!" Amy gasped. "Of course, they probably left Malta when the regiment did and settled over here. We'll soon find out one way or another!"

"Somehow, I don't think Gina left Malta. She was very close to her family and they were all so protective, over protective of her. I would bet that she persuaded Ginger, if he needed any persuading, to get a job in Malta so that she wouldn't have to leave her family. Well, hopefully we'll find out soon enough, or rather you two will."

"We haven't even considered that you might even be a granddad! Your son or daughter might be married and with a family!"

"Goodness, she's right of course Jim."

"Oh dear, I wonder..." Jim seemed to be miles away...in Malta most likely, Amy thought.

CHAPTER 7

It didn't seem very long before the young couple were holding hands and feeling very excited as they were nearly there! Their wide, eager eyes looked out of the windows as they approached Luqa airport. Much to Amy's surprise, as soon as the plane touched down all the passengers starting clapping! Paul had forgotten about that and smiled at her surprise.

The golden rays of the early morning sun made everywhere look light and bright. It promised to be a perfect day. Even at daybreak it was comfortably warm, neither hot nor cold. It seemed amazing, even though it was still very early in the morning. The sun was already peeping out brightly and no trace of a cloud was to be seen.

Amy looked out of the windows at the clear blue Maltese sky that she had heard so much about.

As they walked down the steps away from the plane, her excitement was mounting but at the same time, it was tinged with a little nervousness. Now, finally, she and Paul were going to be able to try and help her dear uncle find out about his love child. She smiled to herself as she thought that she liked what they called illegitimate children in the sixties. Amy wondered how on earth she was going to feel when she managed to find Gina and her son or daughter. In a way she felt very honoured and responsible to be trusted with such a task. All these thoughts were buzzing through her head as she looked around her and tried to take it all in.

Amy followed Paul and joined the other passengers who were boarding the waiting buses. These were taking them on the short ride to the Arrival Lounge at the airport.

Everyone looked relaxed and laid back as people bustled about and queued up to go through Customs. She was impressed by the great open spaces in the building. It was so spacious and so clean. Everywhere shone! The marble floors were so highly polished that they reflected everything. It all looked very grand and certainly impressive. It was all so unlike the airports back in England. Everywhere looked bright and sparkled in the sunlight.

There was some hanging about because it seemed that the friendly custom officers wanted to have a little chat with most of the newly arrived passengers. They were taking their time, smiling away and looking very laid-back. Once they were cleared through Customs, they found their holiday rep waiting to shepherd them out of the building into the beautiful bright morning.

Beaming broadly, Maria introduced herself to everyone in her group. The very attractive and cheerful girl led them to the coach that was waiting to take them to their holiday homes. As the driver got himself ready, Maria started to tell them about all the outings and events in store for those who wanted to join her and other tourists during their stay in Malta. She gave each of them a list of events and excursions and her contact numbers so that they could call her if there were any problems, however small. Everyone seemed relaxed and happy as they boarded the coach and looked eagerly through the windows.

As they drove away from Luqa airport, Amy's eyes darted here and there, taking in the buildings that seemed to be mushrooming all over the place. Acacia trees, full of colourful blossoms lined the roads on both sides until they came to the built up areas. She remembered her uncle describing the scenes she was now seeing for herself. Maria was still talking and interacting with the passengers but Amy was feeling rather strange.

It was all so familiar, if only in her mind's eye. Her uncle had certainly painted a vivid series of pictures with his perfect descriptions. It actually felt as if she'd been there before!

The only difference would probably be the new-looking buildings - mostly holiday flats and hotels. Newish looking houses were built from large, white, sandstone blocks. It was easy to pick the newly built ones because they weren't painted. They all looked very grand. The houses back in England must look like dolls' houses compared to these, the girl was thinking.

The most obvious difference between the houses there and in Malta was the lack of lush green, front lawns. In the built up areas, the only greenery came from the huge rubber plants and palm trees in big terracotta pots. Every house seemed to have these tucked to the side of their front porch. All the new houses looked impressive with wide steps leading to the front doors. Most of them had stone statues among the potted plants. Cherubs and Greek gods and goddesses were indeed popular. The older houses they passed by had brightly painted doors and different coloured facades. These provided a touch of green with their window boxes.

This was all like her uncle had described to her. It was also strange that there was a great deal of traffic which seemed to be coming from all directions! It was just around seven in the morning and yet there seemed to be lorries, trucks, horse-driven carts, vans and bicycles. They were all so noisy! Uncle had mentioned that in summer, all the drivers tried to drive in the shade. It wasn't summer yet, but it was promising to be a sunny day. She grinned as she uttered, "I'll soon see if he is right about that too!" Buses added to the traffic and the noise.

The coach eventually got to Msida and then to Gzira. As they drove alongside the yacht marina, Paul pointed out some of the grand yachts moored there, and remarked "there must be some rich people about." After dropping various groups at different hotels or apartments, the coach approached Sliema.

Since they were the last to be dropped off, Gina could relax and continue to enjoy looking out and taking it all in. She thought it was fantastic to look out of the coach windows and see the blue sea. Here and there were brightly painted fishing boats or "Dghajsa".

They carried on along the coastline with stops every now and then to drop off some more new visitors to Malta. Amy started to feel quite emotional when Paul squeezed her hand and told her that they would soon be at St George's Bay. They were soon going to find out if the bar was still there.

"There seem to be new buildings going up everywhere you look."

"I think that these are probably more hotels and holiday flats." Amy had been thinking the same. "I just wondered what Uncle Jim would say about the changes he'd see after more than twenty years away from Malta. A couple of bumpy bus rides would soon make him feel at home, although some roads look fairly new," she said laughing at her own joke.

Maria encouraged everyone to take a leaflet that gave all the dates of the organised outings. Since it was Easter time, there were quite a few (albeit religious) ceremonies and events well worth visiting.

"Don't forget," she reminded her group," you've got my contact numbers. Hopefully nobody will get in touch with a problem. However, should any of you have one, however petty, please call me," she urged.

Paul thought that Amy looked worried and he could easily guess what was going through her mind. He kept quiet and soon was lost in his own thoughts too. It was only when the coach arrived at St George's Bay that he forgot himself and in a voice louder than he realised exclaimed, "There Amy, there it is!"

"What? Where? You mean the bar?" she whispered. "I can't see it!"

"Over there, look, tucked in the corner. It's exactly as I remember it. There. See it? It's closed of course because it's too early."

True enough, there it was, with a big bright sign saying George Cross bar above the door.

"Look Paul," whispered the girl breathlessly, "that's the house where Gina used to live with her parents. Maybe she still does. Uncle Jim said it had a yellow door. It still is, bright yellow, look!"

"Did you see that? There was a paper stuck to the bar door, a notice of some sort. I wonder what it says."

"We could stop here and find out," suggested Amy rather foolishly. Paul reminded her that they had cases and bags to carry and that the hill was long and steep! She grinned and agreed but in her excitement she wasn't able to think rationally.

It was a great relief when they were finally dropped at the apartment. It was indeed one of the many newly built ones. Here again, like at the airport, everything looked bright and shiny.

"Look at the polished floors Paul, it's amazing… no carpets anywhere. That's what's so different. I should imagine these tiles keep the flat cool in summer. Carpets wouldn't be ideal in such a hot country, would they?"

It was still only eight o'clock but they both felt tired; mentally rather than physically. The journey had been a short one. They didn't travel all the way from Plymouth to an airport in London, because Paul had booked their flight from Exeter. Amy was grateful that there wasn't a lot of travelling involved because she couldn't wait to arrive in Malta. Now they were actually there, she felt a sense of excitement, almost panic. She really needed to unwind.

After a refreshing shower and a snack from the welcome pack they found waiting for them, she began to feel relaxed. They enjoyed their food whilst sitting on the veranda and looking at the lovely blue sea. This was dotted with brightly coloured boats of all sizes. The tepid sun did not yet heat the slight sea breeze and so it felt a little cool.

"It's simply idyllic to relax like this and get into the holiday mood," she said as she sprawled into a comfortable sun lounger. Paul murmured his agreement as he got comfortable. They relaxed so much that before they knew it, they were having their first siesta, albeit a little early in the day!

"I can't believe that I slept for an hour," Amy declared.

"Well, I believe it. You were snoring loud enough to wake me up," Paul teased. "We obviously needed that."

"I'll unpack now," Amy said and soon they were both getting that out of the way so that they could start enjoying their holiday.

"That's it, "Amy exclaimed. "I don't know about you Paul, but I feel wide awake and raring to go. Shall we take a leisurely walk? We could stroll down to the…"

"Ok, ok, I hear you. Come on, let's go and see what that notice says, shall we? You'll die from the suspense if we don't, but it will be a long walk back, mind. I'm not sure about buses."

Feeling energised and ready to start their adventure, Paul and Amy set off, and hand in hand they went down the steep hill, the hill Jim had talked so much about.

There was no need for words because each of them had a good idea how the other was feeling, so they walked slowly down in poignant silence. However, there was a strange aura of excitement about them. You could almost touch it. Since they had no clue how things would turn out or how difficult or easy their task was going to be, they were also rather anxious.

Soon they were going past the so-called private beach. They both knew that the section was originally supposed to be just for the servicemen and their families. Amy repeated what Jim had told her. He'd said that not many single men stayed there to swim and sunbathe because there used to be many kids about. Instead they all trailed down to St George's Bay with its sandy beach and lots of girls sunbathing. Anyway, it was just a ten minute walk away!

Across the bay they could see the rocky part of St George's Bay. There was the Water Sports Centre and bar, which had been so popular with Jim and the other soldiers. Amy looked at the deserted beach and she could imagine it thronged with sun lovers in the hot days of summer.

"If he were here now, I'm sure that Uncle Jim would see lots of changes and improvements. There's no doubt about that!"

"Definitely, he probably wouldn't like it! For a start there seem to be many hotels and new buildings mushrooming everywhere. He wouldn't expect to see so many I'm sure. Anyway, most people get disappointed when they return anywhere after many years."

"Yes, I think you're absolutely right. Still, the sea is still there, as incredibly blue and as calm as he said it would be."

It was still spring and so the beach looked deserted and rather sad and empty. Gina closed her eyes for a moment and imagined how it must look in summer. Suddenly, they were there. Just a few steps away from the bar.

"Let's go and read the notice," Amy urged, pulling eagerly at Paul's sleeve. "If it's in English that is. It might be in Maltese," she said with a frown.

"Yes it's in Maltese, well I think it is, but here you are, it's in English too."

The note said, briefly and seriously, that Anna had passed away at the grand age of ninety-two and that the bar would stay closed as a sign of respect. It would be open in a couple of days with business as usual on Easter Sunday.

"Oh well, that's that," said Paul with a touch of disappointment. "Now we really have to be patient and calm. I wonder who on earth is Anna, or rather was Anna?"

"I haven't a clue. Uncle Jim never mentioned her. It wouldn't be Gina's mum. She would be in her sixties I'd say."

" Hmmm...if she was that old.... Hang on a minute Paul, I think I know who that is, was! It must have been the Nanna, her grandmother. Uncle Jim spoke so highly of her. She was quite a character, according to him. Yes, yes, I'm sure it is, was, her. If that's correct then the chances are that the same family still owns the bar. Then someone will be able to help us find Gina."

"Great, let's hope that you're right. But, what shall we do now? It's still so early.

"There's nothing here except the sea and the bars. There are a couple more not far from here. We could go to the cinema, to one of the clubs at St Julian's, go bowling...what do you fancy doing? We can catch a bus...the bus stop is on the other side."

"I know, we drove past it in the coach. A Sliema bus was picking people up there."

"Oh yes, I remember thinking that there were quite a few considering it was still so early. If you like, we could get a taxi instead?"

"Uncle said that it's fun on the buses and it's not far is it?"

"No I don't think so. OK, bus it is then!"

"To be perfectly honest Paul, I feel sort of deflated and I don't fancy going anywhere you suggested, not yet. We can do all that back home. On the other hand, if we go back to the flat , and we watch television, it will be like an ordinary night at home too."

"Don't look so dejected love, this business of the bar being shut for two days is ideal. We can see some of the island without feeling guilty. We can't do anything yet about Gina. So we might as well make the most of our free time."

"You're right, as always," Amy answered amusedly.

"I'm so looking forward to showing you some fantastic sights. These couple of days will give us time to catch our breath from all the planning and plotting we did back in England."

"How about looking at the list of outings arranged for us? I wasn't paying much attention because I was sort of in a trance while the guide was talking, but I think there might be some event that we can go on to tonight." Gina started rummaging in her handbag. "I'm sure I put that list in my bag...let me see," she mumbled to herself as she tried to find the necessary piece of paper. The couple had now sat on the low wall that ran alongside the road, separating it from the sandy beach.

"Yes she did say something about processions...I can't remember the time..."

"Got it...let me see. Yes, there's an outing tonight to see the Good Friday procession along the streets of Valetta. Pick up time is half past two. That's lucky, it's only just after two o'clock now so we could go to that. What do you think?"

"I'd like to see it. It'll be a traditional event and if I know anything about the Maltese, I'd say it would be packed with people of all ages. Let's see, we have to go to the bus stop to be picked up by the coach. Actually, I think it's quite appropriate that you go to the capital city of Valetta first." Paul was sounding enthusiastic as he gave his girlfriend a spontaneous hug.

"All right, I think it's a good idea. It should be interesting," agreed Amy. "We have plenty of time so we might as well sit here for a while. It was here on this sand that Uncle Jim met Gina you know!"

Sitting there on the low wall with their feet on the sand, Amy knew that her uncle and Gina had spent time making plans when they sat on the very same wall. Now both Amy and Paul appreciated the peaceful atmosphere as they looked out at the colourful boats. These were gently bobbing up and down out at sea. It was so peaceful in the deserted bay and since the road behind them was never a busy one, they sat there savouring the moment. The welcome silence enveloped them. There was not a soul around. No cars had passed by for quite a while, and the only sound was the soft, lapping of the gentle waves on the nearby rocks.

Amy shivered and Paul put his arm round her shoulders. He was wondering what was going through her mind at that moment but he didn't want to break the surrounding serenity. He knew very well that his girlfriend was very anxious and in a way a little frightened by the enormous responsibility that Jim had given her.

To give him his due, Amy's uncle had said that he didn't want to pressure his niece. He wanted her to try to find his child if she possibly could. That 'child' was now twenty-odd years old. However, Jim had made his niece promise that if the search for him or her proved too hairy, she had to leave it and forget about it all.

Paul knew how committed his girlfriend was and that she would do her very best to succeed. They had known each other for about three months and one of the things he liked about her was her strength of character and also the fact she didn't give up too easily. He thought, in fact he was sure, that Amy had the drive and determination to help her uncle. That was one of the reasons why she was so good at her job. She was a quiet girl and people could be misled by that and think that she was timid and weak,. but if Amy believed in something, she was passionate about it.

This was a different kettle of fish though, and Paul was just there to help and support her in every way she needed him to. The fact that he knew his way around Malta was an added bonus. To be on holiday with Amy, in spite of the mission that she was on, was an even bigger bonus!

"I wish it were summer really, even though it's lovely here at the moment," she said softly. "Wouldn't it have been lovely to have seen everything just like Uncle Jim described?"

"It's all exactly like he said, without all the people on the beach of course. You can just imagine it though can't you?

Oh, I just thought…the time, it's getting late! Quick Amy, it's ten minutes before the coach turns up and look, there are four people at the bus stop. I never saw them arrive, did you? Running across the quiet street lifted the couple's spirits up and they arrived breathless and giggling like a couple of kids.

The family group standing at the bus stop soon got chatting to them. They all exchanged their views on their holiday so far, compared notes about their accommodation and before long, the coach arrived. It pulled in so that the passengers could alight without getting off the kerb.

"Good evening, ladies, gents and children," Maria welcomed them with a beaming smile.

"We have to go to Gzira and pick a group up from there. Then off we go to Valetta. I'll wait until every one is on the coach and then I'll tell you all about tonight's ceremony. Has anyone of you ever been to Malta before? I'll try not to bore you if you have," she grinned.

"Well, I was here just over a year ago," Paul piped up. "It was summer so I never had the chance to see the Good Friday ceremonies. I saw all the big village fiestas and their impressive firework displays though! That was simply amazing, awesome!"

Paul turned to Amy and started telling her all about them. He described the grand and elaborate displays that were held in every town and village every Sunday and some that were also celebrated during the week. These elaborate and exciting firework displays were usually organised to start at nightfall. They always seemed to be held close to the parish church or on the Village Square, the Piazza. This went on all through the summer months.

"You have to see it to believe it Amy!" he exclaimed. "The whole area is absolutely choked with the locals and all the tourists who come in coachfuls especially for the show."

"Really? I would love to see that!"

"Hopefully, one day you will. It's such a merrymaking time. All along the nearby streets there are kiosks selling all sorts of refreshments and Maltese products. Honey rings and different sorts of nougat, pea cakes, cheesecakes and the famous pastizzi all sell well. These are flaky pastry parcels filled with ricotta cheese, or mushy peas. They are so good! Cold drinks and ice-creams are sold all over the place too. The atmosphere is simply electric."

"Oh well, hopefully next time it will be a summer holiday," she said with a smile.

"I forgot to mention the brass bands! It's so festive with people throwing streamers from their balconies and verandas... while the band marches through the streets. All the coloured paper floats all around them." Amy could see that Paul really knew what he was talking about. He was so enthusiastic.

"Ladies and gentlemen...ssssshhh, can we have a bit of hush now please? There's no one else from your hotel coming is there?" Maria asked the group of tourists that had just been picked up. The driver started the coach on the drive to Valetta.

After a few minutes banter, and exchanging views and opinions between themselves, the rep. and the driver got on with their respective duties.

CHAPTER 8

Maria started to describe the event that they were going to that evening. She told her eager audience about the pageants that are traditionally held in the afternoon.

"For a Catholic island like Malta, Good Friday is a day of mourning," Maria continued. "All the cinemas and public places of entertainment are closed for the day." She went on to say that Valetta, being the capital of Malta, probably had the most attended ceremony. Other towns and villages held their own processions and ceremonies. However, the one inValetta was one of, if not the major event.

"You'll be amazed by the life sized statues that are carried in the procession. These commemorate the passion, the death and the resurrection of Christ. They're all taken out of their usual place in the parish church and carried through the main streets."

Once the coach dropped them off at Valetta, Maria shepherded them all through the crowded streets to find a good place where they would be able to watch the proceedings. Amy, Paul and the rest of their group found a good vantage point outside a closed shop. Standing on the steps made it easier to see what was happening.

Just as Maria had said to her group of tourists, these huge and heavy statues were indeed all very ornate and colourful. They were carried by a group of strong men. Each group stopped every now and again. Then, they exchanged places with other keen volunteers who looked eager to take over and promptly went forward.

The men who carried the statues wore long, white, pleated cotton shifts. There were also other followers who had their faces covered completely with a hood. This had just slits for their eyes and each person carried a cross. Some participants were dressed in costumes that depicted scenes from the Old Testament.

Maria had told them that there, in Valetta, as in most towns and villages, the streets became transformed into scenes of Roman and Jewish pageantry. These traditional ceremonies were very sombre and full of emotional scenes of religiosity.

Amy remembered to take some photos, remarking to Paul that she felt as if she were on a film set. Many devout people, young and old, followed the processions and prayed or sang hymns all the way. It was all so moving. Maria had explained to her English group of tourists why some people were following the big cross and other statues all the way through the streets. Some were barefooted and others were going slowly on their knees. These very religious devotees were usually keeping a promise of thanksgiving for some great wish; a grace that they had prayed for and which had been granted to them. They were now carrying out their pledges and their promises they made as tokens of thanksgiving.

For others, it was just a show of devotion. The procession finally ended when it reached the church. Everyone then went inside to take part in the closing ceremony.

Amy and Paul decided to go and have a peep inside the church too. Inside that beautiful building, they found somewhere to sit and watch as the procession with all its entourage filled the church .

They had promised Maria, just like the rest of the group did, that they would make sure that they would be outside the church at the agreed time.

At the moment both of them were mesmerised by the pomp and seriousness of the ceremony. The church was indeed grand and full of people. All the big framed pictures, huge candelabras and other ornate objects on the altars, were covered in purple cloth. When Amy wondered aloud what the significance of this was, a Maltese lady near them said that it was a sign of mourning because it was Good Friday-Jesus' death on the cross. She added that all the covers would come off on Easter Sunday.

Once the ceremony ended, the congregation started to leave the church en masse. As they were walking out of the church, the couple saw Maria and they followed her out into the mercifully cool air.

"That was a great experience," Amy remarked as they emerged into the night. "I'm so glad we came, aren't you Paul?"

"Yes I am, but it was rather stifling in that crowded church. The smell of incense and candles was overpowering."

Maria started to count heads as she led her group back to their coach but Paul turned to Amy to suggest that they don't go back on the coach but stay in Valetta. He couldn't wait to introduce Amy to at least a small part of the island.

"Come on Amy, let’s stay around for a while. If you like, we could go for a walk around. I know it's late and all the shops are closed…" Paul said.

"How do we get back then?"

"When we're ready to go back, we can catch a bus down the road in Floriana." he suggested. "It should be easy enough. I know where the bus stop is, because I often caught a bus from under the arches."

"You did?"

"Yes, I was here last summer and I remember it well,"

Maria interrupted.

"It would be best if you go to the bus terminus and check the timings first. The buses are all around one side of the fountain. Be careful though because the St Andrew buses (yours) don't run every few minutes like the ones for the other areas of Sliema

"You also have to remember that there are about three or four different destinations in Sliema. Make sure you get the right numbered bus."

Amy groaned amusedly but Paul, always optimistic, said that it wasn't as bad as it sounded.

Maria was still trying to make sure that the couple would get the right bus.

"Just make sure that you catch the right one for St. Andrew's. All the buses have numbers and they also have the name of their destination in the front, so you should find it easy to get the right one. One thing though, it will probably be the last one of the day, so don't miss it ok? It's only your first day. Aren't you tired after travelling?"

"Not at all. It was only a short flight and we had a rest this afternoon. Don't worry, we shan't miss the bus," Paul reassured her. "Come on Amy," he said taking hold of her arm.

"Thank you, Maria, the Good Friday procession was very moving and worth going to tonight," said Amy. "I'm glad we came along."

"You're welcome. See you again soon eh? Bye…"Sahha"…a Maltese word for you! Don't forget, if you want to join any other outings, turn up at the pick up spot like today or just ring me if you want us to come to the hotel or wherever. Ok?"

"Will do Maria, and "Sahha," they answered with a smile as they started walking towards the terminus and the information boards that gave all the bus timings.

It all felt so strange to Amy.

"I feel that we've been here for a while already. I can't believe that we only arrived this morning!"

"Yes, that's true, but it was very early wasn't it? Also, because we were in our flat so quickly, we managed to unpack, sleep and go out. It has been a packed day really."

"Everywhere is shut and yet there are still many people walking about," Amy pointed out.

"I'm surprised that even young children and babies are still about with their parents at this hour in the evening. I guess they've all been to see the ceremonies and processions."

"I remember Jim mentioning that the Maltese children always had a sleep after lunch and then they stayed up late. He had also told me that their parents took them everywhere with them, if it was appropriate for children to be there, of course."

Before long, they had found out their bus number and also the timings.

The great Triton fountain that reigned in the middle of the bus terminus was all lit up and looked very impressive. They went closer to have a good look and went past lots of young people. Groups of them were sitting there around the grand fountain, talking and laughing. They all looked animated and full of fun. Amy thought that obviously these youngsters did not have the strict rule of not staying out late like Gina did. Then she reminded herself that that was the case when her uncle was going out with Gina over twenty years ago!

She put her arm through Paul's as they turned left and started walking towards Floriana. Paul had worked out that if they walked down to the bus stops under the arches in Floriana, they had at least half an hour before they had to catch the next bus. They didn't have to rush but could stroll slowly. The fragrant air was scented sweetly by all the Acacia and Oleander trees and the rest of the seasonal flowers. Hand in hand they walked slowly down the hill and Paul took great pleasure in pointing out the panoramic view of the Grand Harbour to his girlfriend. After that, they continued in silence. It was pleasant just walking leisurely in the sweet night air without any need for conversation.

"I just wonder what must be going through your uncle's mind." Paul broke the silence at last. "Poor bloke must be counting the minutes, never mind the days until he hears from you," he admitted.

"Well, I think he's got a long wait. I'll try to keep a diary of everything we do and then I'll phone him up - if we've found out anything at all, that is."

"It's going to be difficult for him to talk to you about Gina because your auntie is around all the time isn't she? How on earth will you manage to talk to him? Oh, you'll be able to talk, but he won't. She hardly ever leaves his side!"

"I know, I know, it's a problem and a half! Oh well, when I speak to him, I'll ask when auntie's next WI meeting is. I think it's every first Friday of the month. That makes it this Friday coming, doesn't it? It's the 1st on Thursday, I think. Do you remember that night I phoned you from their house and you came over? I had dropped in for a visit, remember - I went unexpectedly, after uncle was discharged from the hospital. That evening, auntie had a meeting. It was the 1st Friday of the month. I know that for a fact because we had the monthly meeting at work that morning."

"Yes, that's right love. It was Parents' Evening at the school. I brought the map of Malta with me and we studied it," Paul said. "Anyway, I don't agree with you about only phoning Jim if we find anything out. I think that you should phone up whether we have any news or not. He must be so anxious, poor fella. Come on slow coach, we'd better walk a little faster now or we'll miss the bus. Remember it's the last one!"

As they walked briskly towards the bus stop they looked like an ordinary couple with no worries or problems; just young, in love and looking towards a future together. Nobody seeing them would have guessed that they were, in fact, very thoughtful and worried about the enormous task they had taken on.

Paul wondered if Amy would be able to stay detached and not get emotionally involved if the search for her cousin proved futile or turned nasty.

On the other hand, his girlfriend was racking her brains trying to find a way in which she could approach a member of Gina's family. She hoped that she and Paul were right in thinking that the family still lived in the house with the yellow door. If some members of Gina's family still lived there, it would be so much easier for her to make a move. The worry was how on earth was she ever going to make that first move?"

Once they were snuggled up in the bus on their way back to St Andrews and to their apartment, Amy felt strangely at home already. She looked around the front of the bus, at the Holy pictures stuck to the front of it on one side and some pictures of Elvis on the other. In the driver's little cubby-hole there were photos of children and one of him with a lady - obviously his wife.

All the windows were open and letting the fresh air in.

Amy got thinking that none of the girls on the bus seemed worried about the wind messing up their hair.

Jim had told her that when he was stationed in Malta, the girls hated having the windows open. The few that were on the bus with them though didn't seem bothered. It must be because they're now all going home and they're not worried about how they look, she decided with amusement.

The friendly conductor, his face beaming with a big grin, was going round checking the tickets and politely talking to everybody.... Everything was just like Jim had described it. The bus was obviously a new one but it was still noisy and it rattled all the way to Sliema. When they were near to St George's Bay, Amy changed seats and went to sit near a window on the left side. The bus was nearly empty and Paul laughed as he too got up and went to sit on the side overlooking the house with the yellow door.

Amy wanted to look as closely as she could at the house. She got rather excited when they went past and started whispering to Paul.

"Look Paul," she whispered as her eyes lit up. "There are some lights on! I wonder if Gina is in there with her family. I wish I...."

"I know Amy. Me too. I wish we could just go now and find out one way or another, but we must be patient! It really won't be long now."

CHAPTER 9

Easter Saturday dawned bright and pleasantly warm and the couple promised themselves a fun filled day doing things tourists do. There would be no mention of Jim, his daughter or son or even Gina. Today they would be carefree.... a day just for the two of them. It started with Paul taking Amy for a leisurely walk up to the top of the hill where her uncle had been stationed. St Patrick's barracks, which was Jim's home during his stay on the island, looked sad and deserted. Here and there, there was some construction going on and Amy remembered to take photos to show Jim when they returned.

As they started walking back down towards their apartment, both were feeling quite subdued.

Suddenly, they heard a vehicle coming noisily behind them and in the distance, slowly approaching was a bus going to Valetta.

"Do you want to go to Valetta love?" Paul asked. "Look, if I'm not mistaken, the driver will stop for us. Shall we go and do a bit of sight seeing?"

"Yes, lets!" Amy was all for it and Paul stuck his arm out as he'd seen the locals do. Sure enough the bus came to a halt and the couple got on all giggly and happy.

"Thank you!" they both said grateful to the driver for stopping just like that for them.

As they neared the bottom of the hill, Amy, who was sitting next to a window on the right side overlooking the St George's Bar, pressed her nose against the glass. She waited eagerly for another glimpse of the house with the bright yellow door.

Paul knew how nervous she was and squeezed her hand. He too was looking at the house when the door opened and a man came out. Holding his hand was a little boy. The very tall guy then stooped down and swiftly lifted the toddler on to his broad shoulders before he started walking in the opposite direction to the bus. Both Amy and Paul were on the edge of their seats as their eyes followed the man and the little child. When they couldn't see them any longer, Amy turned to Paul. Her eyes were shining and her face was all flushed.

"Did you notice anything interesting, Paul?" she asked smiling broadly and bright eyed. She didn't wait for Paul's answer but went on breathlessly, " That must be uncle's so called friend. Did you see, Paul? His hair was bright red. That must be Ginger!"

"Yes of course, it must be. He looked about the same age as your uncle didn't he? I wonder who the toddler is."

"Maybe he's a grandson. Oh, this is so exciting! I can't wait any longer Paul. I really can't! If that bloke really is Ginger, then he must be Gina's husband. You must be right. That toddler is probably Gina's grandson. Ooh, I can feel butterflies in my stomach and we haven't even been near the bar yet."

"Didn't she have some brothers? I'm sure Jim said that she had two. You see, that little boy might be a grandson to any of them really."

"Of course, you're absolutely right. He could belong to any one of the siblings. Uncle's child will be about twenty-two now and if he or she has a family, that child could well be Uncle Jim's grandchild too! That complicates matters doesn't it?"

"Not necessarily. If Jim's son or daughter is aware that Ginger is not her biological dad, he or she might be glad to know who actually is, her birth dad I mean. If Gina and Ginger never disclosed that fact to the son or daughter, then our task will be harder. We might be met with hostility."

"Yes, if we don't tread carefully and slowly, we might cause terrible trouble in the family. That's my main, my only worry really."

"Paul, wouldn't it be fantastic if everything works out without any hiccups? I must make sure I bring the photo Uncle Jim gave me when we go. I haven't been carrying it around because it's the only one he has and it's obviously precious."

"Where is it then?"

"It's ok, it's quite safe. I put it with the silver chain in the locked drawer back in the apartment. Once we get to talk to the family - whoever we manage to contact first - that photo will be like an introduction won't it?"

"Yes, I suppose so. We're nearly there Amy. Did you know that the buses used to be different colours? I think this is the only country that had a different coloured bus for each location.

Anyway, where shall we go first? I must take you to some of my favourite places."

"Well, I read a lot about St John's Cathedral in Valetta and I'd love to see it."

"Oh yes, of course, we must definitely go to see St John's Cathedral…it is awesome! However, I think that we should see some of your uncle's old haunts first don't you?"

"Yes, I think you're right Paul. We'll do that. I'll take photos for him."

The bus dropped them at the terminus that was busy with people walking briskly towards the entrance to Valetta and just as many coming out and walking towards the buses.

"What's that lovely smell? Hmmm..." It was the mouth-watering smell of the "imqaret". The sweet tantalising smell invaded their nostrils and had them looking around to see where it was coming from. They went past a few kiosks that were busy with people queuing up for soft drinks and snacks. There, at the side, was a stand with a small queue waiting to be served. A wizened looking man was dropping flat folded pastries in very hot oil. When they were cooked until they were golden brown, he rolled them in sugar.

Amy bought some and found out that folded in the pastry was a concoction made from dates. Both were soon licking the sugar off their fingertips and promising themselves some more on the way back out of town.

Walking through the entrance to Valetta seemed very strange. Jim had described the twin archways that led into the city. According to him they formed the entrance. He had described it with a tunnel on each side of the road, long, narrow, dark and historical. It had obviously been an impressive architectural entrance but it was all very different now. It had been replaced by a very wide and plain, but ultra modern looking building with big shops on both sides. As they walked down the middle, Amy pointed to a show of some sort that was taking place to the right of them. There were crowds of people watching some traditional dancing and there was also a television crew bustling around.

To the left, in front of the shops but close to the kerb, there were various small stalls set up. These spread all the way up to the main street. It seemed as if you could buy anything. The laden tables were tempting the passers by with all sorts of goods. Most items were manufactured locally. Lace woven in all shapes and patterns, seemed to be one of the most popular products of Malta. Beautiful tablecloths and doilies and all sorts of goods made out of lace were hung up to show off their beautiful, intricate designs and patterns to their best advantage.

Hand knitted sweaters were another local and seemingly popular product. The tourists who were buying them like hot cakes made this obvious. Amy wasn't surprised that they were selling so fast, because she found that they were very reasonably priced. She promised to buy herself one next time they went to Valetta. Today she just wanted to look around and get the feel of the place.

Paul had promised to take her to Castille Palace where her uncle used to do guard duty. He knew his way around and so he took Amy to the palace first. They were close to the Upper Barracca, so that was their next stop. The paths were lined with trees and statues, and busts and plaques were dotted here and there. From so high up, the view of the Grand Harbour was breathtaking. Paul had read that there used to be a lift to take you down to the Lower Barracca.

It was truly a beautiful sight. The dazzling blue sea was dotted with various crafts. There were cruises going on and people were waving happily as they sailed around the historical fortifications and bastions across the Grand Harbour.

"Look at all those boats, how colourful!" Gina pointed out.

"I read all about them...they are called "Luzzu".... a uniquely Maltese boat, a bit bigger than the "Dghajsa" which we can see a lot of in Sliema. There were many in Msida too."

"Yes I remember, all so colourful. They're used for fishing too aren't they?"

" Yes, but these are different. See! these are all painted in the traditional colours of red, blue and yellow. Apparently they are so sturdy and reliable that they can be put to sea in almost any kind of weather."

"They don't look that strong..."

"Well apparently they are. Though, first and foremost they're really fishing boats. They're also used to carry tourists across the Grand Harbour. Look, look to your right. See. There are a few out there at sea."

"You have done your homework, haven't you Paul?" his girlfriend teased, impressed by his knowledge.

It was handy having Paul around supplying her with some of his little gems of information and it was much better than reading about it all, Amy thought amusedly.

After leaving the garden it was just a short walk to check out another place that Jim had specifically asked them to find. It was the Vernon Club. Jim said that it used to be a very popular social club with all servicemen, friends and families. However, when they got there they were both disappointed because it was now a bank.

"How sad," said Amy.

"Things change Amy, and obviously it was vacant once the British Forces left Malta. That's quite an impressive bank isn't it? It's better to see buildings in use than deserted and neglected isn't it?

"Yes, I suppose so…but it is sad…"

She was secretly hoping that the photos that she was taking might help her uncle to start talking to Meg about Malta. She had admitted to her niece that she'd wondered many a time why her husband never talked about his time on the island. This had perplexed Amy for a long time too. She finally remembered that quite recently, her aunt had reached a decision about this. She thought it was painful for her husband to talk about his stay in Malta because of the accident when he had lost a leg.

"Paul," she said as she put her camera away, "I'm really hoping that maybe these snaps will provide an opening for uncle. Whatever the outcome of our search for the child he's never seen, I feel sure that the photos will trigger a conversation about his stay on the island. Hopefully, finally, he might let auntie into his secret."

"I hope so too. It has seemed to weigh so heavily on his heart for all these years," Paul agreed heartily.

Amy then let Paul lead her round some historical places. His favourite being the ruins of the theatre in Republic Street. It had been left untouched after it was bombed during the war. Paul seemed so knowledgeable about the history of Malta, but Amy was only half-listening. She couldn't wait to go and do some window-shopping.

"I don't suppose you want to come along to the war museum do you? It's absolutely fascinating. No, never mind. Forget I suggested that. Let's just walk down towards the square,-that's known as the Main Guard. There is another palace on the way down. I'll carry on down to the museum at St Elmo's, and you can stop and look at all the shops to your heart's content."
"Oh, that's great. I haven't been near any shops yet!"

"When, if, you have enough of that, just go to the outdoor café that we'll soon pass. Why don't you get a paper and sit in the shade? They sell lovely cheesecakes here…small ones, savoury, not sweet.

Get some and try a gorgeous drink they sell here. It's called Kinnie. It's sort of bitter -sweet."

"I'll do that. How long will you be?"

"I don't really know. Just sit there until I come and find you. I'll also have some cheesecakes then. My tummy 's rumbling. Last time I was here I had some every day I think!"

"What a good idea. Ah, this is the café I suppose...lots of tables but they're nearly all full. Look, there's a platform, a stage, so they must have live music or other entertainment. I'll come and find a table when I feel tired of walking around," and giving her boyfriend a grateful kiss, she stopped while he carried on down to the very bottom of the street towards the museums. She then started her tour of the lovely shops, both on the main street and those in the shopping armada. She mentally bought presents for everybody back home. It was just great to take her time and get ideas on what to get for her friends and family. When she did come back to do her shopping, it wouldn't take as long and Paul wouldn't get impatient.

It was early evening when Amy and Paul started to make their way to the bus terminus. They had walked a lot and because it had turned out to be quite a hot day, they felt doubly exhausted and ready to go back and crash out.

"If I doze off, wake me as soon as we get to St George's Bay won't you?" Amy said as she rested her head on Paul's shoulder.

"If I'm awake! Of course I will," he teased her. "I could do with a kip myself mind. No, no, I'm only joking. My legs are tired but I'm not sleepy, so relax will you?"

True to his word, as they neared St George's Bay, Paul nudged Amy. She had indeed dozed off.

"My dad and your uncle had to walk up the hill when they were stationed in Malta unless they had a taxi. I don't think there were any buses that went that far in those days. I was young so I don't remember much but one thing I do recall is later on my parents and me and my sister had a ride on a"karozzin"...a horse drawn carriage...well, sort of. I've seen a few. Did you see any in Valetta?"

"Oh yes, I did. There were tourists queuing up for rides."

"We used to catch a bus to some part of Sliema. I can't remember the name... where we had to get off. There used to be "karozzin" about and since it was a long walk to the beach, we'd go on one sometimes. I remember mum used to feel sorry for the poor horses pulling us all up the hill and then down to the beach. One day a wheel came off and rolled back down the hill we'd just gone up. I remember laughing my head off but after that, we decided to walk the rest of the way."

"You did say that you lived somewhere near St George's Bay didn't you?"

"Yes, it was somewhere near where our accommodation is now. Anyway, what I was saying before I side tracked, was that occasionally, Dad would give us a ride in these horse-drawn taxis. I loved it!"

Just then, Paul realised that they were nearly home.

"Look, Amy, look…that's got to be Gina's mother…she looks much older than Jim, so it's not Gina, is it?"

CHAPTER 10

"What is she doing? Oh, I see, she's got a buggy."

Amy sat on the edge of her seat so that she wouldn't miss a single detail. She craned her neck to see the lady in question who was all dressed in black. Amy watched her take a pushchair out and then go back inside, presumably to get the child. The bus then went past the house with the bright yellow door, same as usual, before it carried on noisily up the hill. It was terribly annoying then as neither of them could see what happened next.

"This is so frustrating!" said Amy with a grimace.

"Patience, patience Amy. Tomorrow the bar will be open and we can then go and test the water, or have a drink instead," he teased.

That evening, both Amy and Paul were unable to relax.

"It's been a lovely day really hasn't it Amy?" Paul wondered out loud. He thought that it was better to keep talking and keep Amy from brooding about the following day.

"Yes In a way I'm glad the bar was closed today. I've enjoyed myself. Thanks for showing me where Uncle Jim used to go, Paul. At least now I have photos of some of the places he went to before the accident which changed the course of his life."

Since both of them were feeling tired, Paul suggested that they just relax and watch a film on television that evening, but neither of them could concentrate enough to follow it. The tension and anxiety that Amy was feeling touched Paul too. All they felt like doing was sitting on their veranda making plans, so they talked and talked. They discussed and debated how to do things once they went to the George Cross bar. Amy wasn't quite sure what to do.

"I wonder," she began hesitatingly, "wouldn't it be better if we wasted no time and just went and introduced ourselves straightaway….if the bar isn't busy, of course? Then we go on from there. Or maybe it's better if we went straight to the house. Perhaps that would be the best way to go about it. I honestly don't think it's right to go to the bar with strangers all around, all waiting to be served. Yes, I think we should go to the house." She finally sounded more determined as she brought her thoughts to the fore. She did sound, however, as if she was trying to convince herself more than Paul.

"I don’t think so love. I'm really not too sure, about going to the house I mean.. I don't agree with you at all...We can't just go knocking on the door and.... No, no, I honestly don't think that we should just barge in and introduce ourselves. Well, yourself actually. I'll just be there to support you, but only if you need support, that is."

"Well then, since we've only got two choices, it means that you think we should just go straight to the George Cross bar. Then what? Just sit there with a drink and watch them for a while to find out who's who? If we did that, when we eventually do tell them who I am and the reason for being there, they might feel that we'd been spying. I think that might make them feel at a disadvantage. They'll probably ask why we hadn't come forward before."

They kept on and on thinking of various ways and means to approach the family. Neither of them could decide who was the best person to talk to first and they stayed up till the early hours tossing their ideas and opinions back and forth. Finally, Paul decided to call it a day.

"We'd better get some sleep now. It's been a very long day and we're not going to agree about anything because we're exhausted. However, see how you feel in the morning Amy. After all, it's your uncle's child and the person we have come all this way to find is your cousin. I think we should now try to have a good sleep. Tomorrow, I'll go along with whatever you decide to do."

After that long speech, Amy was thinking of something else constructive to say but Paul was asleep before she had thought of an answer.

She sat up, and rubbing the sleep off her eyes looked at Paul who was still sleeping like a baby. Something was different that morning. She tried to figure out what was strange. Something was odd, and for the life of her, Amy couldn't see what it was. She hadn't slept at all well and had tossed and turned all night. When she finally did manage to doze off, she dreamt about babies being snatched and people shouting and crying. It seemed like a big argument was going on, on a beach of all places!

It was a relief when dawn finally crept through the flimsy curtains. Suddenly it came to her. Today, for the first time since they'd arrived in Malta, she didn't wake up with the sun streaming across the bed. It was rather dull in the bedroom. Going through to the veranda, she had a surprise.

"It's raining! It's raining! I don't believe it, I thought it didn't rain until the end of summer" she said out loud as she shook Paul awake to tell him.

"Can you believe it?" she asked.

"Amy! You're wet! Get off, you're dripping. Have you been out like that?"

"Only on the veranda but it was blowing this way and it's so heavy…but it's actually warm."

"It's only April. It'll just be a shower…just because it's been quite warm since we arrived here, it doesn't mean it's the hot season yet."

"Oh of course. You're right, it's still very warm even after such a heavy shower, but I suppose it will be fresh out. Anyway, now that I've woken you up, do you want some breakfast Paul?"

"Yes please, just some toast. If you put the kettle on I'll come and make the coffee. What are you having- toast too?"

"Oh no, I couldn't eat a thing this morning. I have a stomach full of butterflies."

"Did you sleep at all? I know you were tossing and turning for ages."

"I couldn't sleep and at one point I got up and I sat out on the veranda for a while. It was lovely but I was just thinking how I might be on the verge of changing at least one person's life."

"Yes. I can only imagine how you might be feeling…it's such a responsibility, but I'll be with you. As I said last night, you can rely on me for any support or back up you'll need."

"I know, Paul. You are sweet," Amy said as she planted a big kiss on his lips.

The rain had stopped and so they sat on the veranda. Surrounded by such as beautiful view of the bay, Amy began to feel strangely at peace. There were some boats bobbing about on the gently lapping sea. Somehow the surrounding scene of tranquillity rubbed off on the anxious girl.

"I'm all right now Paul. We've come all this way. We planned it, talked about it, and I promised Uncle Jim that I would find his son or daughter. I will find him or her. Yes, I'll do it and I'll do it as soon as possible."

"That's my girl! Now, let's plan how to get on with it. I know that we've decided on certain strategies a few times, and changed our minds just as many times. Now, today, we must get on with it. Let's go down to the bar this evening."

"Oh, why do we have to wait till this evening? It's only nine o'clock."

"Think about it Amy. The family has just lost a beloved member and the bar's been closed for three days. This morning seems inappropriate really. They might be busy after reopening and I don't I think it'll be open in the afternoon. We can try but I honestly don't think we'll find a few minutes to talk."

"Yes, I know you're right. It's just...we're here, so close yet so far from any communication with any member of the family."

"We can't rush it and if the bar...forget it for a while. Let's get ready and go out now, shall we? We can walk down and if it's open when we go past, maybe we could stop for a drink. Hopefully, when we're there, we might learn something - at least who's who. Then we could catch a bus from the same place where the coach picked us up on Friday. We'll go somewhere nice."

"Where? Where can we go, and why? I just want to..."

"We can go to Sliema, maybe go and see a film or just look around. You'll like it. We can even go on a little cruise around the harbour from the place they call the Ferry."

"Oh yes, I saw some of those cruisers from that garden in Valetta."

"Yes, that was at the Upper Barracca. We'll decide when we get to Sliema, shall we?" Paul was trying hard to make the day interesting for his anxious girlfriend.

"Afterwards, on the way back here we'll stop and get something to eat at the bar. I know they do food - there's a board outside remember - it listed the menus."

"That sounds good to me. Hopefully, we'll see some of the family this morning and, as you said yourself, we can 'test' the water!"

Amy made an extra effort with her appearance that morning and Paul teased her mercilessly, wondering if she wanted to impress her long lost cousin.

"Don't be daft... I might not even see him or her yet. I'm putting some make-up on because I feel more confident if I try to look my best and also so that I conceal these huge bags under my eyes. I don't want anyone to guess how little sleep I had last night."

The walk down the hill seemed never ending, and as much as Amy wanted to run away, to forget the whole thing, she was determined to see it through.

The sun was out in all its glory and it felt quite warm once again. It seemed like a good omen to her.

"What happens if when I say who I am…in relation to Uncle Jim, they go mad and get angry? I don't know what I'd do!"

"You do nothing. If that happens, I'll just intervene and we'll leave quietly and quickly."

"We can't just leave…. after all the…"

"Of course we can…if it comes to that, we'd have no choice. Would you want a scene? Remember also that more than likely there'll always be people eating and drinking."

"Oh dear. I guess you were right all along. We can't deal with this in the bar. It's much too public. We'll have to ask outright if we can visit."

"What reason do we give? Any ideas?"

"Either the truth…we could say that we have a message from an old friend or something like that."

"That's a good idea!"

"It won't be a lie and it won't make matters worse. Actually, I just remembered…the photo… I never brought it with me! Oh dear, now what? We're nearly there too."

"Well, if you feel energetic we can go back…we have plenty of time. Or else we just leave it for when we go to the house."

"Look, let's go and sit on that low wall again and think this out before we go for that drink," suggested Paul, who could see that Amy was getting upset again.

"This is so odd sitting here…I feel strange to be sitting here again, yards away from where Uncle Jim and Gina first met."

"Now Amy, we'll go over and get a drink. Then, when there is a break in the stream of customers, I'll go to the counter and speak to whoever is serving."

"What will you say Paul?"

"I told you. I'll just say that we have a message from a friend and that's it." Paul was beginning to sound bored, Amy thought. She knew that she had dithered for too long!

"Ok, thank you…let's go," she said softly and stood up quickly. Standing on tip toes, she gave Paul a kiss for being so understanding and linking arms, they started walking towards the bar and of course, towards the house with the bright yellow door.

Finally, the nervous couple stood in front of the George Cross bar. They had to go past the house with the yellow door, and both of them stared at it as they went past it. One was willing the door to open and the other one was afraid that it would. Amy sighed with relief when the door didn't open because she was still feeling very nervous.

The proprietors obviously didn't think that there would be any more rain that day, because there were some tables and chairs arranged in a semi-circle around the entrance to the bar.

"Shall we sit here, outside?" Paul asked his girlfriend as they reached them. For an answer, Amy just pulled a chair out, and sat down at the table nearest the middle. She wanted to be able to see everybody who was in the bar.

"I see, that's your answer is it? Well, you've chosen a good seat. It's in the best position."

"Yes, I think if we sit here we'll be able to watch everyone coming and going and everything that is going on."

"Clever girl. Mind, you can't see much at the moment. It looks like a coach load of visitors are in there."

"Well at least from here we can wait and see when you, or we, can make a move."

"That's the idea. Good job you sat here. The other tables are filling up now. This is definitely the best position to see what's going on."

"That's what I thought! I mean, what's the point of sitting at one of those tables away from the doorway? I'm here to find out a few things," she said with a nervous smile.

"Well, relax now. Hopefully, we'll have made a move by the time we leave. Now, what would you like to drink? It might take a while because there are a few people waiting to be served."

"That's probably because it's lunch time."

"Yes, but I'm not hungry. Are you?"

"No, not the slightest bit.... I feel sick."

"Come on Amy, chill! Anyway, I'll get the drinks. What do you want? Maybe you'll feel better if you have something... I noticed you threw most of your cereal away."

"I'd like that drink you introduced me to, 'Kinnie'. It's lovely, but no, thank you, I don't think I can swallow anything. I feel too stressed! Look now Paul, I can see two men there, they've served all those hungry tourists."

"They're probably the brothers. Your uncle said Gina had two older brothers but to be honest, I can't really see from here. Oh yes, I can see now. There are two men behind the bar. Funny, but that tall guy looks very familiar. I'll go in and get us some drinks now. You don't want to go get them do you?"

"Oh no, Paul. I am so nervous..."

"Well I am too really, if I'm perfectly honest."

"Well sit down for a few more minutes."

"Yes, ok, but I just want to go and see if I can find anything useful..."

"You will in a minute. There are only a couple left now. Go on Paul, go and just keep your ears open for any..."

"Yes ma'am," Paul tried to make light of the tension he was feeling and he managed to make Amy smile. She gave him a gentle push and he walked slowly into the crowded bar. She kept her eyes glued to Paul's back as he approached the counter.

From her seat, which was directly opposite the bar, Amy could see a young couple being served. It looked like they were ordering some food before they went and found a vacant table.

Paul stood there patiently. Then one of the blokes behind the counter went through to the back. He was short and stocky while the other guy, very tall and thin, was serving somebody with what looked like the popular cheesecakes. Amy knew that they were called 'pastizzi'.

The stocky one returned and finally he turned to serve Paul.

To Amy's surprise she saw him look up, look with surprise at her boyfriend and then he was shaking hands with him. Both men then seemed to be talking excitedly, all the while gesticulating wildly.

The other bloke then joined in and suddenly they were all laughing and talking nineteen to the dozen!

From where she was sitting the trio looked like long lost friends. They got louder and louder and deep laughter filled the air. Amy watched with her mouth wide open. What on earth was going on? Did they know each other? The three of them seemed to be so pleased to see each other and every now and then they patted each other on the back! Then, Paul turned round and waved to her. The two men smiled at her and waved too. She waved back even though she felt really confused.

She then saw Paul pay for the drinks and turn to make his way towards her, while the two blokes behind the bar carried on seeing to the small group of people who had walked in and were waiting to order. They had been standing there, watching the three men's antics and waiting patiently to be served.

When Paul finally reached Amy, she suddenly realised that she had been biting her nails. She wanted Paul to hurry up and tell her what he had found out- if anything. She was bursting with curiosity and a thousand questions were buzzing around in her head.

"Who are those men Paul? Are they the brothers that Uncle Jim talked about? Are they Gina's brothers? Do you know them? When did you meet them?" she bombarded her boyfriend with questions but didn't give him time to answer any of them!

"Hang on, hang on a minute," said Paul with amusement all over his face. He put his hand up to stop the flow of questions.

"One question at a time please love," he said slowly and tantalisingly.

"Oh please, Paul, come on, tell me... look I've bitten all my nails."

"Why did you do that? You weren't nervous were you darling?"

"Paul! You are being so infuriatingly, annoyingly... Oh Paul!"

Her boyfriend just grinned like a Cheshire cat and putting the tray with the drinks slowly on the table, very slowly pulled out a chair and stretching his long legs, picked up Amy's hands in his.

"Paul! Tell me, go on. Do you know them? You shook hands and.... Are they Gina's brothers or not?"

"Aha well...just be a little patient and I'll tell you...

Well, they said it's their bar and that they've always lived here. Their parents, and before them, their grandparents ran it. So, I guess this could be Gina's family."

"Yes! Yes!" Amy could not contain her rising excitement. She dragged her chair closer to Paul's and grabbed his free hand with both of hers.

" Uncle Jim definitely said that the bar had been in the family for generations. I think we're right and her family must still live in the house next door...bright yellow door and all!"

"Well, I'm not so sure. You must remember it's been over

twenty years. It could be any family with two sons couldn't it?"

"No, not if you work it out - when Uncle Jim was here, the bar had been in the family for at least three generations. Anyway, remember we saw Uncle's friend Ginger the other day… when was it? I'm all muddled up."

"Yes of course, I remember seeing him, or rather, the man we thought was Ginger."

"Yes, it's got to be him - it would be too much of a coincidence to have another red haired bloke living there!"

"Hang on a minute Amy. Do you know what Gina's brothers were called? I don't, but these two they're Ray and Martin."

"Oh yes, yes, yes!" Amy was so excited and clapped her hands like a child.

"It's them. Yes it is. Gina's brothers were called Martin and Raymond and being a little older than their sister, they must be in their early fifties. These two look the right age. I think, no, I know, we've made some progress."

"Yes, you're right, you have to be. Besides there are only two bars beside the George Cross in the area. One is that new, modern bistro cum bar and the other …I can't remember the name"

"You mean The Cellar? No, I never even gave that one a thought when I first saw it."

"Well, Malta being such a small island and this place having just three bars, made our search very easy didn't it?"

"Oh yes, besides, " Amy sounded amused. My only worry was that it might have been sold on to another family…we would have hit a brick wall then!"

Amy was sounding much happier, and Paul felt easier too now that he was sure they were in the right place.

"Paul, you still haven't said…do you know the two brothers? How do you know them? I mean, you were acting like long lost friends!"

"Well, they say it's a small world. Malta is very, very small…"

"Go on Paul, for goodness sake!"

"It is! It's only about seventeen miles by nine I think."

Amy was feeling really irate now and virtually jumping up and down in her chair.

"Ok, yes that's very small but that still doesn't explain how you know them. Do you know them? Oh, look one of them is coming over. Now what?" she hissed at him and gave him a menacing look.

"Hi, you're Amy, you did say Amy, didn't you Paul? Pleased to meet you," the tall suntanned man shook her hand. Then, after a quick glance at his brother to make sure that he wasn't too busy, he sat at their table.

"Amy, this is Martin. The other man, the handsome one," Paul said teasingly, looking at the friendly bloke sitting at their table, "that poor bloke who's still busy at the counter, that's Ray. These two men were very kind to me last time I was here on holiday. They were such a welcome sight, and I'm so pleased to meet them again."

"When did you meet? How…?" her voice trailed away.

Paul went on to tell Amy how on his last holiday in Malta, the previous summer, he had hired a car to run around in.

"Dave and I were driving around Malta, in fact we were coming back from St Julian's - you know - where all the nightclubs are. Do you remember me telling you that we were staying at that hotel on the other side of the bay?"

"Do you mean this bay, St George's?"

"Yes of course, wakey wakey Amy," he teased. "Like I said, we'd been to St Julian's nightclub area and had had a great time. Dave was slightly, well more than slightly, tipsy and…."

"Dave? Dave who?" I've never heard you mention anyone called Dave. Does he teach at your school? Who..?"

"It was before I met you Amy. He left and is teaching in Africa now. Anyway, to cut a long story short, we were about half a mile away from our hotel when, suddenly, the engine died. Like I said, it was late. We were tired after having had such a good night. We'd been dancing for hours."

"Yes, you said, then what? You're being deliberately long winded. Come on Paul, for goodness sake!"

With a big grin on his face, Paul went on to explain how he and Dave just got out of the car and stood there not knowing what to do.

"We just had no clue what to do at that late hour. As you know, Amy, I am useless with cars. Dave is even worse, if that's possible. We looked at the engine, but that was a waste of time. We were stumped and there were no garages open. Well, we hadn't seen any."

" Remember it was very late," Ray reminded Amy.

"I'd just decided that we had to walk the rest of the way and leave the car where it was," continued Paul. "I didn't know what else to do. Dave, however, didn't like the idea because he wasn't sober enough to walk he said. So I said...."

"Go on Paul, you are infuriatingly slow on purpose!"

Ray smiled and picked up where Paul had stopped.

"You should have seen them Amy, they were so useless...Martin is good with cars and he sussed out very quickly that it was just a battery lead that had become loose and caused the problem. He gave me a nudge and...."

"Why, you two... it was that simple all the time? Oh boy, I've changed my mind. They're not nice blokes at all Amy", he said, laughing out loud.

"I remember now. Yes, Dave was furious. We had planned to go to Gozo on the ferry early the next day. We were taking the car on the ferry so that it would be easier to see some of that island. Well, we'd planned to take it but at that time it seemed highly unlikely."

"Are you talking about the other close island ..."

"Yes, it's the sister island. I'll try to take you there if we can fit it in. Anyway, we just stood there, looking under the bonnet and hoping for a miracle. Then, a tatty old van came to a halt near us."

"Excuse me," Ray butted in, "are you talking about our old faithful van, the little magic machine that never stops? Don't you insult it mate!" Laughter lit up his dark brown eyes and etched little laughter lines, which only made him look more attractive.

"As I was saying, Amy, this...dirty grey, what was once white van pulled up. Two Maltese men came over and asked if they could help. Yes it was this friend here and his brother, who is still busy inside."

To Amy's amusement, and laughing all the time, Paul carried on with his version of the incident when he met this friendly bloke.

"Dave and I just looked on as this big guy here and his brother Martin, looked at the engine and touched it here and there. They even spoke to it!" Ray was shaking with laughter as Paul was taking his time.

"Stop it Ray. You see Amy, they seemed to be debating what the problem was. We thought that they couldn't agree what was wrong and that we were in for a long night. Of course, Dave and I could only guess at that because they spoke Maltese between themselves. Then, suddenly, I could hear the engine again. It sounded as sweet as a nut." Paul thumped Ray on the back; well it was more than a pat, which amused Amy. She thought that Paul was learning to be tactile like the Maltese.

"I could have kissed them!" Paul said giving Ray a friendly punch on the arm.

"I'm glad you didn't!" Ray quipped.

"Well, it was lucky for you that we were coming back to the bar that late and had to go past you. That was our Friday fishing session. We go fishing at Sliema every Friday in the summer. Since we're always very late back and we're closer to this place, we come here and kip upstairs in our parents' spare room, ready for the next day."

"Ah yes, I remember saying you stunk of fish! I'd forgotten that."

"You were lucky because as you found out, you don't get many cars on this road especially so late at night. Actually, there's a bit more traffic now with that hotel and the holiday flats up the hill."

Paul gave Ray another friendly pat on the back and Amy was totally convinced now that Paul was feeling braver about showing his feelings. She thought that she quite liked him that way. He wasn't usually a demonstrative person, but he seemed to be learning.

"Well Amy, at the time I was feeling tired, anxious and frustrated. I thought that this man here was a whizz kid with cars. After a lot of gesticulating and debating between themselves, it took him all of five minutes to make the engine start. Now, he tells me that it would probably have taken even less if they hadn't acted the comedians. Still, the purring engine was music to our ears."

"Well your mate was in such a foul mood, we thought we had to let him stew, or calm down, at least for a few minutes. He was a bit the worse for wear, unlike you. Anyway, that was our little joke!"

" I was driving so I was only high on cola that night."

"Who recognised who first then? Or do I take it that you recognised each other straight away? Did you?" Amy was impatient.

"I thought so," Amy said after they admitted to have recognised each other at once. "I didn't think you shook hands with all your customers. That's why I was so curious when I saw you doing just that with Paul. "

Amy was feeling odd and not a little bit nervous. She kept thinking that she was actually talking to Gina's brother. It was an awkward feeling knowing that he was unaware of her identity.

"Oh yes, I would have recognised Paul anywhere. He looks just the same except for the fact that now he looks pale. Last time I saw him he was suntanned, but I still recognised you at once didn't I Paul? Excuse me, I must go and give Martin a hand now. He's busy. In fact, I'll take over so that he can come and speak to you too. I hope you'll come back Paul...sort out something with my brother ok. Bye for now. Bye Amy."

Ray hurried back into the bar and after exchanging some words with Martin, he took over and his younger brother walked out towards the English couple's table. Amy didn't have much time to ask Paul any more questions before Martin was there, shaking hands with her. He then took the seat that his brother had vacated

"So this is your young lady, Paul, is it? Amy? Lovely name. It's probably the English version of Amelia. My niece is called Amelia. She's about your age I would say, and just as pretty."

Amy was blushing at the direct compliment from a stranger, but she had to keep her cool. She really needed to keep Martin talking for as long as possible.

"Amelia? Oh that is a lovely name! It sounds kind of a romantic sort of name doesn't it Paul? It conjures up a beautiful, dark girl; a pretty Maltese lady."

"Well, it shows how wrong you can be. She isn't dark at all. She's quite fair, which is unusual in our family. In fact, she is almost as blonde as you, but she has brown eyes. Amelia is not. My nephew, her brother, however, is a proper carrot top, like his dad."

"Would that be Ray's family then Martin? "asked Paul quickly, too quickly.

"Oh no sorry, " he continued. "You just said that the lad had red hair like his dad. Ray has brown hair. So..." He'd noticed that Martin had been just about to say something about his niece, but had stopped himself. The English couple did notice however that Martin had looked flustered for a few seconds.

"How about you Martin? Have you got a family?"

"No, I'm sorry and saddened to say that my wife and I were never blessed with children. My wife and I are Amelia's godparents. She and Robert are my sister's kids. Well I say kids, but Amelia is twenty-two I think and her brother has just turned twenty."

Both Amy and Paul were now sure that Jim's love child was this twenty-two year old Amelia. After that, Amy felt quite agitated and she was finding it difficult to stay focused having just found out that Uncle Jim had a daughter almost her own age.

She found herself thinking that when they went back to the apartment she would try phoning her uncle to tell him about his daughter. Amelia, what a lovely name! She squeezed Paul's knee under the table, hoping that he would take her cue and keep Martin talking as long as possible.

He did indeed understand, because they'd agreed to give each other that signal. It meant that Amy needed some help. She had dried up with excitement after learning about Amelia.

"And what about Ray? Is he married?" Paul hoped that Amy would approve of his delaying tactics.

"Oh yes, he's married to a lovely lady called Lucy and they've got twin boys. They're both married and each of them has a little boy."

"I see, so Ray is a granddad," said Paul.

"Yes, he certainly is a Nannu, as we call grandfathers here in Malta." Martin seemed as friendly as his brother Ray. He was the opposite to him in looks, but both had big brown eyes with ridiculously long eyelashes.

"Where do you live Amy? Do you both live in the same town?" Martin noticed that Amy had gone quiet and so he tried to include her in the conversation.

"Yes, we both live in Plymouth, that's in the South West, a beautiful part of the country. We're lucky in that we live pretty close to the sea and also very close to the moors." Amy became quite animated now she'd joined the conversation again. "What about you, have you ever been to England, Martin?"

"I went to London a couple of times when I was single and I loved it even though it did nothing but rain. It was July too! We tend to go to Italy or to Spain now because Laura loves the sun. She doesn't fancy the unsettled weather you have in England. My darling wife wants guaranteed sunshine on holiday and we get that in Italy and Spain. Actually, my sister and her family are all away in England at the moment. Well, they should be there by now since they flew out this morning."

Amy and Paul tried not to show their disappointment. Both felt their hopes shatter when they found out that the person whom they went all the way to Malta to see, was back in England.

This was an unexpected calamity. Was that going to be a problem or not? Talk about bad timing! Both Amy and Paul needed to know more.

"Really, whereabouts did they go? London?"

"Oh no, they went to Leicester. Ginger, my brother-in-law, comes from somewhere near there and they're all visiting the grand parents."

"Have they gone for a long holiday?" Paul asked knowing full well that Amy wanted to know too. He felt Amy squeeze his knee when she heard the confirmation that the man they saw was indeed Jim's friend.

"Oh no they only went for a week. It's Gina's in-laws' golden wedding anniversary."

Amy breathed a sigh of relief and caught Paul's wink in amusement. Thank God, they might yet achieve what they went to Malta for, after all.

"Well, it seems England is enjoying very warm weather at the moment so they must be pleased," Paul added with a smile. "It'll probably be nice until we return and then, to make us feel at home, it'll start drizzling. Oh look Martin, Ray is waving. I think he's trying to get your attention,"

"Oh yes, it's looking pretty busy in there now. I'd better go and give him a hand. Will you be coming back before you return to England? Where are you staying anyway?" Martin was on his feet and slowly moving away towards the bar.

"We're staying at one of those new holiday flats, not far from St Andrews. It's up there, at the top of the hill, and yes, we'll come back soon. Definitely. We're off to Sliema now, but we'll try to stop here on our way back."

"That would be grand. We get busy in the evening mind."

"That's ok. We might even try one of your Maltese dishes tonight. What do you think Amy? Are you up for it?"

"Yes, that's fine by me, unless we're late back, because then they would have stopped serving."

"Last orders are at half past eight, so do try to get here before that. Now I really must go in or Ray will get mad, and when he gets mad…." Martin walked away laughing out loud.

"We'll try to come for a meal tonight, then. Like I said, we might even be brave enough to try one of your specialities," he said with a big grin on his face. Turning to his girlfriend, he continued, "We'll not eat anything until tonight so that we'll be starving and enjoy whatever we pick!"

"Come on Paul, let's go. Bye you two, see you tonight."

CHAPTER 11

Amy and Paul walked away from the bar with a jumble of mixed feelings and emotions engulfing them. Both of them felt very excited and happy in a strange sort of way. They were also rather overawed that they had already found out about Jim's daughter. It had been so quick and relatively easy so far. Luck was definitely on their side at the moment.

There were some people at the bus stop, so Paul and Amy were almost whispering to each other as they went over the conversations they had just had with the two Maltese men.

"That was really odd," Paul was shaking his head in utter disbelief. "I just can't get my head round it! Of all the places in Malta - granted it's a very small island - but of all the bars in Sliema, they had to be the owners of 'the bar', our bar. It's really unbelievable!"

"It isn't such a coincidence, is it? Uncle Jim told us it was at St George's Bay and he described exactly where it was. Since there are only three and one had a house with a bright yellow door next to it, the other two nearby were obviously not what we were looking for" Amy was very matter of fact as usual.

"What's strange for me is the fact that you never even mentioned them before. It was lucky for you that they came along when they did."

"Yes it was, but like Ray said, they couldn't miss us since it's not a very busy road especially at so late an hour. They had to go past us to drive round the bay to get to the bar."

"Did you actually know that your good Samaritans owned a bar?"

"To be perfectly honest, I'd forgotten all about the car episode and if they mentioned the bar, I honestly can't remember it. We met and got talking to so many people during our holiday."

"But ...surely you'd remember if they...?" she persisted, very eager to find out every single detail.

"Well, they might have mentioned it, but it was very late at night and I was tired. Besides that, it's been a year. I just remember being very grateful to them and then driving off to get some sleep because we were going on the early ferry to Gozo the next day. That reminds me...this bus is late isn't it?"

"We've been waiting for at least twenty minutes. Are you sure there's one due, Paul? Oh yes, it's coming! I can just see it now," said Amy, craning her neck. She was still feeling very excited about the new development. On their short journey to Sliema, she and Paul went over and over the unexpected turn of events.

"I'm so glad you came to Malta with me Paul. I would never have found out all this without you. Thank you," she was almost in tears with the emotional turmoil that she was feeling.

"Oh you'd have found out. There's no doubt about that. It would have taken you just a bit longer to find out what we've already discovered. By sheer luck, we've already started on the journey towards the peace of mind that your uncle craves so much."

"Oh, you are so poetic Paul. That was lovely. You're right though, this is the beginning of the end of secrets. Fancy Gina and her family going to England though, just when we came to Malta!"

"Yes, that's a bit of a stumbling block, but we'll still have about ten days left after they return. The thing is, Amy, now that we've met the brothers, and we found out that we knew each other from a year ago, we have to be even more careful. I mean we've got to decide today how and when we should come clean and reveal your identity. I feel that we should do it as soon as possible. Do you agree?"

"I wondered about that when you told me that you knew them, especially when Ray came over to our table. In a way it's useful, but on the other hand, this could make things worse. I'm positive that if they knew our reason for being here, they would want us to come clean straight away. So much for taking it nice and slow! The fact that you know each other changes everything. So, yeah, we can't hang about now."

“I think they know about their sister's illegitimate child. They're older than Gina and they must have found that out when she married some guy other than Jim, and so quickly after he disappeared! I don't think that it's going to be as hard or as difficult as we feared."

"Oh, I've just remembered something! Paul, did you notice when Martin started looking uncomfortable for a few seconds? He started saying something about Amelia, then he stopped, looking positively flustered, I thought."

"Yes, you're right, he did. I'd forgotten about that. He started saying something, then he seemed to think better of it and stopped. Quick, Amy, we have to get off here." Paul pulled Amy to her feet and they quickly got off the bus at the strand which every one called The Ferry.

Amy pulled her boyfriend by the hand away from the bustling crowds of shoppers. She wanted to go closer to that lovely crystal blue sea. It was so very calm. Gently lapping waves were tapping on the sides of the cruisers. These were lined up, getting ready to take people across the water. They were all advertising cruises that took the visitors to the Maltese islands to see special attractions. These majestic looking cruise ships were all busy with people trailing steadily on board. Paul would have gone on one of them, but Amy was quite happy just watching for the moment. She watched them start their trips to the Grand Harbour and the various historical fortresses and bastions, that made Malta so interesting. There seemed to be crowds everywhere. Everyone looked happy, friendly and very relaxed. All around, in the streets and on the pavements, there were festive scenes. Wherever you looked there seemed to be a lot of shaking hands, hugging and kissing going on. Gone was the aura of mourning and sobriety of Good Friday. Easter was definitely a time for rejoicing.

"Let's have a quick look at those little shops." Amy couldn't resist any shop. Crossing the road was a bit of a nightmare because buses and cars were everywhere and they seemed to be coming from every single direction.

They walked slowly up the hill towards the Savoy area and were soon stopping to admire the shops on the way up.

"Look Paul, those cakes look lovely and look at all the different shapes and colours. They must be traditional Easter pastries because there's a chocolate egg in the middle of each one."

"Those are 'figolli' said a young girl who was also admiring the cakes. "They're almond pastries, traditional for Easter. Mums, and some dads too, make them for each of their children."

"Oh, that's a lovely tradition. Do they get one each then?"

"Oh yes, a different one each. My mum used to stay up very late decorating them with icing, little sweets and silver balls. There were nine of us so you can imagine how busy she was when we all lived at home."

"Thank you, that was nice of you to explain." Amy was so

surprised at the friendliness that she had encountered so far. People who knew that she was going to Malta had told her about the hospitality and warmth of the Maltese people, but she still marvelled when she came across it like she and Paul had done just then.

They went in the shop and bought a couple of figolli...one shaped like a fish and one in the shape of a mermaid.

"Do you want to go and see a film or shall we just mooch around and then walk along the sea front? Do you remember the place where we got off the bus? If you like, we can go back there, check out the cruises and pick one. I saw people getting on and off the boats before we crossed the road. It's up to you really. We can go to the cinema if you like. I'm not fussed what we do to be honest, but let's decide."

"I don't really feel like going to the cinema. Let's just walk along the sea front. We'll go on a cruise another day. It's just nice being out here and seeing all the people looking so animated and cheerful. Look at all the kids too. Most of them have one of those pastries."

"Well, that young girl did say that every child had one. After we look at the shops to your heart's content, lets go down again and wander along the promenade."

"Ok, I did notice that there were people sitting on benches. We can sit down and have some of our figolla when we've walked enough."

"Ok we'll do that but before we go back. I really think that we should decide what we have to do next. One way or another, it makes sense if we make our mind up today and then go for it."

Amy sounded much braver than she was actually feeling. They had already talked in great length and detail about their inevitable change of plan. It was now crucial to lay their cards on the table and to do it as soon as possible.

Seeing so many people out relaxing on the benches laughing and talking out loud made Amy breathe a sigh of contentment.

"This is so relaxing isn't it? Everyone is enjoying the fresh sea air and all these children are having a good time too."

"Yes, it beats staying in and watching television that's for sure," Paul agreed. "Shall we start walking back now? We've walked a long way you know.

Look Amy, there on the other side of that bridge, over there, it's called Manoel Island. I went swimming there when I was here last. I'll try and take you there one day."

"We'd better keep walking because the last thing we want is to miss the bus. I don't fancy walking much, but I have really enjoyed looking around. It's been lovely."

Leaving Gzira behind, Paul and Amy turned round and started walking back to the ferry. It was getting dark, but somehow the lights all along the sea front made the atmosphere appear more festive than it did in daylight.

"Yes, it's been a good evening. Are you limping love?" asked Paul suddenly.

"Yes, I think I must have a blister. These new shoes … my feet ache now. Never mind it's nearly six o'clock. I'm starving, and tired. Let's try to hurry up a little. I can't wait to kick my shoes off."

"We did say that we might eat at the George Cross bar. I'm only going to have a little taste of this pastry because I don't want to spoil my appetite."

"Me too," she said as she broke a piece of her figolla and promptly started to eat.

"Hmmmmm. Very nice Paul. It tastes like almonds, doesn't it?"

"Yes, lovely. That's it, I'd better put it away or I'll eat it all!"

"Paul, we still haven't yet decided what we're doing. Shall I ask one of them to meet us? We could say that we've something important to tell them. They might meet us after they close."

"Hmm…Maybe we can suggest that we stay behind. I wonder how they'll react… suspiciously? Curiously?"

"Well, they've no reason to be suspicious, have they? I know, how about inviting them over to our apartment after closing time? It will still be relatively early after we've eaten. Staying behind will be no good then so I think we should invite them over. Then, you can tell them who you are and what has brought you to Malta."

"Yes, I think I might feel more relaxed and less nervous at the flat. Right, we'll do that. You ask them please Paul, if you don't mind. I'll do my bit when they visit. Oooooh..I'm shaking!"

"Oh come on love, now come on. We've agreed now, and we both need to do our best for your uncle. Maybe you should phone him before we get to the bar and tell him that we've met Gina's brothers."

"I think it's better if I do it tomorrow, when I'll feel a bit calmer. Hopefully tonight will go smoothly."

"Ok, that makes sense. Now, let's hurry and catch that bus back. It'll be all right ...we'll go and have a meal first and then, when I find the right moment, I'll invite them over. It'll probably be after eleven o'clock you know. Anyway, there's our bus. Good, I'm starving!"

"To be perfectly honest, I'm not sure I can eat anything," groaned Amy.

Sitting on the crowded bus and not being able to get a seat next to Paul gave Amy the opportunity to mull over the progress so far. It was half-exciting and half-scary. She was all excited now because she knew that she had a cousin called Amelia and she could hardly wait until she could tell her uncle the good news. Well, it seemed like good news to her. On the other hand, Amy was scared and worried that when she eventually revealed her identity to Gina's brothers, she would then be met with an angry and heated reaction. They might even refuse point blank to help her to get to talk to Gina. That would be so awful, especially now. After meeting them this morning and the warm welcome she and Paul had received from the brothers, Amy felt very worried in case Martin and Ray turned nasty and angry once they found out that Jim had sent them to find his daughter.

Amy hoped against hope that her newly found cousin knew that somewhere in England lived her biological father. She reckoned that if Amelia had grown up with this information, there wouldn't be a big problem to face. It was surprisingly strange that she'd never tried to find him - if she knew that he existed. It was easy to explain why Jim had never tried to acknowledge her since he was sure that he wasn't wanted on the scene.

Then Amy reminded herself of the fact that the family was very religious and had been over protective of Gina in the sixties. Her uncle had mentioned these facts many times. If the older family members were still as strict and religious now as they were in the sixties, then Amelia would definitely not be aware that Ginger was not her birth father. They probably had encouraged Gina to marry Ginger so that a scandal would be avoided. Well, Ginger had been available while Jim was in hospital, very seriously injured.

The bus ride seemed much shorter that evening and Amy stood up almost reluctantly and with heavy legs, followed Paul off the bus.

"This is it! Paul…I'm shaking. I don't know what…"

"Sh…. you'll be all right once we start talking…come on, think of your poor uncle. God knows how he must be feeling. Let's go in. Hopefully, we might be able to phone him with some good news tonight."

"We have some good news for him anyway. I'm sure he'll be over the moon to find out about Amelia," she said. When they arrived at the bar they noticed that there was a big crowd in there.

"Hi Ray, Martin," Paul called out as he led his girlfriend as close to the counter as possible. "We'll just find a table and then we'll look at the menu."

"Hi you two. I'll come over in a minute and see what we can tempt you with," Ray said and true to his word, within minutes he was sitting at their table. Friendly as ever, he tried to help them with their choice of meal.

"As you can see, we do a lot of English dishes because we have many tourists from the UK. Most of them like to stick to what they know. Then here you have the Italian section. That's very popular too. Of course, last but not least is the Maltese selection. Have you tried any of these yet?"

"No, we only arrived early Friday morning. We've been cooking light meals at the apartment. Well, Paul has actually. You like cooking don't you Paul?"

"Yes, anything that goes in a frying pan mostly," he said modestly. "Ray, what's this 'Timpana?'

"Well, do you like pasta?"

"Oh yes I love it."

"Well this is a lovely dish, pasta in Bolognese sauce, only it's not served just like that. It's baked and on top of the pasta there is a layer of lovely golden pastry. It's very popular and if you like pasta and Bolognese sauce, you'll love it."

"It sounds good to me," Amy replied, surprising herself at her newly found appetite. "I think I'll have that Ray. What about you Paul, what do you fancy?"

"I think I'll try the stuffed peppers. I love peppers, but have never had them stuffed .Yes, stuffed with meat please, not tuna."

Both of them enjoyed the meal and the bottle of Marsovin wine very kindly given to them by the brothers. There had been no talk about the subject that was uppermost in their mind, but now that they were nicely sated and feeling more relaxed they had to make a move. Every now and then, either Martin or Ray came to their table and talked to them.

"When they come over again, I'll ask them to our apartment for a drink so we can return the favour."

"It's funny asking two blokes who run a bar to come for a drink isn't it? Maybe we could make it a lunch date - what do you think Paul?"

Paul was trying to catch Ray's eyes but the popular bar had suddenly got busy once again. A door on the right opened and an elderly lady came out.

"Did you see that? That lady came out of somewhere. I can't see…."

"Yes, there's a door which must lead to the house with the bright yellow door. I'm sure uncle mentioned it..." Amy pondered out loud.

The lady in question was quite tiny but seemed rather sprightly. In no time at all she made herself useful by starting to clear up some tables.

"Ma, stop, we'll do that in a minute. Stop it… come here." Martin went over to her and tried to gently pull her away from the table where she was piling dishes and glasses to clear away. "Mum, come over and meet our friends from England. Remember Ray and I were telling you all about them last night?" he said as he gently guided his mum to Paul and Amy's table.

"Paul, Amy, this is my mother. Ma these are our English friends."

"Pleased to meet you. I've never been to England but my son-in-law is English," she explained. In fact my daughter and her family are over there in England now," she said in excellent English. "Have you just arrived in Malta? Do you like it?"

"We came on Friday, but it seems like we've been here much longer than that, possibly because we've been up and about all the time. I must say, you speak very good English, you put me to shame," Paul complimented her. "I can 't speak any other languages, only English."

"Well, we all speak English in Malta," she answered quickly. "Besides, since our son -in-law is from England we talk English most of the time. He has picked up some Maltese, but even after many years living here, he's still not fluent, except in swear words." She chuckled as she continued, "yes, Ginger knows plenty of them!

Mind you those two rascals behind the bar used to teach him a few when he first came on the scene."

Martin walked over to their table, and putting an arm round his mother's shoulders asked, "What's she been saying? I could hear you laughing. Ma, come on, what's the joke?"

"No joke dear. I just mentioned that you and Ray made sure that Ginger learnt enough Maltese to get by," she said, giving Paul a wink. "Mind you, his kids, well they're not kids really, but anyway, they 're fluent in both languages, aren't they Martin?"

"You all seem to be, in Malta," Amy remarked.

It was lovely sitting there talking to Gina's mum and brother. However, Emma's appearance had complicated matters somehow, because Paul didn't think he should ask the brothers over while their mum was there. He would feel obliged to invite her too, and that wasn't a good idea at this stage. He couldn't even tell Amy that they had to write their plan off for another day because Emma still sat at their table. She was very friendly and amusing and Amy seemed to be enjoying her company too. Paul, however, was feeling disappointed because he really wanted to move on and talk to the brothers without any more delay. He turned to Amy and tried to show her by the expression on his face that they should leave.

"I'll just go and pay for our meal Amy, then we must make tracks back. I don't know about you, but I'm so tired. You must be too. You see we walked an awful lot today," he explained to Emma. Then, turning to his girlfriend he added," I won't be a mo." He left the table and walked up to Martin. It had calmed down a bit in the bar and Paul decided to go for it before it got busy once again..

"That was excellent," he started. "It was a lovely meal. Thank you for your advice. It was delicious and we're stuffed but we must be off now. It's been a long day."

"Glad you enjoyed the meal, and don't forget to come again soon ok? You aren't too far are you?" Martin asked.

"Oh yes we'll come back. We must…I mean, we need, we'd love to!" Finally, Paul managed to get a sentence out. Feeling suddenly brave, he thought, "What the heck?" and before he could change his mind, he blurted out, "Tell you what Ray, Martin, why don't you come and see us? Make it tomorrow. I'll cook you an English meal."

"We're always tied up here Paul, sorry."

"Don't you take time off? Come on, don't you close after

lunch? Visit then," Paul tried to persuade them. He was feeling good then, having made an invitation. He thought it had to be a move in the right direction. Ray seemed to be looking for excuses not to go but Paul was persuasive.

"Yes we do, but we do try to catch up on the stock orders, etc. and if possible we have a nap too."

"Oh, come on, old man. You don't have to stay long. We'd love you to come round for a visit."

"Oh all right. I'll ask dad if he'll baby-sit this place. He won't mind as it's not usually busy when we open after lunch. I just want to make sure someone opens up if we're late at your place."

"Right then you two. Shall we say we'll expect you to be there at about two o'clock? Is that ok for you guys? "

"All right, we'll be there but don't blame us if we fall asleep after lunch, ok?" Ray was always the one with the quick, sometimes funny answers.

"Oh no you mustn't do that or it will be another missed opportunity..." Paul suddenly realised that he was thinking out loud.

"What do you mean?" asked a perplexed looking Ray. "What opportunity?"

"Oh never mind, I just..."

"What?... go on..."

"No, nothing Ray, " Paul said quickly, getting more and more flustered by the minute."

"We'll talk tomorrow. I think that wine....that Marsovin is more potent than any wine I'm used to."

CHAPTER 12

"Very mysterious," Ray turned to his brother, "don't you think?" he asked as they stood there watching Paul making his way to where Amy was still talking to their mum. With hardly a backward glance the couple waved and called "See you tomorrow" and left the bar with what seemed a sudden urgency. Martin, who had been busy sorting out the shelves under the counter stood up and stretched.

"What do you mean Ray?" he asked.

"Weren't you listening? Paul said something pretty odd."

"Odd? I heard nothing odd. You two arranged for us to visit them tomorrow, but there's nothing odd about that is there?"

"Oh, I think you must have been in the cellar then, when this was going on. You went to fetch some tonic didn't you?"

"Yes I did. What happened then? I was only away minutes!"

"Well, I said something about not making it there to visit. I said that we might fall asleep when we close for lunch. I was just teasing him, you know what I'm like. The funny thing is that Paul seemed agitated suddenly and said that we must go otherwise it would be another "wasted opportunity."

"Opportunity for what? " asked Martin. He too started feeling a bit confused now." That's exactly what I asked him. I still haven't got a clue. When I asked him what he meant he went all funny and almost ran out of the bar."

"Well, I don't know really. Oh, I tell you what, maybe he's giving us a surprise of some sort. You know what he was saying the other day. He said that he felt bad that he's never thanked us properly for fixing the car that night. He said that he'll pay us back one day."

"Hmm, could be I suppose, but somehow... well, he looked rather worried... flustered. Oh, I don't know, maybe you're right, Martin."

"I'm sure that's it. Now, I think we might as well shut up shop. There's only our old regular there, and old George will stay all night if we let him, poor sod. He's so lonely. Goodness me, look, he's actually going."

" That's mother's doing. She went to clear his table! She's been bustling around him and he's probably had to keep hold of his glass, just in case she'd whip it away!"

"You're right. Poor old George. Night George, see you tomorrow!" Ray called out and Martin echoed his brother's warm greetings.

The two men then started the usual round of jobs that they did automatically at closing time.

Their mother was still bustling about, picking up glasses and ashtrays.

"Mum, you should go through now. It's late. You shouldn't be doing that. Go on, we can manage. Leave those glasses, mum, go on, go to bed."

"Oh all right, I suppose I'd better go. Your dad must wonder why it took me so long to say goodnight," she said with a chuckle, and off she went through the door that led to the house with the bright yellow door.

Once everything was shipshape and up to their usual standards, the two men went out to their cars. They both lived locally, only about twenty minutes' drive away. This made it very easy to get to work and back every day. Martin sometimes cycled to work but not when it was a hot day or when it was raining. On the other hand, Ray never walked if he could drive. Apart from that, the two brothers were quite similar in character, although Martin seemed the softer of the two, and more sensitive, while Ray was funnier and louder.

"See you Ray," Martin called to his brother. "Don't forget, we have a lunch date with Paul and his lovely girlfriend tomorrow."

"Of course I won't forget. Goodnight Martin," Ray called back.

Unlike their Maltese friends who seemed happy and pleased with their lot, the English couple was feeling rather anxious that evening. The day that they'd been waiting for was finally looming. They were both feeling some degree of excitement, but this was also tinged with worry. Next day, without fail, they were going to reveal Amy's identity to Martin and Ray. Hopefully, they would be able to tell them all about Jim and his greatest wish - to acknowledge his daughter. It all depended on how it worked out after the initial tentative approach was taken.

Both of them found it hard to sleep and so the night seemed to drag on and on. Finally, when the first rays of dawn crept in through the curtains, it brought with it happy feelings and positive thoughts. Deep down, they were both hoping for a good reception from the two brothers and that kept them feeling happy and hopefully optimistic.

"Do you know what, Paul?" Amy finally broke the pregnant silence. "I'm so surprised at myself. I actually feel calm and collected. I feel excitement, almost a sense of impatience. It's so strange really, because at the moment, I really can't wait to bring everything out in the open. Then, maybe, hopefully, everyone involved can start building bridges and looking forward to family reunions and gatherings."

"Yes," Paul said thoughtfully. "There'll be a lot of catching up to do here in Malta, won't there?"

"I suppose it really all depends on who knows that Amelia is not Ginger's biological daughter."

"There'll be the same, if not more, catching up to do in England I should imagine. Remember your aunt has no clue about any of this. Then there is Jim's family, his parents, his siblings…and their children - your dad for a start. I know I'm not related, of course, but I feel so involved and I do so hope that what you just said will happen. It would be marvellous indeed if everything goes smoothly."

"If Amelia's never been told about Jim being her dad, then we're bound to be greeted with anger and possibly even with hostility. They'll look on us as troublemakers, won't they?"

Paul could detect a trace of anxiety in his girlfriend's tone of voice as she continued with her speculating.

"Oh dear, I do hope and pray that she knows that Ginger isn't her father. I can't begin to imagine the reception we're bound to get if she doesn't. She has to be told, it's her right, never mind poor Uncle Jim's right in all this."

"Amy, you have to be prepared for that. It was twenty odd years ago and knowing how strict and over protective Gina's parents were - your uncle's words - the chances are that she hasn't been told that she's not Ginger's birth child. If that's the case, I feel sorry for the girl."

"Yes, me too. It's not great to find out that the man who brought you up isn't your biological father. It must be much worse to find that out when you're an adult. If Amelia still has no idea that

Jim is her dad it's our duty to make sure that she gets to know now. Otherwise, it would've been a wasted journey and poor Uncle Jim would be devastated."

"Well it's not really up to us to tell her such an important fact, is it?"

"No, if that's the case, all we can do is to hassle Gina to tell her."

"Yes I agree. Of course it's her right to know that Jim is her father. Actually, don't you think you should phone him?"

" I meant to do it yesterday but I forgot. That wine they gave us must be stronger than it looked. I can hardly remember walking back."

"Yes, you're right it got me too!"

"Now that I can think clearly, tell me Paul, why that sudden rush to leave last night? It was quite rude. I was talking to Emma and enjoying it - she's an amazing lady - and you just grabbed my arm and said goodnight very hurriedly"

"Oh it was just something I said. Don't worry."

"Ah, I see, you could have blown it but you didn't, so never mind. I'm beginning to feel really nervous. They should be here in a minute."

"Yes, but now I really think that you should talk to Jim as soon as you can. It would be best straight after this visit, because you'll have a lot to tell him then, be it good or bad."

"Yes, you're probably right. Hopefully, I'll have some good news to pass on to him. If Auntie Meg is around and he can't talk, then I'll ask about her WI meeting." Amy felt pretty sure that it was on the following Friday.

“Anyway, if he has auntie around him," Amy carried on, “then I'll tell him to just listen and to stay calm before I inform him that he has a daughter."

"Well, personally, I hope you can arrange to phone him on Friday because if you tell him while your aunt is around, his face might give the game away." Paul didn't know what to suggest for the best.

"I'll warn him beforehand, then he'll stay calm and collected. Then you see, hopefully, he won't make a comment and drop himself right in it. Anyway, you still haven't told me properly why you made us leave in such a hurry last night. Just how did you nearly spoil things? What did you say?"

"I blurted out that if they didn't visit us it would be a wasted opportunity. As soon as I said it, I could have kicked myself. Of course, Ray picked up on it straight away."

"What did he say then? He is sharp isn't he? He's really very switched on."

"Ray asked me what opportunity was I talking about and I got very flustered. I just couldn't think of an answer - that wine was my downfall! First it loosened my tongue, and then, when I needed to say something, it wouldn't let me say anything that made any sense! I just wanted to go before I tied myself in knots. So I muttered something about it having been a long day, grabbed your arm, and made a hasty exit."

"Oh dear, it's just as well that they're coming today. I think if we leave it any longer one of us will say something else. That really would ruin everything. They must find out from us at the time we think is best. That time is today, when we're all sitting down and there's no one else about. We should tell them why we came to Malta, who we are, etc, etc. The sooner we do that, the less likely it is that we'll anger them. If we just keep visiting the pub without saying who we are, and why we came to Malta, when we do eventually come clean, they could easily turn round and say that we're devious. It'll look as if we've been taking advantage of their friendship with you Paul."

"I feel like that too. Do you remember that we'd originally planned not to make any move until Gina and her family returned from their holiday? That's totally out of the question now. We didn't know then that I'd already met the brothers. Yes, the more we discuss it, the more I get convinced that it has to be today. When we've got everything out in the open we can hopefully enjoy the rest of our stay on this lovely island."

"Ok, I agree with you. Of course you're right. Since you already know the brothers and you actually owe them a big favour, we can't hang about. As you said, that would make us appear very deceitful. It's best to tell them everything now. After all, it's the first opportunity we have and they won't be able to fault us on that."

"I hope so love," Paul said under his breath.

"Now then, the question is, what lunch are we providing? There's not much left in the fridge."

Paul smiled at Amy because he could see that she was being her normal, practical, self. He knew then that she was obviously calm and collected.

"I think just a nice omelette and a salad would be fine," he replied. "There's enough in the fridge for that. They both said not to prepare a big meal or they wouldn't feel like working when they went back."

"Good. Just as well in the circumstances, or we'd have had to go shopping. Now, let's tidy up a bit and then I'll sort out the salad. Have we got any wine left?"

"There's that bottle that we opened when we came back from Sliema. Yes, here it is," said Paul. "I was definitely a bit tipsy last night, but I'm sure they both said they only drink coffee until the evenings."

"I suppose that makes sense. If they started drinking in the afternoon, they wouldn't be in a fit state to work would they? That would be funny working in a bar, pub, wouldn't it?"

"No, I guess it wouldn't be funny at all!"

"You know what I mean. Anyway, let's get on and get everything ready so that we're not busy when they come." Both of them got on with what they thought needed doing, both keen to stay busy and thus resist looking at the clock every few minutes.

"Remember, Amy, I'll start the conversation and when I squeeze your knee, you just say it as it comes. Don't plan how to say it. If you stay as calm as you seem to be now, you will be great!"

Eventually, both of them were completely satisfied with their preparations for a warm welcome for their very important guests. When the doorbell finally shattered the peaceful aura in the flat, Paul and Amy were sitting on the veranda looking at the beautiful blue sea and at all the boats bobbing up and down, creating a colourful tableau.

Both jumped up, Amy looking suddenly startled.

"Stay Amy, just sit down again. I'll go and let them in. I'll bring them out here shall I?" and without waiting for her answer he pressed her back down in the chair and hurried towards the front door.

"It's just me I'm afraid," Ray apologised, as he walked through the open door. "I would've rung you but we never thought of asking you for your phone number last night. Have you got a phone here? Oh yes, I see it."

"I never thought of it either. I'll write it down for you at once. I wouldn't have known it anyway last night." Paul admitted as he was writing down the telephone number. "Here you are Ray. Will you give us yours please? We might need it. Now, what's happened to Martin?"

"His wife phoned me this morning. He's got a very sore throat, headache, and the full works. Mum and dad gave me a hand this morning because it got rather busy."

"Oh, now if you'd had our number and phoned to say that Martin was sick, I would've come and given you a hand."

"Yes," said Amy, "Paul sometimes works in a pub in the school holidays, don't you Paul?"

"Oh, that 's good to know. I tell you what, if Martin's still sick tomorrow, I might be glad of a bit of help. Just at lunchtime. Anyway, that would be the last resort because one of our cousins might be available."

"Ok, that's settled then. If you need me, just call. I won't mind helping you until about eightish and then my girlfriend won't feel neglected," Paul grinned at Amy. He was feeling rather confused,wondering what was the next best thing to do since there was just Ray to talk to.

He tried to catch Amy's eye, but it was proving difficult because she was being the perfect hostess and asking Ray what he wanted to drink. Paul felt really pleased when Ray asked for coffee. He started to think of an excuse to nip into the kitchen and ask her what she wanted to do. He was sure that Amy was feeling the same way with this new development. Should they carry on with their plan or wait until they were able to talk to both brothers?

Paul was just making small talk with Ray, all the while wondering how on earth he was going to see what Amy wanted to do, as after all, it was her mission. He began to feel slightly panicky, and afraid that it would show.

"Paul," called Amy, "where on earth did you put the coffee? You made the last lot."

"Coming," he answered thankfully. "Excuse me, Ray, I shan't be a minute."

"Clever girl," he whispered giving her a quick kiss on the back of her neck.

"Paul…stop it... I wanted…"

"I was trying to think of an excuse to come and talk to you." In hushed tones, Paul asked his girlfriend if she still wanted to go ahead, and without a moment's hesitation, Amy said "Yes, I certainly do!" So Paul returned quickly to the veranda where Ray sat admiring the view.

The now nervous couple spent a while chatting happily about the places they were going to visit while in Malta. When the conversation changed direction and they were answering Ray's questions about England, and mostly about Plymouth, Paul felt a little edgy. They had agreed to broach the subject after the meal and here was Ray asking questions about their families back home. He didn't want Amy to mention her favourite uncle until after the meal. She was bound to if they carried on in this vein.

"I'll go and make that omelette and then we can eat," he decided as he scraped his chair back and stood up and stretched.

"Amy, I'll let you tell Ray about my fantastic skill in omelette making," he called over his shoulder as he walked through to the kitchen. Fortunately, he really was a dab hand at turning out perfect omelettes and very soon, they were all enjoying the light lunch.

"That was really good Paul. I must say, I can't cook anything. I'm not allowed in the kitchen. However, my wife's a brilliant cook. Did I mention that she does the meals three times a week at the bar?"

"Does she? Was she there yesterday?"

"Oh no, she wasn't. We have a local chef on the two days when Lucy isn't working. Sometimes even Ginger helps if he has a day off. He's a chef at one of the hotels in Sliema."

"That's handy. I love cooking. No Ray, just leave everything, and let's sit in the lounge away from this table. I'll help my gorgeous girlfriend to clear up later. It'll keep."

Ray didn't need to be told twice. He'd only started to clear up because he felt that it was the thing to do. They all took their coffee and trailed through to the bright lounge that was bathed in sunshine. Paul and Amy snuggled close on the settee. Ray was soon looking very comfortable in the huge armchair facing them.

" I must keep an eye on the time," he reminded himself. "We close till tea time now, because it's not as busy as it is in the summer. Most people, mainly locals don't come till late. As summer draws closer, we stay open all day. What time is it anyway? I forgot my watch."

"It's only three o'clock, and it will take you all of five minutes to drive down the hill. Oh, don't forget now. If it gets really busy, just phone me, because we've made no plans for tonight. We might just stay in and maybe just go for a walk.

Hang on, you said something about a relative helping."

"Yes I did. Thank you for the offer, mate. Yes, Andy, that's one of our hundreds of cousins, has already been roped in. He's probably at my parents' house already. Dad had been trying to phone him earlier but he couldn't get through."

"Does he live locally too?"

"No, he lives in Qormi you see, which is a little far away. If he's available, he'll spend the night at my parents' house and he'll be there to help tomorrow. I'll let you know tonight. In fact, do you mind if I call my father and find out if he got through to Andy or not? If he's there already, I can relax because he'll open up...he's come to the rescue before."

"Of course, help yourself, you've seen where the phone is. It's in the hall."

The minute Ray was out of the room, the nervous couple started whispering in as low a voice as they could manage.

"As soon as he comes back, I will, I promise. Yes, please calm down, Amy. I said I will!" hissed Paul. Amy was worried in case Paul was going to put it off. Now that they'd got this far, she was not prepared to go through the anxious uncertainty and apprehension that she was feeling at the moment, all over again.

"Sorted," said Ray happily as he returned to the big, comfortable armchair where he'd been curled up before. Andy is there and if I'm not back in time, he'll open up. Dad said not to rush and I won't. No one will wait long for a drink with the two of them behind the counter. Both are fast workers and very good with people."

"So you're in no hurry now Ray," said Amy unnecessarily, as she dug her elbow in Paul's ribs.

"Ouch, that hurt," he grimaced, while trying to smile and gather up some courage to start.

Ray looked from one to the other with a huge nervous grin.

"Was that just for fun?" he asked Amy.

"No, Ray. Paul needs a little prod sometimes, don't you darling?" she said.

"You can have a glass of wine then Ray. Come on, just the one. I'm going to," tempted Paul as he got up and escaped to the kitchen. He knew that he was delaying the moment but he had suddenly begun to feel worried. He might muck it all up and then...

"Come on Paul," Amy was not giving up that easily. "Ray is all ears, aren't you Ray? He doesn't have to rush back now."

"What do you mean, Amy?" Ray's eyebrows went up.

She waited until Paul had handed Ray the wine and then sat down near her again.

CHAPTER 13

"Well, are you going to start Paul or shall I?" she demanded, throwing caution to thc wind.

"What on earth are you on about Amy? You're being very mysterious. What's she trying to say Paul? What's going on?" Ray was now sitting up and leaning forward as he looked fixedly at Paul.

"I will, Amy, I promised didn't I?" Paul hissed at her. "I tell you what, you just go and get that photograph please. Go on Amy," he urged her. "Just bring it, please.!"

"Now Paul. Why? But that's for Gina...." Amy was taken aback because they hadn't planned on showing the photo to anyone but Gina.

"What are you two talking about? Will someone please tell me? What photo? What about my sister? You haven't even met her have you? So, what...?"

"Sorry Ray, just wait a second until Amy comes back. I didn't mean to confuse you like this. I sort of panicked and now I feel like I went in feet first...Ah, here she is." Amy returned with an envelope in her hand.

"Go on Amy, let Ray see it." Amy stood there looking confused.

Her hands were shaking but Amy managed to take the black and white photo out of the plain brown envelope. She looked at Paul, then at Ray and then, very gingerly, handed it over to the puzzled Ray.

"What the ...this is my sister...and Jim...how... when?" Ray could not get one sensible sentence out. "This was in...let me see, it says nineteen sixty eight at the back...Where did this come from?"

"See, Paul, poor Ray is so confused now. Sorry Ray, this wasn't the way we planned it."

"Planned it? What have you planned? Where did you find this photograph? I wasn't aware that you knew my sister. How do you know her?" Ray would have carried on asking question after question, but Amy felt sorry for him. Feeling brave and quite moved by Ray's anxiety, she stood up and went to sit in the other armchair that was next to his.

"We don't know your sister, Ray. At least, we haven't met her yet, but we know of her."

"How? What on earth do you mean?" Ray was looking more and more on edge.

"Please be patient Ray. I'm about to tell you. First of all, there was the pure and utterly amazing coincidence... the fact that you and Paul had met before."

"I explained that it isn't a coincidence.... we couldn't miss them!"

"OK whatever! We came to Malta to look for your sister and that would have involved you of course. As it happened, when we first came to your bar to test the water as it were, we found out that you and your brother had already met Paul."

"Yes, that's right," Paul picked up where Amy had trailed off. "Then, it became obvious that you are Gina's brothers. When we found out all this, we obviously felt that we had to come clean as soon as possible. This was the reason we wanted you and Martin to visit today. We didn't want to keep meeting you under false pretences."

Amy looked at Ray who looked more confused than ever and because her mouth felt so dry, she looked at Paul and willed him with her eyes to carry on until she had a breather.

"I see, so that was what you meant when you mentioned something about a "wasted opportunity!"

"Yes Ray, sorry, I was a little drunk last night. Anyway, as Amy said, we came to Malta to help Amy's Uncle...Jim."

"Uncle?"

"Yes, I'm Jim's niece, and he asked me to come to Malta and..."

"Cause problems and heartache? You want to cause misery and probably a rift after all these years? Why, the....he never bothered before did he? Why does he want to bother now? Too many years have gone by.... why has he suddenly decided to...?" Ray was looking very flushed and angry. His hands were curled in tight fists and his knuckles looked white. This was what both Amy and Paul had been dreading. He got up and started pacing up and down.

"Please Ray, don't be angry. I, we'll tell you all we know and then you'll understand."

"There's nothing to understand. That ...that uncle of yours

wasn't interested when he found out that my kid sister was having his child. He never had the decency to even answer the letters."

"What letters?" Amy looked at Paul and then at Ray again.

"I wrote twice to him because my parents were absolutely distraught. He'd made my sister pregnant. Those days, illegitimacy was unheard of here in this little Catholic Island. He brought shame to our family. Gina wrote and told him about her predicament as soon as she could and asked him what he wanted to do. She loved him, and she was sure that he loved her. She expected him to write back and arrange to get married as soon as he was better."

"So she did know he was injured?"

"Yes, Ginger had told her that Jim was injured badly. Gina wrote at once and told him to get someone to write to her if he couldn't do so himself. My sister just needed his support. No, we never had an answer to any of our letters."

"How could he reply? He never had them! Although he was still very ill, he would've been given them and someone would have read them to him when he was out of the woods."

"My sister wrote again to tell him that she had married Ginger. She never asked him why he hadn't answered our letters. She believed that he didn't want to know about the baby but she wanted him to know about her marriage. She gave it to me to read and asked me what I thought about it all. Then I posted it for her."

"Well, he got that one. That was the only letter he received and that's how he found out that his girlfriend was expecting his child but had married his best friend. In a mad rage, he ripped it up and never mentioned her name again."

"I can't understand it... he must have got them. We knew that he was ill in hospital. Ginger gave us the address, but..."

"Ray, think of Jim for a moment. He'd just begun to get over the trauma of losing a leg," Paul took over now.

"He what?..."

"Yes, that's right, it was that serious. He was just beginning to show signs of recovery. Then, one day, he was given the one and only letter he ever received from your sister. Like you just said, she told him that she was expecting his child and that she had just married his best friend. It's a pity that she didn't mention the other letters then, isn't it?"

"Poor Uncle Jim then had a relapse. He slowly recovered after spending months in hospital and then in a rehabilitation unit. He never mentioned Gina's name ever again. He never allowed himself to think about her or the child, because he felt so betrayed by the two people who were once so close to him, his girlfriend, and his best mate." Amy's eyes welled up and Paul went to put his arm around her.

"Yes, that's it." Paul helped her out until she recovered her composure.

"That's why it was so painful for Jim to dwell upon it and needless to say, he never heard from his so called best friend either!" Paul was glad that he knew the whole story.

"What happened to those letters then? If he were so ill… no, I don't doubt you Amy," he said quickly, when she almost leapt from her chair. "Someone might have put them somewhere safe until he was able to deal with them. There were four letters, like I said, including the last one."

"The nurses would have helped him with that. They used to read his letters out to him. His brother wrote regularly and so did his parents. If they couldn't visit, they wrote to him. No, the letters never arrived. Well, one did."

"Gina was desperate to find out if he wanted to acknowledge his child. She wanted to do the right thing. It seemed to me then, that my sister was giving him one last chance. She told him once more about her pregnancy and how she and Ginger fell in love and got married. When days, weeks and then months passed and she still had had no answer to this letter either, she finally decided to let sleeping dogs lie and never mention him again. She didn't, because there seemed to be no point if he wasn't interested in his child and hadn't even bothered to reply."

"Ray, believe me, Uncle Jim received one letter…one letter only. It was obviously the last one, the one you posted. He told me what it said and it's exactly what you told us just now. That letter shattered him both physically and mentally."

"Yes," said Paul, " after he read it, the poor bloke never even talked about Gina to anybody, until last month, when he told Amy. His wife doesn't even know about any of this!"

"What I don't understand is why now, suddenly, Jim wants to acknowledge his child. Well, she's an adult now. Did he only tell you about her then, Amy?"

"Yes. Well, he had no idea if he had a son or a daughter. Something that happened recently made him decide to find out. You see, he had a bad fall at work and he ended up with a nasty head injury which left him unconscious for days."

"Poor Jim!" Ray was moved in spite of himself.

"When he came round, he realised how lucky he was to be alive. He found himself thinking about Gina and wondering if she'd had the baby and if it was a son or a daughter. He took stock of his life and that's what brought me, us to Malta. He asked me to find out and give him or her a chain and cross which your sister gave him years ago."

"Huh, how generous of him!" said Ray with a sneer.

"Please hear me out Ray," begged Amy. "He felt that now that he was heaps better, he needed to know. He could have come to Malta himself years ago, but remember, he thought that Gina didn't want anything to do with him. As you said yourself Ray, the letter that he received stated that she was pregnant with his child and it also said that she'd already married his best friend."

"Yes," Paul said. "Jim admitted that he could have returned to Malta and seen for himself, but he actually stayed away because it was a "fait accompli." He didn't want to cause trouble. He thought it was the best thing to do - the best thing for everyone but himself. However, now he is really desperate to know about his child. Oh, by the way he's married to a lovely lady but they have no children. You must understand a little what having a child, well yes, she's an adult now, means to Jim. I do feel for the poor man."

"Well, if he really didn't get the letters…"

"Of course he really didn't get them! He only got the one, I keep telling you! I still can't understand what happened to them though. Did you post them all yourself then? Are you sure they were posted and not forgotten somewhere, maybe fallen behind something?" Amy demanded heatedly. She was feeling rather more and more upset.

"Why, of course I'm sure. Ginger posted them. He had to go past the letterbox on his way back to the barracks. I remember posting the last one because Gina had asked me to read it, for approval, I guess. Then I posted it for her. I remember it clearly, because her husband was away on exercise when Gina wrote it. I thought at the time that she wanted me to make sure that there was nothing in it that would upset Ginger. …. You know, now that they were married. Like I explained earlier, it did seem to me that she was giving Jim a last chance to acknowledge his child. So, I read it and posted it on the way home."

Paul and Amy looked at each other, then they both looked at Ray. Nobody spoke for a few minutes. All of them felt unable to utter out loud what was going through their minds.

Finally, it was Amy who was brave enough to come out with what, to her, seemed so obvious.

"Well, I think it's clear to me and to you both, that uncle's so called friend didn't want Gina and Jim's relationship to carry on. He obviously wanted Gina for himself and didn't post those letters at all."

"Oh no, Ginger's a good chap, a good husband and father to both children, I hasten to add. He never treated Amelia any differently to how he's always treated his son. No, no, he wouldn't do a terrible thing like that. He adores his wife and always has done."

"He might be an 'ideal' husband and all that Ray," Paul went on, "but did he always love her, even when she was going out with his mate? Did he love her so much that he broke up the relationship so that he could step in?"

Amy looked at Paul with admiration. He had put it so well!

"It does look like that. Ray, you've got to admit that it's highly possible that he never posted those letters. Poor uncle, he felt so dejected and then months after an awful silence, he received the letter telling him about the child and the wedding. That must have hurt him so badly."

"Ginger must have known the seriousness of Jim's condition. There's no doubt about it! Didn't he tell Gina about it?"

"Well, he did go to see her and told her that there had been a horrible accident on exercise. Then he started to visit her at home, initially to talk about Jim but I don't honestly know how they… how things changed. Maybe Ginger wasn't her first choice, and we have to remember that there was a scandal to be avoided, but those two are very happily married still. I just can't think that he..."

"Come on Ray, he must have destroyed them, there's no other explanation!"

"I don't know what to say. I'll have to speak to him as soon as I can. I did tell you that they're in England. I still can't believe that Ginger would do such a thing though!"

"He didn't post those letters. That's how it looks to me, or rather to us, to all of us. He is the cause of all the heartache and misery which might emerge when Amelia finds out the truth about her father."

"She doesn't have to find out anything. As far as she's concerned, Ginger is her dad. You mustn't shatter her life."

"Ray, you said yourself that she's an adult, with every right to know her parentage. I'm sure that when someone, probably Gina, tells her the whole story, Amelia will understand."

"Oh well, she's bound to be shaken and upset at first, but then, she might take it better than we think. Anyway, we have a few days to work out what is best for all concerned. We have four days to prepare some sort of plan."

"Look, just stop it. My head's buzzing and I can't think straight. There's Gina to consider too. Oh my goodness, my parents!" Ray looked very, very worried. He was now pacing the floor whilst trying not to get angry. It would just make matters worse for everybody if he did.

"Shall we leave it for today Ray? I mean, let's stop talking about it now and let you mull it over. Talk to Martin about it. Please don't be mad at me," Amy was pleading now. "I saw how it affected my uncle. He really needs to know about his daughter. We must remember that he's the innocent party in all this."

"Yes Ray," Paul was keeping his promise and backing his girlfriend up. "Let's stay calm and as soon as Martin's better we can talk about it all and see what the next step should be."

"If it were up to me there would be no next step at all. I wouldn't try to shatter the family and its security. Martin might think otherwise. He's a softie and has passed the odd comment about Amelia's father. I have to admit that we were all very fond of Jim. Amelia favours him in looks."

"Does she really? I can't wait to see her."

"Well, Martin is her godfather and they are very close. We were recently talking about Amelia and how fair she still is. That was only about a week ago. My brother actually said that Amelia has told him more than once that it's strange, that while her mum is dark, her father and her brother are ginger haired, she is so blonde!"

"Well then, in a way that makes me feel better. Most probably, your brother Martin won't think it'll be as big a deal as you might be thinking. If Amelia really thinks that she is so different to her brother and her parents, then I hope and pray that being told that Ginger is not her biological father won't be such a bombshell." Amy almost felt a ray of hope. She too thought it was best if they left it for the time being though.

"Ray," she began, "you said yourself that Andy can hold the fort tonight. How about us going somewhere, maybe to Sliema and have a meal out. It will be nice if you could. What do you think Paul?"

"That's a brilliant idea. Ray, phone your wife, go on, and see what she thinks."

"I can't take advantage of my cousin. However, he is good. He needs the money and he has my dad and mum if needs be... I don't know. Oh blow it, I haven't had an evening off for ages."

"There you are then, now's your chance. Phone her, go on."

"I'll tell you what, I'll go now and help out until about eight o'clock, and then I'll leave. Let's say eight thirty. You two make your way down to the bar and then we'll go and pick up my wife. You two decide where to book a table then. I noticed that you've got lists of restaurants and pubs etc, near the phone."

"Yes, that was here when we arrived. We'll do that then. We'll be at the George Cross bar no later than eight thirty."

"Right, I'd better be off now. Bye you two," and he shook Paul's hand and gave Amy a hug and a kiss to make sure they knew that there were no hard feelings now. He had calmed down for the time being. He didn't even try to think how he would feel when he faced his brother-in-law. If his suspicions were correct, that so-called 'ideal' husband of his sister caused and was going to be causing, a lot of problems and an awful lot of heartache soon.

CHAPTER 14

The evening turned out to be very pleasant and productive. Lucy, Ray's wife, was very bubbly and friendly and anyone observing the two couples laughing and talking animatedly would have thought that they were either old friends or relations. Ray had told Lucy all about his lunchtime session with the young couple. She was hardly surprised at all. She said that it was more surprising really that Jim hadn't come to Malta and claimed his daughter years ago.

"Well, Amy, like I said to Ray earlier, it doesn't surprise me at all. I mean things have changed now, people are more broadminded and illegitimacy is part and parcel of modern living."

"What do you mean?" asked Amy. "What doesn't surprise you at all? You do mean - I hope - that you're not shocked by uncle's decision to find his daughter after all these years?"

"Yes, and from what Ray has told me, even though the poor man was gutted, he was really very prudent to actually let Gina and his friend get on with bringing up his child."

"I hope that Gina sees it like that too, and then Amelia can be told as soon as possible." Amy was getting more optimistic by the minute.

"It's very difficult to understand how Amelia was never told about her biological father. She's an adult now and it must be harder to accept than if she were told at a young age. She would have grown up with the idea."

"Well, to be perfectly honest Amy, we never talked about - well we haven't for years and years. As far as I know, Ginger didn't want her to know. Gina was all for it, but Ginger adored that girl, he still does really and he wanted to be the only father for her."

"That was a lovely meal." Paul had been eating and not involving himself in the conversation. He had let Amy talk and had carried on eating and enjoying his choice of a typical Maltese dish.

"I've never had rabbit stew before and I didn't realise what I was missing," he said wiping his mouth and rubbing his stomach with a sigh of satisfaction. Amy looked on amused. She never thought that Paul would ever have anything but steak! He had never been adventurous with his choice of meals in the past.

"This has been a lovely evening," Ray looked around at his companions for confirmation and they all nodded in agreement.

"However, I'd like to have a couple of bottles of Hop leaf, but I can't because I'm driving tonight. My lady wife says it's my turn. How about if you two come to our house for a nightcap? I won't be able to drive you back from our house mind, because I'll have had a couple of drinks there. Lucy here has had enough wine too."

"That's ok, we'll get a taxi to our pad. What do you think Amy, shall we go along or do you want to stay in Sliema for a little bit longer?"

"No, I'm quite tired. It's been a heavy day really. We'll come with you, then we'll get a taxi back to our apartment."

The hour or so they all spent at Ray and Lucy's house rounded off the evening very nicely. Although they'd all exhausted the subject of Amelia, it was difficult to keep off it, especially now that Amy was feeling optimistic about the reception she and Paul would get from Gina.

"I honestly think that as soon as Gina and her family return to Malta, well, let's say a day later, you should arrange to meet her. If it helps I'll invite you both here, then you'll be able to talk more easily on neutral ground. I also think that you might feel better with me here, now that I know what you came to Malta to do. What do you both think?"

Paul and his girlfriend were blown away by this kindness. Amy agreed that it would make her feel better if Lucy was there when she told Gina all that her uncle had trusted her with. Ray wasn't so sure.

"What can you possibly do to help? My sister's going to be so disturbed and shocked to hear that Jim wants to acknowledge his daughter after so long. You can't change that. What can you honestly do, Lucy?"

"I think that Amy won't be so nervous if she knows that I'll help if I can…maybe there'll be some awkward moments. What do you think Paul?"

"I agree with you. For a start, you can keep Gina calm. You obviously know her very well." Paul felt that he had to say, "Amy would feel better with your wife there Ray. Lucy, you're so level-headed that I won't worry about Amy getting out of her depth if you're around."

"Thanks Paul, I can see things easier because I'm in the wings, so to speak."

"I also think that you're right about meeting here, Lucy. It's better to meet Gina here than at our apartment or at Gina's house. Do they all live in the house with the bright yellow door? Do your parents live there too Ray?" Amy had woken up and needed some answers.

"Yes, it's rather a large house. There are two communicating doors. The downstairs one leads from the bar directly to the kitchen. Then, upstairs, there's also a door connecting the rooms on top of the bar to the rest of the house. That's our parents' suite."

"It must be lovely for them to have company if they want it and on the other hand, if they want time on their own, they just go through a door to their part of the house. It's a great arrangement!"

"Yes," said Lucy. "Ray and Martin lived there when they were single. When Gina got married, my in-laws moved into the rooms that were made into a lovely self contained suite for them."

"So, Ginger stayed behind then. He must have left the Army, obviously, and stayed in Malta since."

"Yes, it would've broken my parents' heart, if Gina had left Malta. There was Nanna too. She passed away recently."

"Yes, we guessed it was your grandmother. When we arrived in Malta we went to the bar and read the note which was stuck to the closed door."

"I'm sorry folks," Amy butted in, "I feel so tired now. Can we phone for a taxi please?"

"I'll order it for you," said Lucy kindly. "Poor Amy, you look really worn out. It's been exhausting for you, more mentally than physically, I think."

It was mercifully a very short time before the taxi arrived. They only had enough time to hastily arrange to talk more the next day. On the way home Amy found it hard not to shut her eyes and sleep, but she managed to keep awake until the taxi dropped them outside their holiday home.

That night, both of them slept peacefully because they felt that they had safely gone over the first of many hurdles. However, this time it was Ray who tossed and turned all night.... he was just unable to decide what was the best thing to do next.

The shrill ringing of the telephone woke Amy up. She looked

at the big clock on the chest of drawers and couldn't believe that it was nine o'clock! Paul was nowhere to be seen so she quickly got up and rubbing her eyes, went to the kitchen to put the kettle on.

"Good morning, sleepy head," Paul pulled a chair for her and dropped a kiss on top of her head, as he got up and walked towards the teapot. "You looked so peaceful, and you were obviously exhausted, so I tried to be quiet. Here's a nice cup of tea for you. Shall I make some toast? I'm starving but I waited for you."

"Yes please, I'd love some. This bread is absolutely lovely. It doesn't keep though, but it's lovely toasted isn't it?"

"Yes, I'm not going to be so keen on the sliced bread when we are back home. By the way, who was that on the phone?"

"It was a wrong number I think. I picked it up and as soon as I spoke, the other person hang up."

"It woke me up. Just as well mind, I don't want to sleep the hours away while we're on this beautiful island."

"There's your toast, eat it, don't wait for me. Talking about this beautiful island, what shall we do today? I feel that we must keep talking to Ray and of course his brother, when he's better.. However, we must have some fun as well, because let's face it, we can't do much else while Gina and her family are away."

"Don't let your toast burn, Paul. Mmm, I'm making some more. Of course, we have to wait till they return. What about going to the Silent City? I read about it in one of the brochures we were given. It sounded worth visiting."

"What a great idea, Amy. I went there, but it was ages ago when my dad was stationed here. I was very young but I remember the quiet streets and the big buildings. It's a way off though. We'd better find out about buses before we set out."

"Shall we walk to the George Cross bar and have a chat with Ray and Martin if he's there? Then, we can ask about buses."

"Yes, we'll do that. We must keep talking to them as we said last night."

"Yes, but we mustn't say anything if the parents are about though. God knows how they'll take it!"

"They most probably think that things will never change and that their granddaughter will always remain blissfully unaware that the man she calls dad is not her father."

"I hate the thought of causing them any grief and worry, but then, uncle deserves to be recognised. On the other hand, his daughter deserves to know the truth about him. Don't you think that she should know why it's taken him so long to come forward?"

“Absolutely, yes of course I do. I think we should try and leave all that for a while now though. Come on Amy, let's make a day of it, shall we?"

"Good idea. I'll get ready quickly. Come on then, you'd better get on with it Paul, so that we have a day out in that lovely sunshine." Paul was bustling around getting ready but he went on planning the day...he always liked to have plans laid out clearly.

"We'll have lunch out, and come back when we've had enough. What do you think?"

"Yes, I'll try and read all there is about The Silent City. There's a leaflet about it on that telephone table. Hurry up Paul, we should be on our way down the hill by now."

Paul finally emerged from the bathroom dripping all over the tiled floor. He always hurried Amy, but she was always ready first. This time was no exception. She was ready and so while she waited for Paul, she was reading all about Mdina (as the Silent City was also called).

"We have to catch two buses, Paul," she said. "I think the best way is if we go to Valetta, get off at the terminus and then, catch a Rabat bus. They used to be dark blue but they're all green now."

"Yes, I saw them when we were there on Good Friday. Gosh that seems ages ago. See, I'm ready, let's go."

"Ray hasn’t phoned you has he? He obviously doesn't need you." Amy just remembered that Paul had offered to help." I'm glad actually, because I do want to see a bit of Malta now that we're here. Uncle Jim wanted us to have a good holiday if possible, didn't he? So, today, we'll enjoy ourselves."

"Talking about your uncle, Amy, you were supposed to phone him the other night."

"I tried, didn't I? The line was engaged for ages, then we went out and I forgot to try again when we got back. It was late anyway."

"When was this?"

"I told you, yesterday, when you were in the shower."

"When was that? In the morning? Oh you said before we went out didn't you? So it must've been before we went out for a meal with Ray and his wife."

"Yes, I kept trying, but I didn't get through. Then, when we got back, it was too late to phone up. I feel awful now. I could do it now but I don't feel like getting all emotional, not when we 're on our way out."

"He must be thinking that we haven't made any progress. However, I did say on the postcard that I'll phone him on Friday."

Their conversations always seemed to end up about Jim and the purpose of their holiday in Malta. True to form, as they were walking down the hill they again felt some of the emotions which Jim had somehow passed on to them every time he had talked about St George's Bay. His fond memories and vivid descriptions fitted perfectly with their surroundings. Soon, they reached the now familiar bar, just next door to the house with the bright yellow door.

The bar wasn't very busy and there was Ray talking to his brother at one of the tables. Paul held Amy's hand and led her towards them.

He could see that she was suddenly very nervous. Squeezing her hand, he tried to reassure her that it would be fine. He pulled a chair out for her and both of them sat and smiled nervously at Martin. They were both wondering if Ray had told him all, and they were on tenterhooks to find out how he felt about it all.

"How are you feeling Martin? You weren't expected to be here working today. Are you alright?"

"Yes, thank you Amy. I do feel much better today."

"You should take it easy though," Ray butted in as he was setting some drinks on their table.

"I will take it easy. Huh, there's no choice really. Andy is still here, he's stock taking because, as you see, we're not exactly run off our feet!"

"Well, that's just as well. Just don't push yourself if it does get busy. By the way, we're going to Mdina today. Is it a hassle to go by bus?" Paul asked. "What about hiring a car Amy?"

"Oh yes, Paul, yes!" said an excited Amy. "That would be marvellous. We won't have to change buses, and anyway, the buses that come all the way up here aren't very frequent. Ask Martin here to recommend a car hire firm, Paul."

"Self drive? You want to hire a car? Yes, I can certainly help you there. As it happens, my father-in-law owns a small car hire firm. He'll give you a good deal. When do you want it?"

"Today. Now!" exclaimed Amy a little bit louder than she'd intended. The few people, mostly tourists that were having a quiet drink, turned to look at her.

"Oops, I shouted did I?" she asked, turning bright red.

"Don't worry, we all shout here, especially when someone is feeding the jukebox. I'll tell you what, you two have a drink and I'll go in the back and give Victor a ring. It's unlikely that all the cars are out. If it were summer, I wouldn't even bother phoning."

"Really? Is he that busy then?"

"Yes, very. He's got a very good reputation and he's usually all booked before the tourists arrive here. A few visitors, mostly English, actually book a car when they book a holiday. He has quite a few regulars too. Now, I'd better go and phone up."

It was only a couple of minutes before Martin put his head around the door that led to the little office.

"Paul, you'd better come and sort out what you want," he called, inviting Paul to walk through the back. "You go through as well if you want Amy."

Amy followed Paul through to the little back room that served as an office. One wall was completely covered in framed photos. While Paul took over from Martin and sorted out a car to hire, Amy stared at all the photographs. She recognised Ray and Martin's mum because she'd met her in the bar. She presumed that their dad was in the photo next to Emma.

Ginger, whose photo was next to a very attractive lady, was easily picked out. His hair was a dead give away. Amy was looking at Gina. She hadn't changed much from the photo that Amy had been given to take to Malta with her.

"Come on Amy, let's go. It's all sorted. Good old Martin! In fact the car's going to be ready for us in ten minutes, so we'd better leave now. We have to go to St Julian's."

"Paul, look this must be Amelia. Isn't she pretty? It's got to be her."

"Are you sorted?" Martin had come in to see if Paul needed any help. He found them standing in front of Amelia's picture.

Both jumped back guiltily. Amy felt herself blushing and tried to say something, but words couldn't come out.

"I see you're looking at my goddaughter. Ray told me all about your mission here, as it were. We need to talk, all of us together, even my parents, but not here, not now."

"You're right of course," Paul said, and thanks for your help. George said he'd have a car ready in ten minutes. I have my driving licence and you have my passport in your bag haven't you Amy?"

"Yes of course, you know I do."

"Just checking...we'll arrange to meet tomorrow maybe. Today's going to be a day off for us. We need to have few hours of relaxation. Would you and Ray decide the best place to meet and talk to Martin? We haven't got any plans for tomorrow."

Ray had served everyone and so he went over to where Martin and the English couple were standing. As soon as Paul explained that he and Amy had to go and pick a car up, Ray very kindly volunteered to drive them to the garage.

"Oh that's kind of you, but you don't have to do that."

"I know, but I want to. It's only a ten minute drive, but it'll take you a while to find it. It's in one of the back streets. Come on, let's go. We can talk in the car."

"Thank you Martin. Hopefully, we'll see you tomorrow."

As soon as they were on their way to the garage, Ray said that they had to meet and talk because his sister and family were due back soon. He echoed his brother's concern about telling their parents. Before they could decide on a solution, Ray was pulling up in front of a big open garage.

"Here we are," he said. "We'll phone you tonight. If for some reason we don't, we'll ring you tomorrow morning. It'll be before we open, so maybe a little too early for you, but it's better at that time because mum and dad are unlikely to be down. We'll sort something out, but we must meet tomorrow.

There's Victor. Hi Vic, here they are. Ready to take it away. I said you'll look after them and give them a good deal."

"Of course, don't I always.... to your friends anyway?" His laugh was loud and contagious.

"Nice to see you Ray, long time no see. How's your mother? She is a lovely lady, his mum is," Victor said addressing Amy. "She was my childhood sweetheart...my first love at seven years of age."

"Oh yes, we heard it all. She gave you her apple every day at school until her mum found out and she ticked you off!"

"That's it, that was the end of my first love affair. Lovely lady, she was a lovely little girl and she is a lovely lady now."

"Well Vic, I have to go back. I didn't think we'd be busy, but there are a few tourists having lunch already. They're still on their Easter holidays. Anyway, I left Martin on his own. How come you opened today then? I thought you weren't open until Friday. You used to have the week off before."

"Martin twisted my arm and as we Maltese are renowned for our hospitality, I wasn't going to break the record. I'll close the door as soon as these two lovebirds have gone. I'll get an earful if I don't." Turning to Amy with a big grin on his face, he explained, "It's my lady wife, you know, she wants me all to herself!" and he laughed out loud at his own joke.

"Oh, you're so kind to help us today," gushed Amy and she impulsively planted a kiss on the leathery, brown cheek. He smelt of aromatic pipe tobacco. She surprised herself, but then it was very kind of him to open just for them.

Ray started walking towards his car saying that he was leaving them in Vic's capable hands.

" Be careful now. Drive safely. We'll speak later tonight or in the morning. Bye bye, Victor."

"Say hi to your dear mother Ray. Make sure you do."

"I will, "Sahha."

"Sahha."

Martin was right. Victor was a great chap and he gave them a very good deal.

"Any friend of Emma's boys is a friend of mine," he said loudly, thumping Paul on his back in very friendly and boisterous way.

"Here you are," he said as he handed Paul an A-Z street map of the area. "I don't suppose you 've got one of these have you? Well, I don't need it," laughed George. "Someone left it in the car so you might as well have it. Anyway, let's see what I can do for you."

It took all of ten minutes for the deal to be all done and dusted and the two were soon speeding away happily.

"This A-Z is useful, but I do need to look at a road map Amy, so let's stop at the place they call Ferry. Remember that's where we bought the figolli. We should be able to buy a map there and I need to fill up as it's only a quarter full, so keep a look out for a petrol station, please love."

The drive was different to say the least. Paul soon joined the horn chorus. He laughed as he sounded it back at the drivers who used theirs for any reason, be it to tell everyone they were coming, to warn other vehicles that they must make way for them or simply to attract someone's attention. There were a few pretty girls about, so the horn chorus was quite busy!

"I can see that there's some truth about drivers staying in the shade," Paul said with a big grin on his face. “I can actually understand a little."

"Yes it's quite hot today, even though it's only April. Have you noticed that all the men have their arms resting out of the window as they drive?"

"I noticed that a year ago when I came here with Dave. We had a great time here. I actually remember that initially, I was quite scared to drive! Then, I just joined them! It's all coming back now! It's alright when you're driving.... you have to go with the flow as it were."

"Don't take any risks, Paul. Please drive carefully. Slow down, please. There, that looks like a newsagent in the corner. Well, they obviously sell newspapers. Hopefully they sell road maps. Stop and I'll run and buy one."

"Ok, here you are. Take all the change," and Paul emptied his pockets. That should more than cover it. Amy, don't be long now, I can't stop here for long."

Amy virtually skipped to the door and was surprised to find that the shop that looked so little from the outside was much smaller when you went in it. An old man was sitting at the back smoking a pipe. His twinkly green eyes shone when Amy entered the shop. He took his faithful old pipe out of his mouth, twirled his moustache and tried to catch Amy's eye, but she was too busy looking around. She felt mesmerised. What an Aladdin's den indeed! It seemed there was everything one needed for a good holiday in that little cubby-hole of a shop. As she paid for the map the sprightly old man gave here a cheeky grin and said that he hoped to see her again. That was after he'd asked her if she needed any film for her camera, batteries or sun cream because it might get hot, even in spring. She might get burnt, he warned and did she need any headache tablets?

Amy felt highly amused and promised that she would go back if she needed anything while she was in Malta. He would have kept her talking about England but she'd promised Paul that she'd be quick. As she walked to the car quickly, she wondered if she could ever live like that and spend all day cooped up in a little room. He was obviously starved for company, but he was, nevertheless, a very charming and cheerful character. She meant what she said and would go back if she needed anything that he kept in his little shop. Smiling to herself, Amy came to the conclusion that her new friend kept everything in that little shop.

Hurrying back to where her boyfriend was parked, Amy waved at him with the map that she had just bought. As soon as she was in the car, Paul sped off at once, not wanting to waste any more time than was necessary. He couldn't wait to go back in history through the streets of Mdina.

"Paul, there seems to be a traffic jam ahead. You can't see can you, stuck behind that big lorry? I think we'll be ages now." Paul could tell that Amy was getting impatient.

"Shall we go a different way? Is there a different way, or do we have to go to Valetta first?" She bombarded him with questions, proving that he was right. She was getting very impatient.

"Just wait a little please. I'll park up as soon as I can. We'll study the map because I haven't got the faintest idea about the route. Remember that I told you I was only a youngster when mum and dad took us to the Trade fair. I remember it was in a place called Naxxar. Even though it's been years and years, I never forgot the name. I'm probably wrong, but I think it was close to Mdina. I'm not sure. When I came on holiday with Dave we went to Mdina and I think Rabat is thereabouts."

"Let's park there, look. We can study the map for a few minutes and refresh your memory."

Paul took a few minutes to find the best route for Rabat and on to the Silent City and then they were off once again.

CHAPTER 15

They were both determined to try and have a normal, enjoyable day. Amy was hoping that it would be refreshing and more importantly, restful, to be away from the concerns and worries surrounding the secret with which her dear uncle had entrusted and burdened her. It was indeed a revelation that was soon to either destroy or strengthen the family bonds which Gina and her relatives enjoyed and took for granted.

As they walked through the walled citadel, they felt a million miles away from all their worries. It seemed as interesting, and really as historical, as Paul had enthused about to Amy. His being a History teacher made him see more than the average tourist could see, even if one had an eye for everything historical.

Amy had been prepared to find that his enthusiasm about his pet subject had, at least slightly, exaggerated the wonderful ambience of the place. She soon found out that he hadn't! She could feel the tranquillity that reigned in those quiet streets. Paul was right. It enveloped them and seemed to wrap them in a calming aura that's so difficult to find in most modern towns and cities.

She was mesmerised by the amazing charm of the streets of the ancient city and the silence that reigned supreme there.

"You were right Paul. It's so calming here. Oh, look at those walls!"

"Yes, those thick walls separate Mdina from Rabat."

"I'm not surprised that you wanted to come back here. All this architecture! You must know all there is to know about it. I bet you've read everything you could lay your hands on."

"Yep, but I didn't want to bore you. I'll just say that it's mostly Norman and Baroque."

"I've just thought... this must be like a busman's holiday for you!" Amy exclaimed, but Paul just smiled. He was in his element.

As they walked through the clean, quiet streets, they went past several palaces and Amy was utterly surprised to learn that these were being used as private homes. Many of their shuttered windows were draped in bougainvillea.

"The people who live in these palaces are descendants of

noble families you know." Paul seemed, as usual, very knowledgeable.

"Really? They're so grand, and look, we can stop for lunch here. Let's!"

Very enterprisingly, some inhabitants had converted space into gift shops and tearooms.

After a light lunch they resumed their walk in what seemed like an old world. One small group of tourists was listening attentively as their guide talked about their historic surroundings.

"We never checked to see what excursions, if any, there are laid on for today, did we?" Amy suddenly asked. Seeing the groups of tourists had reminded her.

"Well, to be honest, I forgot too. However, now that we have a car we might as well go where we want, when we want."

"Ssssh Paul," Amy was listening to the group's guide as she was talking loud enough for them to hear.

"She just said," Amy whispered, "that the lack of noise is due to these narrow and curved streets."

"Well I read that they were designed to stop arrows and vehicles."

"Whatever it was that created such peace, it's certainly worked!"

In spite of numerous people around, and teeming with tour groups, respectful silence seemed to be the order of the day.

"Shall we make our way towards Rabat now?"

"Yes, but listen, I can hear singing.... it must be the nuns. This is a convent. Look Paul."

"Yes, I can hear it. It is, I don't know - kind of moving isn't it?"

Suddenly, the bells of the cathedral started tolling. Oddly enough, that made the tranquillity feel even more pronounced!

When they left the Silent City and its surprising peace - in spite of it being fully inhabited, Amy was amazed how noisy the streets of Rabat were in contrast! She wondered how much noisier it would be on a normal working day because some shops and businesses were still closed for the Easter week.

For the English couple who had set out with the intention of having a relaxing day, it had been just that. They were enjoying themselves doing the normal things tourists did.

This time, for a change, hours had passed by without either of them thinking, or worse, worrying about facing Gina and then probably getting turned away without making any contact with Amelia. Today Paul and Amy forgot their worries and concerns about the probable pending problems which were about to surround the family who lived at the house with the bright yellow door.

In the meantime though, it was simply a great pleasure just to walk hand in hand through the peaceful public garden at Rabat and then to stop at a kiosk and buy the delicious 'slice' (as the name suggests) of ice cream. This delicious concoction was enriched with nuts, cherries and other pieces of fruit and held together with two light and crispy wafers. Paul introduced it to Amy, and now she didn't think that she had ever tasted anything so delicious in her whole life.

Since they now had a car at their disposal, Paul and Amy didn't have to plan around the bus timetables which gave them more freedom to just go about anywhere without constantly time keeping.

They were tempted to stop at a big kiosk, which seemed to be doing a fair trade. Paul bought some 'Hobz biz-zejt', which he ordered in Maltese showing off his knowledge of the language, impressing his girlfriend..

"What's in them Paul?"

"Oh, these crusty baps are really, really delicious...they're filled with tomatoes, olives, capers and some tuna fish. Some are spread with tomato puree instead of having tomato smeared on them. Both kinds are tasty. Take the drinks off me please, before I drop something, quick love."

"We've only just had lunch!" laughed Amy.

"Well I've decided to take you to a beach. We saw some beautiful pictures in the brochures. I'm thinking of Mellieha Bay at the moment. We might get hungry walking on the beach in the fresh sea breeze. Come on, let's go and see how it all looks without its multitude of sun lovers"

They were soon on their way there, and the empty beach looked so much bigger than it did in all the photos they'd seen. All those summer crowds made it look smaller somehow.

Paul and Amy were carefree for the time being, and they looked it. The deserted sandy beach provided a perfect setting for the picture they unwittingly made, as they walked barefooted in the golden sands with the gentle waves tickling their toes.

"This sand feels quite cool even on such a sunny day. I bet it's too hot to walk on in the summer," said Amy.

"Very!" said Paul.

"That must be why everyone wears flip-flops. Uncle said that everyone did in summer. That reminds me..."

"What?"

"Uncle Jim told me how he met Gina, the very first time. Apparently, he nearly tripped in his new flip-flops. She'd been sprawled out on a towel, reading a book. He was walking on the beach and, in trying to stop himself from falling, he managed to cover her and her book with sand."

The day was turning out to be a lovely relaxing time for both Amy and Paul. They sat on the sand and picnicked on the fresh bread rolls which Paul had had the foresight to buy at the kiosk.

Inevitably, after a while, the subject of Amelia came up again.

"Paul, I think we should try and decide what the next step should be. Ray or Martin will be phoning, I know, but we should decide on some plan or action before we get roped into something, which might not be ideal. What do you think?"

"I think you're right. We've had such a lovely day away from Gina and co. I think that now we're rested, we might see the way ahead more clearly."

"Yes, well, let me see. Ray suggested that his mother be told next. Remember, Gina and her family return this Friday. What do you suggest we do now?"

"I think we should take Lucy and her suggestion into consideration. I don't think we should meet the parents in some restaurant or any public place." Unsurprisingly, Amy was as practical as ever.

"Yes, I 'm with you on that. Gina's parents might get angry and it would be embarrassing and awkward for everyone. They might walk out or raise their voices. No, I agree it would be better if we meet at Ray's house. Lucy will think of a good excuse for meeting there, I'm sure."

"Yes, she made me feel very confident. I really took to her. She's like a breath of fresh air and seems very calm and level headed!"

"Yes, she'll probably keep things from getting out of hand because she knows Gina so well.

Oh dear, I just wonder what your uncle would make of all this?"

"That's a point. There's a phone box across the road. Look, just there."

"Why? Do you want to try and get through now?"

"I might as well try. I have lots of change. You stay here, Paul. If uncle can't talk with auntie around him, I'll try my best to find out if he'll be on his own Friday evening. I'll see if auntie has a meeting then. If she has, I'll arrange to phone him again then."

"What are you going to tell him, if you get through, that is?"

"Only that he has a daughter called Amelia and that we've talked to her brothers. That should be enough to get on with."

"Yes, definitely. At least like this, with a little information to start with, he won't, hopefully, get anxious and give his wife cause for concern. Go on love, careful how you cross the road. Watch out for those mad Maltese drivers!"

Paul sat on the sand, undisturbed by the traffic that zoomed past the long curving road behind him. He had his fingers crossed that Amy would get to talk with her uncle. When he looked back at the telephone box and he could make out Amy...she was smiling. She looked up and waved to him before she put the phone down and crossed the road.

"Well, are you going to tell me or are you going to carry on smirking?"

"I don't know really. Now, what should I do? I'll think about it for a few…" She didn't get to finish the tantalising sentence. Paul had grabbed her feet and dragged her along from where she had sat down next to him.

"Let go, Paul! Let go...I'll tell you..."

"Promise... Promise" he said as he dragged her further towards the water. Both were laughing hysterically. Amy could hardly talk, but managed a throaty, "I promise, I promise!"

He let go and she would have run across the sand but her legs felt weak because he'd grabbed them so tightly to drag her.

"Ok Paul, you win."

"And...?"

"There's nothing to tell really," she uttered, a wicked smile playing on her lips.

"What do you mean by that? You were ages. I saw you talking. What did you say? How did Jim take it?"

"Slow down, Paul. Goodness, you sound like me when I get excited, or rather that's what you tell me often enough. You always say that I fire the questions out. Let's walk back to the car now and I'll tell you word for word what was said. You have to put your shoes on, remember?" she laughingly reminded Paul who had really forgotten about his shoes.

"I felt so comfortable barefooted on this sand," he explained. He took them out of the bag they had with them and proceeded to put them on as quickly as possible.

Paul did not start the car up but turned to Amy who was now quite recovered from her laughing fit.

"Well, uncle said absolutely nothing," she said before Paul had a chance to start interrogating her again.

"Why not? Come on Amy."

"Uncle Jim said nothing, because he wasn't there!" she said with a satisfied smile. "It's not funny really, but anyway, he was at the outpatients for a checkup. His friend took him because he shouldn't drive yet."

"So, who were you talking to? I saw you…"

"Auntie Meg. She stayed at home because the television was playing up and the repairman is there at the moment. I couldn't say anything but then before I knew it, I said that I'd met my girlfriend I'd spoken to Uncle Jim about. Auntie then said she didn't know I knew anyone in Malta. Oh boy, I nearly tied myself in knots then."

"So what did you say then?"

"I said I'd told uncle ages ago and she might have been in the kitchen at the time. Anyway, auntie will tell him that I found my old girl friend, and hopefully, he'll get the message and realise that he has a daughter."

"Hmmm…you're a clever clogs Amy. Yes, hopefully he'll click. It's a shame that he wasn't there though. It would've been good to tell him what we know."

"Yes, it would have, but I did find out that auntie's WI meeting is on Friday, just as we thought."

"How on earth did you find out without making her curious?"

"I just said that I'd be phoning again on Friday. She replied that it would be great if I did, because Uncle Jim will be in on his own. Then, she went on to explain about her meeting."

"Well done, you did well. Now I think we should get back. I'm feeling quite tired. I don't know about you."

"Yes, I feel very tired now. It must be the sea air. Walking so much at Mdina and then at Rabat helped too I think."

Paul jumped up startled at the shrill ringing of the old

fashioned telephone. He was just going to say something scathing about phone calls so early in the morning, when he looked blearily at the big clock on the wall. It was ten o'clock! He got out of bed quickly and ran to pick the phone up.

"Oh, good morning Martin. No, no, that's no problem. We were out all day yesterday and walked a lot on a lovely beach. All that sea air made us very tired. Anyway, I suppose you want to let us know what's on the books for today then."

Amy was just as surprised that it was ten o'clock. She made her way to the kitchen and busied herself busy putting the kettle on and then started making some toast. She could hear Paul talking to Martin in the background. It sounded as if they were going to be meeting Gina's parents that day. Paul seemed to be agreeing with whatever he was being told. She hoped that he would tell her what was going on, before he gave his word.

As if he had read her mind, Paul said, "Excuse me a minute Martin, let me just tell Amy," and he called her to see what she thought of Martin's suggestion.

Apparently, the brothers had talked for a long while and debated what would be the best way to tell their parents about Jim.

"They can't get away from the bar, not together. The plot is for us to go to the bar for lunch today and we can make the proper plans then."

"Fine, we'll do that. I'm so glad that we're finally making some headway and I think that the parents should be there or else be told first, before anyone else."

Soon they were having breakfast on the veranda, which at this time of the day, was, as usual, bathed in sunshine. It was so peaceful and calming.

On the other hand, lunch time at the George Cross bar seemed pretty hectic. Besides the few tourists that were seduced by the lovely smell of good food, there seemed to be a lot of local workmen about. A group of men, mahogany skinned and covered in limestone dust, were obviously working on some of the new hotels and holiday apartments that were being constructed around the area.

It wasn't surprising really, that all these workmen went there for lunch. There was a very good and varied choice of snacks and hot dishes on offer, and none were too expensive.

Martin found a vacant table close to the counter and called Paul and Amy over with a wave.

"Here's the menu," he said giving Paul the usual firm

handshake and Amy the customary kiss on each cheek.

"Have a good browse. See if anything takes your fancy. Ray or I will come over for a chat as soon as it calms down a little."

His wife, Laura, was cooking today and he promised that he would introduce her to them when there was a lull in the orders. Soon he was busy once more out the back.

They both decided to try a popular Maltese dish. Laura came out of the kitchen looking all flushed and shy. She was pretty and looked much younger than her fifty odd years, but she wasn't easy to talk to because she wasn't very confident speaking in English. It was a shame, because when she did speak, Paul and Amy found out that she was very fluent. They had taken her advice and were both trying one of the traditional dishes - rabbit stew. She assured them that they would love it and promptly went back to the kitchen to get on with the cooking.

Later, when they were enjoying the delicious lunch, Laura came out to see how they were doing. She had lost a little of her reserve and when Martin came to their table, they were soon all laughing and talking at the same time...just like the Maltese regulars.

"Martin," called Ray, "lend us a hand. Maybe we'll be able to shut up shop a little bit early today."

"I'll help too since the kitchen is closed now. Excuse me Amy, Paul." With those words, Laura hurried through to the back of the bar.

The couple had finished their meal and since they had agreed to stay behind, they waited until Ray and Martin finished the jobs they did automatically after closing. Finally, the two brothers, satisfied that everything was shipshape, called Amy and Paul to follow them through the back to the house. Amy looked at Paul with eyes that were shining with hopeful anticipation. They were finally going into the house with the bright yellow door! Amy pinched herself. She couldn't believe that she was going into Gina's house, where, all those years ago, dear Uncle Jim had spent many happy hours.

Ray and Martin explained that their parents had gone to Sliema to do a bit of shopping, but they were due back soon. Ray wanted to close the bar as soon as the last punter had left because he hoped that they'd be able to decide how best to tell the older couple. It was better to thrash some ideas about while their parents were still out. Bearing in mind that Gina, Ginger, and their family were returning to Malta in a few days' time, there was really no more time to waste. The parents had to be told as soon as possible. The brothers had convinced Amy and Paul that if they won the parents over, half the battle would be over.

"Remember they are very protective of Gina and Amelia and would not hurt a hair on either of their heads. I suggest that you, Martin, start….."

"Me? Why me?" Martin sounded panicky.

Amy was oblivious to the discussion. She looked around the big table in the very big bright room. Amy felt a sort of déjà vu sensation because it was all just as Uncle Jim had described just a few days before. She was feeling rather strange because it was all just like the vivid picture she had conjured up in her head, when her uncle had talked about it back home. She'd make sure to phone him that evening. Whatever the outcome of this gathering, she would tell him about the house and about everything else she could think of.

"Are you alright love?" Paul asked under his breath.

"Oh yes," she smiled broadly. "I was thinking that this is just as my uncle described it to me."

"Apart from decorating every so often, my sister has left everything the same here. Whenever we have something important to discuss, like there is at this moment, we gather here, around this table. This room is the heart of our family house, our home. It has held many important gatherings. Anyway," Ray stopped himself going on, "we think that the best thing to do, is to get dad…" and he stopped because the shrilling noise of the telephone broke the flow of his sentence.

"Excuse me folks," and with a couple of strides Ray was talking on the phone.

"Hello dad, you're a bit late today. Have you stopped for a cup of coffee somewhere? What? Oh no! … How? Poor mum, is she…. really…dad? Are you all right? You don't sound too sure."

"What's happened Ray, what?" Martin had leapt up and wanted to take the receiver away but Ray carried on talking.

"One minute, Martin. I'll tell you in a minute. Yes dad. Ok, we'll do that. Are you sure now? Ok then…. Bye, bye."

Breathing deeply, Ray went to his chair and slumped down.

"Have they had an accident Ray? Who's hurt? What's happened to mum? Ray! Come on, tell me for heaven's sake. I gather something's happened to her."

CHAPTER 16

"They had just finished shopping and were walking to the car which was parked around the corner. As they turned into the street, a crowd of youths dashed around the corner. They were chasing each other. One of them bumped into mum and knocked her over. She fell badly and broke her wrist. Poor mum, she must've been in agony."

"Oh my goodness, where is she now?"

"Is she alright?"

"Has your dad taken her to casualty?"

"Which arm is it?"

Everyone was talking at once. Martin, who was usually the quiet one, took control of the situation.

"Ok, please, let's all calm down. Sorry, Amy, Paul, obviously we can't do anything that would cause mum any distress at the moment. So, we'll just have to talk later."

"I understand, of course we can't. Look, Ray, Martin, I think Paul and I should go and let you get on. We're in the way now. Before we do go, please tell us Ray, how is she really?"

"Well, dad said that they're still in casualty. Her wrist is in plaster and apart from that she's a bit shaken by the accident. When mum is allowed to leave they're going to the canteen to have a cup of tea. Dad said that it would give mum a chance to calm down a bit more before he drives her home. He sounded very worried about her and he needed to steady his nerves I think."

"Poor dad must be shaken too," said Ray. "I think I'll get a taxi to the hospital and then drive them back myself in dad's car. What do you think Martin?"

"Yes, that's a very good idea, Ray. Go on, get ready. I'll order a taxi for you. Then I'll phone the casualty department at St Luke's and tell dad to wait for you. What time is it? Gosh, it'll soon be time to open the doors."

Martin was soon on the phone and leaving a message for his father. He then remembered that he would normally be taking his wife back home at around this time.

" Laura, I'm afraid you'll have to wait until Ray gets back. I can't take you home like I usually do."

"That's fine. There's no urgency. Anyway, your mum might do with some help. We don't know if it's her right or her left hand do we?"

"No, Ray didn't say. We'll phone you later, Paul about the other matter. Oh dear, it looks like I'll be busy." Martin was looking down from the balcony. He saw the taxi arrive and then pick Ray up.

"That tour group are heading this way," he pointed out to Paul, who was out on the balcony too. "I'd better get a grip or they'll walk away. Oh dear, I haven't even…."

"I can give you a hand Martin. Just tell me what to do…"

"Will you really? Are you sure? Oh, that's brilliant. Amy, you might as well keep Laura company. Come down, both of you, please. Mum will probably want to go and lie down. It must've been quite traumatic for a lady of seventy-four years of age. Besides, they missed their siesta today."

"Amy, why don't you take the car and take Laura to our apartment? I'll phone you when I'm not needed any more. Then, you can bring Laura back here and pick me up at the same time."

Amy didn't volunteer to take Laura home, because she didn't feel very confident driving on the busy streets. She didn't mind taking her to their apartment though, because this was only a quiet road, so she liked this idea very much. The two ladies were soon off up the hill, but before they walked away Laura gave her husband a quick shout over her shoulder. She reminded him to hurry up because there were still people outside looking for a drink!

Crowds of tourists were indeed gathered outside the door. They looked as if they were debating whether to wait for the rest of their group who were approaching slowly and seemed in no hurry, or go in without them. Finally, as Martin opened the big brown door they trooped in. As he turned back into the bar ready for the thirsty crowd, Martin gave Paul a grateful smile of thanks.

Paul proved to be fast, friendly and familiar with bar work and Martin was really thankful for that. They were kept very busy with a stream of thirsty patrons who were still coming and going through the door.

Martin was getting quite concerned because his parents and his brother hadn't made an appearance yet. He was busy in one of the stock rooms when Ray came through the connecting door.

"Oh hi Paul, I see you're busy. It's nice of you to help. Where's

Martin?"

"He went to fetch some mixers. I stayed to help because there were people waiting for the door to open. It's been busy, non-stop since then. Anyway, how's your mum?"

Just then, Martin walked back into the bar.

"Mum seems alright. She's having a lie down, but poor dad's still shaken. He said her wrist looked so awful, all purple and swollen and the drive from Sliema to St Luke's Hospital seemed to take forever, when it really took barely twenty minutes. He was so worried because mum was in agony."

"I'll go up and talk to them. Ray, Paul has been great. Did you know that he's experienced in bar work? It came in handy today."

"Go on, before she falls asleep. Have a cup of tea with dad. We'd forgotten that our Gina is coming back tonight. They get back at about eleven tonight. I thought that if mum and dad have a rest now, they wouldn't be too tired to wait up for Gina and the family. They'll wait up. They always do."

"Yes, I'll see if I can persuade dad to have a lie down too. I won't stop long," and he walked though to the house with the bright yellow door.

At one clock on Friday morning, and with a lot of noise and laughter, Gina and her family hurried into the kitchen followed by Ray, Lucy, Martin and Laura. They were all talking at the same time, full of excitement at being all together again.

The parents were looking like their normal selves again, and in spite of having her arm in plaster, Emma was looking excited and happy to have her daughter and all the family back together. The only ones missing were Ray's sons and their families who all lived in Gudja. This was a bit too far for them to pop in for a visit at one in the morning!

Ray and Martin had debated when to tackle their brother-in-law about the letters that had never reached Jim. They'd agreed to let sleeping dogs lie for that night, mainly out of concern for their mum but also because it was so late. Next day was a Saturday and they were the only members of the family who would be working.

The day dawned as usual for all the family, but the two brothers were very subdued at work in the bar. Both found it difficult to be their usual genial selves when they were dealing with their customers.

Martin kept checking the time and wondering when Ginger would make an appearance but Ray told him to relax because nobody would get up early after travelling from Leicestershire to London and then to Malta the night before.

Gina was the first one to show her face in the bar. She sensed at once that something was on Martin's mind, but he reassured her that nothing was wrong.

"I know something's up Martin. I know you. Come on, what's the matter?"

"Nothing Gina, honest."

"Come on, something's wrong. Ray, do you know? Look, there's no one waiting to be served. I'm not stupid. Something's wrong. You both look down in the mouth."

"Please Gina, leave it heh. This isn't the right time…"

"I knew it, so there is something wrong!"

"I never said that…I…well…the thing is…"Poor Martin was tying himself in knots.

"Martin! We agreed to speak to Ginger first."

"What on earth is the matter? Why speak to Ginger? Is one of you going to tell me what's going on or not?"

"Oh my God! Please Gina, it's lunch time and Laura is busy in the kitchen. Give her a hand if you feel like it."

"I just want to know…"

"Let's leave it until we close, please, Gina. Then we can talk. Look we're nearly done here. Laura's getting the last order ready. Then, we'll close as soon as we can."

"I'm worried now. Is it serious?"

"Well, it depends... leave it Gina. We can't discuss private matters in the bar. You should know that."

"Yes, of course I know that, but, if it looks like it does involve me…oh alright, I'll wait. I don't have a choice do I? I'm going back to do some unpacking and washing. Please come through as soon as you close, after lunch as soon as you can."

"Yes, of course. Are mum and dad up?"

"Yes, they're in their sitting room watching an old film. Why? Is it something to do with them? You said Ginger…"

"Gina, please, is he awake? What about the kids?"

"Amelia's in the bathroom and Ginger and Robert are still sleeping. Look, I don't have a clue what all this is about, but I hope it's nothing bad. We've just had a week's holiday which was a bit of a nightmare what with constant rain and Ginger and I arguing most of the time."

"Thank God, there's just one person left there finishing his meal. He'll be gone soon. Go on Gina, Martin and I will finish off here and then we'll come up as soon as possible. I promise, go on."

Martin and Ray weren't feeling very good about the situation. They were really worried about the effect it would have on their mum and dad. It was all turning out to be the opposite of their well-laid plans. First of all, Amy and Paul weren't there. In spite of their belief that their parents should be told before anyone else, there'd been no opportunity to talk to them, and so the old couple were still in the dark about Jim's decision to acknowledge their granddaughter. To crown it all, Emma had had that traumatic accident the day before. To add a bit more to their grave concerns, their sister was already miserable. It looked like the holiday had been a bit of a disaster.

With a deep sigh, Martin shut the big strong door and was about to start picking up glasses and ashtrays.

"Come on Martin, we have to get on with it. Gina won't let it rest, you know what she's like. I hope mum and dad don't get too upset. Hopefully, they'll stay in their suite with the TV very loud as usual. Do you want me to confront Ginger or would you rather? I don't really fancy the job. You're more tactful than me."

"You do it. Oh please Ray, you're much better than me at putting things across. I'll help. Come on, let's get this over and done with. There's no point dragging our heels now."

Laura, who'd been waiting for someone to tell her what was happening, followed the brothers through to the house with the bright yellow door. Sitting around the long table were Gina and her husband. Empty dishes with the remains of a hastily eaten lunch cluttered the table. That was proof that their sister was in a bit of a state because she would normally whip the plate away from you before you'd finished if she could, so that the table got cleared at once. Amelia, who was as usual, still eating her lunch, sat opposite them. She was always a slow eater and nothing much riled her. She looked up, beamed at her uncles and carried on eating her spaghetti Bolognese.

"What about mum and dad, are they still having their lunch or what?"

"They were just clearing up. Do they need to be here too? I hope not. I don't want mum to..."

"What don't you want me to do Gina?" asked Emma, walking in, totally unaware of the tension that some members of her family were feeling.

"Where's dad?"

"Oh, he went to lie down. He didn't sleep very well last night, I think. My accident affected him more than it did me." She looked round the room that was the heart of the house and made her way to her usual chair.

"Where's Robert?" Emma had a soft spot for her grandson.

"He won't be long...he's on the phone, talking to his girlfriend."

"Aaah," grandmother said indulgently as she glanced at her only daughter but then she noticed her drawn face.

"What's up Gina love? Is something wrong? No, don't deny it, I can see it. You two haven't been arguing again have you?"

"No, mum. Gina is worried because she knows that I have something to say that might...."

"Might what? For heaven's sake Ray!"

"Ok, there's only one way to say this. I m sorry sis, but we just found out..."

"Who's we?"

"Martin and I, we've just found out, that your dear husband, yes, Ginger, you might as well look worried, because after all these years, we have found out that you never posted those vital letters to that poor man, to Jim! The only letter that Jim received was the one that I posted. Remember, Gina, you gave it to me to post? Ginger was away on exercise at the time."

The man in question seemed to be shrinking into his chair and seemed to be getting smaller by the second.

"You, in fact, changed the course of my sister's life."

Silence fell over the room. You could have heard a pin drop. Then, five seconds later, pandemonium broke.

Ginger, looking whiter than usual and his freckles looking much darker in his pale face, was trying to bluff his way out of his wife's screaming accusations. She went berserk and would have lashed out at him if her brothers hadn't pulled her back.

Amelia stood there with her fork in mid air, shocked to see her mother so angry. On the other hand, her grandmother seemed to be incredibly calm, almost detached from what was happening around her.

Then Robert walked in on the loud, angry scene and went to his grandmother for a reassuring hug, before dragging a chair close to her. This gesture that was quite normal usually, seemed to jolt Amelia.

"What on earth are you so angry about mum? What letters are they talking about dad? Who on earth is Jim Anderson?"

"Oh my God, Amelia, sorry dear, in my anger, I forgot about you…you shouldn't be…"

"What mum? What did you forget? Mum, you look awful. Are you alright?"

"I don't know where to start. This man, Ginger, your so called father…"

"Mum, we had enough of that on holiday. You were arguing all the time, and mostly it was because of me. How do you think that makes me feel? There, it was because he wanted me to have more freedom. You kept accusing him of not acting like a good father. You're just old fashioned and you forget I'm an adult! Tell me…what is it this time, dad?" beseeched Amelia.

Ginger had his head down on the table. Amelia ran round to him and made him look up. He looked in such pain with tears running down his cheeks. Amelia started to cry.

"This must be serious. What on earth is this all about? Will someone…please tell me...dad? Is anyone going to tell me...Mum?"

Gina couldn't tell her daughter anything, because for the first time in her life, she passed out.

Emma flew across the room as fast as her arthritic knees would let her and pulling everyone away from her daughter, started telling them what to do. No one argued with her, and soon, Gina was on the big comfortable settee and the colour was back in her cheeks. Laura was busy in the kitchen making a pot of tea. The men stayed in the kitchen out of the way and you could have cut the atmosphere with a knife.

Amelia returned to the kitchen where Martin was talking very quietly and seriously to her brother. Ray made her sit down, put his arm round her shoulders and talked calmly to her until her sobs died down for a while. He would have told her everything, but he really thought it was best coming from her mum.

Ginger was still just sitting there, like a statue. Martin, who was usually the mild tempered one, suddenly left his nephew and facing his brother-in-law, started to attack him verbally. He said that he might well be responsible for splitting up the whole family, but mainly he could kill him for what he was going to put Amelia through. Not only for finding out that her so called father..."

"Martin, shut up!" shouted Ray. "It's not the right way or the right time for..."

Amelia looked up and ran across the room to face her Uncle Martin.

"What do you mean? How is dad going to hurt me? Dad, what does Uncle Martin mean?" she shouted, and once more, everyone was talking at once. Ray couldn't believe his brother had started it all again."

"Of all the stupid...Martin!"

"Sorry, but look at him, just look at him!" pointing at Ginger. Martin, usually so calm and level-headed, looked as if he was dying to hit him.

"What has he said about it all?" Martin was finding it hard to bite his tongue. "He has caused so much trouble. But then you probably thought you'd never get caught didn't you? Look, he hasn't even shown any remorse... just self pity."

"What on earth is happening here? I was trying to get some sleep but it sounds like world war three has broken out."

Ray gave his brother a menacing look. Their dad was the last person they needed there.

"Sorry about the shouting dad. Go back to sleep. It'll be quieter now," promised Martin.

"Oh no, I can't, not now. I asked what the shouting was all about. Go on tell me... Ginger what the heck is up?... Are you crying, man?"

Amy, feeling calmer now that her beloved Nannu was there, went to him and led him to his favourite chair.

"I've been asking that for ages, but no one will tell me. It must be something bad 'cause mum was so upset and she fainted. It's ok, Nanna's with her, and Auntie Laura is there too. Nannu, it's something to do with me because Uncle Martin said..."

Ray quickly butted in to stop her.

"Don't worry about that please. You'll soon find out," he promised the worried girl.

Back in the lounge, Gina's mother was sitting at her daughter's side on the big, comfortable settee.

Suddenly, raised voices could be heard from the kitchen. Gina could hear her normally quiet brother raising his voice and calling Ginger a few choice names. Ray was making himself even louder as he tried to shut Martin up. Gina now realised that her dad must have woken up. She could hear him telling his sons to control themselves and their temper, but it didn't seem as if he was having any success. Next thing, a distraught Ginger dashed into the lounge, looked at his wife for a few seconds, then in a hoarse cry shouted, "I only did it because I love you. I always did. I loved you from the very start. I let Jim win you over and make you his, when all the time I was going crazy inside." He stopped and walked towards Gina and tried to take her hand but she pulled away from him angrily, as if his touch had burnt her.

"I let him win you over, yes I did, but then when I knew that he wasn't coming back...you loved me you said, you loved me too."

Amelia had followed Ginger into the lounge, scared at the scenes she was witnessing. She stood rooted to the spot, staring at the mother she loved so much turning into a crazy shrieking woman.

"Go, just go!! Get out of here. I can't bear to see you! " Gina screamed at her husband. "We've been living with your deceit all these years, and all the time, letting me think that Jim...oh God, sorry Amelia. Please don't cry. Come here. Just look at her, just look at your daughter!! Your daughter!!!"

Ginger looked with pity and sorrow at his wife and daughter. He glanced round the room until his eyes fell on their suitcases, left there in the early hours of that morning. Without looking back up at anybody, he picked up his suitcase, which he hadn't yet unpacked, and ran out of the room and out of the house.

Amelia tried to say something but nothing came out of her mouth. The noise of the door slamming very hard jolted her into action, and she ran the length of the hall to the front door. Her hands were shaking so badly, that she couldn't open it. Screaming and calling her dad, she started kicking the bright yellow door in frustration. Nobody helped her. Her grandfather was calling her, asking her to go and tell him what was wrong. Her uncles and Robert just stood there like statues. Nobody dared say anything. Nobody knew what to say.

She was oblivious to everything around her and giving up on the door that wouldn't open, she kicked it in frustration. Looking all flushed and with her hair wild around her worried face, she ran up the winding staircase taking them two at a time, and then flew across the front bedroom. Flinging the door to the veranda wide open, she looked down and saw her father reversing the car out of the garage. Amelia screamed and called him as loud as she could, but he didn't seem to hear her. As she saw the car drive off, she rested against the wall and finally, resignedly, slid down to the floor, sobbing uncontrollably.

It had been an incredibly traumatic twenty four hours. Nobody could possibly have foreseen the awful events that were to be triggered by Ginger's angry departure.

Very late the night before, after he left the house in such a black mood, Emma decided to bring everybody together and demanded some answers. She waited until her daughter was feeling better. Then in no uncertain terms, she said that she wanted to know the whole story. How had all this come out now - more than twenty years on? What had Ginger actually done? What had made her daughter faint like that? Why was her granddaughter so hostile towards her mother?

Everyone knew that Emma was right. They all needed to talk but also try to keep calm. Her sons were still there because the bar had remained closed that evening. No one wanted to leave because the house with the bright yellow door was in such turmoil.

Only Ginger was missing. He wasn't there to defend himself, but Ray, Martin and Gina knew from his reaction that there was no doubt about his guilt.

Until then, the big, long table, made by Edward when the children were little, had witnessed such happy gatherings. Birthdays, anniversaries, and every special occasion for the family had meant that happy, smiling and bubbly family members often surrounded the table.

That fateful evening, angry, confused and sad faces surrounded that same table. Ray and Martin, Lucy and Laura were all sitting opposite Gina. Her son was sitting next to her, looking pale and lost.

The grandparents were seated at the top of the table and Ginger's usual place remained empty. He'd been gone for about four hours and everyone was concerned. They were hoping that he went to the cinema to calm down, as he loved going to see a film as often as he could.

The brothers had decided between them that if he hadn't returned by midnight, they would go and look for him, but thought he'd need some time.

Emma wanted them to do something as soon as they had finished their family 'meeting.'

First, she and their dad must talk to them all. So Emma went to her granddaughter's bedroom and coaxed her to come and join them in the big kitchen. Emma told her granddaughter to get up and act a bit maturely. If she went with her, she would get the answers to all her questions. Looking angry but sheepish at the same time, Amelia let her Nanna lead her to the table, and reluctantly gave in. Emma made her sit down next to her.

"Do you want to start Ed, or shall I?" she asked her husband who was patiently waiting for everyone to be quiet."

"We must get on with it before Ginger comes back, so you must all keep calm and try not to interrupt. Then, when he comes, please don't let's have another scene."

"I'll start, Emma. I guess some of the blame is ours, Gina. We did encourage you to forget about Jim and to look closer at Ginger who was there for you when Jim wasn't. Well, yes, of course now we know why the poor chap wasn't there. Please, don't.... don't stop me Amelia. You'll soon understand. Just be patient, love."

Slowly and calmly, her grandfather spoke with directness and honesty about the scandal that would have blotted the family's good name at a time when illegitimacy was taboo. Back in those late sixties, they didn't want their only daughter, a good Catholic girl, to be an unmarried mother.

His sons had told him all about Paul and Amy's revelations and how the poor young man, who was so critically ill, hadn't received the crucial letters. He made a point of saying that Jim hadn't found out about his love child until after Gina and Ginger were already married.

When Edward related all this to his family, his eyes remained on Amelia. He wanted her to sympathise with her mother. Even though it was obviously still painful for his only daughter, Edward reminded those who already knew, and revealed to Amelia how her mother had cried herself to sleep, night after night for a long, long time. She was heart broken when no answer came from Jim.

"Can you imagine Amelia how rejected your mother felt as the days passed and still no answer came from Jim, the father of her unborn child,...no answer to her letters telling him about her pregnancy, about you." Amelia looked sheepishly at her mother.

"To be totally honest now, it's time for us all to be frank. Your mother " he said, looking at Gina, "your Nanna " he said addressing his granddaughter, "and I, we encouraged Ginger when he came to visit. We knew he was in love with her and that he didn't need much encouragement. As it turned out, it's been a good marriage, but you, young lady, should be ashamed of the horrible things you said to your mother. You should now see why she was so angry with your dad, with Ginger. By not posting those letters, he changed the course of our lives especially yours and your mother's, and let's not forget Jim."

"Where is the man now?" Ray wondered as he glanced at the big clock on the wall for the umpteenth time.

"God knows," whispered Martin.

Edward noticed that his wife had put her arm around Amelia. His granddaughter then lifted her head and with eyes that looked so red and puffy after all her crying, she glanced at her mother and quickly looked away again.

"Gina," her dad asked gently, "do you want to tell your daughter that Jim...?"

"No, dad, you might as well..." Gina replied in a voice which was not much above a whisper

Well, darling Amelia, as you must have guessed, Jim is the man who fathered you. Look up, love, and please look at me. We all know that you already have a good father in Ginger. Nobody can take that away from you. He has been an ideal dad and husband. Now, you must try to understand how your mother felt to find out about the letters. She loved Jim and he adored her. She was so hurt and devastated when she had no answer to her letters.

We have gone over all this already, but I want you to remember that your mum felt rejected. Rejection is painful, especially when one is carrying... Your mother has only just found out that your birth father, Jim, had not rejected her at all. The poor man had no idea that you were on the way."

By now, tears were running down Gina's cheeks as she turned to look at her daughter. Amelia was looking straight at her grandfather. Then, as the room fell silent, she turned her head very slowly, around the table. Her sore, streamy eyes looked at every member of her family. When they finally rested on her mother's face, she tried to say something. She swallowed a couple of times and in the end, shaking her head, got to her feet and would have run off but her grandmother held her back with her good hand, and begged her to stay. To lighten the atmosphere, she told her not to pull away again like that. She already had one arm in plaster and didn't want to hurt the other one. A nervous giggle went round the room.

When Amelia had resignedly seated herself again, Emma said that she thought that her sons should take over and carry on with any more information or details they now knew.

"Please Ray, and you Martin, it'll help this young lady to understand why her mother flew off the handle as she did. I want you to explain to her all about the letters, because no one has told Amelia yet. Not properly anyway. Please, just do it," their dad backed his wife.

"No one has mentioned the horrific accident Jim had when he was in Benghazi. No wonder he never came back to rejoin his regiment. We only just found out how serious that accident was. Gina knows, and Amelia, you should know everything now. We all realise that it's painful for you dear," Emma told her granddaughter, "but, remember it's much more painful for your mum"

"Your Nanna is right, Amelia. Try to understand her pain. Ray or you, Martin, you tell her the rest and I suggest that if Ginger comes in now, you all stay calm. Please, don't get angry or accusing …enough has been said."

So Martin looked at his niece and told her everything that he had gleaned from the English couple. He had already told his family that Paul and Amy had planned to tell them their reasons for coming to Malta. However, things had come to a head unexpectedly.

"When did Ray and Martin tell you about the letters dad, mum?" Gina wanted to know.

" I'm confused…how long have you known, mum?"

"When you were asleep, I left Laura to keep an eye on you and we had a long chat. Anyway, it does look pretty obvious that Ginger never posted those letters. Now, don't start getting angry and upset again Gina. We must stay calm and think of Amelia."

"Yes, I hope Ginger's back soon. I'm more worried than angry now… I was so mad at him, and, well, I am still but…as you two said, he is a good man. Nevertheless, he had no right to..."

"I know, we all know, but don't start getting yourself upset again. He was only young remember that. Look at your daughter! We should be thinking of her now."

"Amelia, please understand. You're an adult now, but I really wish we told you when you were old enough to understand. We thought then that we didn't have to. I now realise that we were wrong, very wrong." Gina was finally pouring her heart out to her distressed daughter.

"Listen to your mother dear. We're asking a lot of you, we all know that. It's a shame you had to find out like that. It's a great enough shock to discover that your biological father is not the kind, good man who brought you up. It should have been done quietly and lovingly many years ago."

"Yes, Nanna's right. We re mostly to blame there. It was our fear of a scandal in the family that made us keep quiet. However Amelia, please believe me, nothing has to change. As to Jim, he was, and I am sure he still is…

"I don't want to talk about him…" cried Amelia hoarsely interrupting Gina. "None of you ever told me anything about him before, ever. You were all too worried about your reputations. Now, I just find out that…no, no, I don't want anyone to talk about him."

"OK love, OK. When you're ready."

"Ginger is my father…I don't need this..." She couldn't even say the name. "Ginger will always be my dad…oh where is he? We haven't been back twenty four hours yet, and now this!"

"If he is not here soon, we'll go for a drive and see if we can find him, but let's make sure that you don't have any more unanswered questions Amelia. We'll tell you all we know, everything you want to know that is." Martin was very patient with his highly-strung niece. He still told her, even though she tried to stop him, that Jim didn't come forward before because he thought that he wasn't wanted. He respected that wish until circumstances made him change his mind and that's what triggered him to try and trace his offspring.

Finally, everything was out in the open. No voices were raised. Everyone helped in one way or another to keep the situation as calm and rational as possible. The proof of that was clear when, suddenly, Amelia stood up and for a moment, the family group thought that she was going back to her room. Instead, she went to her mother to give her a hug. Mother and daughter cried together, each one having regretted words they had said that day. Everyone present swallowed and there wasn't a dry eye in the room. Robert got up too and joined the two in a loving embrace.

They were hugging and crying together, while across the table, the grandparents were beaming at each other. The old couple were feeling relieved and not a little pleased with themselves as they and the rest of the family witnessed mother and daughter embrace and get close once more.

In spite of their misgivings and worries, both Emma and Edward had stayed calm. Somehow, they had managed to make Amelia understand her mother's anguish and to forgive her shocking outburst, the outburst that had made Ginger storm out. Gina understood her daughter's pain and that helped her to forgive Amelia's words, terrible words, full of hateful accusations.

Ray and Martin too, were breathing sighs of relief, now that everything was out in the open. Their wives got up and made themselves busy, getting everybody a well-needed cup of strong tea.

"Let's have a cup of tea and then I'll go and drive to Valetta. Ginger's ex-army mate lives there. He took me there a couple of times and he might just have gone there. He lives in the flat on top of his café in Merchant Street."

"Yes," said Gina, looking a little hopeful." You mean Tony don't you? We always go there for a snack when we go to Valetta. There's his phone number in the note book, but it 's pretty late now isn't it? Maybe it's best to phone."

"I think it's best not to phone and embarrass him. I'll just go. Maybe you could take Lucy home for us Martin?"

"Yes, but I'd rather wait..."

It was then that the front door bell rang. Two quick rings shattered the fragile peace that had begun to settle down on the family once again.

"It's ten o'clock, who on earth can it be? It's probably Ginger…I don't suppose he took his keys," grumbled Edward, as he went to open the bright yellow door.

Everyone in the kitchen had gone quiet. They were still all silent as Edward returned to his loving family, followed by two grim faced police officers.

CHAPTER 17

Amy and Paul were feeling really good and happy with themselves. She had just had a rather long chat with her uncle. Paul too, had managed to talk at length to the man who was already sounding so much happier than he had been when they had last seen him.

Jim admitted to Amy that he'd been hoping that he had a daughter. He too was amazed at the similar names of his child and his beloved niece.

He told them that they had made him a happy man. First Amy, and then Paul, warned him that the most important people in the frame were still in the dark.

"There's bound to be some trouble when everyone, especially the grand parents, get to know the reason for our arrival on the scene," Paul warned him.

It was very worrying really because neither of them could tell how the family in the house with the bright yellow door were going to react.

However, Jim only picked up what they told him about his daughter. It tickled him to find out that she was very fair, just like him. He was also very pleased when Amy told him that Amelia had noticed how different she was from everybody else in her family. Jim was looking at all the positives so far.

"I just hope," he said in a voice that sounded husky with emotion, "that when Amelia finds out that Ginger isn't her real dad, she won't be…

I don't know, I guess what I'm hoping, is that it won't be so great a shock to the poor girl."

"But Jim…," argued Paul, "come on, it's bound to be! She's an adult for goodness sake and all her life she has only know Ginger as her father! To find out suddenly that he is not…"Amy was getting a little concerned. It seemed that Paul was getting rather impatient with her uncle.

"You both said that she has queried her unusual colouring."

"Yes that's true, but…anyway, we'll keep you posted Jim, I'll pass you back to Amy." He gave her the phone and shook his head at the thought of Jim's growing confidence. He seemed to be wearing blinkers at that moment.

Both Paul and Amy tried not to build his hopes up too much, but it was proving difficult. They left him with the promise of another phone call the next evening, but only if there were any changes in the development. At that stage, neither of them knew what to do next. They had to be patient and wait for a phone call from the brothers. Amy said that it might be a while because they would have to make sure that their mother was alright before they said anything.

"I just wish," she said, "with less than a week left of our holiday, I wish we could talk to Amelia now. I can't wait to tell her all about her father and why he hasn't come forward and claimed her before now."

It was getting increasingly difficult not to keep bringing the subject up, so in the end, Paul suggested that they go out, since it was hardly likely that they would be summoned that night.

Paul knew that Amy hadn't yet seen any nightlife in Malta, so that evening they went to St. Julian's. It was vibrant and teeming with locals and tourists. She was pleasantly surprised with the trendy nightclubs that were packed with people. The atmosphere all around was alive with the loud music blaring from the bars and clubs. It was really a surprise that such a small island had so many modern and popular venues of entertainment - and that was just at St. Julian's near Paceville!

While the English couple were having a really good night, having made a conscious effort to leave all their worries behind, the Maltese family at the house with the bright yellow door were going through a very traumatic experience, as Amy and Paul were to find out soon enough.

It was late when the carefree couple made their way to the apartment that evening. They were still buzzing and the adrenaline was still flowing when they turned into the road that went all around the bay and then on to the now familiar hill.

"I really feel as if I'm on holiday now Paul," Amy said. "I really enjoyed myself tonight, in spite of a very sore throat. I have to say that I was pleasantly surprised. The nightclubs here are as good, if not better than those in Plymouth."

"I knew you would like it there. Oh Amy, look..." Paul slowed down as they approached the George Cross bar and the house with the bright yellow door.

"My goodness, what's happened? Stop, Paul stop!" she shouted and Paul went past the house and stopped the car close enough to be able to see what was going on.

They both looked worried and very puzzled when they saw all the cars outside the house. The bright yellow door was wide open. There was a police car a little further down too. There were lights on all over the house.

"Something awful must have happened," Paul said very quietly. "It's nearly midnight. Those are Ray and Martin's cars. I don't recognise the other two cars. That police car ...the officers must be in the house too. What shall we do?"

"There's nothing we can do Paul! We can't go to the house and ask. Someone has come out. Look, who is it? It looks like Ray."

"Yes, he 's gone back in. Oh, I wish we could do something."

"Well, we can't. Come on, let's go. We'll find out in due course, but I have to admit that I do feel quite worried. Come on Paul, I've got such a bad headache and my throat hurts. I must get to bed."

"Yes, me too, but I won't sleep a wink tonight. Maybe we ought to phone in the morning and find out. Hopefully you'll be feeling better by then too."

"We can't phone, we're not relatives, or friends really. I'll tell you what, maybe we ought to phone Martin or Ray at their house. We've Ray's home number haven't we?"

"Maybe either Lucy or Laura will be there on their own and they can tell us, but I'm not sure we should Paul. It's not our business really. Why would she tell us? They, well, the brothers have only just met us really. Ok, they'd met you before, but ...let's go now. I 'm really tired. It's been a long day."

"Alright, I suppose we'll find out soon enough," Paul conceded, and rather reluctantly, he started the car up and off they went.

"Oh no," groaned Amy, when the shrill ringing of the old fashioned telephone woke her up. For a few moments, she didn't know where she was and actually thought that it was her alarm clock.

"Who can it be this early? Amy, aren't you going to answer it?" asked Paul, as he tried to push her out of bed. She just sat there, rubbing her eyes and feeling slightly disorientated.

"Oh, alright, it's only seven o'clock and my head is thumping," she complained. Rather reluctantly, she made her way to the hall to answer the phone. It was very frustrating when, as soon as she was just about to pick it up, it stopped ringing.

"Oh, for goodness sake! That got me up for nothing. I wish I had not been drinking last night," she moaned and made straight for the kitchen for a glass of water. She was walking back to the bedroom with a cup of tea for Paul, when the phone started ringing again. It made her jump and she very nearly dropped it.

This time, Paul leapt out of bed and was at the phone in no time at all.

"Hello. Oh, hi Ray," he started cheerfully. Amy put the tea down and moved nearer Paul. It had suddenly gone very quiet. Paul hadn't uttered another word.

"Oh my God," he gasped, suddenly. "Oh Ray, I'm so sorry. We saw the lights on when we drove past…oh Ray. It 's a tragedy but, …please, no…no…don't say that…it is not…Ray! Ray!" he shouted. Visibly shaken, he replaced the receiver and, like an old man, walked slowly to the lounge and sank in one of the deep armchairs.

Amy, looking pale and alarmed, followed him. She propped herself up on the arm of his chair and put her arm round his shoulders. She could feel him shaking.

"What on earth did he tell you Paul? Wait, I'll fetch your tea," and she had to hold his cup because it was rattling unsteadily in his shaking hands.

"Oh Amy, poor Gina. Ginger…Ginger is gone…gone, and Ray is blaming us. They're all blaming us."

"What do you mean gone?" Amy, though frightened, had to ask.

"He ran out yesterday, very disturbed and in a state, and…and…terrible accident..."

"You mean, do you mean, he's dead?" and, nodding his head Paul told her the bad news. Amy's eyes welled up and she broke down in great sobs that went straight through him. He could only hold her close and let her cry it out. He could say nothing to help. So he didn't even try.

It was too painful to tell her anything else at that moment. When she had calmed down a little, and he felt able to take any repercussions, he would have to tell her the rest of the things Ray had blurted out angrily at him, over the telephone.

Paul was dreading having to tell the distraught girl that the family who lived in the house with the bright yellow door, did not want to see them or hear from them again. They blamed him and Amy for the arguments, rows, heartache and tears and for the loss of a dear husband and father. The problem was how were they going to tell Jim that all his hopes were now dashed?

A tragedy had shattered that lovely family and Amy and Paul were being blamed for it all. Paul did not understand how that was, because Ray had not explained. He was rambling and accusing the couple of instigating such a tragedy. He mentioned the argument, which eventually led to Ginger storming out, never to be seen alive again, but he didn't say what it had been about.

Ray was adamant that it was all their fault. He made it very clear that it was all their doing. The big argument between Gina and Ginger which resulted in such a tragedy, would never have happened, if it weren't for their interference and raking up the past after all these years!. If they hadn't gone to the George Cross bar to find Jim's offspring, if...if... it was all if ...that lovely close knit family would still be as happy as they were before Amy and Paul turned their world upside down.

It seemed so tragic, that in order for one man's wish to be granted; to find a daughter he had never let himself acknowledge for twenty odd years, Amelia and Robert had now lost a father they had both adored and Gina was now a widow.

CHAPTER 18

The George Cross bar had remained closed the night before and it would now stay closed for a few days as a sign of respect. The traditional black strip of material was pinned to the door as a sign that the family was in mourning. The bright yellow door had the same black strip pinned across it.

Inside, there was great turmoil. Everyone was wandering around from room to room like ghosts. Gina was in bed, heavily sedated.

Very early on that sad Saturday morning the grandparents were up and about, subdued and pensive. They hadn't gone to bed at all. Both had dozed on and off in their armchairs, too disturbed to sleep soundly. They were worried sick about their daughter who was crying and screaming desperately. She kept ranting on that she was sorry, she hadn't meant to send him away, and that she could never, ever forgive herself. It was a great relief for the elderly couple when the sedative worked.

Before he left, the family doctor urged them to go and get some sleep. Both promised they were going to, now that Gina was asleep. First they wanted to check on their grandchildren. Robert had hardly said a word since he'd found out about his dad's tragic death. He had not moved away from his mother's bedside.

Amelia on the other hand had become angry with her mum and blamed her for the tragic accident. After she vented her anger at her beloved mum, she'd gone to her bedroom and stayed there. One minute she could be heard sobbing and screaming for Ginger. Then, she would go all quiet and one of the uncles or their wives would try to talk to her. They all tried hard to reason with her, to make her see sense and not to condemn her mother.

However, nobody could get through to her. She didn't want to talk to anyone. Her brother, himself grieving for his father, tried to reason with her. He had lost his dad too and his sister was acting as if she was the only one affected here! Robert started feeling bitter against his sister. He even told her in a spiteful outburst that she was alright, she had another dad, one who was ready to step in, unlike him who had just lost his only father. At this, his sister went mad and started throwing anything within her reach at him.

Robert didn't recognise his sister any more, but as soon as the words were out, he realised that he shouldn't have said what he did.

"Sorry Amy, sorry, but listen.... listen to me," he tried to keep calm in spite of feeling so upset. "Just think how mother feels, knowing that she sent dad out and now he is never coming back. She must be racked with grief and regret. Think of her for a change," and slamming the door behind him, he left her.

Their grandmother went to see what was happening now and as she opened Amelia's bedroom door, she could almost touch the pain that her granddaughter was going through. She started to slowly stroke Amelia's back as the young girl lay face down on her bed. In a very calm and soothing voice, Emma began to talk to her distraught granddaughter, slowly and gently. She was hoping to make Amelia see how upset and betrayed her mother was feeling at the dreadful time when she had told Ginger to leave.

When the family found out about the fatal accident, Amelia had gone absolutely berserk. Emma kept thinking how her granddaughter had shouted with hatred at her mother, telling her that she would never forgive her. Never!

After talking to her for a while and getting no answer, she walked out of the young girl's bedroom feeling defeated.

Her grandparents then decided that it was best to leave her. They were both going to their rooms to try and get some much-needed rest. Martin had finally managed to persuade them to go. He and Ray were rather worried about their parents who had been marvellously strong for everybody else. They needed a rest. So, after their sons promised to stay around for as long as they were needed, Emma and Edward went to get some sleep. They couldn't switch off as easily as they needed to. Too much had happened.

"What a night, Em," her husband said.

"Yes, and it's going to get worse when Gina wakes up and remembers again that she sent her husband away."

"What a tragedy! Amelia's anger at her mother makes everything so much worse. We had only just managed to make her feel pity for her mum rather than hatred. It was so moving when they hugged wasn't it? Now it's worse than ever."

Back at the apartment Amy had eventually fallen asleep exhausted on the settee. Paul put a duvet over her and let her sleep.

Before he went to bed, he tried to think what they were supposed to do now. First of all, he thought that they had to phone Jim as soon as possible and tell him about Ginger and about the telephone call that had distressed them so much.

When he looked at his girlfriend Paul noticed how flushed she looked. She had mentioned a sore throat and a headache so he wondered if she was getting the flu. They'd heard that it was going round.

He felt her forehead, and yes, she was burning up. That's all they needed now. They were on the last week of their holiday and if Amy wasn't better... he didn't want to think any more.

When she woke up, Paul was there with a drink and some tablets for her.

"I feel awful. I thought my head hurt because of the drink last night, but my throat is so painful. Oh dear, I hope I feel better soon."

"Take these pills now to reduce your fever and they'll help your throat too. I've been thinking about your uncle."

Amy put the cup she had been sipping down hard, and alarm showed in her face as she looked at Paul.

"What about my uncle?"

"I think we should tell him about Ginger. It's highly unlikely that we'll ever see or get to speak to Amelia now. Last time we spoke to Jim, he was so optimistic, it was worrying. Now, it looks like we have to disappoint him."

"I think we should wait a day or two...."

"Why? We were given our orders as it were. We're not welcome at the George Cross bar. They don't want to see us or talk to us now. Why wait?"

"I don't think I can decide anything with this sore head. It's painful to talk. Maybe if I rest my throat it'll get better quicker."

It was such a lovely day with the sun high in the cloudless sky, but Amy felt too ill to go out or even venture out onto the veranda.

Later on, when it was still early evening, Paul was looking forward to going out for a while. He had been doing the few chores that needed doing, and was now going shopping.

"Make sure you have everything you need near you, let me see, and then I'll pop out for the bits and pieces we need. I'll go to the chemist and get you some flu tablets, that is if I find one that 's still open. Some places close at lunchtime on Saturdays." Paul fretted as he took a closer look at Amy who seemed rather flushed.

"Are you sure you want me to go? I know we need milk and bread so I have to go to one of the big shops in Sliema. I don't know where else would be open so I might be a while."

"You have to…go on. I'll be fine, don't fuss. Just get me a magazine to read."

"OK, will do. Now try to get some sleep and get better or you'll have to spend this last week of our holiday in bed. I'll be quick, and hopefully...oh the phone, I'll get that." Paul ran to the phone.

"Oh hi, who is it? Gina? …oh my….Gina. I'm… Amy and ...and I…" Amy could hear her boyfriend stuttering, but couldn't quite catch what he was saying.

"I need to sit down," he said as he walked into the bedroom to tell Amy about the odd and long conversation he'd just had with Gina. Her brother Martin had first apologised to him and Amy for the phone call Ray had made earlier.

Then, Gina, sounding very choked and subdued, spoke to him. The family had talked and talked and decided to get them both to visit. They all thought that if Amy and Paul went and said their bit, Amelia would hopefully get rid of some of the bitterness that she was feeling at the moment.

"Do you know what, Amy? Gina said that her brothers said some complimentary words about us, but she ended by saying that we cannot make things any worse than they are already anyway."

"Oh dear, and here I am feeling so rotten," croaked Amy.

"If you're better, they want us to visit in a couple of days, after the funeral. I said yes of course. Now I must go before all the shops are closed."

Amy felt a little happier with the thought that the family in the house with the bright yellow door wanted to talk to them. At that moment, she felt too ill to do anything but sleep, but as she closed her eyes, she decided that if she were not well Paul would have to go and face them all on his own.

Next day Amy was stuck in bed with all the symptoms of flu. It looked obvious that she was going nowhere for a few days. She was feeling worse than ever. Knowing that she wasn't able to go to the house with the bright yellow door made her feel really miserable. She couldn't even talk to her uncle so Paul had been on the phone to him.

It had proved rather difficult to talk to him because Jim let him know at once that Meg was bustling around him. However, Paul managed to tell him the bad news about his ex-best mate. Jim then said that he was going to talk to his wife about that. He said that it would be a start. Promising him another call as soon as possible after that evening's meeting, Paul put the phone down and went to talk everything over with Amy. But she was fast asleep again, so he left her and went to watch television with the hope that he would relax a little that evening. The meeting planned for the next day was bound to be emotional and maybe disturbing, but he had to go. He never thought that he would have to represent Jim and tell the family Jim's side of the story. Paul hoped that he would be able to stay calm and not to get angry if anyone of them got really angry.

Neither he nor Amy was aware that the family had been through so much during the last three days. They knew about the argument that resulted in Ginger's fatal accident, but they had no idea that the family had already dealt with Amelia's emotional outbursts and tears after she learnt that the man she knew and loved as her dad, was not her father at all. Paul and Amy were totally unaware of this. Paul would have felt much better if he knew that it was all out in the open.

As it was, he spent most of Sunday worrying how he was going to cope with all the questions he would undoubtedly be asked the next day.

On the other hand, Sunday had been a long, sombre day for all the family at the house with the bright yellow door. Gina had spent most of it in bed sedated. Amelia and Edward had just wandered around making cups of tea for anyone who turned up to give their condolences. Ray's boys and their families didn't stay long because their children were too boisterous and noisy. Normally the little boys were encouraged to run around and entertain them all with their antics, but on this occasion, their parents knew that no one could cope with them. So, they made the visit as brief as possible.

Monday dawned wet and miserable, totally in keeping with the mood of the family in the house with the bright yellow door.

The funeral was over and now they were back home and,

trying not to worry about that evening, they all found something to do. In a few hours, they were all going to gather round the table and talk to Paul and Amy. They all hoped that after today, all the family members could start to rebuild their lives.

Gina felt apprehensive, but in a bizarre sort of way she was almost eager to talk to someone who knew Jim. She wanted to find out what he'd been through since that day when he left for Benghazi and never returned. She hoped that talking to Jim's niece would help her daughter to start thinking of her biological father with some kindness. Then she realised that the two girls were cousins!

At the moment, they were all treading on eggshells around Amelia, but at least she wasn't so angry with her mother any more.

Poor Robert had been wandering around all silent and pensive until his granddad asked him to lend a hand with some job that needed doing in their kitchen. It was precisely what Robert needed.

Gina's parents had been towers of strength all the way. Now that she was actually out and about in the house, and not drugged up to her eyeballs, Gina told her brothers and her children that they must all try not to give their parents any more cause for concern. After all, they were both in their seventies, and they were just getting over Emma's accident when this tragedy happened.

Her brothers were home with their families and they were to return that evening to talk to the English couple. They would open for business the next day.

Amelia was calmer because she knew that her mother was right to be concerned about her grandparents. She still felt bitter towards her mum, but she was trying to curb her temper.

Her mother wanted to keep her busy and she had reluctantly agreed to help sort out her father’s big, cluttered desk.

He wasn't the tidiest of men, and papers and books were everywhere. Receipts and invoices surrounded his computer because he did all the accounts for his brothers-in-law.

Amelia was engrossed in sorting the invoices first and her mother was amused to hear her daughter scolding her late father for the chaotic state of his desk.

"God knows how he managed to keep on top of everything. Mind you, once he got started he always got it all done in no time at all," Gina spoke indulgently.

"This is organised chaos, "Amelia agreed. "It's going to take ages. Let's sort these papers - invoices first I think, because there are invoices everywhere. Mum, I already emptied those drawers. Oh no, not the middle one. I couldn't open that one. He must have money in there," and Gina saw her daughter smile again. She admitted that she had absolutely no idea where the key could be.

"I have never bothered touching this desk or any of those papers, because I never knew where to start. In fact, I did once, just the once, and Ginger went mad because I tidied everything up and he couldn't find anything! You carry on while I go and fetch your dad's bunch of keys. With a bit of luck it will be amongst that lot," she spoke as if he were in the other room. She was so relieved that her daughter was with her but she was afraid to say anything that might chip away at the fragile peace of the moment.

Within minutes, the peaceful scene changed completely. Both women were on the big bed with their arms around each other, sobbing their hearts out.

Robert had gone to find them to ask them if they wanted a cup of tea since he was making one for granddad. He was shocked when he saw the distress on their faces as they pulled apart.

"What now? I thought you said we were to stay brave and calm, mum. Granddad might walk in too. What's this?" he looked puzzled as he picked up one of the sheets of paper, which lay on the floor. "This is dad's writing. Where was it?...What?…it's addressed to you !" he said, staring at his sister.

His sister wiped her eyes, picked up the rest of the papers and hugged them close. She looked at her brother.

"Yes, we found this letter in one of the drawers. Read it, Robert."

"Where's mine then?" he asked, not without a touch of resentment. "What's in that other envelope…one for me?" and looking at the writing on it asked, "Jim …? I thought it was a letter for me."

"There was no need to write you a letter…."

"Oh, I see. You, the precious daughter, who in fact was not…"

"Robert!" Gina tried not to get angry. "Please, what your sister meant is…look, read it please, just read it."

Scowling like he used to when he was little, Robert started to read.

"My Darling Amelia - Goldilocks,

I hope that it will be a long time before you get to read this letter. Today you are twenty one... a beautiful young lady any father would be proud of. I am so proud of you. If I haven't told you in so many words, I am so sorry. You have always made me so proud to be your father.

I have watched you blossom and grow into a beautiful young lady. Since that moment when I saw you come into the world, I can honestly say that I have tried my best to look after you, to protect you.

I have never forgotten your tears at cutting your first tooth (I took my turn, and spent many a sleepless night, pacing the floor with you screaming in my arms). How can I forget your first step, which you took towards me? Your very first word was 'dada'. Everyone said that it was just the easiest sound a baby first utters, oh no. That was my darling daughter calling me.

Oh Amelia, you must remember that I was always there, next to your mum to hold your hand whenever your little stubborn mind let me.

I loved every stage in your journey from childhood to adulthood. That includes sitting on the little uncomfortable chairs at those school plays and assemblies. I always felt you were the best one there, and I know that I embarrassed your mum when I clapped the loudest. I remember my eyes welling up when you played Mary at your first Nativity play.

When your baby brother was born, you became a proper little madam and wanted to help with all the feeding and changing. I still think you are the best sister to him, best daughter to us.

Please, dear daughter, when you have read this letter, try not to get angry with me. However, if it stops your tears after I am gone, then rant and rave and stamp your feet just like you used to when you were little. Please, stay close to your mother and your brother. You will be able to comfort each other when I am not there any more.

I want you to know the truth about the injustice I did to your dear mum and to some one who used to be my best friend. Then I would like you to do something for me. You decide whether you want to do it or not... I won't blame you if you decide not to, but think it over and do take your mother's advice. I wish I did. I was a coward, who having taken my best mate's girl, I didn't want to risk losing that same mate's daughter. I loved you too much…"

Robert stopped for a moment and looked at both women. They were watching him trying hard not break down, while tears poured down their own cheeks.

Robert swallowed a couple of times, and was ready to carry on reading.

"Well, you know about this bloke already, so it's not a shock now," he said looking up at Amelia. "Still, I suppose hearing it from dad's own…." and poor Robert finally broke down.

Gina took the letter and read on, every now and then stopping to wipe her tears. She read how Jim got injured so badly and how with him out of he way, Ginger made the most of it and stole his girlfriend. Ginger admitted that he got rid of those letters, which would have told his mate that his girlfriend was carrying his child.

"Whatever you do now, please don't get mad at your mother. If I had listened to her, there would have been no need for this letter. She went along with my wishes. I never wanted you to know that you were not my daughter by birth.

I did a terrible thing, I know, and when this comes out your mum might hate me."

This set Gina off again as she remembered her reaction when she had found out.

"My excuses are that I was a young man, away from home and I was so in love with your mother. I had kept quiet about my feelings because my best friend started courting her. When he got hurt and was sent to England, I made the most of his absence to offer her comfort and to make her see me as more than a mate. She trusted me, but I was madly in love with her, so in love with her that I destroyed those letters that would have got to Jim and maybe…who knows?

I have to say in my defence, that in those days an illegitimate child would have rocked the family's world. Your mother's reputation would have been ruined. What I am trying to say is, that I was encouraged by other members of the family to make an honest woman out of her. I didn't need any encouragement. I loved her.

I am so sorry, but not for loving her and having you for a daughter. I will never regret that.

As you have surely guessed by now, Jim, who was my best

friend, is your father. Please, don't hate my memory, or me. To me you have always been my darling daughter. I tried my best to be the best father a girl could have. I hope you feel that I succeeded, if only a little."

Gina was unable to read any more, so her son took over once more.

"I now have to ask you to do me a great favour. Please, I'm begging you and I know that it's a lot to ask but I am sure that you will find a great comfort if you do it... One day, when you have stopped being angry, confused or worse, please go to England and give the other letter to Jim. He deserves an apology, even at this late stage.

I am no longer there to look after you. I hope you will grant my wish and so, hopefully, let Jim take my place at long last. He deserves to meet his wonderful daughter and, you could if you want, let him be your father. I can see you shaking your head."

Robert had tears running down his cheeks as he looked up and smiled at his sister.

"Jim was, must still be a great guy, so kind hearted and honest. He always had a very dry sense of humour, but during our days in the army, he was also fond of practical jokes. Does that remind you of anyone? I seem to remember poor Robert screaming when you put a frog in his boots…."

"He is right too!" Robert added. That was horrible….."

"Jim was very blonde just like you Goldilocks, with dark blue eyes…your eyes are like your mother's but…. Look in the mirror Amelia. You said yourself how different you look from the rest of us."

"Oh mum," her daughter was laughing and crying at the same time.

"Ssh, let Robert finish. It's nearly finished isn't it?"

"Yes, he just gives you his blessing. Hang on,"

"PS…I would like to show Jim that I have looked after his daughter. I hope that one day, he will see for himself…I really want him to know that I haven't done a bad job of it."

"Will you do it sis? Will you go and find your real dad?" Robert seemed quite moved by the letter but he wasn't sure what his sister, half sister, was thinking.

"I don't know. It's too much to take in. It would have been

much better if I found out about him through this letter than the way I did on Friday. As far as I'm concerned, Ginger was my real dad and not this…"

"Well the poor guy has been betrayed hasn't he? I think you should…."

"Leave it for now, son. We'll talk it over tonight when we have the family conference. Robert, I hope you understand now why your sister said that you needed no letters."

"Yes I do mum. Sorry sis, I shouldn't have said…"

"That's ok, Robert. You weren't to know. Mum, I've just realised something. Poor dad, do you realise that all the time Uncle Martin and Ray were accusing him of deceit and even you…. My poor, poor dad …" and the girl was once more in a flood of tears.

"Yes, I know what you're trying to say, he took it all, including my horrible attack while all the time, this letter was in his desk and had been there for the last year. If only he told us instead or let you read it, I'm sure that we would have reacted less horribly."

"Mum, like you said just a few minutes ago, you weren't to know. That 's why you reacted as you did."

When Monday came round for Amy and Paul, the dull and unusually grey day didn't help to lift their spirits.

Paul had done all the little jobs that needed doing and even did some washing that morning. In between chores, he made sure that Amy was comfortable. He was trying to keep himself occupied or his girlfriend would have noticed that he was very nervous about going to the house with the bright yellow door.

At six o'clock, Paul dropped a kiss on her hot forehead and left Amy tucked up in bed. Magazines, drinks and other things that Paul thought she might need, surrounded her. She was feeling very sorry for herself but she had no choice in the matter. There was no way she could have gone along with him when he went to visit the Maltese family. To think, she had come to Malta to find her cousin and now that they had found her, Amy was too ill to meet her.

Her boyfriend had not bargained for things to turn out like this at all. He was not feeling his best because he had spent a very restless night. He'd promised to support Amy in her efforts to help her uncle to find his offspring. Now that Amy had the flu he found himself, not in a supporting role, but actually taking Amy's place.

"Any moment," he was thinking, "I'll be inside the house with the bright yellow door." After he parked the car across the road, next to Ray's cavalier, he walked slowly towards the house.

Very nervously, Jim picked up the tarnished looking doorknocker which when he saw it last, was highly polished. Rather reluctantly, he knocked twice on the bright yellow door. He felt like a school boy who would knock and run away, but he couldn't move from the spot, even if he tried!

Paul was remembering how back home, Jim, Amy and he had talked in such length about going to face the family. They had planned and debated which way was the best. Now, all that seemed to have been such a waste of time. He had to face the family on his own."

"If someone doesn't open soon," he muttered under his breath, but didn't finish the threat. He was expecting one of the brothers to open the door, but no, when the door finally opened, he found himself looking at a beautiful girl, who, in spite of the sadness etched around her big luminous brown eyes, still managed to make him catch his breath.

Her long blonde hair was tied back. He found himself thinking that the rather severe hairstyle only managed to show her perfect features to their best advantage.

"You must be Amelia," he managed to say finally as she opened the door wide and asked him to go through. She said she was and in a rather cold manner, led him through the very long hallway and into the big, airy dining room cum kitchen. He saw a blur of faces as he took in all the family members that sat around the table. They were all in black and nobody said anything until Ray, and then Martin, welcomed him. They wanted to know where Amy was.

Paul found himself seated near the grandparents, and there opposite him, was Jim's lovely daughter. He had to stop himself from staring at the blonde girl, but he kept finding himself drawn back to her. She just sat there and stared at him. Paul could not work out if she was just arrogant, or, he hardly dared think it, interested in him. Whatever it was, he was always the one to look away. Amelia never flinched.

It did seem weird sitting in that room surrounded by all those people. They were all in one way or another involved and touched by what was until recently, a secret buried in Jim's heart.

Finally, Gina spoke and introduced everyone. She made him

feel a little relaxed when she told him that he was not to worry. Later he remembered thinking that she must have seen his nervousness.

Paul noticed that her brothers stayed quiet and let their sister take the lead.

She went on to reassure him that they were not going to get angry. They had been through a great deal of sorrow and heartbreak since they came back from their holiday.

They had done their crying. Gina said sadly that now they just needed to know all the facts. She hoped that Paul could bring them up to date with Jim's life. He was the innocent party after all. Gina was talking very fast and somewhat nervously. It seemed as if she would never stop to catch her breath, but soon she had to.

After swallowing a couple of times she carried on, "You see Paul, now we all carry a sense of guilt because we've been thinking so badly of him for so long."

In spite of her sadness, Gina was really trying to encourage him to open up and tell them what he and his girlfriend had wanted to achieve. Had they already informed Jim that he had a daughter? Did they tell him about Ginger? She wanted to find out how Jim was. She went on to ask if he was still feeling bitter towards her after all these years. As far as Jim knew she had never got in touch, that is, not until after she had married his best friend. It was then that he found out that she was carrying his child.

"You see, you're not going to drop any bombshells here, not now," she said. Paul looked rather taken aback. Suddenly, he felt a great rush of relief. It had finally registered in his mind that there were new developments in this saga. He had come to this house worrying how they would receive him and what he had to tell them. Ray then admitted to the family that he had phoned Amy and Paul and told them in no uncertain terms that they were not to get in touch, or to come round anymore.

"I don't see why you felt the need to do that," said his dad.

"Well I thought you would all hate them…for causing all this."

"They didn't cause it. If everything you said to your mum and me about the letters is true….."

"You can stop looking so worried," Gina said trying to put Paul at ease. "We all know now why you and Amy came to Malta. I wish I could turn back the clock. I wouldn't have lost…."

She could not carry on for a moment, but sighing softly she

struggled to go on.

"It would have been much better for me coming directly from you, and not the way that I found out…. about the letters I mean."

"It would have been even better if Ginger had admitted it himself or if he gave Amelia the letter on her twenty-first instead of leaving it in his desk!" Emma said heatedly. They all turned to look at her, surprised at the outburst.

Composing herself, Gina shakily admitted that she had started all this. "It all boils down to me mum. You see, I noticed that Ray and Martin were looking very worried about something. They wouldn't admit it for a while but I would not let it rest. The more they protested that there was nothing wrong, the guiltier they looked. It was obvious that something was drastically wrong. Finally, I managed to bully them into telling me. That's how I found out about the letters that never got to Jim. Unfortunately, I…I...got so"…and despite her good intentions, Gina broke down again. Her daughter ran to her and held her as Martin picked up where his sister had stopped.

"It was really me and my big mouth. I was so angry with Ginger that I couldn't wait to confront him. In my anger I said too much and Amelia heard," Martin admitted.

"Gina's upset because she got so angry with Ginger who then stormed off," Ray explained.

"That's when he drove off and...but, I must take some of the blame too. I was the idiot who blurted it out to Gina. That was after my brother had told you not to say anything that might hurt the family! I don't know what came over me, anyway, poor girl," he indicated Amelia with a nod towards his niece, "she very promptly picked up on the fact that she was somehow involved." Feeling somehow confused, Paul looked from one to the other.

"Does that mean that Amelia knows about Jim then?" he asked Martin in a low voice. He didn't dare ask her outright and risk upsetting her even more. She looked so sad after seeing her mother so distressed.

He found himself looking at her again, and when she spoke, he just listened to her husky voice. He really had to concentrate hard in order to find out what she was saying.

"Why don't you ask me?" she snapped. "I don't think it has anything to do with you anyway! I don't need you or anybody else to tell me about this, this Jim bloke," she almost spat out. Her grandmother reminded her quietly that she had promised to be civil and not to get angry.

"Amelia, please love, we have done enough shouting. We need to stay calm now. Your mum must not be upset any more."

"Sorry Nanna, mum….it…it's just so..."

"I know, love. I know," her mother said resignedly. "Go on, answer Paul's question," she encouraged her daughter.

"If you must know, yes. I do know about this ..about Jim." She seemed to have difficulty saying the name. "My 'dad,' yes Ginger told me everything."

Her answer got Paul rather confused. When did Ginger tell her? He wondered for a while, until Gina, looking at her daughter, then explained all about the letter Ginger had left for Amelia. She refrained from mentioning the other letter that was addressed to Jim. That was left to her daughter and she herself, had to decide what to do about it.

Suddenly, Paul felt really relieved that nobody was angry with him or with Amy any more. He still felt bad because the fact was that if he and Amy hadn't started the search for Amelia, there wouldn't have been such a tragedy. He looked slowly around the table at all the faces that showed the marks of recent tears and sadness. His eyes finally rested on the grandparents.

Until then, the lovely old couple had taken a back seat in all this, but now, they started talking about Jim. They both admitted that they had once hoped that he would marry their daughter, well before she had found herself pregnant. They all spoke highly of him and went into great detail about the evenings he spent with them. They were enjoyable ones, full of laughter around that very same table. All the family had thought it was very unlike him to ignore his girlfriend in her predicament. They couldn't understand how Jim could do that when he seemed so fond of their only daughter, so obviously in love with her. Of course, now they knew that he didn't have a clue about it. He was, in fact, the victim in all these years.

Gina and her brothers started asking questions too. It was obvious that they wanted to know everything Paul could tell them about Jim. He suspected that all these questions were mostly for Amelia's benefit because, although she had made it clear that she wasn't interested, she really needed to know some important facts about her birth dad. She obviously wasn't prepared to ask him anything herself. Even though he had just met her, Paul could tell that she would never admit that she had the slightest interest in her real father! Amelia had made that pretty clear to him.

He wished Amy were there. It would have come so much easier to Jim's niece to tell them all about her beloved uncle and godfather. Besides, Jim's daughter was disconcerting him. When Gina asked him to describe Jim, Paul remembered the photograph that Amy had given him to show them. Taking it out of his inside pocket, he stretched his arm across the table to give it to Amelia. She rudely ignored the gesture and so her mother gave her daughter a stern look and took the little black and white photograph off him herself.

"I 've got a copy of that somewhere," said a blushing Gina.

"Do you mum? How come you kept it then if you were so angry and upset with him?" This was Robert who had been a bystander until then.

"I don't know, but I suppose I still thought of him as Amelia's father. Even though Ginger was the perfect dad, I knew that one day, she would have to be told about her biological father. We never agreed on that. I thought you should be told Amelia, but he...you know the rest now.

"Yes, he told me in the letter," Amelia snapped. Then to, everyone's amazement, she started to talk!

"I still think he was the perfect dad. I can now see though, that sometimes, he might have been trying to prepare me..." Amelia moved closer to her mother. "He used to tease me about looking so different to the rest of the family, didn't he?"

"Yes he did," agreed her grandmother. "He called you Goldilocks and I seem to remember that you always gave as good as you got though."

"I did," Amelia admitted whimsically, "I used to say that he, mum and Robert were the three bears. Oh..."

Amelia wiped her eyes, but tears still rolled down her cheeks. It seemed that once she started talking about Ginger, Amelia couldn't stop.

"Yes," she carried on almost in a whisper now, "I always teased him too. I used to say that I was glad I was not another carrot top like him and Robert. Now I wish I were! Then, there would not have been...."

" Don't, dear girl," her grandfather said tenderly. "Poor Ginger, it must have been difficult for him too. Your blonde hair must have been a constant reminder of his Army friend."

"Yes, more importantly, it must have reminded him of the injustice he did to both your mum and to Jim," continued her Nanna.

Edward had not said much so far, but now he sat forward in his chair and looking at his granddaughter, he carried on reminiscing. He reminded his wife and Gina how sunburnt Jim was when he first went to visit.

Gina then told her daughter that Jim and his friend Ginger had learnt a valuable lesson about sunburn, very early after arriving on the island. After that first painful experience when they had slept on the rocks at midday, they were both very careful not to sunbathe during the hottest hours of the day." Amelia looked at her mother who seemed to be far away as she talked softly about Jim but she was soon brought back when Emma looked at her grandaughter and smiled.

"Amelia has got a lovely suntan now, but she has to take it very slowly at the beginning of the hot days. Don't you dear?" her grandmother asked looking indulgently at her.

"Yes, Nanna, I do…you always nag me about that," teased Amelia and to Paul's delight she looked positively radiant when she allowed herself to smile.

"Well, Jim is still very fair and in great contrast to Meg. His wife has got very dark hair and eyes."

"What about their children?" Amelia surprised herself when the question came out without her thinking about it.

Everyone was surprised to hear her. She was finally showing a bit of interest in her father! The rest of the family looked at each other with great amusement and Amelia did not miss their looks of surprise.

"Well, Jim and Meg have………"

"Never mind, it has nothing to do with me anyway," she said quickly. Looking at her mum, she suddenly stood up and said that she wanted to go and see her friend before it got too late.

"Now?" asked Gina. "It's a bit rude don't you think, to leave after Paul came on purpose to talk to all of us? And it's late, too late to walk."

"Mum, I need to…I promised her."

"Let her go Gina, she's not a child. I think we've said enough for one day, but it's getting late dear. Your mother's right."

"You know it's not far, only a ten minute walk at the most, and she'll give me a lift back as usual."

"I really should be going now too." Paul excused himself and stood up. "Poor Amy must be wondering how I got on. We've both been very worried about the reception that waited for me here." Looking at Amelia, he said, "If you tell me where your friend lives, I could give you a lift, if you like."

She was already shaking her head and was about to make some excuse when her Uncle Ray said that it was a good idea and it would give her more time with her friend if she had a lift, wouldn't it?

With a shrug of her shoulders, the sullen girl made for the front door and waited for Paul to take his leave. Before he left, Paul had to promise them that he would give them a call. He said that as soon as Amy was well enough to go out, they would come and visit them together.

Once they were in the car, Amelia gave him directions and then she sat there without saying another word. Every now and then, Paul caught her giving him the odd sideways glance. He was amused at a girl her age acting almost childishly.

There was a pregnant silence in the little car until they arrived outside her friend's house.

Paul didn't want her to leave him yet, so he said the first thing that came to his mind.

"Believe me, Jim's a really great bloke, Amelia...honest, it's true," ventured Paul bravely, because he thought that she might bite his head off. She did!

"I don't want you to tell me anything about him. I've just lost my dad, and you... and they all...they all want me, expect me to..." and to his great dismay, Amelia burst into tears and soon her heart wrenching sobs were echoing in the little car.

"Oh, sorry love. I'm so..."

"How, how do you open...?" the distraught girl turned to get out and was trying to open the car door but she couldn't manage it.

"Please, please wait. I didn't mean to upset you," but her sobs grew louder and without thinking what her reaction might be, Paul put his arms around Amelia. After an initial half hearted struggle, she relaxed, cried into his warm shoulder and let him hold her. She almost admitted to herself that it was quite pleasant to be held by such a handsome man. However, Amelia wouldn't let herself do that.

Very reluctantly, she shrugged him off. After all, she mustn't let herself down and show that she was weak. Oh no, that wouldn't do ...not for proud Amelia!

"Thank you for the lift," she whispered hoarsely. "Now, will you please open this door for me?"

"Let go, I'll do it." Paul was not put off by her bold attempt to appear indifferent. "That handle needs replacing but I haven't bothered to take it back to the hire firm yet." Paul leaned across the tearful girl to open the door for her. She quickly grabbed her bag, which was at her feet, and made ready to get out of the car.

Her perfume engulfed him and impulsively, he put a hand on her shoulder to stall her. Then, wiping the tears away gently with one thumb, and surprising even himself, he gave her a kiss on the cheek, tasting her salty tears. He then moved back quickly thinking with some amusement that she might very well slap him. Instead, Amelia blushed as she looked up at him. Looking surprised she just stared at him, then almost in slow motion, she lifted her right hand and shyly touched her cheek. Next, without saying a word, she quickly got out of the car.

Amelia started walking away and then suddenly, she stopped. Paul thought that she might have forgotten something and so he looked where she had been sitting, but there was nothing there. He saw her turn round and start walking back towards the car. Very quickly, Paul wound the window down to hear her what she had to say.

"Are you coming back for a second helping?...Oh, sorry," he said thinking that he probably really had overstepped the mark this time.

"No, erm..., yes but..., no I mean... I just wanted to say I'm sorry I was so rude in the house," she said sheepishly.

"That's OK," he reassured her, quite surprised by her apology and knowing full well that it had cost her a lot to say what she did. "It has been a very sad and difficult time for you, I know that. Everyone understands how tough it's been, especially for you and your mum. I can only begin to understand. Go on, off you go now. Spend some time with your friend and relax a little... Is that her in the window?"

"Yes, that's Rita. Bye bye and thank you."

"Bye, see you soon," he said hopefully.

CHAPTER 19

When Paul let himself in, he thought that Amy was looking much better. She'd been watching TV in the lounge and had fallen asleep in the big comfortable armchair. He was pleased because he didn't want to have to talk at that moment. He just wanted to think of that lovely girl, and go over again all that she'd said to him. She truly was an enigma.

He couldn't understand how she'd got under his skin so quickly. He had a lovely girlfriend and during the three months he'd been seeing Amy, he hadn't given any other girl a second glance.

That was a fact, until this evening. A few hours earlier, he had met Jim's lovely daughter and now he couldn't stop thinking about her. In spite of her churlish behaviour and the curt words she'd used at the house with the bright yellow door, Paul had felt a spark of chemistry, a pull towards her. He couldn't really explain it any better than that to himself. At first he'd been shocked at her rudeness and arrogance, but then he'd seen another side to her. He couldn't forget the compassion she'd shown towards her mum. When her grandmother gently chided her, Amelia showed only respect towards her.

As far as he was concerned, this made up for her rudeness. She was really a very sensitive girl who had tragically just lost her beloved father. The poor girl had then also found out that her father hadn't really been her father after all!

But he just couldn't think what had made him feel so flustered when he heard her talking.

For a few minutes, he just sat there with his girlfriend asleep opposite him. He felt quite guilty for thinking about Amelia and the impact she'd had on him. He was really touched when she turned back to thank him and when she apologised for her earlier behaviour. Paul was pleased to see that the cold front, which that poor grieving girl showed to everyone, had slowly started to thaw for him.

"Oh, hi. You're back!" Amy sat up and tried to get out of the chair, but still feeling rather fragile, she decided to sit back for a while longer. "How long have you been sitting there?"

"Not long. You looked so peaceful that I didn't want to disturb you. No, don't try to get up.

Take it easy, Amy, you do look better, but you 've been quite feverish until now. I'll make us a cup of tea and then I'll tell you everything."

"Paul!" she cried impatiently. "Forget about the tea. I've been waiting patiently and I can't wait any more. Tell me, was it awful?"

"I'm coming," he shouted from the kitchen. "As you saw for yourself, I'm still in one piece so stop worrying."

Both settled down and Paul told Amy everything that was said during the family meeting at the house with the bright yellow door.

"What are you telling me, that everything was already out in the open? Did Gina already know that Uncle Jim wants to acknowledge his daughter?"

Paul got up and passed Amy her cup of tea because her voice was getting croakier.

"Does his daughter know about him already then?" She would have carried on struggling to ask more questions but Paul put his hand up and stopped her.

"One question at a time please Amy. Yes, they must know all that. It seemed like it anyway."

"So they know how seriously injured Uncle Jim was?"

"Yes they do know that and why he couldn't write himself to start with. We told the brothers, remember? I think we told Ray."

"So it turned out better for you then? That's a great relief isn't it? We'd been so worried about the way the family would react to what you were going to tell them! Tell me, how does Amelia feel about Uncle Jim?"

"Don't ask," he replied quickly. "She's very touchy but then who can blame her? I tell you what Amy, she is a real stunner with blonde hair like yours, that's Jim's genes I guess, and she has big brown eyes, but she is rather abrupt and bad tempered. In fact she was downright rude. There's no excuse for that, is there, not really."

"The poor girl has just lost the man she always regarded as her father. What do you expect? It's too early to replace him with a total stranger who claims to be her real dad!"

"Well, it's not just a claim, is it? Her relatives know him and she's seen a photo of him with her mum. However, you're right, of course. Mind you, later on she mellowed slightly and apologised. She'd been looking so surly but when she finally smiled, it was pure magic."

"My my, I think you like her Paul. Oh yes you do, go on, don't even try to deny it." Poor Paul blushed like a schoolboy.

"Don't be daft Amy, I...I...just..."

"Paul, you're blushing! I think I should try to get up. I'd better come with you next time. Is there going to be a next time?"

"Don't be silly. I mean, yes, of course. We'll both visit when you feel up to it. Now, as far as Amelia is concerned, yes I think she's a real beauty but we didn't hit it off."

As soon as he said that, he wondered why he didn't mention the episode in the car. She hadn't got mad when he kissed her, although it was just a peck. Amelia didn't really push him away, well, not very convincingly anyway. When he had dared to put his arms around her, he got the feeling that she liked it. These thoughts kept going round in his head and he didn't feel like telling Amy about any of this. That fact somehow made them seem of some significance.

"Bye the way, you should be phoning your uncle now, shouldn't you?"

"Yes, you're right. My throat's still very sore, so I'll be brief. He must be wondering how things are, if we've made any progress."

"Wait Amy, I've just realised that it's almost eleven. Isn't it a bit late for him? He might be in bed."

"No, don't worry, he never goes to bed before twelve. He's said more than once that he slept enough when he was poorly. Anyway, it's ten o'clock there remember, they're an hour behind us."

"Let's call him then. It's best if you talk to him even though you're a little hoarse. If your throat starts hurting, pass me the phone."

"Oh, ok, I'll talk to him. If I start coughing, just take over please."

Paul helped her to get comfortable and as she dialled the number, he started wondering if she would be all right to travel on Friday. He had to go back to school on the following Monday, so he couldn't change his flight date. However, Amy could change hers if she still wasn't feeling well enough to travel, because she had more holidays than he did. She had planned to spend them with her grandparents in Somerset after returning from Malta. Obviously that was all up in the air now.

"Can't you get through yet?" he asked her. He was getting

worried about her as she was looking increasingly pale.

"No, not yet Paul. I hope he's told Auntie Meg about Amelia. Do you think he did?" she asked as she waited for someone to pick the phone up.

"It's ringing, but I don't think they're in...sssh Paul," she whispered.

"Hello, hello," and covering the mouthpiece she explained, "uncle is saying something, I can't understand." and looking confused, she asked "What is it uncle?" He sounded rather odd.

"Uncle Jim, it's me, no, it's not Auntie Meg, it's Amy. Why, is she out? Uncle Jim...speak to me!" A distressed Amy handed the phone to Paul.

"Something is very wrong. I can't understand him. I think, I think, he is drunk. I think he's crying." Amy was distraught.

Paul took over and tried to make some sense of the mumbling that Jim was coming out with on the other end of the line.

"Jim, Jim, what on earth? How much have you had to drink, man? Calm down, please, you're only worrying your niece. No, no, we haven't heard from Meg. We only phoned to tell you that we, that I just met your daughter...yes,...Amelia. She is absolutely...what?"

Amy looked up, frightened now that Paul had raised his voice.

"What do you mean, gone? Gone where?"

Amy stared at her boyfriend who seemed shocked. She nudged him, impatient to find out what was wrong with her dear uncle.

"All right Jim, we'll talk to her. We'll do our best anyway...of course, of course. Yes, we'll do that promise, I promise. Yes, yes I think you should go to bed now. We'll phone you tomorrow. Try not to worry Jim. Yes, I know, but she probably just needs a little space to get used to the idea. Yes, I think so, I honestly do think so. Goodnight now. Take care."

"What on earth...?" Poor Amy dragged herself to the settee and waited for Paul to speak. He seemed to be taking his time, as he always did. He always kept her waiting and it really infuriated her. This seemed serious, and since she was feeling rotten already, she said that she might as well hear this latest drama. It sounded like a drama, which no doubt was going to make her feel worse.

Paul looked sadly at Amy. She was looking very worried now as she begged him to tell her what was wrong with Uncle Jim.

"I think I heard him correctly. It seems that when Jim told Meg about Amelia, there was a big row. He wasn't talking very clearly as you know, but I think he said that he'd had a couple of drinks for Dutch courage before he told Meg. Unfortunately, he was very nervous and made a total mess of things because it all came out wrong. Your auntie walked out…Jim reckons that she won't go back. He said she went on about her not having children, when all the time he had a daughter. Poor Meg, we can only imagine how that made her feel!…She was so distraught and after packing a few belongings, she left. Jim says that your aunt ran out and she said that she didn't want to see him ever again!"

"Never! Auntie is the sweetest, kindest…"

"Well, she's left and he thinks that she is staying at her sister's house. Have you got an aunt living in Exeter?…Joyce? Jim thinks she might be there as the two sisters are very close."

"Yes, I have, but I don't understand…"

"That's where Jim reckons your auntie is staying... I promised him that we'd speak to her soon, so maybe we should phone her tonight. Oh, no, I didn't ask for her number. Have you got it? I know you brought your address book."

"Yes, I have it," she said in a sad voice. "Why hasn't he phoned her himself and tried to sort it all out?"

"He said that he's tried, but her sister answers the phone and says that Meg isn't there, but he's convinced that she is..."

"Oh dear, and he hasn't been out of hospital long!"

"He did say that he was given the ok when he went to the Out Patients Department and that he starts work in a week."

"I wonder though, with Auntie Meg not being there, if he'll motivate himself." Amy was really worried. "I suppose this happened just after we phoned up to tell him about Ginger. He must have told her about his ex-army mate and how he destroyed those vital letters."

"Yes, I'm sure you're right, Amy."

"In a bizarre sort of way, that tragedy brought things out in the open didn't it?" continued Paul. "Well, it obviously gave him an opening, and it could have been done so well, but he blew it."

"Yes, it sounds like it." There was a hint of resignation in Amy's voice, but she wanted to talk.

"Paul, do you know that it was Auntie Meg (she was a Military nurse at the time) who took that letter to him? She saw him tear it to shreds. She must have remembered that if uncle mentioned the episode. It should have been quite easy to tell auntie about Amelia after that."

"We don't know how he went about telling her but the fact is, she's left him now. I feel sorry for both of them really."

"Well, we can do our bit by phoning Auntie Meg's sister and seeing if she's there. "Amy wiped her forehead with the wet flannel she kept close by. "I'm feeling hot again and my throat is hurting," she finally admitted.

"Come on, let me help you. Get back to bed, and I'll fetch your medicine and a drink. Then you must try to sleep."

"I'm really not feeling very well now Paul, and my head feels so heavy."

Paul helped her to get back to bed and made sure she was comfortable.

"Here you are, drink this. If you feel better, you can phone in the morning. When we get back on Friday, we must try to help them sort things out," Paul said, but he didn't sound too optimistic. Poor Amy was still not over the flu bug she had.

Paul was feeling quite doubtful that Amy was going to be well enough to travel to England on the Friday. He wanted to prepare her for the possibility that he would probably be flying back home on his own, leaving her behind until she was fit enough to travel.

"Amy, it's just three days before we're due to fly back. What happens if you're still not fit to fly? I've got no choice. School opens on Monday and obviously I have to go. I'm just concerned that you might not be over the flu by then."

"I honestly can't think straight at the moment. My head is throbbing and…" she couldn't continue. Paul rushed to fetch her a drink of water as she was having a bad coughing fit. When she had stopped coughing and could breathe a little bit easier, she reminded him that she had the following week's holiday too, so she could change her flight date if she had to. However, she really didn't fancy doing that at all.

"Let's try not to worry about it yet. If you're still not well by Wednesday, we might have to do something about changing the flight date for you. If it comes to that, I'll make sure that everything is sorted, down to your lift to the airport and I'll meet you at the other end. Don't worry yet, but I felt I had to say it now."

"Alright, Paul, I know. I'd better take some more cough medicine. My goodness, it's one o'clock!"

"So it is, come on, let me cool you down a little bit love. You're burning up again. Come on drink up. "

Paul was really concerned about Amy. He didn't think that she would be feeling well enough to fly in three days time. He wondered if maybe Laura or Lucy would help. The holiday flat was paid for but it was only booked for two weeks. If the worst came to the worst, he hoped that one of the women would help by putting Amy up for a few days until she was fit to return to England. He didn't want to think of Amy stuck in a hotel on her own feeling poorly.

If Lucy and Ray could put her up, he wouldn't feel so bad about leaving her behind. Paul was thinking more of Ray and his wife simply because the two women had hit it off so well. He also reminded himself that Laura worked in the kitchen of the George Cross bar three or four days a week but he wasn't sure. Lucy, on the other hand, was at home all day.

With that reasoning going on in his head, Paul made a mental note to approach Ray about the problem first thing in the morning. After that, they would just take the rest of their holiday one day at a time, and hope for the best.

CHAPTER 20

That night was a rather strange one for Paul. He was woken up a few times when Amy started to mumble in her sleep. She was feverish for a while, and he was back and forth getting drinks for her. Then, every time he nodded off, he had to get up again to give her some cough medicine or else to cool her down with a cold flannel.

When he finally did manage to grab some sleep, he dreamt of a very blonde girl who was shouting and yelling at him. He woke up startled and confused. Someone - the blonde girl - was calling him. It was Amy who was very hoarse, saying that she was so thirsty and would he please give her a drink of cold water.

It was a relief when morning finally arrived. It had been a very long night and Paul felt more tired when he got up than when he had actually gone to bed.

He noticed that Amy did not look so flushed that morning, but she was breathing rather heavily and sounded quite chesty when she coughed. That made him decide to talk to Ray as soon as possible. He had to see if he and Lucy would look after Amy until she could fly back to England, or else he had to sort out some other accommodation as soon as possible. It was really very doubtful that the poor girl would be better by Friday.

After helping Amy go to the bathroom and then giving her a cup of tea, Paul made sure that she was as comfortable as possible. He had just decided to go and see Ray, rather than have a long-winded conversation with him on the telephone.

Waving bye bye to him, Amy knew that she had no choice in the matter. She agreed with Paul that she would rather stay at Lucy and Ray's house than in a hotel. It was just her rotten luck to get ill on holiday. It hadn't really been an ordinary holiday. It had seemed more of a mission for her and for Paul. No, she just couldn't see herself being fit to travel on Friday.

She was just glad that when she and Paul could, they did see some interesting places. Amy kept thinking of the sights that they had managed to see. It seemed ages since they were on that lovely beach eating the Maltese sandwiches. She was just grateful now that they'd managed a bit of sight seeing. She hoped that one day she would go back to the Silent City again. She definitely would return to Malta for a proper holiday.... it might even be on honeymoon.... and her daydreaming got her so relaxed that she was soon sleepy.

Before she fell asleep the poor girl crossed her fingers. She just hoped that Lucy would be kind enough to put her up for a few days. She knew that she couldn't fly when she felt so ill and so she then made a mental note to make a couple of phone calls. First she had to tell her parents what was happening and then she would also try to get in touch with her Auntie Joyce to find, hopefully, her dear Auntie Meg's whereabouts.

Paul parked the car and walked out into the morning sunshine past the house with the bright yellow door and into the bar. He decided that it was better not to go to the house. He was trying to be loyal to his girlfriend and not risk seeing the girl who had unnerved him so much. She had really got under his skin and though he tried hard not to, he still kept finding himself thinking about Amelia at the oddest times.

In spite of trying so hard to be noble, Paul was pleasantly surprised to see the girl in question serving drinks at the bar.

He felt a twinge of guilt at the way he felt about her, but he consoled himself with the thought that he had at least tried to avoid seeing her.

She looked beautiful that morning, maybe because she had a big smile on her face as she served the little crowd of tourists.

Paul just waited his turn and was quite amused to notice that Amelia had looked up through her ridiculously long eyelashes and looked down again without acknowledging him, not even with a smile.

He decided that she was obviously going to play it shy this morning, or was she playing games? You never knew with her!

When it was finally his turn, Paul could have kicked himself. To start with he was tongue-tied but when he finally managed, "Good morning," he was off! He started talking and going on and on, without stopping to catch his breath.

"Do you help out here too?" he asked. "I never saw you in the bar before. I...I mean, we, we came here a few times to meet your uncles, but you were...never here...oh, I just thought...of course I... I mean we, we never saw you. You were in England until..." and he would have carried on if she hadn't interrupted him with a great big smile that lit up her entire face. How did she do that? How did she manage to make him feel so self-conscious? He actually felt himself blushing and very quickly asked if her Uncle Ray was about.

"As to your first question, no, I hardly ever do, help here, I mean. Uncle Martin is helping mum sort out dad's clothes to send to some charity, and as for Uncle Ray well, he's gone down to the cellar to fetch some stock."

Paul felt totally hypnotised. What was the matter with him? She was really making him feel weak at the knees. Even though she was dressed all in black and her hair was pulled back severely, she looked gorgeous and somehow managed to make him either tongue-tied or else turn him into a waffling idiot. He finally managed to ask her if she had the day off work.

"I actually had two weeks holiday left this year and I was saving them to go to Italy in the autumn with some friends." She suddenly looked very distressed and stopped to control herself before she went on.

"After the funeral, I decided that I couldn't face going to work just yet and act normal after… I also thought that mum might feel better if…anyway, my boss was very understanding. He said I could take as long as I need before going back to work. I was on the phone to him at eight o'clock this morning."

"That's early," said Paul.

"Yes, he's always at work before everybody else, but tell me, what brings you so early here? You didn't come to see me, that's for sure!"

"Is she flirting with me?" he asked himself. She looked coquettishly at him and he felt that magnetism once again. "Who wouldn't be flattered?" he asked his niggling conscience.

"Amelia, watch out for his smooth talk. He has a lovely girlfriend," teased Ray, who walked in carrying a crate of soft drinks.

Amelia looked a little embarrassed. She lowered her head and sneaked a quick look at Paul. She had a customer waiting, so she got busy. The two men sat at one of the empty tables and started discussing some sort of arrangement. She could hear Amy's name mentioned a few times and wondered what this was all about, but she couldn't really get close enough to listen.

Eventually, both of them seemed satisfied with whatever they had agreed on and Ray asked his niece to get Paul a Hopleaf while he finished off his jobs in the cellar.

"How is your girlfriend? Are you two engaged then?" and as soon as she said that, Jim's daughter wanted to bite her tongue.

"She's still suffering, poor girl. This flu bug is vicious. As for your second question, we have known each other about three months, and no, we're not engaged or anything," Paul said. Straight away he asked himself why he'd said that, then to make himself feel better he asked Amelia if she wanted to meet her new cousin.

At first, Amelia declined because she didn't want to see the girlfriend of this gorgeous man. She was persuaded however because Paul told her that Amy had something to give her. It was something that Jim sent with his niece for his long lost daughter.

"What has she got for me?" she asked quickly, looking a little excited.

"I can't tell you, I'm sorry. That's between Amy and her uncle. It has nothing to do with me. It's really not my place to tell you."

"Go on, Paul, please, "she pleaded in that sexy, husky voice.

Paul suddenly realised that Amelia had changed her tune. Up until the night before, she didn't even want to hear Jim's name mentioned. She 'd got really angry and been rude when anyone even dared to mention him. Now, she wanted to know what Jim had sent her with Amy.

"I promised not to tell you about it, sorry. Amy wanted to carry out Jim's wish, and since she can't go out yet, you must visit her."

"Oh, I'm not sure about that. I don't..."

"How about tonight? If Amy is up to having visitors, I'll pick you up at seven o'clock." Trying not to look too eager, Amelia hesitated a little and then agreed. She said she wouldn't mind meeting his girlfriend, really. Her smug smile showed that she had another reason for accepting the invitation. She worked out quickly that she would see Paul again in ten hours! Little did she know that the man in question was thinking the same and hugging the thought to himself.

"Amy is very fond of her uncle so you'll get a good picture of him."

"You're talking about him again! I wish people would..."

"What do you wish? Don't you want anyone to mention him at all?"

She was off again! She was up and down like a yo-yo. It was

proving to be difficult to keep up with her quick change of moods.

He decided to be a little assertive as maybe it would be a better approach.

"Just listen for a minute please. Like I said, if Amy isn't too bad, I'll come and fetch you. You can come to our flat and meet her."

"I can't!"

"Yes, you can. You have already agreed to come. You'll enjoy talking to Amy. She is devoted to her Uncle Jim and his wife, Meg. Your cousin, oh yes, she is your cousin. It's no use you shaking your head. She is without a doubt, the best person to tell you all about him, if you want her to of course."

"Is she better now?" asked Amelia, finally resigned to the fact that she was going to meet Amy.

She seemed a little better this morning. Hopefully, she'll have improved even more by tonight. You can ask her whatever you want to know about your dad.... Your birth father."

"I don't really want to think about.... about that man.... it's too..."

"Ok, don't think about him. Just be ready when I come for you. I'll be here at seven o'clock. Is that alright?" Even though she would be going to meet Amy, Amelia suddenly felt really excited knowing that she and this attractive Englishman would have some time alone together.

Instead of feeling disappointed when he had to leave, she started counting the hours until Paul would call for her. She was going to be alone with him, in that car again. He had kissed her in that car. Amelia began to wonder if this time...

Her uncle then brought her back from her daydreaming.

"Amelia, give us a hand please. You look like the cat that's swallowed the cream. If Paul managed to put the smile back on your face he deserves a pat on the back. However, his girlfriend wouldn't be smiling if she knew that he was flirting with you, her newly found cousin."

Meanwhile, back at the holiday apartment, Paul could see that Amy was feeling a bit better after sleeping for a couple of hours. When Paul suggested fetching Jim's daughter for a visit, Amy thought that it was an excellent idea.

"Thank you Paul. I'm dying to meet her. I have the necklace

ready, all wrapped up for her. I hope she takes it as it has great sentimental value."

"Of course, I hope so too. She was a bit unsure about meeting you at first."

"Why? She met you!"

"Yes, but you're actually related to her biological father and so you're related to her too. You'll like her, Amy. She's very blonde just like her dad. She's like him a lot actually, now I come to think of it, especially in the way that she comes out with things, straight to the point. However, she can be rather abrupt and prickly, but you'll get to like her. I'm sure you will."

"When she's here, we must remember to take some photos to show uncle. Before I forget, do you think we ought to phone him again?"

"Yes I think you should, but after Amelia's been. Then, you'll be able to tell him about his gorgeous daughter."

Amy thought that Paul was being a bit too complimentary about her newly found cousin. She was going to say so, but decided against it. She was probably just being too over-sensitive.

If Paul had realised what Amy was thinking, he wouldn't have gone on about Amelia, but he went on to tell Amy that the lovely girl had been serving at the bar that morning. He seemed amazed to see that, in spite of being all in black and wearing no makeup, she had looked very attractive behind that bar.

"She really has impressed you hasn't she?" Amy asked quietly. "You seem to know her so well, so quickly."

"I only spoke to her today and yesterday, but she's quite a character. You'll see for yourself this evening. Are you staying in bed or do you want to try and get up? I'll help you, if you want to come into the lounge."

"I don't know yet," she said," but I'm dying for a cuppa." So Paul went through to the kitchen and put the kettle on.

As soon as he was out of the room, Amy sat up and swung her legs round so that she could sit at the edge of the bed. Then she tried to stand up. She wanted to try to get out of bed without asking for help, but she felt light headed and her legs felt weak.

"No, I can't ...I can't get up yet, Paul," she had to admit as she lay back once more and waited until he came back from the kitchen.

"Did you try to get up? Amy! You should have waited. I was just making you the cup of tea that you asked for. I think you'd better stay put. Look, it's still ages before Amelia visits, and I can help you freshen up a bit whenever you like. Mind you, if you'd rather she didn't come…."

"Oh no, I really want to meet her. Then… when she leaves, I'll phone Uncle Jim. I'm so worried about him and Auntie Meg."

"Yes, it's a shame that such a lovely, devoted couple are going through such a traumatic time. It would be a disaster if on finding his daughter, Jim loses his wife."

Suddenly, Paul noticed that Amy was crying.

"Oh love, come on, don't get upset now. They'll probably make up soon. Their marriage is strong and they are so devoted to each other. You'll see. Meg just needs some time to get used to the idea of Amelia"

"Oh I do hope so!"

"Come on, you just drink this tea and try to sleep a little bit longer. If you need anything, just call this time. I'll be in the lounge tidying up."

"Paul, I just remembered something. Did you manage to speak to Ray about me possibly staying with him and Lucy after you've gone?"

"Oh yes, sorry love, I forgot to tell you. Ray said that he would help out. He spoke to his wife on the phone and then told me that they would love to have you for as long as you need to stay."

"Thank God for that. I was so worried. I like Lucy, but I'll hate to see you going without me. It won't be for long will it?"

"No, just a few days I would say, but you might want to stay a bit longer once you feel good again. Anyway, Ray said it would be better if we move you on Thursday at the latest so that I can leave the flat clean and tidy etc. It would be nice to see you settled in before I went back. At least, with Lucy around to look after you, I know that you'll be in good hands," Paul admitted, sounding almost relieved.

"That lady will be a tonic for you."

Amelia was looking out of one of the upstairs windows when Paul arrived to pick her up. He had barely pulled up outside the bright yellow door before she opened the window, and waving to attract his attention, she called him a couple of times. He wasn't sure if he was expected to wait for her in the car, or to go up to the house. The decision was taken out of his hands because within seconds, Amelia came out and walked to the car.

Somehow, she managed to look gorgeous in a short but plain black dress, and once again she overwhelmed Paul. He had to remind himself that the girl was in mourning for the man she called her dad, and therefore she was still very vulnerable in spite of her show of bravado. She seemed to be prone to extreme shows of emotions. She would burst into tears and rant and rave one minute and be as sweet as anything the next. Sometimes she just looked lost and sorry for herself but then she could also appear so cheerful, and like now, look on top of the world.

“Is Amy any better now?" she wanted to know as she let herself into the passenger seat. Paul told her that the poor girl was still not quite right but she had insisted on meeting her cousin.

On the short drive up the steep hill, Paul found himself stealing the odd sideways glance at his attractive passenger. She just sat there looking cool and all the time twirling a strand of hair that had fallen away from the usual severe ponytail. He was thinking that she looked even more attractive and distracting with that lovely hair framing her face.

He felt rather than saw Amelia stealing the odd glance at him. Her perfume filled the car with a sensual aura, which was not helping him to stay cool towards this seductive girl. She was beginning to have a rather ridiculously disturbing effect on him.

He noticed that her short black dress had somehow managed to ride up her long brown legs. As he parked the car and turned towards her to speak, he felt himself bowled over by her big brown eyes and for the life of him, he couldn't say anything!

"Are you going to open this door or…" she asked seductively, putting her hand on his knee.

I seem to remember that you had to open it for me last time," she said smiling.

"Of course…I…I…" stammered Paul as he leant across her, breathed in her perfume and before he gave himself time to think, started kissing her long and hard.

There was no telling how long that kiss would have lasted were it not for a passing car. The cheeky driver decided to have a bit of fun with the loud horn. He laughed out loud, seeing that he had made Paul pull away. The latter shook his head in confusion. A soft moan escaped his lips as he looked at Amelia's red lips smiling seductively at him and then at her half- closed eyes. Once again he felt guilty. He had to watch out. He had to try and ignore the strong pull that there was between them. He had the strange feeling of, "the spirit is willing " etc, going round and round in his head.

"Sorry, I shouldn't have…" he started, confused and slightly embarrassed. At the same time he had to admit to himself that he was feeling over the moon because this lovely girl had not pushed him away but, wonder of wonders, she'd returned his spontaneous kiss.

"Ssssh," she whispered in her husky voice. She put her finger on his lips to stop him saying anything else. "Let's go in and see Amy. We can talk later."

"Oh no, I'm sorry. I don't know…"

"Please, don't apologise, I liked it," admitted Amelia with a big smile on her face. " Let's go in now. Come on, and open this door. I see you haven't sorted it yet...I wonder why…" she was grinning knowingly.

Amelia's sexy voice made Paul feel in desperate need to clear his head before seeing his girlfriend. He felt rather awkward. Would Amy be able to tell? He was just about to open the front door when Amelia called him huskily. He sighed when he saw her still sitting there with a satisfied smile. Even though he'd pushed the door open from the inside, she'd just sat there and waited for him to go round and open the door properly for her. At that moment he just wanted to escape!

"It's a hired car and I'm returning it tomorrow so there was no point in taking it to be fixed," he explained, trying not to look at her amused expression as he went round to open the door and let her out.

As soon as he opened the apartment door, he let Amelia walk in first into the cool hallway.

“Amy, we’re here!" he shouted as soon as they went in. He wanted to give her a bit of a warning before they barged in on her but he was also giving himself some time to compose himself, before he faced Amy.

CHAPTER 21

She was still on the settee where he'd left her and despite looking rather pale, she looked happy to see them. Turning towards the Maltese girl, she said that she had waited months for that moment. Amy felt quite emotional and had to pinch herself to make sure that she was actually talking to her uncle's daughter.

When the subject of Jim's heartache and all the painful feelings of rejection came up, Amelia herself felt slightly emotional and could see the different emotions that Amy was going through. Very tentatively, Amy started talking about Jim finally receiving the one and only letter from Gina. Amelia didn't say anything, as her new-found cousin explained why Jim had made no effort to find her before. Amelia just listened when Amy repeated all that Jim had said about the moment when he received the one and only letter.

Amy admitted that she felt so sorry for all the years of uncertainty and rejection that her uncle had been through. He had suffered so much pain as a direct result of a jealous mate's actions. That mate had wanted his girlfriend and he had got her through his deceitful ways.

At this stage, both girls were in tears. Amelia was doubly upset. She now felt sorry for her birth father because hearing it all from Amy, she finally believed how much the poor man had suffered. At the same time, she felt some compassion mixed with a little shame when she considered that Ginger had caused all this grief.

Paul was really pleased to see the Maltese girl getting quite emotional - she usually had that cold, icy exterior showing. It was good to scc hcr so moved about her birth father's suffering.

Paul stood up and gave each girl a hug before he walked to the kitchen.

"I'll make you both a nice cup of tea and then I'll go for a walk so that you two can get a little acquainted," he said very thoughtfully. Amy was grateful but Amelia didn't look too happy. The fact that she followed him with her eyes until he went out was not lost on Paul's girlfriend.

"I think you should open the box now," Amy suggested

quietly. She had handed it to Amelia while Paul was in the kitchen but the nervous girl had just put it down on the arm of her chair and had ignored it since.

"Go on, it's nothing spectacular, but," and she stopped talking while Amelia gingerly picked the little packet up. With trembling fingers, her new-found cousin ripped the pretty paper and opened the box. Lifting the cross and chain, she looked up at Amy. She looked almost disappointed Amy thought, until she told her to look at the back of the cross.

Amelia then saw her mother's initials and what she now recognised as her birth father's initials and promptly burst into tears.

Amy was looking flushed and tired, but she was feeling quite pleased to have Lucy looking after her and fussing around her. She had felt awful and quite tearful when she left the flat. It had felt odd leaving Paul there, but Lucy had kindly volunteered to go to St Andrew's to pick her up and to take her to her house herself. It seemed a sensible idea at the time.

"Now, Amy," she said, as soon as the English girl was settled in a pretty bedroom that was filled with sunshine and fresh flowers. "Now you must try and get better so that we'll be able to have some fun before you go back to England. Paul said that he had a chat with the travel agent and that they were very sympathetic.

When you feel better, you must go to get your new flight date and ticket. Don't worry, I'll take you." Lucy was just the medicine that Amy needed. She was kind but there was no nonsense about her. At that moment, Lucy was talking and fussing so that the young girl wouldn't have time to brood about leaving her boyfriend and more importantly about his leaving her behind when he returned to England.

"I suppose your family back home are aware of all this?" she asked, practical as ever. "I mean, do they know that you won't be back home yet?"

"Oh yes, I spoke to mum and dad last night. Thank goodness, they even suggested that they talk to my boss. I'd forgotten about her. Mind you Jane, my boss, well, she's really lovely! So, everything's sorted. I do still need to talk to Uncle Jim though…maybe tonight."

"Does he know that you and Paul have met the family?"

"Oh yes, he knows all about that. What I haven't told him yet is that I've finally met his daughter. Last night, after Amelia left, I felt very emotional so I didn't think that it was a good idea to phone. I also need to tell him that I gave her his necklace." Lucy looked puzzled and so Amy explained about the silver chain and cross that Gina had given to Jim on his birthday and which Jim now wanted Amelia to keep.

The two women chatted for a while. Lucy reassured her guest that she would remind her to phone her uncle that evening, especially after Amy had explained about her godparents' separation.

Then, after making sure that she was comfortable and hoping that Amy would sleep, Lucy left her and went to make a start on her housework.

Poor Amy found it difficult to relax. She was too worried about Amelia and her very obvious attraction towards Paul. He seemed to be revelling in the attention. Amy just hoped it didn't go to his head.

"I must stop being silly. It must be the flu making me extra touchy," she chided herself. She tried hard not to let herself get upset. Finally, the sounds that Lucy was making as she got on with her chores around the beautifully kept house, lulled her into a sound sleep.

Back at the flat, Paul was feeling rather odd too, and not without any guilt. At the same time, he felt relieved that someone else was looking after Amy. He was flying back the next day and the flat really needed a tidy up. He had to get on with his packing too, but first he wanted to go to Sliema and buy some souvenirs. He and Amy had meant to do that much earlier, but somehow, they never got around to it.

He was feeling somewhat deflated now that Amy had gone and not a little lost. He shook himself thinking that he had to get on with it but he didn't feel like doing anything.

Paul was filling the kettle to make a cup of tea when the phone rang. He had a lovely surprise when he heard Amelia's sexy voice.

She wanted to know how it felt with his girlfriend leaving him.

"She didn't exactly leave," he said, finding her question rather odd. "She had no choice, I am going back home tomorrow night."

"Still…are you all ready to go?

“No, not really, I have to clean the flat to start with, then I still have the packing to do. Oh, yes and I have to go to Sliema..."

"Why?"

"I must get some souvenirs...I don't know where to start. Honestly, this place is a shambles now."

"Would you like some help?" How did she manage to make such an ordinary question sound sexy?

"Eh...better not, thank you...but...."

"Why not? It won't take me long...I could get on a bus and...."

Paul tried, at first firmly, but then rather feebly, to refuse her offer.

"I need to talk to you anyway. I need your advice," she said. He felt slightly light-headed when she said that she would be there in about twenty minutes or so. If she had hoped for a lift, she was disappointed because to give him his due, Paul was trying to fight the pull he felt where Amelia was concerned. He didn't think he should put himself in such a situation again...so close to her.

"What advice?" he was totally puzzled.

"I'll tell you when I get there. Oh, by the way, what time do you leave tomorrow?"

"The flight leaves at eleven at night. Why?"

"See you soon," she said and promptly, put the phone down. It seemed that somehow Amelia would continue to unsettle him. Much as he tried to fight it, he had to admit to his innermost self that he was losing control of his willpower. It was only natural to be attracted to her. She was like no other girl he had ever met before. Amelia was unpredictable. She was fire and ice. No one could tell which would show first, the ice or the fire. He certainly couldn't, although he was feeling the warmth more often than the coldness now. Paul was trying hard to convince himself that it would be alright, that this time he wouldn't even touch her hand. That way, there would be no need for any guilty feelings.

He gave himself a mental shake, put the phone down, walked back to the kitchen and came down to earth with a bang. The tap was still running and the little kitchen was flooded!

True to her word, Amelia was soon knocking on the door and a rather harassed Paul quickly let her in and asked her to follow him.

"Where, you're not inviting me into your boudoir are you?" she asked cheekily.

"I wish," he muttered under his breath, as he led her to the kitchen where several towels were spread out on the flooded floor.

"It's your fault really," he chided her jokingly.

"How do you work that out? I came to help…"

"Yes, but you kept me talking on the phone……"

"I never did! You cheeky….. You went on and on about the work you had to do……You sounded so like a bored housewife."

"I…. I.." Paul seemed to have lost his tongue again. The chemistry was there alright and he kicked himself before knuckling down to drying the floor as fast as he could.

Amelia turned out to be a fast and thorough worker and soon the kitchen looked all clean and almost dry.

Once that was done, Paul felt much better and while Amelia helped by tidying up the rest of the flat, he got on with his packing.

All the time he was very aware of the girl who kept flitting from one room to the other. She seemed to be doing her utmost to invade his thoughts and to make a mockery of his resolutions not to get involved.

His conscience told him that he was already involved. Then he thought of Amy…she was a nice girl who didn't deserve to …but they weren't engaged. They were good friends. Thoughts like these swirled round and round his head.

He forced himself to concentrate on what he was doing and tried to hurry up, when Amelia went in the bedroom and promptly sat on the bed. Paul tried to carry on and finish off his packing while all the time he was very conscious of the girl who was invading his peace of mind.

She seemed determined to unnerve him. He was nearly done.

Looking up at him innocently she said that it was a shame that he was going back alone.

Paul was surprised that she was thinking of Amy, because so far she had almost tried to dismiss her completely, if even he mentioned her in passing.

"Yes," he answered her. "Poor Amy must feel so cheated …it hasn't been much of a holiday really. Still, we found you. I'm sure she told her uncle all about you last night. He must be so thrilled about that."

"Will you stop talking for a moment? " She was her old self again, quick and to the point. Yes she was so like Jim!

"I meant," she said, "I meant it's a shame that you're going to be all alone…."

"It's only a short journey…." he said.

"Paul, you're making it harder for me to say what I'm thinking…I am asking you outright, would you like it if I came along?"

Paul dropped the shoes he was just about to pack, and looked up open mouthed at this complex girl.

"You… you…want to go to England? You've only just returned from there." He was looking at her, but it was difficult to read her expressive eyes this time. However, something told him that she was serious. Paul couldn't make her out at all. Was she saying that she was ready to meet her biological father? Had she had a change of heart? Up until the night before, Amelia hadn't even wanted to talk about him. Paul had to be direct now and find out if he was getting the right message. On the other hand, he was well aware that in the mood she was in, she might bite his head off.

"You're not suggesting to go …to go and meet your …Jim?" He thought it was impossible that she was thinking about Jim, not after all her protestations.

"Yes," she almost whispered. This time, she looked really serious. Yet there was softness around her features that sometimes got lost if she was angry and went on the defensive or if she got all prickly and snapped at whoever dared to mention Jim.

"Yes, Paul, I know. I've shocked you now haven't I? I'm not surprised at your reaction, not after all my anger and bitterness towards, towards...Jim...I can't call him..." She couldn't even say the word, but she was struggling to carry on.

"I can't …I'll call him Jim."

"I'd say that that's perfectly normal. Please, don't worry about it now." Paul sat next to her, and, thinking that she was getting upset again, he put an arm round her shoulders.

"Nobody expects him to replace Ginger, your dad. I understand that and so does everybody else. However, what is really puzzling me is, what happened since last night to make you change your mind? You weren't even keen to learn anything much about him. What has happened that made you even consider going to England to see him?"

"My dad, Ginger…and don't say he wasn't my dad," Amelia quickly snapped.

"I wouldn't dream of saying anything like that!" Paul saw her getting all serious and close to tears again, so he didn't say another word because he was rather afraid that she might clam up and not say any more.

"My dad left me a letter you see. I can't remember if you were told about it..." and looking at Paul, Amelia saw him nodding. He reminded her that her mum had told him about the letter when they'd had that get together, after the funeral.

"In that letter, he asked me to do something for him. .He left another letter you see. You didn't know about that one because mum thought that it was up to me whether I would tell anyone about it or not."

Amelia looked at Paul who in turn looked puzzled. This was news to him.

"I didn't want to tell anybody about it. I guess I was afraid of being pressured to do what my dad asked me to do." Amelia leant back against Paul and in a quiet voice that showed that it was difficult for her to speak, she carried on, determined to tell him.

"This other letter is for... for Jim, and, and, dad said that he wanted me to deliver the letter personally to him."

Paul was quite happy with his arm around Amelia, his nostrils teased by the fresh smell of her long, shiny hair. He had to force himself to stand up. He pulled her up onto her feet and taking her hand, he led her into the sun filled lounge.

He sat opposite her because he wanted to keep a clear head and she had a way of unnerving him if he were close to her.

"We need to talk this through, rationally and seriously," he began. "First of all, what would your parents...Sorry, oh God...sorry, I mean what would your mum...?"

He didn't get to finish because Amelia quickly butted in to say that she had talked to her Nanna and asked her opinion. She said that her beloved grandmother would talk to Gina. If she needed persuading she would remind her daughter that Amelia was a grown woman and should make her own decisions.

"Nanna said that if I did manage to get a flight - it would obviously be ideal to go with you - I can stay with my grandparents in Leicester or find...."

"I have a spare room in my flat and I don't live too far from your.... sorry, from Jim."

He noticed that Amelia's eyes lit up when he said that. He suddenly wondered if he was doing the right thing, but somehow his mouth had take over his brain. He quickly said that he was going to Sliema for some souvenir shopping.

"If you come along with me now, we can find out if you can get a seat on the same flight. I think the first and only thing we can do at the moment is to go to the travel agent and see. Then, we can go from there. You might be lucky but if not, you could get another flight to Exeter and I'll be able to meet you. It's the closest airport to Plymouth - less than an hour's drive."

The two of them were soon on their way to Sliema, to the same agent Paul had gone to in order to sort out Amy's ticket. Keeping her fingers crossed, Amelia followed Paul into the cool office.

She studied his brisk efficiency as he explained the situation to the girl behind the desk. He seemed very persuasive and quite at ease as he somehow managed to make the girl smile a lot and get her to help out efficiently and promptly. Amelia was totally impressed by his charm.

A very happy looking couple came out of the busy office into the afternoon sunshine. Amelia gave Paul a quick peck on the cheek and full of excitement, she was almost skipping along the narrow pavement.

Paul curbed her enthusiasm a little because he was still unable to get his head around the new development. As soon as it was all done and dusted, he began to have doubts about the whole idea of Amelia going with him and meeting her birth father so early after losing the man she had known as her father.

He had allowed himself to be carried away by her impulsiveness and her eagerness. Now, he was seriously worried. However, seeing the change in his companion, seeing how full of life she suddenly seemed, he decided that it was a fait accompli and he had to go with the flow.

Paul led the way to an outdoor café not far from the Ferry and after the waiter brought them the coffee and 'pastizzi', he tried to remind Amelia that she had to make sure that she had made the right decision. It seemed like shutting the gate after the horse had bolted since she had the air ticket in her hands and was happily examining it.

"Amelia," he started tentatively, "I said you can stay in my spare room, and also that I don't live very far from Jim, but I honestly don't know if he's ready to see you. I'm just thinking that he has only just found out about you. Then there's the worry about Meg and their marriage."

Paul felt he should tell her about Jim and Meg's separation and what had led to such a split. The beautiful girl suddenly looked quite worried but true to form, she soon looked up and declared that if she couldn't meet him, she'd go and stay with her grandparents, Ginger's parents again. She wanted to spend some days with them anyway.

"Remember, I have two weeks leave. I explained that to you yesterday didn't I?"

"Oh yes, I know that. The best thing to do now is to get back so you can tell your family, do some packing, and well, do whatever…I must tell Amy that you…"

"Do you have to? Do you have to tell her, I mean?"

"I think it's only fair….I feel guilty enough that I.."

"Kissed me? You still feel guilty? Come on Paul, it happened. You liked it and I certainly did, so what's the harm?"

Her straight talk still amused him. He now felt that he too had to be honest and admit that she had not been far from his thoughts for any length of time. She looked overjoyed at the frank admission from this man who had always appeared to be in control. He certainly was, until they got in his car that is, she mused to herself. Once in that little car, he wasn't so good at hiding his feelings or in keeping them in check.

She remembered that when he took her home last night, he'd not used the dodgy door handle as an excuse to get closer to her. He needed no excuse that time. That goodnight kiss was a little longer and a lot more lingering than one would normally expect from someone who was pretending to be cool and detached. He had been very quiet on the way home, but when they got there, he'd parked a little away from the bright yellow door. Then, turning towards her, Paul asked her if she wanted him to let her out.

It was dark, but she could just about make out his chiselled profile and then his white even teeth as he smiled. Amelia shrugged her shoulders, in a feeble gesture of indifference as she replied, "It has become a habit for you to lean over and…." His lips stopped her in mid sentence, and this time, he felt her arms ride up around his neck. Last night she had stopped pretending that she wasn't interested. She found herself returning his hungry kiss with the same frantic urgency. He groaned and suddenly he pulled her arms away from his neck and opened the car door very quickly. He almost pushed her out in his effort to be off and away from her.

"Goodnight. Go on, please go," he urged. "I'll just wait here until you go in," he said huskily. He was telling her to go when all the time she knew that he wanted to say the complete opposite to her.

Paul watched her walk tantalisingly slowly up to the door, turn, and give a little wave. She stood under the light for a moment. Then, turning her hand, she kissed her palm and blew the kiss to him. In a second, she was gone through the bright yellow door, into that warm welcoming house.

"You were miles away," Paul brought her back from her daydreaming. "What were you thinking about?"

"I was thinking about last night..." she said looking up at him through her dark eyelashes. Oh well, he had more or less admitted that he had feelings for her now, strong feelings, just as she herself had for him.

"You have really..." And, lost for words, he looked at the girl opposite him and grabbed her hand across the table.

"Can't you ever finish a sentence at all?" she asked as she threw back her head and laughed out loud.

"We've got to accept it, Paul," she was surprising even herself at her directness. "We both feel the same way, don't we? Let's not fight it, and please, please, remember, you said yourself that you and Amy are, were not serious about each other."

"Yes, I've tried to stay away from you. I tried not to let you…but I couldn't…I can't help it...I …."

"I love you," Amelia said with triumph. "Say it Paul…It's easy, just three tiny words. I love you," she said again.

"Yes, I believe I do," he managed. Paul was suddenly amused to find himself acting so unlike his usual self. With old girlfriends and even with Amy, especially with Amy, he had always taken the lead in the relationship. He had never said those three little words to Amy, and they'd been happy together for over three months. Yet here he was now, telling a girl he'd met yesterday, yesterday, that he loved her! What had got into him? Yes, this rather tempestuous girl was definitely now in the driving seat and, for a change, he was enjoying the experience of being led. Yes, now that he'd admitted that he was attracted to her, he suddenly found himself loving every minute.

CHAPTER 22

Back at the house with the bright yellow door, Amelia stunned her mother and her brother. She had waltzed into the house and told them straight away that not only had she decided to do what Ginger had asked her to do, but that she was going to England the very next day, in just over twenty four hours in fact. Then, to make matters worse, she said that she was going with Paul.

They were both amazed at the obvious transformation in the girl. As usual, when there was some talking to be done the three of them were sitting around the table. In a very short time, the discussion had got rather heated.

Gina thought that it was much too early for her daughter to meet Jim. She pointed out the obvious fact that she had only just lost her dad just one week ago. Gina was quite worried because she felt that Amelia had not really thought this through. She couldn't believe her ears when she heard the confidence in her daughter's voice as she made her announcement.

"A few hours ago you went absolutely crazy if one of us even as much as mentioned Jim. Now you're telling us that you have already booked a flight so that you can go and meet him. I can't believe it! I really can't." Gina sounded very troubled and completely shocked.

Fortunately, Emma and Edward chose that moment to walk in from their suite and so with their usual calm and positive reasoning, they managed to cool the sparks that were flying in the room.

"I'm not going on about it any more," Gina promised, if only half-heartedly. "You have to admit though," she continued, "it's out of order that Amelia's going abroad with Amy's boyfriend, and then, actually staying at his flat with him!"

Amelia had really stunned her family this time. Her face seemed to be lit up with an inner glow and she was looking rather smug as she explained the situation and looked amused at everyone's reaction.

"I thought you'd be really pleased mum. I thought you wanted me to meet…"

"I do want you to, but not yet, not just yet," her mother stopped her. "For heaven's sake, we've only just lost...." Amelia was now shocked to see her mum crying again.

None of them could understand the change in the girl sitting there in her plain black outfit. It seemed that there were no half measures as far as Amelia was concerned. With her it was from one extreme to the other.

Gina, still very much mourning her husband, and slowly coming to terms with her part in his death, was not ready for more problems and complications. In spite of trying hard to bite her lips in order to stop the pain showing, she had to blink back the tears which were threatening to run down her cheeks. At times like this it was impossible to stem them.

"How can you do that to poor Amy?" Gina sounded as upset as she looked. "I'm not impressed by Paul either," she told her daughter. "I would like to give him a piece of my mind."

"Mum, mum," Amelia had ran quickly to her mother's side and giving her a big hug, she explained that Paul felt the same way as she did. There was really no need to worry because, according to Amelia, the English girl wasn't going to be hurt.

"How do you make that out?" Robert too was shocked by his sister's revelations. He just didn't recognise the curt, sulky girl of the last few days. He glared at his sister who was now looking so pleased with herself.

"Robert! They're not engaged or anything like that!" She sounded as if she were trying to convince herself as well as them. "Paul told me that they've only really known each other for a very short time, and I believe him. They are just good friends. Anyway, we both feel the same. We can't help it."

The whole family felt unhappy about the situation, but after much deliberation and argument, they all agreed that after all, the people concerned were all adults. It was just a shame that in spite of Amelia's protests about the matter, Amy was sure to be devastated.

Grandmother was only concerned about trying to keep her daughter from getting hurt any more. Very softly, she declared that sometimes, young people - and the not so young too 'get into these situations without really trying.' She pointed out that Amelia looked so happy even if she had fallen for someone else's boyfriend. "Well, it does happen sometimes, doesn't it?" she asked, nodding wisely.

Looking straight at Gina, she was willing her to understand her last words without hurting her.

To Emma, it almost seemed that history was repeating itself...she felt it was a betrayal. Fortunately, since there was no sign of an engagement between Paul and Amy, Gina and all the family had to be thankful for small mercies.

"Does Amy...I mean, is the poor girl aware that you two, that the two of you..."

"No, she doesn't know how we feel about each other yet."

"So when are you two going to tell her? Who is going to tell her? The poor girl is at Lucy's. She's probably already feeling bad, because she has the flu and cannot go back with Paul tomorrow."

"I don't honestly know. We haven't discussed it yet, mum."

"Well, your mother's right," said her granddad, who, until then had appeared to be dozing. He opened his eyes wide and looking straight at his granddaughter said, "you should do the decent thing and be honest with her, both of you."

"Oh all right, I'll talk it over with Paul later today. Now, if you lot will excuse me, I'll go and pack," she informed them. With that, she skipped out of the room.

They all stared at each other in silence. Then, as if on cue, they all started talking at once.

It wasn't long before Ray walked through to the kitchen. They had heard raised voices in the bar because somehow, the door had been left open. So Ray left his brother to deal with the thirsty customers, and went to see what was happening. He made absolutely sure that he shut the door behind him. Suddenly, Ray felt alarmed because when he looked at Gina, his sister looked as if she'd been crying again.

His father was usually very calm and level-headed. However, at the moment, he seemed to be arguing with Gina, and what was more, his mother was also having her say.

"What on earth is all this shouting about?" he exclaimed. "We have customers trying to have a quiet drink, and everyone could hear you all shouting. Yes, dad, before you ask, unfortunately the door had been left open."

"Well it shouldn't have been open!" snapped his dad.

"Anyway, what's the matter now? What on earth has happened?"

"My darling sister, your dear niece," started Robert with sarcasm dripping from every word, "Wait for it. Are you ready for this?"

"Come on, Robert, spit it out. What has Amelia done?"

"She has only just informed us that tomorrow night, she is going to England! Yes, she is," Robert repeated, when he saw his uncle's jaw drop. "She has suddenly decided to go and meet her...her real father!"

"She has? Has she already made up her mind to meet Jim? I don't believe it!"

"You'd better believe it," his sister said in a broken voice.

"As soon as she's packed a case, she is off to Paul's flat. She's ordered a taxi because she didn't want to ask you or Martin for a lift."

"Why won't you just accept it Gina? " Emma was being very patient with her daughter and spoke very softly to her.

"It's really her choice and we have to respect that. I say that we should try to help her because at the moment, she is so very vulnerable."

"You haven't heard the best bit Ray," continued his distraught sister.

"What else can there be? Go on, tell me, but I think that mum is right, Gina. There isn't much anyone can do. You know her. Once she makes her mind up. I think we can only help by preparing her.... just in case."

"Just listen Ray. Amanda has 'stolen' Amy's boyfriend. It's awful because she doesn't have any regrets about the other girl, her cousin. On the contrary, she appears to be over the moon."

"What do you mean 'stolen'?"

"She has fallen in love with him...or so she says. Can you believe it? They've only just met and she says he feels the same way about her. Guess what? They're going to England together. She's even managed to get a seat on the same flight as Paul."

"Oh my, I should have seen it coming. I thought there was some chemistry there when I saw them in the bar."

"When was this?" Gina looked angry.

"Calm down, sis. Do you remember the other day, when she was helping out? Paul turned up unexpectedly."

"He did, did he?" sneered Gina. "I expect that was why the madam volunteered to help. She must have known that he was coming."

"No, Gina, you are wrong. First of all, I asked her to help because we were expecting some groups of new tourists from the

Hotel down the road. Amelia didn't volunteer at all. Secondly, Paul came over just to speak to me. He wanted to see if Lucy and I could put Amy up until she was fit to fly back to England. He had only just decided to ask me that very morning".

"What did you mean when you said that you might have guessed that they…?"

"I meant that Paul and Amelia looked as if they were really getting on. Anyway, that's beside the point now." Ray was not surprised at his sister's concern. They all knew how very impulsive Amelia could be.

"Where is she staying? Is she going back to Ginger's parents?" he wondered out loud.

"Oh no, I wouldn't mind so much if she were going there. She's staying at Paul's place. Apparently, he doesn't live very far from Jim." Gina was all flushed now.

"Gina, you must calm down dear, she's not a child," her mother said gently. We've been through all this already. The girl is upstairs packing and we must accept her decision. I believe that we must also be there for her because she has had such a traumatic time recently. I know you have too, Gina. There is no denying that but, anyway, I think we must now all try and pull together."

"I think what mum is saying is right, Gina. We have to be ready to support her in case things don't work out. All we can do is be here, ready to pick up the pieces, if she needs us to."

"Exactly, Gina," her dad added gently. "As we've said before, she's very vulnerable at the moment and probably she's not making the right decisions. That 's why we just have to be patient."

"Your dad's right. Come now, Gina," her mum said. "You've got to accept that there's absolutely nothing else you can do really."

"Yes, mum's right as usual. Aren't you, you old so and so?" asked Ray, trying to lighten the mood.

"Away with you," laughed his mum, "off you go. Your brother must be wondering what's up. I'm just surprised that he didn't come through as well, and left all the customers to help themselves!"

"Now that's an idea, why didn't we think of that, a self service bar eh?" Ray answered quickly and before his mum could come up with another witty answer, he got up and went through to the bar as fast as he could.

As soon as she was up, Lucy went into Amy's bedroom to see

if the young girl was awake. She looked down at the still sleeping girl. Her cheeks were a little flushed, but she hadn't coughed for a while, so hopefully she was on the mend. She didn't want to wake her up but very gently, Lucy moved the blonde hair away from Amy's face. She suddenly found herself thinking that the sleeping girl actually looked like Amelia. She hadn't noticed the resemblance before. It was possibly more obvious now, because Amy had lost a bit of weight. Yes that was it. Now, her face looked much thinner, just like Amelia's.

Lucy then went quietly out of the room, shaking her head sadly. She felt sorry for the poor girl. She had been so upset the night before. She spoke to her aunt on the telephone and it seemed that her godmother, her Auntie Meg, had left her husband after more than twenty years of marriage. It all happened because she found out that her husband had a secret child. Meg had only just been told about Amelia. Understandably it was a great shock to her to find out that her Jim had kept such a big secret from her all through those years they'd been together.

Well, Amy had really tried hard to make her aunt understand that her husband had only kept such a secret because he loved her and didn't want to hurt her. She urged Meg to return to her home, and kept on reminding her how she and Jim loved each other, and that this was hurting them both. Amy was virtually begging her aunt to return to Jim, but she didn't succeed. Meg just wasn't prepared to accept what she saw as deceit on her husband's part.

Amy didn't manage to tell her aunt that she wasn't flying back yet. Amy was just trying to make her aunt go back and even went on to tell her how her uncle was a broken man without her. It seemed that he was probably drinking too much too.

It was hardly surprising that she completely forgot to say about her postponed flight back to the UK.

When she finally put the phone down, she cried with frustration.

Lucy wasn't worried that this Meg didn't know about Amy's flu so she told Amy not to worry. "Listen, dear," she tried to calm her, "your parents know. I'm sure they'll talk to your aunt and uncle about your staying in Malta a bit longer than planned." All that mattered was that Amy's parents knew.

That difficult phone call to her aunt had left Amy in no fit state to talk to her uncle. This made it easier for Lucy to persuade her not to bother phoning him as she had originally planned.

"He'll find out soon enough," she said logically. "You've done your bit for him Amy. Listen to me, dear. You must think of yourself now, and concentrate on getting better."

"Yes, you're probably right. Paul will talk to him when he returns anyway, I'm sure," she reassured herself.

"That's true, he will, no doubt about it," Lucy agreed and was pleased to see that now she had stopped crying, Amy was almost asleep, utterly exhausted. She went out of the room and hoped that things would look up soon for the unlucky girl.

It was only seven in the morning and Lucy was in her kitchen making a pot of tea. She was well aware that Amy would be quite upset that day. As soon as she woke up, she was sure to remember that Paul was going back to England in a few hours time.

It was rather odd, she reflected. You would have thought that he'd have phoned his girlfriend or even called to see her, at least on the night before his departure. She couldn't understand why there'd been no word from him since she'd gone to fetch Amy from the apartment she had shared with Paul. The more she thought about it, the more Lucy was glad she'd brought her to her home, her lovely big house at Paceville. If Amy thought it strange that Paul had made no effort to speak to her, she didn't let on.

Lucy hadn't had a good night's sleep herself. After all that bother with her aunt, it was a wonder if the English girl had slept at all.

She was bustling about in the kitchen when Amy surprised her by walking in and sitting at the breakfast table. She looked pale, but at least she was smiling.

"Good morning dear, it's so nice to see you up and about. The kettle's nearly boiled. Do you fancy a cup of tea or coffee?"

"Tea please, Lucy. I feel almost human today," she grinned and admitted that surprisingly she'd slept like a baby.

"Good, you needed that. Hopefully by Monday you'll be able to go out. Then, we can go somewhere nice. What do you say?"

"That would be lovely," said Amy. "I'd love to go to the Silent City again."

"Ok, the Silent City it is. I haven't been there for years. We tend to take these historical places for granted really."

"First I have to sort out my return ticket, and then yes please, I would love to see some more sights and places before I go back."

They were soon having some toast and planning where to go once Amy felt well enough to venture out.

"By the way, Lucy, could you please see if my watch is in your car?" Amy changed the subject. "I can't find it anywhere. I can't remember if I was wearing it or not when you came for me."

"No, love, it's definitely not in the car. Ray cleaned it right through yesterday evening. He would've mentioned it if he found a watch. Just a minute, I'm about to take his first cup of the day to him," she said with some indulgence. "I'll ask him, just in case he did find it and he forgot to mention it," she said helpfully.

Lucy went into the bedroom to find Ray reading the paper in bed. She asked him about the watch, and then went back to the kitchen where Amy still sat cupping her drink in her hands.

"Sorry, Amy, no luck. What's it like?"

"It's lovely with an oval face and it's silver. The strap is very pretty, sort of plaited silver."

"Was it a present? " said Lucy. "Don't worry, it's probably somewhere safe. You haven't been out for days have you? You probably left it in the apartment. Where did you keep it when you were staying there?"

"I always put it in the little drawer of the bedside table. I hope it's still there because it's a special one. My parents gave me it on my twenty-first birthday."

"Do you want to phone Paul, see if he found it?"

"I'm sure if he found it, Paul would have said. Anyway Lucy, I can't phone now. It's still very early, so I'll wait a while and decide what to do."

Amy seemed to be thinking out loud, "Actually, I thought he might have phoned me last night. He didn't phone while I was asleep, did he?"

"No, Amy, I'm sorry to say he didn't. To be perfectly honest with you, I expected him to phone... still, I suppose he was busy cleaning the apartment and packing etc."

Amy said that she was going back to bed for a bit longer. Then, trying not to get upset, she lay on her bed, but before she knew it she was once again thinking of Paul leaving Malta that night. She had so looked forward to seeing her uncle and telling him all she knew about Amelia and Gina. She suddenly remembered that she still had two films to develop. Oh well, at least she'd have time to do that before she returned home. She knew that her Uncle Jim was going to be so pleased to see photos of his old haunts and those she took of Amelia when she was given the necklace.

Amy kept looking at the clock on the chest of drawers because she'd decided to phone Paul at eight. He didn't stay in bed longer than that usually and while they were on holiday, he'd only slept in once. That was when they'd gone to the nightclubs in St Julian's. That's what she thought anyway.

Amy went through to the lounge, made herself comfortable and dialled the number. Her throat was still sore and croaky, but she couldn't wait to talk to Paul.

Just then, Ray popped his head around the door.

"Bye Amy, be good. Bye Lucy." He then gave his wife a kiss, and left for work. Lucy made a fresh pot of tea, took a cup to Amy, and noticed that the girl was looking worried.

CHAPTER 23

"He's not answering," Amy said. "Now that's strange. Paul's always quick to answer the phone," she explained to Lucy.

"Oh, hello, hello, sorry, I must've dialled the wrong number." Amy was just about to put the phone down and then she started talking again.

"Just a minute, it's Amelia, isn't it?" Amy suddenly recognised the husky voice and the slight Maltese accent on the other end of the line. She looked confused and her mouth felt dry.

"Amelia?.. Is that Amelia? What are you doing...? You sound as if you've just woken up. You have…? You have... but… what are… where's Paul?"

Lucy, who had been on her way out, stopped. She just stood there frozen to the spot. She was staring at the girl who had suddenly turned very pale.

"Amy, Amy," she walked back to the girl who just sat there, gripping the receiver and staring vacantly. "What's wrong love?"

Amy shrugged and Lucy took charge of the situation. She held the cup to Amy's lips and made her drink a little, then she gently prised the phone from Amy.

As Lucy started chatting away in Maltese, presumably to Amelia, all the colour drained from Amy's face, then she got up and walked away. She made straight for her bedroom and throwing herself on the bed, she burst into tears.

What was Amelia doing at their flat? She had obviously spent the night there. She'd admitted that she'd just woken up…did she and Paul...? had they...? Of course they did! They'd slept together! There was only one bedroom. There was a big settee though, she might have spent the night there. Why would she do that, when she lived just down the road? All these conflicting thoughts were buzzing in her head. Amelia had sounded very odd. She had! Of course she'd slept with Paul. Totally shocked, Amy wondered just how long it had been going on.

In spite of her being so upset, her mind suddenly cleared. Everything was fitting into place!

Now this was a fine kettle of fish, Lucy thought. That niece of hers was so unpredictable and impulsive. Everyone knew that. If she wanted something she'd always done everything in her power to get it. Now Lucy found herself in a very awkward position. She had no choice but to deal with the result of Amelia's latest escapade. She had to be the one to comfort the poor girl who was sobbing her heart out. It now appeared that her spoilt niece had really hooked Amy's boyfriend, hook line and sinker!

Oh how could Amelia do this? She could have had her pick of any man she wanted. She always seemed to have a boyfriend in tow, but this time she obviously fancied Amy's. It was unfortunate that Amy had to find out that her new found cousin was at that very moment, there at the holiday apartment. She'd obviously spent the night with Paul.

Good job they had talked in Maltese, or Amy would have been even more upset. Amelia told her aunt that Paul had been in the shower, and she'd been half-asleep or she would never have picked up the phone.

"I see, so you weren't going to let the poor girl know that you've been sleeping…"

"Auntie Lucy, it wasn't like that…we didn't plan it… it just…"

"Oh yes, it just happened, so innocently... Is that what you normally do? It just happens and…?"

"No, of course not, we love each other..."

"Love? You've only just met, for heaven's sake." The conversation had carried on heatedly until Lucy finally hung up. Before she did, however, she got another bombshell.!…Amelia informed her that she was going to England with Paul when he went back that very night! How on earth was she going to tell Amy about that? Amelia had pinched Amy's boyfriend and now she was also going to England in her place.

As it happened, Amy admitted that she shouldn't have been that surprised. Between sobs, she told Lucy that she had noticed that they both seemed to follow each other around with their eyes. Amy also remembered that Paul had gone on and on singing Amelia's praises, and come to think of it now, there did seem to be some chemistry between the two of them. When the Maltese girl was visiting the apartment, Amy had definitely felt that the two of them seemed a little bit too friendly for her liking.

"I thought that I was being paranoid because I wasn't feeling well," she said in almost a whisper. "I convinced myself that maybe

I was being rather over sensitive."

"Oh well, dear," Lucy tried to help the sad girl, "try not to get yourself even more upset. You deserve better. Now, how about if I go to the apartment myself and find out if your watch is there, maybe still in the drawer, like you said?"

"Would you do that? Won't you feel awkward?"

"They should feel awkward not me! I just feel angry... but, don't worry, I won't make a scene. I'll just ask Paul if he found your watch and nothing else, promise."

Amy said she really wanted to see Paul so badly, but Lucy persuaded her that it was best not to. She would only make herself feel worse.

"I don't think that I can feel any worse, do you?" she asked meekly. "Oh Lucy, I just thought of uncle…what's he going to feel like? I won't be there with Paul, but…"

"Is he supposed to meet you at the airport? It's Exeter if I remember correctly."

"Yes, it's Exeter. We picked it because it's so close to Plymouth. No, uncle won't go to the airport. Paul drove us there and the car will be there for the drive back."

"I'm glad about that. So Jim doesn't need to know yet that you won't be going back tonight."

"No, he doesn't. Please, Lucy, when you go to the apartment, will you make sure that Paul doesn't tell uncle that I'm having to stay behind for a few days? If he talks to him on the phone, I mean, but I don't think he'll be doing that anyway."

"I'll tell Paul, just in case. You're right. Why worry the poor man? Of course, if your uncle had arranged to meet you at the airport, he would need to be told about you and Paul, about … If I were you, I'd phone Jim myself on Saturday, tomorrow, because most probably he'll be expecting a phone call from you anyway. He'll be thinking you 're back home by then, won't he?"

"Yes, of course, he'll be thinking that I'm back. Thank you Lucy, you're so practical. I'm very grateful."

"Don't be silly…but look, dear, I think I'll go now and see if I can get your watch for you, ok. Will you be all right?"

"Yes, of course I will. Don't worry, I'm feeling better in spite of..."

"Listen Amy, I could phone Laura to come and keep you company if you like. She and Martin live only two streets away, as you know."

""No thanks, I'll be all right."

" I know she has Fridays off, so she'll be glad to help."

"No, thank you Lucy. I need to be alone to sort my head out."

"Are you sure…really sure?"

"Yes, really, really sure," and in an effort to convince her host, Amy put the television on.

Then she made herself settle down in front of it. Amy hoped that by acting as normal as possible, she would stop Lucy looking so worried at her. It worked! Amy seemed to be quickly engrossed in the programme on the television, so Lucy didn't feel too bad about leaving her alone. She let herself out of the house. Soon she was on her way to the holiday flat. She knew her way, having picked Amy up from there the day before.

Paul had seemed so attentive last time Lucy had seen him, so concerned about Amy's welfare. He kept promising her that he'd see her soon. Little did Lucy dream then, that that young man who had seemed so devoted to Amy would, in such a short time, take another girl into his bed. To add insult to injury, the other girl just happened to be his girlfriend's newly found cousin!

Now Lucy knew that by taking Amy to her house early, she had unintentionally, given Amelia and Paul the freedom to cheat on the poor girl.

As she approached the apartment, she kept telling herself to keep calm. She would curb her tongue because after all, it wasn't her business. However, she knew that it was going to be very difficult for her to act as if nothing untoward had happened.

Paul was still in his bathrobe and he blushed to the roots of his hair when he answered the doorbell and found Lucy on the doorstep. He opened the door a bit wider and waved her into the hallway.

Without mincing her words, she said that she'd only called to see if he'd come across Amy's silver watch. She didn't want any confrontation. Seeing Paul's guilty and embarrassed look was enough satisfaction at that moment.

He shook his head but then Lucy suggested that he looked in the drawer of the bedside table, the one on Amy's side of the bed.

"Silly me, it's Amelia's side now isn't it?" she asked with a sneer, and she had the satisfaction of seeing Paul wince.

Amelia, who had heard all of that from the bedroom, opened

the drawer and there it was. It was a very pretty watch indeed. She very quickly wrapped a sheet around herself and went to give it to Lucy before Paul had the chance to go and look for it himself.

"Here you are auntie," her niece said with a touch of triumph in her voice as she handed the watch to her aunt. Lucy was absolutely amazed that her niece seemed unabashed. In fact, if truth were known, she appeared rather pleased with herself.

Lucy almost grabbed the watch and was about to leave, when she remembered just in time to give them Amy's message. She told them that they were not to tell Jim that Amy was poorly...if they spoke to him on the phone, that is.

"Amy doesn't want to worry him unduly, not when he has enough on his plate already," she added.

"She'll speak to him herself when she feels a bit better. Obviously, if he remembers that you're due back tonight, he'd probably expect a phone call."

"I'll give him a call sometime tomorrow night, because by the time we arrive in Plymouth, it will be about four in the morning." Paul had no choice but to promise.

"It's just as well that he won't be meeting you at the airport, isn't it?"

Lucy was in full flow then. Once she started, she had to finish!

"Just imagine his reaction at not seeing his beloved niece with you and instead..." Lucy was glaring at her own niece...

"It could very easily give the poor man a heart attack. Both you, Paul, and Amy, said that he has been very ill," she felt she had to remind him.

"Yes, he was, but he said he was going back to work soon so he must be much better. Yes, please tell Amy that I'm sorry, I didn't plan..."

"I think you should be man enough and tell her yourself!" Lucy snapped at him.

"That's it, I've had my say. Now I'm off. I mustn't leave the poor girl on her own for too long," she finished abruptly and turned to the front door.

"Bye," both said sheepishly and with a curt "Good luck," Lucy opened the door and let herself out. In spite of wanting so much to slam it, she managed to control her anger and she closed it very gently.

She felt so angry and ashamed of her niece. It was really ironic that Amy had only gone to Malta to find Jim's child and then to try and unite Amelia with her birth father. Now, it seemed that she had lost her boyfriend into the bargain.

The problem was that now, Lucy had to tell the girl who was probably waiting on tenterhooks for her, that Paul was taking Amelia with him when he left for England that very night. She just didn't relish the thought of hurting Amy even more, but she had to be told. Paul was acting the coward because he had told Amy nothing. If she hadn't phoned to ask about her watch, Amy would still be in the dark about her boyfriend and her Maltese cousin. It had been a horrible way to find out that he was cheating on her.

Lucy was still debating the best way to tell her when, approaching St George's Bay, she suddenly had an idea. She slowed down and going as close as possible, she parked up, got out of her car, and was soon knocking firmly on the bright yellow door.

Gina looked pale when she opened the door, but she welcomed Lucy as warmly as she always did. She was fond of her sister-in-law, and found herself wondering what had brought her out that morning. Gina remembered Lucy telling her that she wouldn't be seeing her for a few days. She said that she'd be at home looking after the English girl.

"I won't be long. I left her watching television. I need to talk to you," Lucy explained, but first she asked if she could use the phone.

She just checked that Amy was alright, and when she told her that she had her watch, Lucy heard a big sigh of relief. Then Lucy said that she needed to speak to Gina, and would Amy mind if she were a little bit longer? Amy reassured her that she was fine. She was alright, watching a good film on television. "Give my regards to Gina," Amy said before she put the phone down.

"Are your mum and dad out shopping? " Lucy asked, looking around.

"Yes, and they said that afterwards they were going to Mass at twelve. I did'nt go with them in case Amelia came by while I was out."

The two women were soon discussing the affair and Lucy explained that she had had no choice but to discuss it with Amy that morning. She added that it was horrible for the poor girl to find out the way she did.

"I'm sorry to heap more worries on you Gina," she apologised to her dear sister-in-law.

"Now I feel that Amy should be told that Amelia is going to England with Paul, effectively, in her place. The thing is I don't fancy upsetting her any more."

Without any hesitation, Gina volunteered to go and see Amy herself and tell her that her daughter was leaving with Paul late that night.

"Oh thank you Gina," her sister-in-law said very gratefully. "It must be equally awful for you, because you must be very concerned about your daughter."

"Yes, I'm very worried. She was angry when she left yesterday morning. We've heard nothing since!"

"Please try not to worry so much about her. We all know that Amelia can look after herself. I'm sure she'll be alright. She might even chicken out at the last minute and not meet Jim at all."

"Oh, I don't think she'll change her mind. She seems stronger now she's with Paul. Do you know that she was with him yesterday, then she came over, packed some clothes and went to the apartment at St Andrew's again. Like I said, we haven't seen her since. She's acting completely out of character. I know she can be impulsive, but this is different…I don't think she knows her own mind any more."

"Well, she's been through a lot these last few days, same as the rest of you, you especially. She's bound to feel more…well, vulnerable, to act so impulsively, even for her! "

"It's just, I had hoped that she'd give herself enough time to be well prepared before she met Jim. She might be either pleasantly surprised or bitterly disappointed and coming on top of losing Ginger, that could…well it could really hurt her. She hardly knows anything about Jim, and yet, she's ready to go and…"

"Yes, I understand what you're saying. I just spoke to her a few minutes ago. She seems so…so…high. However, it's nice to see her smiling, even if it's at poor Amy's expense! Gina, I'm sure she'll drop by on the way to the airport."

"I hope so. I think they've got to be at the airport at about eleven tonight. Is that too late to pop round and see Amy? I think it might be."

"I suppose we might as well wait until tomorrow, then she won't get more upset just before bedtime."

"How about elevenish? I'll bring some fresh Pastizzi. You get the coffee and we must try to keep it as low key as possible…poor girl, I do feel sorry for her."

"I do too. This business with Amelia and Paul was the last thing she needed. Last night, she was quite distraught and feeling guilty about having started the chain of events, especially about Ginger." Lucy stopped, not wanting to get Gina upset now.

"Did you know that Jim's wife left him when she found out about Amelia?" she said, trying to change the subject, then realising that they were all linked."

"No, I didn't," Gina replied, concern written on her face.

"Apparently she had no clue at all until a few days ago. As soon as he found out that he had a daughter Jim told her."

"That's odd. I would have thought he'd have told his wife. We were together long before he met her anyway."

"Remember Amy or was it Paul, said that his wife was one of the nurses who was looking after him after he had his horrific accident. She knew that he'd ripped up a letter, which had upset him, but he never mentioned it and its contents to anyone, including her. Since he didn't tell her then, he kept you and his love child a secret for all these years."

"Yes, of course, I remember now."

"The couple couldn't have any children, so the revelation…only a few days ago, mind…that her husband had a secret offspring all along, really caused a big row. She packed her bags and has been away since."

"Oh no, how awful! So many people have been hurt as a result of…."

"Sorry Gina, I haven't been very tactful have I? Look dear, thank you for the coffee…

Give my regards to your parents when they return from church. I 'd love to wait and talk to them, but I must be off now. I must go back to Amy. Stay there, I can see myself out," Lucy said as she made her way through the long hallway and out into the bright sunshine.

Amy was still curled up in the armchair, the television was still blaring and walking in to talk to her, Lucy found that her house guest was fast asleep. She went and fetched a light blanket to cover her up with because although it was warm, Amy was still not quite over the bad bout of flu, which had really dragged on.

Looking down at her, Lucy found herself thinking that a lot of responsibility had been loaded on those young shoulders.

Her uncle had wanted to make up for his years of uncertainty about his offspring, but it had been a costly experience for so many. She promised herself that she'd try and help Amy at the first opportunity. The young girl had repeatedly declared that she felt guilty that she had started all this trouble. Now, Lucy was hoping that Gina would keep her word and back her up. Between them, they would try to tell Amy that Amelia was going in her place. Most of all, they needed to reassure her that she mustn't feel responsible for the tragic and sad events. She was only carrying out her uncle's wishes.

As she drove back home, Lucy had planned to remind Amy that her uncle had unburdened himself on her and he'd virtually begged her to go to Malta to find his daughter. It did seem obvious though that Jim's plea to find his offspring amounted to nothing short of emotional blackmail. Amy had to believe and accept that it wasn't her fault that Gina had lost her husband and that Jim's wife had walked out on him. The poor girl had paid a price too when her boyfriend betrayed her with her newly discovered cousin.

All these thoughts were still flitting around Lucy's head but since Amy was obviously still tired, she didn't want to disturb her. The kind lady closed the door gently and went to get on with her usual chores.

It was difficult not to think about the dramas that had unfolded since the English couple had arrived in Malta. Lucy could hardly believe that somehow these events had touched everyone, one way or another. She kept thinking of poor Gina, now a widow and having to live with her guilt at having sent Ginger away. Moreover, her sister-in-law was going through more heartache, because her daughter was going to England that very evening. Gina was naturally very worried that Amelia had already decided to meet Jim. It was too early to embark on a new relationship with her birth father. Not now, when she hadn't even had enough time to mourn the man she had always known as dad.

Every now and then Gina stopped whatever she was doing and listened. She kept thinking that she'd heard the front door open, but it was just wishful thinking. She was hoping that her daughter would come round and see her before she went to the airport. Gina tried not to bring to the fore the frightening thought that her daughter might decide to stay in England. She had lost Ginger. She did not want to lose her as well. She was worried that, because Amelia was so vulnerable at the moment, she wasn't able to make the right decisions about anything, never mind crucial issues.

However, for the time being, all Gina could do was wait patiently in case her daughter dropped by.

Lucy, always level-headed and practical, felt that she had to do something. She wanted to help her sister-in -law who had been through so much, and who was now so concerned about her daughter.

On impulse, Lucy picked up the telephone in the kitchen and got the phone number from the operator. Paul answered the phone. When she asked to speak to her niece, he tried to put her off saying that Amelia was very busy and maybe it would be better if they didn't talk at all, because it would only lead to more upset.

Lucy said that if he didn't call Amelia to talk to her, she would have to go round there again to speak to her in person.

Reluctantly, Paul called Amelia to the phone, and Lucy was quite amused to hear him tell her niece to watch her temper.

"Hi auntie, what have I done now?" she asked with sarcasm. "You've only just seen me!"

"Amelia, there's no need for that. You tell me, have you been up to something else? You do sound rather hyped up."

"I don't know, I don't think I've done anything, but I can think of something, if you'd like me to."

"Stop it Amelia, stop it please. Just listen for a moment. After I left you, I dropped by to see your mother. She doesn't look too good. What's making her worse is the fact that you haven't been round since yesterday morning. Can't you go and have a chat with her? Then maybe she'll feel a little better and maybe she will start sleeping at night. At the moment she looks really miserable and exhausted after a sleepless night. You mustn't leave things like this. Then there are your grandparents to consider……Amelia, are you still there? Are you listening?"

"Yes, of course I am. You weren't there yesterday. They all went on and on at me. I just had enough…"

"Well, never mind that now. They're all missing you. You must do something. Please listen to me Amelia. Don't leave without saying goodbye to your family. You left in a huff yesterday, didn't you? Well, you've got plenty of time to make up before you go. It's all up to you now. I just had to try to get through to you, because I could see what your mother is going through."

"Oh ok, I ...yes, you're right ...I'm not happy about the situation either."

"Well, there you are then. Do something about it. Phone up and make your peace or better still...."

"I'll stop by on the way to the airport. We can drop in at home on the way to the airport can't we Paul?" she asked in a loud voice. He had obviously left her alone.

"Ok Auntie Lucy. I'll do that, promise. Believe it or not, we had already talked about stopping by, so don't worry. I'll talk to mum," she promised.

"Good, I'm glad. Now take things easy ok? Don't rush headlong into situations that might hurt you, or hurt anyone else for that matter. That's it, I've had my say, end of sermon." Lucy then gently reminded her niece that she must try to reassure her mum that she was going to be careful and that she wasn't going to rush things.

"You must remind your mother that you're old enough and mature enough, so she should stop worrying about you and start looking after herself for a change."

"Yes, I will." Amelia sounded so subdued now. Lucy, thinking of ways to help all concerned, asked to speak to Paul.

She knew that he was reluctant to come to the phone, because she heard her niece coaxing him.

"Don't worry, Paul," she said softly. "No more sermons, promise. I just wanted to give you a little bit of advice. It's up to you whether you take it or not."

"Ok, I'm listening..."

"Amelia promised me that she's going to see her mum and make peace with her. How about you and Amy? Why don't you drop by, or if it takes less courage to phone, why not call her? She deserves that at least. It will also make things easier for you when you talk to her uncle. From what you both told us, Amy is the apple of his eye. Most importantly, she deserves an explanation, some sort of apology, don't you think?"

There was a loud silence on the other end of the line.

"Paul...Paul are you still there?..." Lucy thought she might have over done it.

"Yes, I'm here, and yes, you're right of course. Ok, I'll think about it. No, I promise I'll talk to her, one way or another."

"Ok, bye then."

"Bye, Lucy."

Lucy felt much better after all that. It felt good to know that she had at least tried to help. Amelia was now going to make peace with her mum and Paul was going to speak to Amy. She felt pleased that she had made the call and now she had better check on her patient.

CHAPTER 24

The first thing that Amy saw when she opened her eyes was her watch. Not wanting to disturb her, Lucy had put it in a prominent position on the coffee table. She rubbed her eyes and tried to stretch but she was all curled up in a big cosy armchair. In the distance she could hear the droning noise of a vacuum cleaner.

When she remembered where she was, she suddenly felt sad and miserable. Today she was supposed to be going back to England. She was still not well enough to travel yet. But then she suddenly remembered that her boyfriend had slept with Amelia. He was going back on his own, probably with his new girlfriend seeing him off at the airport. That thought set her off again and when Lucy opened the door to check on her, she was moved to see Amy sitting there with tears running down her cheeks.

"Come on now Amy, come on. Look, did you see it? I got your watch back." Amy hiccupped and took the tissues that Lucy thoughtfully handed her.

"Before I forget, Gina said that she 's coming round to see you tomorrow morning. Are you ok with that?"

"Oh yes, I'd love to see her. But what about Amelia and... and Paul?"

"I talked to them both," she started, "and there's nothing I can say that will make you feel any better, but if it's any consolation, it's better that you split up now," and as Amy started to protest, Lucy carried on. "It's much better now than later. I'm sure that it would have happened with somebody else sooner or later. It's just unfortunate that it had to be Amelia."

Lucy pointed out that it would have hurt much more if Paul had fallen for someone else later on in their relationship. Then, they might have been engaged or even married.

"He's obviously not the right one for you. You want someone who will stay faithful, someone strong. Now, don't upset yourself any more over such a weak guy who changed his affections at a flutter of a pair of dark eyelashes."

"We were only seeing each other for about three months, but…"

"I know…it hurts, of course it does. Excuse me Amy," she said as the telephone cut her off mid sentence.

"Hello, oh hi. Yes, yes, she's here near me…hang on," said Lucy as she handed the telephone to Amy.

"Who is it?" whispered the girl who was suddenly looking pale and nervous.

"Paul," mouthed Lucy, and as Amy was going to put the phone down, Lucy covered the mouthpiece and encouraged her to at least listen to what he had to say.

"Go on love," she urged her, "or you'll always be wishing you had listened to him and wondering what he wanted to say."

Amy was visibly shaking but she somehow managed to carry on a conversation, however stilted. Lucy had left the room so that Amy could say whatever she wanted in private.

A few minutes later, a very calm but sad looking Amy went in the kitchen. She knew where to find Lucy.

"Let's sit down and have a cup of tea," she said, giving Amy the opportunity to talk if she wanted to.

Amy did. To start with, she found it difficult to say his name, but with Lucy's help and gentle prompting, she opened up and said that Paul had apologised for not being honest about his feelings towards Amelia.

"He has now admitted that he felt attracted to her from the first time he set eyes on her at the house. I was ill, so I didn't go along. The thing is, at the time, he told me that she was arrogant and rather rude."

"She was, very rude. I remember, I was there. Amelia was downright impolite and snapped at him and at everyone else."

"Then Paul said… he said… well, whenever he realised that he was, that she was...." It was obviously difficult for Amy to say more. After drinking some of the scalding tea, which brought some colour to her cheeks, Amy carried on.

"He said that he really tried to fight the attraction, but, well, we know the rest."

Amy managed a weak smile and said that she didn't want someone who was attracted so much to another girl anyway!

"I'm pleased that he called and that I spoke to him. Thank you for bullying me into it, because, well, we've got to stay civil, if only for uncle's sake. If Paul really is the man for my uncle's newly found daughter, we're bound to meet up some time or other. It would be rather awkward if we're not on speaking terms wouldn't it? I've got to carry on as normal, because I certainly won't stop seeing my uncle because of this…this…" She faltered before adding rather wistfully, "Hopefully, Auntie Meg will be back home soon."

Lucy was feeling much better listening to Amy's practical words and positive thinking. She was finally talking resignedly about her ex-boyfriend.

"Yes, Lucy, you were right. I'm so glad I spoke to him," she said yet again. She was obviously still thinking about the day in the future when Amelia would go and meet her dad. More than likely, Paul would be there with her.

Lucy suddenly remembered that Amy was still unaware that her new cousin was going to England with her Paul. It was just great to see her looking a little like her old self. That would probably change when Gina told her about it the next day.

"Well, I think it was brave of him to call don't you? He must have been feeling very guilty to admit all about his cheating. I do think that his phone call took some courage didn't it, Lucy?" asked Amy, always so pleasant.

It took a good kick up his backside too, Lucy mumbled laughingly to herself.

She had been worried about Amy's reaction to Paul's phone call, but now she was feeling really pleased with herself for bringing it about. It seemed to have calmed Amy down and it was such a relief to see her almost resigned to Paul's deceitful behaviour.

"You're looking much better," Lucy admitted as she realised that there was a bit of colour on Amy's cheeks. "I think that you might feel like going out this weekend. Let's see, you just stay here and have a relaxing day tomorrow, and then, if you feel like it, we'll go somewhere on Sunday."

"That would be great. Where can we go? Actually I feel guilty that you've been tied to the house because of me."

"Don't be silly. I don't go out much during the week anyway except maybe to visit our boys. We do try to go out at weekends though. So, if you're up to it, we'll think of somewhere to go this Sunday. We mustn't overdo it though ok?"

"No, of course not...Oh shall I get that?" Amy volunteered to answer the telephone since she was close to it.

"Yes please," said Lucy.

After a couple of minutes, she looked on amusedly at Amy

who seemed to be chatting away quite happily. Lucy wondered who on earth was on the other end of the line. The English girl was smiling and looked almost coy as she talked about herself to whoever it was. She seemed to be explaining why she was staying there.

When she finally passed the phone to Lucy, Amy had a distant look on her face. Watching her leave the room, Lucy was pleasantly surprised to see her looking almost like her old self.

It was Robert's friend on the phone. George was no stranger to Lucy's house. Now he was asking about Amy. He'd seen her around when he'd gone to see Robert and he wanted to invite her to a barbecue on Sunday. He was pleased she'd answered the phone herself, he said," because I've been bugging Robert to introduce us, but you know what he's like. No one can rush Robert!"

Later, when they were having their dinner, Lucy asked Amy if she'd go to the barbecue..." If you feel well of course," she encouraged. "It's nice of George to ask you," she told her, hoping she wasn't pushing her luck.

"He's a flirt," Amy said. "He said that he'd been at Robert to introduce us and hadn't believed him, about me being poorly I mean....and...I don't know if I want to go..."

"Just don't make your mind up yet, Amy. Remember that earlier on, we were saying that you might feel like going out."

"But I don't even know him!"

"I know him, he's a lovely guy."

"Lucy's right, George is a nice lad," Ray volunteered. "You'll, like him," he said.

"I didn't want to say yes, in case... anyway, I don't fancy meeting lots of strange people..."

"Maltese people are not strange Amy," butted in Ray, laughing his head off.

"You know what I mean, Ray... I don't know anybody."

"You know Robert," Lucy reminded her, as she began tackling the washing up quite happily. It was good to see the English girl looking a little brighter than she had been looking for ages!

Gina was overjoyed and once more moved to tears. This time, they were tears of joy because she had finally heard her daughter's voice calling her as she opened the bright yellow door and let herself in. Amelia walked timidly through the long hallway that led to the big bright kitchen. Mother and daughter hugged and then grandmother walked in from the back yard.

"I thought I heard my Amelia's voice. Come here, child," she ordered her granddaughter who was soon giving her a big bear hug.

"Sorry mum, Nanna, sorry I left in a huff yesterday, but please be happy for me. Paul and I love each other, we just can't help that. I'm sorry that Amy has to lose out, but there obviously wasn't a strong enough bond between them."

The three women, of three generations, talked and talked and talked and there were no angry words or recriminations this time.

Robert was pleasantly surprised when he walked in on them. He too had "a big hug" for his big sister, and felt relieved that there was a little happiness back in the house.

It had been horrible since he lost his dad and the only way he was coping had been to stay out of the way as much as possible. His sister, or half sister, he thought wryly, was all wound up. She created a tense atmosphere too often for his liking. Whenever it became too much for him in the house with the bright yellow door, he called on one of his good friends for some company. He was actually looking forward to Monday when he was due back at the office of Andrew's Financial Advisers. He had been working there for a year and enjoyed the work.

He'd heard his sister's voice and gone to wave her off. Robert knew that his mother had been worried about Amelia. That's why she was making her promise to phone them regularly and keep them all up to date with whatever was going on. Amelia then promised that she'd take Nanna's advice and take things slowly. She'd wait a while before deciding whether and when to meet Jim."

"When do you start work sis? I start this Monday."

"That's a point...." Gina hadn't thought of that.

Amelia then reminded her mum that she had two weeks holiday left but her boss had also encouraged her to take another week on top of that. Now she had enough time to decide when, if, she wanted to meet Jim.

"That's what I was trying to explain earlier Nanna," she added. "There's no rush."

Finally, just before her daughter left, Gina asked her if she would do her a favour. Amelia smiled as she took a large envelope from her mother with Jim's name on it.

"Have you told him your life story mum?" she joked.

"More or less," her mother admitted.

"Now Amelia, if you decide not to meet Jim after all, no, don't look so amused, you might very well change your mind, please post my letter, ok. Keep the other one, Ginger's. You have to give him that personally, whenever you are able to."

"Ok mum. I'll do that, I promise. Now here is Paul's address and telephone numbers. Right, give us a kiss because I have to go. We have to check in soon."

"Where is Paul?" grandmother asked.

"In the car... he was scared to face you.... say bye to Uncle Ray and Uncle Martin for me. Don't forget granddad... no Nanna, let him sleep. I must dash, really!"

They followed her to the door and watched her go to the car. Amelia nudged Paul and told him to look up. Emma waited until he looked at them, then she beckoned Paul over. He was feeling worried and embarrassed, but could not ignore the old lady.

"I don't bite," she said. "Look Paul, none of us is pleased with your actions, but we know it takes two to tango as they say. You are our Amelia's choice. You'd better look after her now, and watch out for her, or else...." She stood on tiptoes and opened her arms to give him a hug. Gina followed suit.

"Remember what my mum just said," Gina added. "Amelia's a treasure, look after her."

Paul walked fast to the car and got in next to an amused Amelia.

"I see you didn't get your head bitten off," she smiled as she waved like mad to her mum, Robert and her grandma.

When the house with the bright yellow door was out of sight Amelia turned to Paul, and giving his knee a squeeze said that he was taking her to a new beginning. Smiling seductively at him, she said that she had found her man and that she was going to make sure that he'd always be there, by her side.

"Good, that's all I want to hear you say. Lead on, Amelia," he laughed out loud as he put his foot down to get going to Luqa airport.

It was a typical spring night in England. As the plane was approaching the runway at Exeter airport, many passengers looked out onto the early morning skies to see the drizzling rain. A few of the travellers groaned and said that their suntan would soon disappear in this weather.

Amelia held Paul's hand and he squeezed it tightly while he looked at her and for a moment he thought how like Amy she looked. Both had long blonde hair and were the same height and roughly the same weight. That's where the resemblance ended. While Amy was a lovely, quiet and calm girl who wouldn't say boo to a goose, this sexy, provocative girl was outspoken, impulsive and determined to get what she wanted in life.

The happy couple joined the other passengers who were all waiting for their luggage to start going round on the conveyer belt. Then there was more hanging about, with all the passengers trying to identify and pick up their cases.

At last they found their luggage, and after going quickly through Customs, Paul led the way through to Arrivals.

When he slowed down to let Amelia catch up, Paul felt a sense of exhilaration as he noticed how radiant she looked. He had never dreamed when he had gone to Malta just a short while ago, that he would be returning with a different girl....a beautiful girl who had mesmerised him from the first time he set eyes on her. This was no ordinary holiday romance. This was the real thing. He felt like shouting it to all the people around them, those hurrying out to find their friends or relations and those waiting eagerly for their loved ones to appear.

Paul was quite amused as he looked at the waiting crowds. They all seemed pale compared to the holidaymakers who had just come back from sunny Malta.

"Just follow me now Amelia," he said. "I hope I can remember where I left the car."

"We'll find it," she said optimistically, hoping that it was going to be easy to find.

Suddenly, Paul heard someone calling his name. Turning round, he saw a man pushing his way through to the front. He had a slight limp, which made Paul look again.

"Oh no, it's Jim! He wasn't supposed to be meeting us. He must have remembered the date and everything."

Amelia had stopped in her tracks, and looking rather pale in spite of the suntan, asked Paul what they were going to do. What were they going to say? She felt herself panicking slightly. This wasn't the way she had planned it…

"Oh Paul I must go to the toilet…it's nerves," she explained.

"Go on, it's not far, it's over there, on your left. Please hurry,

I'll wait here."

She looked almost scared and when Paul gave her directions to the toilet, she literally flew in her bid to play for more time.

Then fixing a smile on his face, Paul turned to face Jim who had caught up with him and was soon giving him a welcoming handshake.

"Jim, this is a surprise.... How come you're here? I have the car remember."

"I know, but I thought I'd surprise you. I took a coach from Plymouth seeing as though the doc won't let me drive yet. I got a single ticket, sure that you wouldn't mind me going back with you. You know we've got loads to talk about. I couldn't wait to see you both and ... hang on a sec, where is she? Where's she gone? Where's Amy?"

"It's a long story Jim, it's best if we wait until we're in the car."

Paul was scanning the crowded lounge for a sighting of Amelia. Suddenly Jim saw her approaching.

"There she is!" He exclaimed looking quite excited.

As the Maltese girl approached slowly and proudly, Jim looked perplexed and utterly confused.

"No, that's not Amy!. Who...was... Where is...?"

Paul started walking towards Amelia. Jim then pulled at Paul's sleeve to stop him walking so that he could face him. Was he going mad? This girl looked like Amy. In fact, he'd thought it was Amy, but as she got closer, he could see that it wasn't!

Jim then turned to the attractive girl who was standing there. He could see that she was looking quite confident and sure of herself. Strangely, at the same time, there was definitely a hint of shyness in the half-hearted smile, which never quite reached her big brown eyes. This was not his niece at all.

"What's going on Paul?" he asked, utterly puzzled. "Will you kindly stop looking so...I don't know, so dumbstruck... and tell me...who is this young lady?"

Paul swallowed a couple of times, looked at Jim, then at Amelia. He took her hand in his, hoping that it would give him a little courage.

Then, in a very husky voice charged with emotion he said, "Jim, meet your daughter Amelia."